John Gilmary Shea

United States Catholic Historical Magazine

Volume 3

John Gilmary Shea

United States Catholic Historical Magazine
Volume 3

ISBN/EAN: 9783742817761

Manufactured in Europe, USA, Canada, Australia, Japa

Cover: Foto ©Lupo / pixelio.de

Manufactured and distributed by brebook publishing software (www.brebook.com)

John Gilmary Shea

United States Catholic Historical Magazine

UNITED STATES

CATHOLIC

HISTORICAL MAGAZINE.

PUBLISHED UNDER THE AUSPICES OF THE UNITED
STATES CATHOLIC HISTORICAL SOCIETY.

VOLUME III.

NEW YORK:
Press of the Society,
1890.

CONTENTS.

    *We apologize for the error on p. 41, where this gentleman's name is printed Andrew.

iv   *Contents.*

UNITED STATES CATHOLIC
HISTORICAL MAGAZINE.

Vol. III.)	(No. 9.

EARLY HISTORY OF THE REDEMPTORISTS IN THE UNITED STATES, 1832—1850.

Read before the U. S. Catholic Historical Society, Nov. 25th, 1889, by Rev. Charles Warren Currier, C. SS. R.

It is related of the great Doctor of the Church, St. Alphonsus de Liguori, that as he once looked out upon the Bay of Naples, he beheld a vessel about to sail for New Orleans; turning to his companion, he assured him that one day Fathers of his own Congregation of the Most Holy Redeemer would be established in that city. The prediction of the Saint has been verified, and to-day, more than half a century since the first Redemptorist set foot upon the soil of the New World, the Fathers of the Congregation of the Most Holy Redeemer have charge of three churches in the capital of Louisiana. The second founder of that same Congregation, Blessed Clement Mary Hoffbauer, had, in the days of his deepest affliction, when he beheld his dear Congregation proscribed in the Austrian Empire, turned his eyes wistfully toward the New World, and even publicly declared that in case he were exiled from his country he would go to America. It was from that very Austria, the country of Blessed Clement, that the first Redemptorists came, and planted the banner of St. Alphonsus upon the soil of the United States. In the year 1828 Bishop Edward Fenwick, of Cincinnati, sent his Vicar-General, Rev. Frederic Résé, afterward Bishop of Detroit, to Europe to obtain help for the extensive portion of the Lord's vineyard that had been committed to his care. At Vienna, Father Résé made the acquaintance of the Redemptorists. It appears that neither he understood the nature and circumstances of the Congregation, nor had the Redemptorists any knowledge of the mission Father Résé offered to them.

The Fathers of the Congregation were believed to be richly endowed with the goods of fortune, and to possess many influential friends, and several of the young members were ardent in their desires to devote their energies to the service of the American Missions, little reflecting on the difficulties they would encounter in trying to lead a Community-life according to their rules.

In the eyes of Redemptorists, acting according to the spirit of their Founder, this life of Community is of the most vital importance. Of this fact Father Résé seems to have had but a very imperfect idea, and imagined that the Redemptorists would be similar to secular Priests, entirely at the disposition of the Ordinaries of the diocese.

However, after the preliminary negotiations, the Superiors of the Congregation accepted the American Mission that was offered to them.

The General of the Congregation, at that time, Rev. Celestine Cocle, resided at Nocera' de Pagani, in Italy, a city where the illustrious Founder had spent the last years of his life. Having become Archbishop, he was succeeded in 1832 by Father Camillo Ripoli. The Transalpine branch of the Congregation was governed by Rev. Joseph Passerot, who had his residence at Vienna, and bore the title of Vicar-General.

The members of the Congregation appointed to begin the American foundation, were Rev. Simon Saenderl, Rev. Francis Haetscher and Rev. Francis Xav. Tschenhens, with the Lay-Brothers James Kohler and Wenceslaus Witopil. They set sail from Trieste on April 15th, 1832, and, on the 20th of the following June, arrived at New York. They celebrated their first Mass in America on the Feast of Cor-

pus Christi, in Christ Church, on Ann Street, New York.
In that great city they found nearly a thousand Germans,
attended by a Spanish Priest, who understood a little
of their language. Father Saenderl was requested to
leave one of his Priests in that city; but, as he had
promised his services to the Bishop of Cincinnati, he
could not accede to the petition.

On June 28th the Fathers continued their journey,
going by steamer to Albany, thence by canal to Buffalo,
whence they started via Cleveland for Cincinnati, where
they arrived on July 17th.

Instead of immediately forming a community, as they
had desired, circumstances forced them to separate. Father
Tschenhens and Brother James remained at Cincinnati to
take charge of the Germans, while Father Saenderl, with
Brothers Wenceslaus and Aloysius started for Detroit, where
they sojourned with the pioneer Priest Father Richard.
On August 16th the Bishop, who had been travelling in
Michigan, arrived at Detroit. On the 13th Father Haetscher
had also arrived in the same city.

Father Saenderl was sent by the Bishop to Green Bay
to take charge of a church that had lately been erected
there. In the meantime on his way north, Father Haetscher
had given his spiritual ministrations to the Germans at
Norwalk, Ohio; Tiffin, Ohio; and at other places, while
Father Saenderl had done the same in Detroit. After the
latter's departure, Father Haetscher continued the work he
had begun, and rendered great service during the cholera
epidemic that then raged. Bishop Fenwick and Father
Richard, having both fallen victims to the disease, he was
left alone for a circuit of about twenty miles.

At the request of Father Baraga, Brother Aloysius was
sent to Arbre Croche, Mich., to teach the carpenter's trade
to the Indians.

Brother Wenceslaus had accompanied Father Saenderl
to Green Bay, so that Father Haetscher was left alone at
Detroit, where he remained until about October, when he

joined Father Saenderl at Green Bay. There the Fathers labored for the salvation of souls amidst numberless difficulties and the greatest poverty.

Their congregation consisted principally of French-Canadians and Indians. Two gentlemen, an American named Law, and Mr. Grignon, a French-Canadian, showed themselves very charitable toward the Fathers in their necessities. Some years ago, as I was giving a mission in Green Bay, the two daughters of the latter, ladies advanced in years, having heard that the Liguorians had arrived, called on us. They were children when Father Saenderl first came to their city.

Meanwhile Father Tschenhens had left Cincinnati and was laboring in another portion of Ohio. After spending three months in visiting different stations, he finally arrived at Norwalk where he gave a mission, and where he sojourned for some time, having sent Brother James to Green Bay. There was, at this time, a small frame-church at Norwalk. Father Tschenhens constructed a log cabin for himself, and also built a small school.

In August, 1833, Father Saenderl was sent by the Bishop to Arbre-Croche, Mich., to take the place of Father Baraga, who had been transferred to Sault St. Marie. Father Haetscher remained at Green Bay. Father Saenderl could now speak English, French and two Indian dialects. His proficiency in the latter was such that he even made a dictionary of those languages. He established three Indian villages, and, for a time admitted weekly twenty or thirty catechumens to baptism. The life of these Indians was admirable. Morning and evening they came together for common prayers, assisted at Mass daily, and prepared themselves with great fervor for the reception of the Sacraments. If space and time allowed, much could be written of the fervor of these neophytes. Father Saenderl labored amongst them until the middle of the year 1835.

In the spring of the preceding year, Father Haetscher had been sent by the diocesan Bishop to Mackinaw Island, near the straits of that name, between Lakes Huron and

Michigan. From here he departed to Sault St. Marie, and began to labor with the utmost zeal in the upper Peninsula of Michigan, both for the Indians and French-Canadians. He obtained a deserted barracks from the Commander of a military post and converted it into a church. It was shortly afterward burned by idolators, at the instigation of the Methodists. With it perished the fortune of the devoted missionary, the sum of ten dollars. After the destruction of his church at Sault St. Marie, Father Haetscher returned to Mackinaw.

Father Saenderl having left Arbre Croche, removed to Ohio, where he took charge of Canton, in Stark County. In the summer of 1835, the three Redemptorists met once more at Norwalk, Ohio; after a separation of nearly three years. They celebrated together the Feast of the Most Holy Redeemer, and again separated; Father Saenderl, at the request of the Bishop of Detroit, returned to Green Bay, Father Haetscher went to Sault St. Marie, and Father Tschenhens remained in Ohio.

In 1835 two Fathers, Rev. Joseph Prost and Rev. Peter Czackert were added to the American Mission. Father Prost was appointed Superior, and, on his arrival in America labored for a short time among the Germans in New York. Thence he repaired to Rochester, where circumstances forced him to sojourn for some time. Father Czackert, meanwhile, had gone to join Father Tschenhens at Norwalk, whither Father Prost followed him. He shortly after joined Father Saenderl at Detroit, whence they both started for Green Bay.

The following year, 1836, Father Prost left for Rochester, N. Y., to undertake the care of the Germans in that city. Here he sojourned with the Pastor, Rev. Bernard O'Reilly. In the spring of 1837 Father Haetscher returned to Europe.

In 1838, a mission having been offered to the Redemptorists in Jasper County, Indiana, Father Czackert was sent thither. The foundation, however, did not succeed.

The Redemptorists had now been more than six years in America, and all their efforts to bring about the foundation of a regular Community had failed; it was not until 1840 that they finally succeeded in their endeavors. The first community was established at Pittsburgh, in that year. Its members were Fathers Prost, Tschenhens and Czackert, with the Brothers Aloysius Schuh and Louis Kenning. Father Haetscher had departed for Europe, and Father Saenderl, after laboring in Wisconsin and Michigan, had gone to Rochester, N. Y. The edifice they used as a church at Pittsburgh they dedicated to St. Philomena.

In 1840 Father Prost, being invited by Archbishop Eccleston to the Provincial Council of Baltimore, preached while in that city in old St. John's Church. A short time after, the church just mentioned was given to the Redemptorists. Its pastor, Rev. Father Bayer, left for Europe, and on his return to America entered the Congregation of the Most Holy Redeemer. Thus began the work of the Redemptorists among the Germans in Baltimore.

The time had now arrived when the first novice was to be admitted into the Congregation in America; one, namely, who was to become its most distinguished member and brightest ornament. We mean Rev. John Nepomuc Neumann, afterward Bishop of Philadelphia, and the cause of whose canonization has been introduced at Rome.

John Nepomuc Neumann was born at Prachatitz, an ancient and beautifully situated city of Bohemia, on March 28th, 1811. He studied at Budweis, the episcopal See, and later at Prague. After a youth spent in the exercise of piety and study, he came to America in 1836, to consecrate himself to the work of the missions in that distant field of the Lord's vineyard. He was admitted into the diocese of New York, and received Priest's Orders on June 25th, 1836, having previously been ordained Sub-Deacon and Deacon at New York, by Bishop Du Bois. Immediately after his ordination he started for the field of labor allotted to him, around Niagara Falls, and began with great zeal to work for the salvation of souls. On his way he stopped at Rochester.

A year previous to these events, Father Prost had arrived at Rochester, on his way from New York to Ohio. On the same Sunday that Father Neumann began his labors July 10th, 1836, Father Prost was again in Rochester.

This was the first meeting of Father Neumann with a Redemptorist. At the request of Father Prost, he remained in Rochester a few days longer. Father Neumann, says his biographer, the late Father Berger, C. SS. R., describes his new friend as a saintly, amiable priest, whose acquaintance awoke in him the first desire to enter the Congregation of the Most Holy Redeemer.

Father Neumann worked most zealously as a secular priest until the year 1840. He had grown more and more acquainted with the Redemptorists, and the desire of joining them was gradually awakened within him. "For four years," he writes in his journal, "I strove earnestly to animate my people to fervor similar to that which I remarked in St. Joseph's parish, Rochester; but I did not succeed. This, added to a natural, or rather a supernatural longing to live in some society of priests, so as not to be left to myself in the midst of the thousand and one dangers incidental to the world, inspired me with the thought of entering the Congregation of the Most Holy Redeemer. On that same day, nay, at that same hour, September 4th, 1840, I applied to the superior, Rev. Father Prost, for admission. On the 16th of the same month I received permission to enter, with directions to repair to Pittsburgh. Immediately on receipt of this letter, I notified Right Rev. Bishop Hughes, administrator of the New York diocese, of my intention, begging his blessing and requesting him to send a priest, or rather priests to take charge of the different parishes. Reluctantly, and only after long deliberation and repeated refusals, did the Bishop grant me my discharge."

Father Neumann finally entered the Congregation of the Most Holy Redeemer, October 18th, 1840, at Pittsburgh. His brother, Wenceslaus, followed him on the 13th of November, and entered the Congregation as a lay-brother. Brother Wenceslaus is still alive and was one of the witnesses in the cause of his deceased brother's canonization. Father Neumann was the first Redemptorist novice in America. He received the habit of the Congregation in the church at Pittsburgh, on the Feast of St. Andrew the Apostle, Nov. 28th, 1840, from the hands of Father Prost.

Towards the end of the year 1840, five more Redemptorists arrived in America; they were Fathers Alexander Czvitkovicz, Gabriel Rumpler, Louis Cartuyvels, Mathias Alig, and a Professed Student, Joseph Fey. Father Alexander succeeded Father Prost in the office of Superior. The latter, some time after, returned to Europe. On June 5th, 1841, Frater Joseph Fey was ordained a priest.

Another priest had entered the congregation in America namely, Rev. Benedict Bayer, former pastor of the German congregation in Baltimore.

By a decree of the Holy See, dated July 2d, 1841, the Congregation of the Most Holy Redeemer was divided into six Provinces: the Roman, Neapolitan, Sicilian, Franco-Suabian, Austrian and Belgian. The Provinces outside of Italy were governed by the Vicar-General, Rev. Joseph Passerat, while at the head of the entire Congregation stood the Rector-Mayor, who resided at Nocera dei Pagani, in the kingdom of Naples. The mission in the United States remained directly subject to the Vicar-General until 1844.

Meanwhile the novitiate of Rev. John N. Neumann had drawn to a close, and on January 16th, 1842, he made his vows at the house of St. James in Baltimore, and on the 2nd of July following, Father Bayer was admitted to his profession. About the same time Rev. Joseph Mueller entered the Congregation. He was a native of Austria, and had come to this country as a priest. The Redemptorists at Baltimore attended to the spiritual wants of the Germans of that city, and also visited many stations dispersed throughout the states of Maryland, Virginia and Pennsylvania. Thus Cumberland, Harper's Ferry, Martinsburg, Richmond,

Frederick, York, Columbia, Strasburg, and other places were at intervals witnesses of their zeal.

Father Tschenhens, occasionally assisted by the other Fathers, still labored in Ohio, and beside Norwalk, attended to Tiffin, Mansfield, Wolf's Creek, Thompson, and other localities.

The year 1842 witnessed the establishment of the Redemptorists in the city of New York. Until 1833, the Germans of that city had been almost entirely destitute of spiritual aid; although, as we already mentioned, a Spanish priest who had some knowledge of their language, occasionally ministered to them. In 1833 Father Raffeiner took upon himself the charge of these spiritually destitute souls, and in course of time erected a church that was dedicated to St. Nicholas. During six years Rev. John Raffeiner labored for the Germans in New York. After his departure for Williamsburg, several Priests attended St. Nicholas' Church, until in 1842, when it was offered to the Redemptorists. Father Gabriel Rumpler was the first Father who was sent thither.

About the same time a foundation was begun at Buffalo, N. Y. The Congregation had thus begun to spread, and with the increase of labors an increase of workmen in the Lord's vineyard became necessary. To obtain aid Father Alexander went to Europe towards the close of the year 1842. In April, 1843, Rev. Ernest Glaunach, and the novice Francis Xavier Seelos, afterward known for the sanctity of his life, arrived in America. A few days after they were followed by Father Alexander, who brought with him from Belgium several workers, namely: Fathers Peter Cronenberg, Louis Gilet, Francis Poilvache, and the student Henry Tappert. Father George Beranek, who is still amongst the living, and Father Francis Krutil arrived from Austria in June. The same year witnessed the arrival of Rev. Joseph Helmpraecht from Bavaria.

About this time the station at Norwalk, Ohio, was relinquished; some time previous the Redemptorists had also ceased to work for the Indians in Wisconsin and Michigan. If the pioneer-life they had been forced to lead in the beginning was a thing of the past, their field of activity was being widened in another direction. Regular Communities were being organized according to the spirit of their rules. They had establishments at Pittsburgh, Rochester, Baltimore, New York and Buffalo, and in 1843, they began one in Philadelphia. The Germans of that city who dwelt too far from the Church of the Holy Trinity, requested Bishop Kenrick to allow them to build a church of their own; the request was granted, and the new congregation offered to the Redemptorists. This was the beginning of St. Peter's parish, of Philadelphia.* About the same time St. Paul's Church was being built, and it was to have been dedicated to the Prince of the Apostles; but, acceding to 'the request of the Germans, the Bishop decided that the German Church should have St. Peter as its patron, and the other church be dedicated to St. Paul. A third foundation was begun in Pennsylvania in the same year.

In 1842 a German colony had been established in the western part of the State, in Elk County. The land had been sold to the Germans by some speculating company of Boston, Mass. The original idea of the community was socialistic in its nature, and property was to be in common. In 1843 Father Saenderl arrived in their midst to administer the sacraments. He remained among them about six weeks.

In course of time the Redemptorists established themselves for good at the colony, and continued their labors there for many years.

In 1844 the American missions belonging to the Redemptorists were united to the Belgian Province of which Father Frederic von Held was Provincial. The Congregation also acquired several new members in Fathers

---

*The Congregation for a time worshipped in a frame chapel. Rev. George Baraneck, C. SS. R. was the first pastor, and he was assisted by Rev. H. Tappert, C. SS. R.

Schaeffler, James Nagel, and Nicholas Petsch. In the same year Father Seelos was ordained priest. There now existed at Baltimore two communities, that of St. Alphonsus and that of St. James. Father Czackert had also labored at New Orleans and laid the foundations of a future establishment in that city.

In 1744 the Redemptorists also obtained a foundation at Munroe, Mich., offered them by Bishop Lefevre. Fathers Louis Gilet and Francis Poilvache were sent thither. In order to provide for the education of the children in that city, Father Gilet founded, with the approbation of the Bishop, a Congregation of Sisters, originally called Sisters of Providence, a name that was afterwards changed to that of the Immaculate Heart of Mary. The first sister with whom Father Gilet began the foundation is still alive at the community of West Chester, Pa. The Congregation has at present a large convent at Munroe, Mich., besides many missions in the dioceses of Detroit and Grand Rapids, and · flourishes also in the dioceses of Philadelphia and Scranton.

In 1845 the American Redemptorists received an increase of members by the arrival of Fathers John B. Hotz, Anthony Schmid, Thaddeus Anwander, John B. Hespelein, Louis Coudenhove, Giles Smulders, Martin Hasslinger, and Christian Kauder. Father Czackert became superior instead of Father Alexander.

At New York the Fathers not only attended the German Church, but visited many outside missions, such as Albany, Poughkeepsie, Elizabeth, Paterson and other places. In the diocese of Philadelphia too, they visited the Germans at Easton, Wilkesbarre, Renwick, Waldy, New Albany and other stations.

In 1847 Father Neumann became Superior of the Redemptorists in America. In the same year the first death occurred among the Sons of St. Alphonsus on this side of the Atlantic, when the Lay-brother Joseph Bayer was called away. He was followed to the grave the year after by the first Redemptorist Priest that died in America.   This was the saintly Father Francis Poilvache.

This remarkable man was born at Eben Emael, in Belgium, on March 15th, 1815.   From his earliest youth he was distinguished for his piety.   Having studied at the Royal College of Liege, and at the Petit Seminaire of Rolduc, in Limburg; he entered the Congregation of the Most Holy Redeemer at St. Trond.   After his profession he completed his studies at Wittem in Limburg.   Many were the trials he had to encounter; but he came victorious out of the combat. Shortly after his ordination he was sent to America, where he arrived on April 20th, 1843.

He labored for a while at Rochester, and then he was sent to Monroe.   To the present day his memory is held in benediction, and all speak of Pere Francois as of a saint. Some years ago, while engaged in collecting material for a biography of his, I met many who had known him and who were persuaded that God had given him the gift of miracles.   Some wonderful occurrences were related to me.   His career was brief and suddenly cut short.   A contagious disease, the spotted fever, raged at Monroe, and Father Poilvache fell a victim to it.   Though ill only a short time, he did not die unprepared.   He foretold his death, that occurred on January 27th, 1848.   Father Smulders, who was his companion at Monroe at the time of his death, has assured me that he appeared after his decease in a glorified state, and at the same moment, to all the members of a family several of whom were Protestants.   They were gathered together in a room, and all beheld the apparition.   Each inquired of the other whether he had seen Father Francis, and all admitted having beheld him.   The conversion of several of the Protestant members of the family was the result.   He certainly died in the odor of sanctity.

Another foundation had been accepted the previous year ; namely, in Michigan, in the city of Detroit.   St. Mary's Church had been given to the Redemptorist Fathers.

The old church has since been replaced by a splendid edifice, erected by the Franciscan Fathers, who succeeded the Redemptorists in St. Mary's parish. A foundation was also established in New Orleans, La., in 1847. The Redemptorists were thus gradually spreading over the entire country. The house at New Orleans has cost the Congregation the lives of many of its members who have fallen victims to the yellow fever. The first to die was Father Czackert, who succumbed on September 2nd, 1848.

A few months later there arrived in the United States one of the most eminent members of the Congregation of the Most Holy Redeemer, Father Bernard Hafkenscheid. This renowned missionary was born at Amsterdam, in the Netherlands, on December 12th, 1807. Having completed his studies at Rome, where he possessed among his fellow students the Sovereign Pontiff Leo XIII, and having been ordained a Priest, he soon after entered the Congregation of the Most Holy Redeemer. He made his vows in Austria, October 17th, 1833, and soon after began his labors in Belgium and the Netherlands. He attained high distinction as an orator, and to the present day is spoken of in Holland as a most powerful preacher. There is hardly a hamlet in Holland where the name of Father Bernard is unknown.

In 1845 he accompanied the Belgian Provincial, Father Frederick von Held to the United States, to make a canonical visitation of the recently established communities. This was only a passing visit to the country. In 1848, however, he was appointed Vice-provincial of the Redemptorists in America, where he arrived on January 8th, 1849. He took up his residence in Baltimore. He then made a tour of the country, visiting Pittsburgh, Cincinnati, St. Louis, New Orleans, Philadelphia, New York, Rochester, Buffalo, Detroit, Munroe and other places.

In the middle of the year 1850, he returned to Europe to assist at a meeting of the Provincial of the Congregation at Bischenberg, in Alsatia. On June 22nd of the same year, Pius IX erected the American houses of the Redemptorist

Congregation into a separate province, and Father Bernard was appointed first Provincial, and thus crossed the Atlantic for a third time. He remained three years in this office, when he returned to Europe. He labored in Great Britain and in his own country until his death, that occurred September 2nd, 1865.

Since the erection of the first American Province, the Congregation of the Most Holy Redeemer spread rapidly, and to-day it has two Provinces in the United States, the headquarters of which are at Baltimore and St. Louis. The successors of Father Bernard at Baltimore, were Fathers Ruland, De Dycker, Helmpraecht and Schauer, the present Provincial. The Provincial of St. Louis is Rev. William Loewekamp, who succeeded Father Jaeckel in 1877.

The Redemptorists have at present twenty-two houses in the province of Baltimore, and seven in that of St. Louis. Their work is no longer confined to the Germans and French, as it was, to a great extent, in the beginning; but many of their houses are now attached to parishes, the members of which claim English as their native tongue. The province of Baltimore possesses three houses in the Dominion of Canada, at Quebec, Toronto, and St. John, N. B. The communities of St. Anne de Beaupré, near Quebec, and Montreal belong to the Belgian Province. The three provinces give missions throughout the length and breadth of the land, and the Province of Baltimore has carried its apostolic labors as far as Newfoundland. About half of the young Redemptorists in the United States at present are of Irish descent.

Most of the Redemptorist missions at present are given in the English language. They, however, also give many missions in German and French, and of late years have also preached these exercises in Dutch, Bohemian and Italian.

God has blessed the grain of mustard seed, watered by the sweat of the pioneer Redemptorists, and the Congregation of St. Alphonsus, in America, has, although through many tribulations, reached a high state of development and gives much promise for the future.

The saintly Bishop Neumann, whom we had occasion to mention, died in his Episcopal See at Philadelphia, on January 5th, 1860. The cause of his canonization has been introduced at Rome, and we hope soon to number him among our American saints. We raise our eyes to heaven where we believe he lives to-day and hope that he may look down upon his confrers who may try to walk upon his footsteps.

A PRIEST AMBASSADOR TO THE UNITED STATES.

"Died at Lisbon, in September last, aged 74, Abbe Joze Correa Da Sarra, counsellor of finance, knight of several orders, member of several learned Societies, formerly minister plenipotentiary from Portugal to the United States, and well known in Europe and America as a distinguished botanist, and as a gentleman possessed of an uncommon share of Literary knowledge. In all the different countries in which he resided, during a long, active and useful life, a just tribute of respect was paid to his talents and genius, which, together with the kindness of his disposition and the brilliancy of his wit, ensured him everywhere the most friendly reception. His public services justified the high confidence of his government; his government, his literary merits have been acknowledged by several learned institutions in Europe and America, and by them, as well as by a large circle of friends, his loss will be deeply regretted."

Federal Gazette and Baltimore Advertiser, March 20, 1824.

THE CATHOLIC CHURCH IN CONNECTICUT—THE FIRST PRIEST IN THE COMMONWEALTH.

Read before the U. S. Catholic Historical Society, 1889,
Rev. Thomas J. Shahan, D.D.

The Seceders from Massachusetts Bay and the English Independents, who were the first settlers of Connecticut and Quimipiac, the present Hartford and New Haven, had small sympathy for any religion save their own. With them it was a settled matter that their shade of Calvinism was the correct color, and their form of Church discipline the proper one for Christians.

The ministers of the new settlements in the fertile valleys and along the charming shore were well agreed that the civil arm should be employed to sustain both doctrine and worship.

They were men of positive character, strong will, and, it cannot be denied, were gifted with patience, boldness, and foresight ; witness the foundation at Saybrook, of Yale College. Their influence was paramount in the settlements from the beginning, and they have handed it down to their successors, so that it is safe to say that nowhere in this country is the influence of the Protestant ministry so widespread and far reaching in state, society and education, as in Connecticut.

From the beginning stringent measures were adopted to exclude all other denominations. These were especially severe in the New Haven Colony. The attendance at Congregational service was compulsory, under pain of fine, and on the same page of the New Haven Colonial records may be seen fines of equal severity for missing service, getting drunk, laughing at the minister, and leaving one's matchlock at home. The support of the Church was by public tax, and the civil tax lists were used for apportioning the tithe. No other service could be held save that of the Congregational order.

The Bible, as the Ministers and Elders interpreted it, was the law, and it was always referred to for light, advice, precedents, solutions, etc., even in open court.

The original settlers, in great part, had left England for hatred of the Church by law established, and their first act in the silent depths of the forest was to establish by law the most intolerant of churches.

The first item in the Norwalk town records provides for the restraint of wandering swine, and the second for the erection of a minister's house. One of the earliest laws of New Haven made it expulsion for a priest to cross its borders, death to return, and every inhabitant a constable to apprehend him.

The first code of Connecticut made the settlement and support of a Congregational minister binding on every town and the civil power collected unpaid Church taxes by distraint.

In the course of time the necessities of social life, the ceaseless petty wars, the levelling action of commerce, the jealousy of the lay spirits, and the steady influx of newcomers seriously modified the simple theocracy which John Davenport had aimed at founding in New Haven, and the example of other colonies, together with the pressure of the home government, always hostile to New England, compelled a larger share of toleration in both settlements.

In the year 1706 the doctrines of the Church of England began to be preached in Stratford, and in 1722 a minister was settled there. In 1727 the general court granted to the Episcopalians liberty to organize a worship of their own, and freed them from the obligation of contributing to the support of the "Standing Order."

In 1729 this privilege was made to cover the case of Baptists, and even the detested Quaker, under the reign of Queen Anne, began to meet with toleration.

In 1743 a more general though guarded, act of toleration was passed in the following terms : " Be it further enacted that for the future any of his Majesty's subjects, being Protestants, inhabitants of this colony, that shall soberly dissent from the way of worship and ministry established by the laws of this Colony, that such persons may apply themselves to this Assembly where they shall be heard."

However, individuals were still subject to be taxed for the support of the Congregational Church, and by law were so liable until the year 1818.

As for the Catholics they were by law proscribed until the year 1791, when the first amendment to the Constitution made it possible for them to organize public worship without fear ; up to that time they labored under every disadvantage in Connecticut, for while a Protestant, of whatever sect, might, in the last century become a naturalized member of the colony, without violating his conscience, the Catholic could not, for he had to take the oath of abjuration, allegiance and supremacy, which obliged him to renounce the Pope, and deny the Blessed Sacrament.

In fact in the year 1773 Francis Fourgue, a native of Toulouse, domiciled in Fairfield, and in 1775 Don Gabriel Sistera, a native of Barcelona, domiciled in New London, applied to the General Court for naturalization, and were admitted on fulfillment of the condition above mentioned.

Finally, in the year 1818, thanks to the exertions of such men as Oliver Wolcott and Jared Ingersoll, the old charter of Charles II and the Encrustation of puritan custom, privilege and interpretation were abandoned, and, by a small majority, and after serious compromise, a liberal constitution, in line with that of the United States was adopted, Thenceforth all legal union of the State and Congregationalism disappeared.

Under such circumstances as have been related, few

Catholics ever sought the intolerant soil of Connecticut during the first hundred and fifty years of its existence, and these few it is hard to trace. Had they come in numbers they would have met with persecution. The loss of blood and treasure in the French wars, the large Irish Protestant emigration in the eighteenth century, the common perusal of such books as the "Simple Cobbler of Aggawam," [Springfield,] and the "Master-key to Popery," the dense ignorance of Catholic tenets, the teachings of the ministers, and the ancestral dislike and contempt for the Gael, would have been sufficient reasons to provoke a bloody welcome. It took the patriotic sacrifices of Irish and French Catholics in the Revolution to unlock the doors of Connecticut, which for one hundred and fifty years had been barred against the Roman Catholic religion.

Until the very end of the last century, a drunken crowd of sailors and townsmen paraded annually through New London, a grotesque figure of the Pope, which they finally consigned to the waters of the Sound, after the groggeries had paid tribute to their thirst.

When Hartford and New Haven were settted, England had been a full century in the bonds of heresy, and for this and other reasons, it is hardly probable that many of the original colonists were in any way connected with the ancient faith. But it is a strange thing that three of the most noted English puritans had Catholic brothers, equally noted in their respective spheres. The brother of John Davenport was the famous Christopher Davenport, alias Francis à Sancta Clara, a Franciscan, who did good work in the darkest half-century of the Catholic Church in England.

The brother of Lord Kimbolton, a supporter of the Puritans, and afterwards Earl of Manchester, was Walter Montague, Jesuit, well-known for his "pernicious" activity in furtherance of the Catholic Cause. The brother of the parliamentary Colonel and regicide William Goffe, was Dr. Stephen Goffe, who became Superior of the famous Paris Oratory, and the friend of all English exiles on the Continent, during the stormy years of Cromwell's Protectorate.

The first priest we meet with in the scanty annals of the infant settlements is the Rev. Gabriel Druillettes, one of the heroic band of Jesuit Missionaries who coupled the teaching of Catechism with the practice of Statecraft, and were as much at home in the councils of rulers as in the wigwams of the savage.

"On the last day of August. 1650," says the historian of the Catholic Church in the United States, "though spent with a laborious winter mission on the shores of the Gulf, (St. Lawrence,) he took up his staff to accompany the Indians to their lodgings on the Kennebec. The patient, self-denying Jesuit went also in a new character. He bore letters accrediting him to the governing powers in New England, with whom the Canadian authorities proposed a free inter-colonial trade, and to whose humanity they appealed for aid or volunteers to check the Iroquois, who menaced all that was Christian." After attending to the affairs of his mission, and consoling the affectionate Abnakis, the patriarch, for such he was called, even in New England, set out in November for Boston. "He was accompanied," says Dr. Shea, "by Noel Negabamet, the Chief of Sillery, embarking at Merry Meeting Bay, with John Winslow, whom the missionary calls his Pereira, alluding to the friend of St. Francis Xavier.

At Boston, [Charlestown,] Major General Gibbons received him courteously. Father Druillettes says: "He gave me the key of a room in his house where I could in all liberty say my prayers and perform the exercises of my religion. As he would naturally carry his missionary service with him, we may infer that Father Druillettes offered the holy sacrifice in Boston, in December, 1650. He delivered his credentials, urging the cause of his countrymen and the claims of his neophites, which he pleaded also at Plymouth. At Roxbury he visited Eliot, who pressed him to remain under his roof till Spring; but winter had no terrors for him. After receiving a reply from the governor and presenting his case to the leading men, he sailed early in January for the Kennebec, and in the following month resumed his missionary labors.

He returned to Canada in June, but was again accredited in a more formal manner, as envoy with Mr. Godefroy, to the Commissioners of the New England colonies, who were to meet at New Haven.

Thither the missionary and his associate, Mr. Godefroy, proceeded, and in September, 1651, the Catholic priest pleaded in vain for a brotherhood of nations, and for a combined action against a destroying heathen power.

"When the commissioners were at New Haven, says Trumbull, in his history of Connecticut, Monsieur Godfrey and Monsieur Gabriel Druillettes arrived in the capacity of commissioners from Canada. They had been sent by the French Governor, Monsieur D' Aillebout, to treat with the Colonies. They presented three commissions, one from Monsieur D' Aillebout, another from the Council of New France, and a third to Monsieur Gabriel Druillettes, who had been authorized to publish the doctrines and duties of Christianity among the Indians. In behalf of the French in Canada and the Christianized Indians in Acadia, they petitioned for aid against the Mohawks and warriors of the Six Nations. They urged that the war was just, as the Mohawks had violated the most solemn leagues, and were perfidious and cruel. That it was a holy war, as the Acadians were converted Indians, and the Mohawks treated them barbarously because of their christianity. They insisted that it was a common concern to the French and English Nations, as the war with the Six Nations interrupted the trade of both with the Indians in general. Monsieur Druillettes appeared to be a man of address. He opened the case to the best advantage, displaying all his art, and employing his utmost ability to persuade the Commissioners to engage in the war against the Six Nations. He urged that if they would not consent to join us, they would at least permit the enlistment of volunteers in the

United Colonies for the French service, and grant them a free passage through the Colonies by land or water, as the case might require, to the Mohawk country. He also pleaded that the Christianized Indians might be taken under the protection of the United Colonies. He represented that if these points could be gained they would enter immediately upon a treaty for the establishment of a free trade between the French and English in all parts of America.

The previous year, 1650, Father Druillettes had written to Governor Winthrop, of Connecticut, asking for his good will and influence before the General Court at Hartford, and personally with the Commissioners for Connecticut and New Haven. The letter is in Latin, and directed to the most illustrious lord, Sir John Winthrop, Knight, at Pequott River, New London.

In this touching letter the old Jesuit pleads principally the cause of his Indians, whom he tenderly styles: "prae cœteris omnibus mortalibus Ovis illa Centesima Errans, et derelicta in Deserto, quam unam, relictis nonaguita novem, quaerit sollicite, ut inventam gaudens in humeros imponat Dominus Jesus Christus." He appeals to Connecticut pride by referring to the successful war against the Narragansetts, and signs himself: "ubicum terrarum me detineat Dominus Jesus qui me vocavit ad vitam et mortem inter barbaros docendos agendam, tuæ universa Familiae vivam et moriar, ac potissimum Ver eximie.

Tibi addictisimus in Domino Jesu, pro quo, quia pro fratribus ejus Barbaris Christianis Legatione fungor

GABRIEL DRUILLETTES, S. J.,

Presbyter-docens in Kenebek.

Father Druillettes had arrived in Boston from the Kennebec in the last half of August, 1651, and went on to New Haven in the company of the Massachusetts Commissioners, doubtless across the present territory of Rhode Island, by the settlement at Providence. At Groton he crossed the Thames to New London, where he probably found time to spend a few hours with the brave, learned, ingenious and courtly Winthrop, and to say mass by the same courtesy he received at the hands of the rough soldier Gibbon, at Charlestown. From New London the road led on to Saybrook, and who will deny that it warmed the Jesuits' heart to look, on an August morning at that meeting of the waters—the mighty river and the placid sea. The land he stood on was claimed by a Fenwick; but little did the Missionary think that the first Catholic Missions in Connecticut would be opened up by a bishop of that name. The trail or path lay thence along the shore to Branford or Montowese, and when in the early September he entered the palisaded borders of Qunnipiac, he must have been struck with the beauty of the site, the sweetness of the air, the prim and orderly arrangement of the hamlet, the activity of the people, and the strict military discipline within the enclosure.

If he were gifted with prophetic vision, his eyes, as he entered the Puritan settlement would rest upon a slight elevation to the south-west, where the first Catholic Church would one day be built, and where that elevation dipped into the sea, he would behold a Puritan temple, made over in time to the then proscribed Catholics.

As he crossed the Quinnipiac he would see the oyster-beds at its mouth and among them, in time, when the encroachments of commerce should have caused them to be filled up, a stately church arising to be dedicated by a papal Nuncio.

If he spoke in the first church, and it is not probable that the meeting was held elsewhere. his eye could rest on a spot in the ample common where a great stone temple, in honor of the Mother of God, would one day lift its head in the very Arx of Puritanism.

Where the shadow of the great East Rock fell upon the plain, a large Asylum for the saving and educating of Catholic waifs and orphans would be visible to him, and down by the edge of the great common, where the sea came up to Oak and Commerce Streets, he would behold the churches of two nationalities, not one of whose citizens had yet visited New England.

Doubtless he would know from common report or from the conversations of one John Davenport, the mover of this new enterprise, that his brother Christopher was a Franciscan friar in England, and the Jesuit might see across the Quinnipiac in the flat, reedy plain a populous quarter, and in its midst a Catholic Church, dedicated to a Franciscan Saint, even the father of the Brotherhood.

But, as a matter of fact, the Jesuit, instead of meeting with a small share of success, found the commissioners opposed to him.

Previous to his arrival in New Haven, he had written a letter to the Commissioners for Connecticut and New Haven, asking that the meeting be held at Boston, where, doubtless, he thought he had more friends, and where a more liberal spirit prevailed. He also detailed the arguments for his petitions. To the first point it was replied that it was inconvenient to go to Boston; to the second "such answer was made as might have stopt all further proceedings." It must have therefore, been more evident to him that he would meet with failure at New Haven. However he had orders to meet the Commissioners and from them jointly to receive his answer, which was a polite and guarded dismissal of all his requests. With regard to his Indians, he was told indeed that "the English looks upon all such Indians as receive the yoke of Christ with another eye than upon others that worship the Diuell." This was hardly satisfactory language to the man, who wrote to Winthrop a letter breathing the Apostolic spirit of a Saint Patrick or a Saint Boniface. To his request for aid against the Mohawks, answer was made that "the English desire by all just means, to keep the peace [if it may be] with all men, even these Barbarians."

To the proffer of free trade they made reply that they

desired it not if they had to take it on such terms as the Company of New France gave to the unlicensed French traders within its territory. Complaint, moreover, was made that the French on the borders, and the Dutch resident at Hartford, sold rum to the Connecticut Indians. They might have added that Father Druillettes was ahead of his time in Connecticut with his scheme of brotherly union, his apostolic love for the savage and his generous willingness that a Protestant commonwealth should exercise a protectorate over Catholic Indians. They might also have added that they desired not overmuch close dealings with Priests and Catholics, lest the godly become degenerate, and be attracted to a more alluring fold.

Their policy seems to have been illiberal and unchristian and such was, without doubt, the conclusion of the little embassy, as the priest and his companions wended their way back to Boston, thence to set sail for his mission on the Kennebec, to which he had consecrated his life ; the gentle Abnakis, who in return have preserved to this day, the Catholic faith of Druillettes.

In the same month the battle of Worcester was fought, a Puritan King was enthroned ; all necessity of conciliating the French settlements disappeared, and the long conflict was entered on that ended only in the disaster, first, for France, which lost her possessions in North America, and then for England, when the disappearance of their French enemies emboldened her colonies to strike for their own liberty.

THOMAS J. SHAHAN, D.D.

SKETCH OF FATHER LOUIS ANDRÉ, S. J.
AN EARLY WISCONSIN MISSIONARY.

BY REV. A. E. JONES, S. J.

FATHER LOUIS ANDRE was born in 1623, and previous to his coming to New France he had entered the Society of Jesus as a member of the province of Toulouse. As a Canadian missionary he was within the jurisdiction of the province of France. Father André reached America on the 7th of June, 1669.*

1669. But a short time elapsed before he was sent to the Western Missions, where Claude Allouez, Jacques Marquette, and Claude Dablon, together with the coadjutor Brother Louis Le Boesme, were already toiling in the Master's vineyard. Allouez, who was stationed at the mission of St. Francis Xavier, Green Bay, informs us in the Relation of 1670, but in somewhat ambiguous terms, that " le P. Louys André, arrivé icy l'an passe, destiné du premier abord a cette mission, ou il est donc allé, apres avoir fait icy un an de noviciat de mission, parmi les Algonquins qui y font leur demeure." †

Allouez, whose sphere of action was, as we have said, in the vicinity of the " Baie des Puants," had gone for a time to Sault-Ste. Marie, which was the original destination of André. The confusion in the passage quoted arises from the fact that Allouez speaks as if he were writing from the Bay and from the Sault at the same time.

André's year of apprenticeship to a missionary life was made, we presume, in part at St. Francis Xavier's at the Baie des Puants, and in part at St. Ignace, Michilimakinac. The latter was founded as a mission in 1670.‡ Father André

---

* Martin's Catalogue, 1886.

† Rel., 1870, edit. Quebec, 1558, p. 101, col. 2. Conf. Rel., 1671, p. 81, col. 2.

‡ Rel., 1671, p. 89, col. 2.

seems to have passed the summer months at the Bay and the winter season at St. Ignatius; for he himself tells us : "cette Isle fameuse de Missilimakinac, ou nous avons commencé l'Hyver dernier la mission de Saint Ignace."§

1670. On the 20th of May, ‖ Allouez, leaving the neighborhood of the Bay, had set out for the Sault, and from him we ascertain the fact that Father André had already reached that post with Father Druillettes, who had journeyed with him. To be able to form an adequate idea of the hardships endured by F. André, and to obtain a graphic account of his apostolic labors, the Relations themselves should be consulted, as therein the facts are given often in his own words.¶

I would beg the reader to bear in mind that my intention in giving this notice on Andre's life is to present a simple record of dates and facts, and to supply references which may enable all without difficulty to find in published documents the full details of his career. These details are too lengthy to find place in the present sketch.

On the 28th of August* Father André set out for the mission of Mississagué (wide-mouth river), on the northern shore of Lake Huron. He arrived there three days after. As soon as the exercises of the mission were ended, he proceeded to Ouiebitchiouan,† an island in the same lake lying opposite Ekaent8ton [Manitoulin,] where he remained twelve days.‡ After sojourning on the latter island, continuing unremittingly his apostolic labors in spite of famine,§ he finally reached Lake Nipissing,‖and there spent three months instructing the 8tisk8agami (long-haired).¶

As the ice broke up* he returned to Ekaent8ton, and for three weeks he preached to the Amik8e,† or Beaver nation, who had taken up their abode on the island. Provisions were

---

§ Loc. cit.   ‖ Rel., 1670, p. 101, col. 2, and p. 100.

¶ *E g.*, Rel., 1671, p. 31, col. 2, et passim.

* Ibid.   † Rel., 1671, p. 32, col. 2,   ‡ Ibid.

§ Ibid., p. 33, 34.   ‖ Ibid., p. 35, col. 1.   ¶Ibid., p. 36, col. 1.

* Rel., 1671, p. 36, col. 1.   † Ibid.

now more plentiful, as the hunt of the moose had proved successful, and God gave him, as he says, wherewith‡ to "couler doucement la fin de l'hyver." This, to all appearances was toward the end of the winter 1670–1671. The summer months of 1671 he passed at the Baie des Puants.§

1671. We next find F. Andre at Michilimakinac, where he spent part of the winter‖ with the Etionnontatehronnon Hurons,¶ and other Indians, who had returned there as exiles to their old habitation.

On the 15th of December, 1671, he set out to return to Green Bay.* After a tedious and perilous journey, owing to the ice especially, he reached his destination, and occupied the remainder of the winter journeying from village to village† and evangelizing the tribes settled in the neighborhood.

It was in this year, 1672, that the old Relations were discontinued.‡ So, to follow F. André, we must consult the "Relations Inédites," published by F. Felix Martin, S. J. (Paris, 1861), from the original manuscripts preserved in the archives of St. Mary's College, Montreal, and supplemented by others found in Paris and Rome.

1672. Father André was stationed at Green Bay in 1672, and I might say permanently. He had for his companion Father Allouez. André records in the beginning § of his Relation that on the 22d of December, 1672, his wigwam having caught fire, his writing materials and his diary were consumed. He, however, recalled to mind that it was on the 16th of November, 1671,‖ the very day of his arrival at Chouskoanée, that he had taken informal possession of the St. Xavier mission in the Baie des Puants, or what is now Green Bay. Later on, the new superior of the Ottawa mission, or upper lake region, Father Henri Nouvel, appointed him in a more formal manner.¶ He spent three months of this year at Chouskonabika,* assiduously instructing the Indians of that

---

‡ Ibid.   § Rel , 1672, p. 39, col. 1.   ‖ Rel., 1671, p. 37, col. 2.   ¶ Ibid., col. 1.
  * Rel., 1672, p. 39, col. 1.   † Ibid., p. 40, col. 1.
   ‡ Why? See " Relations Inedites," I Vol., Introduction, p. xxii. et seq.
§ Rel. In., I. Vol., p. 103.   ‖ Ibid. p. 104.   ¶ Ibid.   * Ibid., pp. 117, 118.

locality.

1673. On the 15th of February, the first day of Lent, 1673, he repaired to the village of Oussouamigoung,† where his labors were crowned with success.   But, owing to a promise he had made F. Allouez, he reluctantly left his neophytes, on the 6th of March,‡ to return to the residence at the Bay. Here, day after day,§ from morning to sundown, the Indians flocked to his cabin to be instructed in the Christian faith. On the 24th of March,‖ the Indians struck their tents, intending to camp nearer the mouth of the river,¶ and on the day following, F. Allouez returned from a mission to the Outagamis, thus leaving F. André at liberty* to go on his own annual eight days' retreat, which time is spent in seclusion, prayer, and meditation.

Toward the end of April of this same year, 1673,† F. André undertook a mission to the Maloumines or Folles-Avoines, but he does not specify what length of time he spent among them.

1674. In the following year, 1674, he returned the mission of Ouassatimoun (sic), and premises by saying that it was hif third visit.‡   On the 16th of November, the river of the Folles-Avoines, or Maloumines, being completely frozen over, he was prevented from following the Indian bands to the extremity of Cape Illinois, and saw himself in the necessity of patiently awaiting their return at the end of January, 1675.§

Dablon, in one of his letters dated Quebec, 24 Oct., 1794,* thus speaks of André and his labors: "The first residence (of the Ottawa mission) is situated on the shores of the Baie des Puants, and bears the title of St, Francis Xavier.   The residents are F. Allouez, that saintly and accomplished missionary, F. Marquette, of whom I have just spoken, and Louis André, who reaps an abundant harvest, thanks to his constancy

---

† p. 118.   ‡ p. 120.   § Rel. In., 1 Vol. p. 121.   ‖ Ibid., p. 122.
¶ Fox or St. Francis Xavier's River.   See Ibid., p. 122 note.
* Ibid., p. 122.   † Ibid., pp. 223, 224.   ‡ Ibid., p. 229.   § p. 233.
*Rel. In., II. p. 7.

and indefatigable assiduity." And in the body of the Relation. 1674-1675, we are told that "the next mission (to be
mentioned) is that of St. Francis Xavier, located a little further than the Baie des Puants. It is as it were the rallying
point of a great number of different bands, who dwell in the
neighborhood. F. André labours among those who live
along the Bay. By his firmness he has managed to tame
these savages, the fiercest and most superstitious of the tribes,
bringing them little by little by his determined efforts under
the yoke of the Gospel. We might add that this church has
received its formation from him. It is composed of four or
five hundred Christian believers. The Father, in the course
of last year baptised as many as one hundred and forty."†

1675-1676. André continued his labors at the Bay throughout the year 1675, and in giving an account of his mission, in
a latter dated 30th April, 1676, mentions six ‡ nations as
settled along either shore of the Baie des Puants. One of the
unconverted Indians burnt down his cabin, but he persevered
undismayed. The first fifteen days of his labors were spent
with the Folles-Avoines, and after residing, at the expiration
of that time, three more weeks among the Otiaraouatenon,§ he
passed on to the Winipegoucks. A band of Aia8as or Mas-
coutin-Nadouessis, who dwelt about six hundred miles further
west and who had wandered to the vicinity of the Bay, profited
also by his ministrations. This nation spoke the same language ‖ as the Puants or Winipegoucks. In this Relation
some of F. André's curious observations on the rise and fall
noticed in the waters of Lake Michigan are recorded.¶

1677. In the Relation of 1677 a few pages only are devoted
to the Ottawa or Lake Michigan missions. F. Charles Albanel
was then local Superior;** he had come up the previous year.
It might be of interest to indicate here the different changes
which had taken place in the Ottawa, or upper missions, since
F. André's arrival. I find them recorded in the annual catalogues, the only copy of which in America, as well as I have

---

† Ibid.   ‡ Ibid., p. 118.   § Ibid., p. 119.   ‖ Ibid., p. 120.
¶ Ibid., pp. 120, 121.   ** Ibid., pp. 229.

been able to ascertain, is preserved in the archives of St. Mary's College. It is in manuscript, and copied by F. Felix Martin, while in Rome. Unfortunately, even the Roman collection is incomplete.

The first change occurs in 1673, and I give the status of the mission as I there find it :

Ad Outoua. P. Hen. Nouvel, Sup. in lac. Huron. cum 2 fam.

P. Gab. Druilletes curat miss. S. Mar. ad Saltum.

P. Claud. Allouez et Ludov. André in miss. S. Francisc.

P. Jac. Marquette in miss. S. Ignat. A verno tempore suscepit iter versus Mare Pacificum seu Sinense cum gallis comitibus et Algonq.

P. Philip. Pierson, miss. Huron. S. Ignat. curat cum fam. Coadj. Ludov. Le Boesme.

P. Bailloquet, miss. Nipissin, cum 2 fam.

1674. Ut supra, Insuper P. Ant Silvy cum P. Jac. Marquette reduce.

1675. Ut supra.‡‡ Insuper P. Ant. Silvy ad S. Franc. Xav. et alter coadj. Ægid Mazier.

---

†† The death of Jacques Marquette is not recorded in the above extracts. He died in 1675, on a Saturday, the 18th of May, and not the 19th, as is erroneously given in the original manuscript, which has been reproduced by J. G Shea and copied by others. This date I adopt out of deference to the original manuscript itself. On page 42 (confer " Discov. and Explor. of Mississippi," Shea, 1852, p. 58) it is stated : " La veille de son trepas qui fut un vendredi." And whatever ambiguity there may be in this expression it is cleared away by the explicit statement made on p. 50 (confer Shea, Ibid., p. 65): Aussi lay a-t-elle accordé la faveur qu'il anoit tonsjours demandée, de mourir un *samedy.*" Now, in 1675 there was no Saturday falling on the 19th of May, but the 18th fell on a Saturday. Moreover, 19th May, as the date of his death, is not contained in the body of the manuscript properly speaking, but is rather inferred from the heading of one of the sections on page 46: " Ce qui s'est passé au transport des ossements du feu Père Marquette, qui ont estéz retiréz, du sepulchre le 19e May, 1677, qui est le mesme Jour qu'il mourut l'an 1675." (Confer Shea, Ibid., for a free translation, p. 61). The headings might easily have been added at Quebec to an original account sent from the West, and now no longer extant, the better to divide off the matter in making the draught of the manuscript we still possess. The same mistaken date was adopted in the narrative of Marquette's death in the Relations of 1674–1675, sent by F. Dablon to the R. F. Pinette, his Provincial in France (see Rel. In., I. Vol., p. 31): " Il rendit paisiblement sa bienheureuse áme á son Créateur un samedi 19 de mai eutre ouze heures et minuit." Consequently he died in the night of Saturday and Sunday, but on Saturday, the 18th of May, 1675.

1676.   Ut supra. Insuper P. Carolus Albanel profectus est ad illas missiones.

1677.   Ut supra, except. P. Allouez miss. Illinen.   PP. Albanel et André curant miss. S. Xav.; PP. Silvy et Pierson miss. S. Ignat.

F. André, throughout 1677, continued working assiduously among the Indians of the Bay, and regenerated by baptism one hundred catechumens.   Twice this year had he incurred the dangers of being wrecked in the frail canoes of the natives.*

The "Relations Inédites" of 1672-1679 give no further particulars concerning F. André; but with the aid of the manuscript extracts from the catalogues,† we are able, with the exception of a few years, to follow his movements with certainty till his death.

1678-1684.   From 1678 to 1681 we find him still at Green Bay; in 1682, at Michilimakinac.   In 1683, he is with the Indians at Kiskakin.   This was the last year of his missionary labors in the West.

1684-1690.   He was now in his sixtieth year, and was recalled to Quebec, no doubt, with the intention of affording him a little rest after many years of hardship and apostolic toil.   From the old registers in the archives of the Archbishopric at Quebec, we learn that F. André visited the Gulf of the St. Lawrence in the summer of 1684, proceeding as far as Ka8i and Anticosti.   It was no doubt as a kind of holiday trip.   He was then named professor of Philosophy in the Jesuits' College at Quebec, a post he occupied in 1684 and 1685.   And, though venerable in years, he did not think it beneath him to accept an appointment as professor in the lower forms of Quebec College.   This duty he fulfilled from 1686 to 1690.

For a man of his ability and experience, blessed with a robust constitution and inured to toil, the task of teaching Latin rudiments and even more advanced classes, were mere

---

* Rel. In., II., p. 280.
† Archives of St. Mary's College, Montreal.

child's play. But his superiors no doubt had an ulterior object in view in his appointment. It was, we may presume, to afford him an opportunity and leisure of turning to account for the benefit of future missionaries his thorough knowledge of the Algonquin language. His Algonquin and Ottawa dictionary bears no date, but the little compendium, "Preceptes, Phrases et Mots," written, to all external appearances, about the same time, furnishes us with a clue. At page 45 we are given to understand that Allouez had already been about thirty years on the Indian missions : "Sylvestres alii aliis melius et clarius loquuntur etiam si nesciant se bene aut male loqui, sicut nostrates rustici, et P. Claudius Alloez, qui circiter 30 annos versatus est cum sylvestribus dixit mihi se non reperiisse duos sylvestres eodern omnino modo loquentes, presertim cum aliqua vox erat enucleanda, imo sœpe idem improbat quod dixerat, quod accidit ex·mixtione nationum ; nam quoad possunt ducunt uxores ex alia natione quam ex sua, quod invehit ingentem vocabulorum multitudinem et diversas dialectos."

Now, Claude Allouez landed on the 11th of July, 1658, and died the 27th of August, 1689,‡ giving an interval of 31 years between his arrival and his death ; so that the compendium was not certainly written before 1688, though it might have been written after, as F. Allouez died after *about* thirty years of missionary life.

Besides the Dictionary and the collection of Precepts, 'etc., there were other of his works which survived him, but which I have not yet been able to discover. We are informed of this by the following inscription in a strange hand, written on the inside of the paper cover of the compendium :

COLLECTIO
SEQUENS EST CONSCRIPTA
A P. LUDOVICO ANDRE, QUI
FUIT SILVICOLARUM MONTANORUM
MISSIONARIUS AD ANN. M.D.C.XCIII

---

‡ Martin's Catalogue.

ALIA MANUSCRIPTA EJUSD. SCIL CATE-
CHISMUS, RUDIMENTUM, ET EXHOR-
TATIONES SERVANTUR IN ARCHIO
TADUSSAKENSI, SUB N ᵒ . . . *

1691. In 1691 André is again on the missions, this time at
St. Francis Xavier (Chicoutimi) and Lake St. Peter. † This
was in the Lower Algonquin mission. It is well to remark
that the Lake St. Peter here mentioned is not the well-known
lake of to-day, which is merely an expansion of the waters of
the St. Lawrence, and which lie between Montreal and Quebec
but the one which bore also the Indian name of Chobmouchouan. This is evident from the fact that that same year
and in the same Catalogue F. Vincent Bigot and F. Sebastian
Rale, both belonging to the Abenakis mission, are marked as
missionaries at St. Francis (de Sales), which is on the south-
eastern shore of our present Lake St. Peter, Those who have
the good fortune to possess a copy of the English edition of
Charlevoix's " Voyage to Canada," etc., (Baldwin : London,
1763), will find therein a map on which this Lake St. Peter
is set down (49⁰ lat., 74⁰ 3′ long.), though it is to be
found on no modern government map of the province of
Quebec.

In the archives of St. Mary's College, Montreal, is still
preserved an old missionary map of Lake Chobmouchouan,
with the surrounding region and Lakes. A mission-house,
marked " L Ange Gardien," stands on a peninsula to the
north, and at about 40 miles to the S. E. lie the portage and
Lake of St. Francis Xavier. Chobmouchouan would seem
to extend fully 30 miles in its greatest length from N.W. to N.
E.; it is drained from its northern shore into Lake St. John
by a circuitous route taken by the river which bears the same

---

* The following Collection was written by Father Louis André, who was missionary of the Montagnais Indians down to 1693. Other of his manuscripts, to
wit : a catechism, a grammar, and short sermons, are preserved in the Archives
of Tadoussac under the Number....(in blank).
The Archives of Tadoussac have long since disappeared.
† MS. Cat., 1691.

name. This stream may be said to be all but unnavigable even for canoes, as it is but one long succession of rapids, seething and foaming over an uneven and rocky bed.

Father Claude Godefroy Coquart, in his yet unpublished "Memoire sur les Postes du Domaine du Roy," addressed to the Intendant Francis Bigot, and dated the 5th April, 1750, says : ‡ "Chom8kch8an (sic) was dependent formerly on (the post of) Lake St. John. The Indians brought thither their peltry, or as it is still practiced, the men of the post went after it. Winter cantonments had been made there several years in succession ; but it is now ascertained that it was all but a useless expenditure, it being quite enough to repair thither at the breaking up of the ice. The post of Chom8kch8an lies back of Three Rivers, and it would be well to prevent the trips of the Indians to that town, in which event instead of 8 or 900 marten skins, the amount now secured, the supply might be greatly increased. The Indians are enticed to Three Rivers by the fire-water given in exchange for their furs, and which they bring back with them to their homes. This road has not been successfully blocked up to the present."

"The agent at Chek8timi usually sends up a trader, whom he supplies with merchandise,* together with two Frenchmen and a few Indians of his post. By the end of July they are back again from their trip. The Indians (of Chom8kch8an) are a worthless set ; they cannot be distrusted too much, for their intercourse with Three Rivers has utterly demoralized them. It would be a great advantage for Chek8timi if they could be kept at home, and if the traders of Three Rivers could be prevented from sending either French or Indians to trade with them for spirits. Dergroseilliers had made successful expeditions several years in succession to Chom8kch8an, whatever Mr. Cugnet may assert to the contrary. What is wanting now is a trader who can manage to make a trip each year, either by wintering in Chek8timi, or by setting out in the very early spring, and it is my opinion that he

‡ Orig. MS., p. 20.   * Orig. MS., p. 21.

would be in time enough should he start from Quebec at the end of April."

In comparing the respective difficulties of a journey to Lake Mistassini and one to Lake Chobmouchouan, Father Coquart says : †

" For the last three years it is an employee from Tadoussac who makes the journey (to Lake Mistassini); it is as fatiguing as that to Chom8kkch8an, but takes less time; for, the one, to Chom8kch8an, is a succession of rapids to ascend, and the other a series of portages." It would appear also from Fr. Coquart's " Memoirs " that the natural outlet for trade from the Mistassin Indians was to Hudson's Bay, while that from Chobmouchouan was to Three Rivers, as he alleges the following reasons for not removing the agent of Chicoutimi, one Joseph Dorval: ‡ " The agent of Chek8timi has been in charge of the post for fourteen years. He is a favorite with the Indians, difficult of their nature to manage in this canton. He has a knack of encouraging them, and if he were removed, it is to be feared that the Mistassins, who are attached to him, would carry their peltry to Hudson's Bay, from which they are not separated by so great a distance as from Chek8timi, and those of Chom8kch8an would carry theirs to Three Rivers."

If I have entered into these particulars, it is that the Relations do not extend down to the time of the settlement at Lake Chobmouchouan, and because that region is all but forgotten to-day. What I have quoted concerning it. is from original, unpublished documents, which are almost equally unknown, and certainly not within the reach of your readers. As for the Lake itself, it was never visited by a white man previous to 1661, and probably not for some time later. The region in which it lies was unexplored. This is expressly stated in the relation of that year: § " Lake St. John is the term of French exploration, no one having dared to penetrate beyond, either because the beaten tracks are too rugged or because

---

† Orig. MS., p. 21.   ‡ Orig. MS., p 27   § Relat., 1661, p. 14, col. 2.

they are as yet unknown." In fact, that same relation contains a letter of Fr. Claude Dablon and Fr. Gabriel Druillettes, dated the 2d of July, 1661, from Nekouba (lat. 49° 20/, long. 305° 19/, Paris), a half-way station to Hudson's Bay, and in it we are told* what account the Indians gave of these regions, hoping thereby to dissuade the missionaries from proceeding on their journey: " Precipices on all sides, where the French may well expect disaster, as they (the Indians) themselves, inured from early youth to this kind of navigation, have not always escaped shipwreck. The rapids here are not the usual ones met with, but yawning chasms walled up on either side with towering rocks rising perpendicularly from the river bed, in the midst of which, if the canoe deviates but a paddle's breadth in her course, it is dashed to pieces on a sunken rock or whirled into an abyss. That the most daring amongst them confessed that they grew dizzy when they encountered these torrents, and that the day passed before they quite recovered."

Such was the nature of the journey northward which Fr. André had to undertake. in his 68th year, to reach Lake St. Peter, or Chobmouchouan.

1692, 1694. In 1692 Fr. André was still in the Montagnais missions with the Papinachois and at Chicoutimi. In 1693 and 1694 we find him back amidst civilization and stationed at Montreal.†

1695. He is again on the mission, at the Seven Islands on the northern shore of the Lower St. Lawrence below Tadoussac.‡

1696–1699. From 1696 to 1699, inclusively, he is not mentioned in the catalogue, save in the erroneous statement at the end of 1696: " Obiit P. André Cadomis (at Caen), 30 Apr., 1696." This certainly referred to some other Fr. Andre, for we shall see by the sequel that the sturdy veteran was not

---

* Relat., 1661, p. 15, col. 1.

† MS. Cat. 1692; Old Registers, archiv. of Archbishopic, Quebec.

‡ MS. Cat., 1695.

ready yet to shake off his mortal coil. He appears again in 1700,—where was he in the meantime? I have not been able to discover. Even the Miscellaneous "Liber" and the old registers preserved at Quebec are silent on the matter. But both, unfortunately, are incomplete.

1700. This year his name is marked on the catalogue among those of the community of Quebec College. Though now in his 77th year, he still bears the title of "Missionarius,"which, under the circumstances, could only mean resident missionary at Quebec for such of the Algonquin Indians who might come up or down to barter at the capital of the colony.

1702-1715. It was only in 1703 that the title of "senex" was added to that of missionary, and it became evident that his waning strength would never admit of his again leaving the sheltering walls of Quebec College. In 1705, his title of missionary is dropped from the catalogues, and the significant suffix of "senex" alone remained. He was indeed a veteran now, and entitled to a well-earned but to him a distasteful repose. It was not, however, until ten years later, on the 19th September, 1715, that he was called to his eternal reward, at the ripe old age of 92.

The following circular was sent by his superior, as was customary on those occasions, to the other houses of the Order. It is the first time it is published :

QUEBEC, 1 November, 1715.

REVEREND FATHER,
  PAX CHRISTI:

We have recently lost, in the person of Father Louis Andre, a missionary labourer loaded down even more with the weight of merit than that of years. It is now over forty-five years since he devoted himself to the conversion of the Indians, and it may be justly said that in so painful and laborious a vocation he accomplished all fhe duties of an excellent missionary. There is no doubt but that it was with natural repugnance he adopted the Indian mode of life, and that he underwent many hardships in the long any weary journeyings in which he ac-

companied his Indians. These never disheartened him, for
he reckoned fatigue as naught when there was a question of
God's glory or the salvation of souls. He laboured on the
mission until he had nearly attained his eightieth year, and if
at any moment of his life he was called upon to do violence
to himself in the practice of obedience, it was when his superiors, touched at the sight of his many infirmities and the
suffering inseparable from missionary labour, he must needs
have endured at so advanced an age, put a stop to his departure and retained him at Quebec.

Though Father André possessed all the other virtues of a
perfect religious and of a zealous missionary, he was especially remarkable for his patience and for the evenness of
his temper, which was proof against any untoward eventu-
ality. We furthermore admired in him a regularity that
never failed even unto the end. Already, from far back in
life, had he prepared himself for death, and he awaited in
perfect confidence the moment when it should please God
to call him from this life. It was on the 19th of September last, well on to four in the morning, that he went, as
we have every reason to believe, to receive the recompense
of his labours. Before death he had the consolation of receiving the last sacraments of the Church, and he crowned
a life rich in good deeds and merit with that perfection of
patience which might have led us to believe that he was
insensible to bodily pain, were we not aware, from other
indications, how intense were his sufferings. You will accord him, Reverend Father, the usual suffrages of the
Society, and for myself I beg a share in your Holy Sacrifices, in union with which I am with profound respect,

Reverend Father, Your Reverence's most humble and
obedient servant,

                              JOSEPH GERMAIN, S. J.[*]

---

[*] Translated from the copy of the original manuscripts preserved in the Archives of the " Gesu," at Rome.

The name of Father André, though he had toiled so long in evangelizing the Indians, is not one familiar even to the admirers of the early Jesuit missionaries. If these disjointed notes succeed in drawing the attention of the student of our early history to so meritorious a career, it will amply repay the trouble and research required to bring them together, meagre though they be. They will at least, I trust, serve as pointers for his future biographer, who will find in the correct references to the early Relations, given in this paper, an easy means of filling out his pages with a thousand interesting details I have omitted; but which are on record as illustrations of the life of this remarkable missionary of the West.

ST. MARY'S COLLEGE, Montreal, 27th April, 1889.

————

THE FIRST CHAPEL OF THE JESUITS IN NEW ORLEANS.

According to the reminiscences of Mr. Charles Deranco, an old citizen, given some years ago :

" The suburb St. Mary was no doubt named after a Catholic Chapel erected under the Jesuit Fathers, bearing that name, and which I saw as late as 1816 in Delord Street, on this side of what then was called " Les Jardins d'Elisa," being a public garden opening upon the adjoining estates of M'me Poeyfarre, surrounded by orange fences and flower parterres." Is there any extended account of this Chapel, its foundation and destruction?   D.

DeCourcy's " Catholic Church in the United States " appeared in French in the "Ami de la Religion," Paris, beginning August 3, 1854.

HISTORY OF
THE OLD CATHOLIC CHAPEL AT PRIEST'S FORD,
IN HARFORD COUNTY, MD.

Read before the Harford Historical Society, Oct. 26th, 1889.
By G. W. Andrew, M.D.*

On the very summit of one of the many picturesque
hills that diversify the lovely scenery of Deer Creek valley
stands a quaint old building of other days, the roof sloping
from the central top down to each of the four walls, giving
it an expression at once foreign and antique.   Although
but a single story in height, it covers a considerable area,
presenting, in these days of lofty mansions, a rather squatty
appearance from its high perch.   Its walls of stone are
massive, and its interior arrangement is so peculiar that it
draws at once the attention of any stranger who crosses
the threshold.

This old building has an interesting history, though
unfortunately the greater part of that history is lost to the
world. Born on an adjoining hill, in full sight of the old
building, I had it in my eye almost every day, and many
times a day, for more than twenty years.   During my childhood it was to me a much greater mystery than it is now,
and an infinitely more useful one. For there were strange
and weird stories of its past that were by no means re-
assuring to a credulous and impressionable boy. Had it
not been for the fact that it was at that time, and had
been for years, occupied by a most estimable family, whose
purifying presence seemed quite sufficient to exorcise any
evil spirit that might once have haunted it, I should no

---

* We owe this paper to the courtesy of Dr. Archer, and print it because of
its interesting account of an old Catholic Mission. We would not mutilate his
paper, but leave some points that readers will naturally question.

doubt have looked upon it with even more awe than I did. Even as it was, I used to think that the old building, set up there on the towering hill, with its whitened walls visible for miles in every direction, was making itself entirely too conspicuous for an uncanny habitation,—and, indeed, for any but one of immaculate purity in the past.

The mode by which these impressions were made on my youthful mind only shows too well how an evil seed cast by ignorance upon a mental evil cultivated on exclusive principles, may take root and ripen to a fruitage of unreasoning prejudice and rank injustce. They came from the older and more superstitious negroes belonging to my father. They delivered their oracles mostly in the old " quarter," at night, to all willing listeners,—and I was not often one of the unwilling. Their stories and traditions were conveyed, as is the wont of their race in such matters, in vague terms and dark hints which, while affording nothing substantial to take mental hold upon, made none the less a deep impression. In fact, the only really palpable story that I ever heard from that source about the mysterious building signally failed of its intended effect, simply because I was able, child though I was, to bring reason to my aid. They assured me, with awful solemnity, that a priest was buried directly under the main entrance, and that he had on a pair of iron shoes that he might walk through purgatory without getting scorched. My reply was to the effect that anybody with with a grain of sense ought to know that the iron shoes would soon get red-hot and only make matters a great deal worse, if possible, for the purgatorial ranger. After that sockdolager I heard none but impalpable concoctions as before, which reason could not grasp and wrestle with. And, so, the shadows of them rested darkly on my youthful imagination. As years advanced, all this, of course, passed away ; and although I have often since crossed the threshold of the old house, and sometimes have sat by the hour with the hospitable family in the little porch directly over those imaginary iron sandals, purgatory had no place in my mind, being kept aloof by thoughts of a more earthly and far more pleasant sort.

To understand properly the mode of establishment and history of this old Chapel—which we may take as a type of all of its kind throughout the State—some introductory remarks are necessary concerning the then alternating conditions of toleration and persecution in the province, to which alone the existence of this class of religious buildings was due.

Although volumes have been written in admiration of the tolerant rule planned by the first Lord Baltimore, and carried out by his son and grandson, the truth is no one can tell whether their toleration had any merit or not, simply because none but the All-Seeing eye can read human motives. This much is certain—and I think it completely annihilates all their claims to merit on that score : The Lords Baltimore could not have acted otherwise than they did in the matters spiritual, without being at once stripped of all their proprietary rights. The mother-country's Protestant King, Protestant parliament, and overwhelming Protestant population would have indignantly hurled any Proprietary from his seat on the least intimation of his persecuting those of the dominant faith. But this is not all. Even if King, parliament and people beyond the sea could have remained indifferent, the colonists themselves would promptly have averted such an attempt, or, if they did not, must have proved themselves dastards indeed, since, from the very first, a large majority of them were Protestants.

I am well aware that this has been a thousand times denied, but there can be no doubt of it. The proofs are numerons, but I shall only adduce one, which, strangely enough, seems to have been overlooked, although sufficient in itself to sustain the assertion. It is to be found in the famous "Journal" of Father White, the pioneer priest of Maryland. After describing the long and stormy passage of the first colonials, (whom he accompanied,) he goes on to say, " During the entire voyage no person was attacked with any

desire except that, at Christmas, wine having been freely distributed in honor of that festival, several drank of it immod-
erately; thirty persons were seized with a fever the next
morning, of whom about twelve died shortly after ; of these
[twelve who died] two were Catholics." That is to say,
the non-Catholics who died were two—or five to one of the
Catholics who died, Now, unless we could blasphemously
suppose that the Almighty brought about this drunken
debauch on the anniversary of the Lord's birth, with the
special object of thinning out the Protestants, and that he
guided its ravages almost entirely in that direction, we are
bound to accept these numbers as presenting a tolerably,
fair proportion of Catholics to non-Catholics in the very first
colony to the province. And as the non-Catholics could
not well have been Mahometan, Buddhist, or Pagan, or anything, in fact, but Protestants, it is fair to infer that they were
of the latter faith. At any rate, it proves beyond all doubt
that a large majority of the first colonists were Protestants.
And I believe that no one has ever denied that a very
large majority of those who subsequently settled in the
province were also Protestant. It may be that the three
Catholic Baltimores, even if their power had been supreme
in the land, would have proceeded precisely as they did ;
and from their sterling virtues and their noble characters, we
have every reason to think that such would have been the
case. But there was certainly no merit in doing that which
they could not help doing if they acted at all.

Let the merit of its establishment, however, belong to
whom it may, and whatever the motive for it, it is an
undeniable fact that toleration existed wherever Cecilius
or Charles Calvert was at the helm of government and
wherever this fell into other hands, toleration ceased. All
Christians enjoyed equal rights in matters of religion throughout the province, from its founding until 1692, with the single
exception of four-years rule by Puritans, who had flocked in
from Virginia—having been expelled thence by law—and
found protection under Baltimore. They soon obtained

control of affairs, and with an ingratitude seldom paralleled, decreed that none but Puritans and their like should exercise their faith without molestation. Upon the collapse, in 1658, of this brief alien rule, toleration again prevailed and continued uninterruptedly for thirty-five years. At the end of that period, however, in 1692, despite the prevalence of equal rights the Proprietary was deposed by a rebellion of Protestants incited by a few factious spirits, the chief of whom was an impious renegade. Under the new regime an Assembly was convened " for deliverance," as they expressed themselves, " from a tyrranical Popish government under which they had long groaned." This, however, was only " buncombe " addressed to the Protestant king and parliament, and, as we have seen, had no foundation in fact.

By an act of Assembly of the same year, the Church of England was established, for whose support all had to contribute whether they believed in its doctrines or not ; and if after that, they had any means left, they were graciously allowed to expend it upon their own churches. This was bad enough for both Catholics and non-conformist when received in the light or the present day, but far worse was in store for Catholics, and came apace in the act of 1704, by which under severe penalties, no Catholic priest could exercise the functions of his calling, nor could any Catholic, whether priest or not, instruct the young, or even board them, without being sent to England to be prosecuted. Thus, for a brief period, the Catholics were deprived of both schools and churches, being reduced to the deplorable condition of the most benighted heathens. Soon this infamous act, being condemned by public opinion, was softened down to the extent of allowing the Catholic priests to officiate in private residences, and this, strangely enough, was called an " exemption." Rooms in Catholic houses were now consecrated; soon private chapels were erected under the family roof; and afterwards, in a few instances, separately. This last, though a violation of the act, was mostly connived at, in view of the harshness and cruelty of the restriction, and the oppressed even ventured to open a few schools in private residences, under the same kind of sufferance. One such school was established by the Jesuits at the head of Bohemia river, in Cecil County, where Archbishop Carroll, and possibly his brother, Charles of Carrollton, were in part educated.

Meanwhile, the line of Baltimore became Protestant, and in 1714 the province was restored to the heir with all proprietary rights. This of course brought about no further amelioration in the condition of Catholics. Thus we see that during the first half of the last century they were in a truly pitiable condition so far as their spiritual facilities were concerned. In the very land they had established, and in great measure built up to prosperity, the faithful priests, seeing their little flocks hungry for spiritual comfort, had to wander up and down on periodical visits from house to house, often taking with them their vestments and sacred vessels, and erecting at each station a temporary altar mostly of the rudest description.

Such was the state of affairs when this old Chapel was established at some time before the middle of the eighteenth century. There is one other important point to be considered before giving its history :

No corporation or society, ecclesiastical or temporal, could at this period, hold lands in the province without special license from the proprietary. Cecilius Lord Baltimore, who, although a staunch and sincere Catholic, was by no means priest-ridden, had a severe struggle with the Jesuits about their acquisition of lands not many years after the establishment of the colony. That hard working society, going boldly forth upon their mission into the wilderness, had obtained from the Indians, who highly venerated them, large bodies of land remote from the settlements, and when called to a reckoning by the government, claimed that they held these lands under a certain ecclesiastic law, not of Maryland, or even of England, but of Rome. For while they virtually set Baltimore's authority at defiance. But his lordship was

not so easily brought to terms.   He at once applied to Rome
to have the Jesuits removed from the province, and it was
not long before an order to that effect was actually issued
from the Eternal City.   The Jesuits, however, making a
virtue of necessity, in order to avert expulsion (which of
course, would have involved the loss of all their labors and
acquisitions, both spiritual and pecuniary), executed a release
of the lands they had acquired from the Indians. Baltimore
took prompt and effective measures to prevent a repetition
of such a flagrant encroachment upon his rights, and Maryland feels to this day, for good or ill, the effect of his energetic action—she being the only State in which lands cannot be sold, given, devised to a religious body, or for a religious use, without the consent of the legislature.   Whether or
not there was any difficulty in procuring from the provincial
authorities the necessary license to establish the Deer
Creek Chapel there is nothing to show.

I will now give such facts as are known in the history of
the Old Chapel, filling up some of the numerous gaps with
conjecture, which, though often disastrously misleading, may
sometimes be the best we can do, and is, of course, always
held subject to revision in the light of future developments.

Mr. John Gilmary Shea in his recent " History of the
Catholic Church in Colonial Days," says :   " It was apparently while the future of Catholicity looked so dark that, about
1747 the missioners in Maryland purchased a tract of land on
Deer Creek, near a spot still called Priest's Ford, in Harford
County.   Here they established the Mission of St. Joseph
and erected a house such as the laws then permitted, embracing a Chapel under the roof of the priest's house.   The
first missionary stationed here of whom we have any note,
was the Rev. Benedict Neale, in 1747, and he is probably
the one who erected the building which is still standing,
and which was referred to about the time we mention as
' Priest Neale's Mass House.'   The building has passed out
of Catholic hands, but remains unaltered, and the graveyard
where the faithful were interred has been respected by the

present owners.

" 'The building stands on an eminence, and is a long one of stone, giving room for a chapel, which is now the kitchen. The walls are of great strength and solidity, nearly three feet thick, and the roof and woodwork seem to have been made of most durable and well seasoned wood. A room below, at one end, was the reception room ; above it the priest slept, most of the interior being devoted to the chapel."

This description, though in the main correct, has two considerable errors. The kitchen now used—built some thirty years ago—is of wood, and entirely outside the original walls. Nor has the chapel portion at any time been used as a kitchen. It is possible, however, that the reception room may, at one time, have been so used. Indeed, the statement of the historian that the chapel—which he says embraced most of the interior—was used as a *kitchen*, involves an absurdity in domestic arrangements. Two changes were made in the interior soon after its purchase from the church authorities by the ancestor of the present owner : a very small chamber was partitioned off from the main apartment, or chapel, and a pantry from the rear of the reception room. The historian has strangely neglected to make any mention of the comfortable chambers, almost counterparts of each other, at the end of the building opposite the reception room. The partition between these twin rooms is of brick ; those dividing them from the chapel, and the latter from the reception room, are lathed and plastered in the usual way. There is a fire-place, with a chimney, in the reception room and also in each of the two original chambers, but none in the chapel, which is left out in the cold, so to speak. This was a common, if not a universal deficiency in the day in churches of all denominations. The devotional fervor of the soul seems to have been sufficient to keep the body at a complete temperature.

The attic in which Mr. Shea tells us the priest slept was entered by a flight of stairs leading from the rear of the chapel, being the part now embraced in the little chamber since added. His Reverence certainly had a rude dormitory, with an unobstructed view of the shingles and rafters, the roof being entirely unceiled. But hardships and privations, which would be nigh unto death for most ministers of the gospel, seemed to be essential to the Jesuit Fathers and to give additional energy to their works. Mr. Shea gives, in his work, a very creditable cut of the old building, sufficiently correct to be at once recognized.

The walls measure, exteriorly 46 feet by 26, the chapel (as it originally stood before the small room was taken from it) being 22½ by 17½. Each of the chambers at the end is a little over 11 feet by 12, and they remain just as they were. The reception room was originally 12 by 22½ feet.

The origin of this old chapel is involved in as much obscurity as the sources of the Nile—with the difference, that the whole mystery of the great river is likely some day to be cleared up, while there is but little hope of ever reaching the *fons et origo* of this once sacred edifice. In a letter which I lately received from Mr. Shea, he says : " The Deer Creek Chapel is the oldest Catholic buiding in Maryland used for church purposes." Of course this means, the oldest now in existence—not the first erected in the province. Really, the first Catholic Chapel in Maryland was the rude hut generously assigned by the savages to Father White as his lodging-place, soon after the first colonists landed, and which he consecrated and used for holy purposes until a permanent one could be erected. There have been many since—some better, none probably worse—but this old Chapel at Deer Creek is the oldest of all that is now left.

I find, in a deed among the records of our Circuit Court, that in 1750, Henry Beach conveyed to Rev. Bennett Neale *

---

* His name is written " Bennett," by Scharf, and in the Harford County records, as well as in old ledgers. On the other hand, not only Mr Shea's deed, but a copy of the deed among the Woodstock papers gives his Christian name as Benedict.

Since writing the above, I have found in the "Vestry Proceedings" of St. George's Parish, in this county, that about 1755 (I have not the exact date). The Rev. *Ben nett* Neale, being one of those whom the vestry had taxed as bachelors, certifies that not having property to the amount of £100, Maryland currency, he is not subject to the tax.

18 acres of "Maiden's Bower Secured," lying on Deer Creek. This afterwards became part of the farm on which the old building stands. It was a narrow strip, almost like a ribbon in its proportions, being about five-eighths of a mile in length and twenty perches wide, on the south side of and a few hundred yards from the Creek; and one cannot but wonder at the object of such a purchase by a Jesuit father.

"Thomas's Beginning," a tract of fifty acres, was taken up by Thomas Shea in 1721, and the "Addition to Thomas's Beginning," sixty-five acres, at a later date. These two tracts, extending from the eighteen-acre strip to the creek, constituted the farm on which the chapel building stood and were were conveyed by Shea, Oct. 8th, 1764 to Rev. Benedict Neale "without any manner of exception, only that one-half of an acre of ground where the burying-place now is, which the said Thomas Shea reserves for a burying-place for himself and his family." The consideration for this conveyance is that the Rev. Mr. Neale would allow the said Shea "lodging, board, and all things necessary during his life."

The motive actuating Mr. Shea in this transaction is perhaps not far to seek. He must now have been growing old, since it was nearly fifty years before, that he had taken up one of these tracts, when he. must at least have attained his majority, and was probably a good deal older. He could not therefore have been less than seventy years of age, and having other farms in the vicinity, as shall presently appear, and death not being far off, he probably felt that he could afford to make his peace with heaven and the church of his choice at the cost of a good part of his possessions.

One of the records of the Society of Jesus states that Father Neale was at Deer Creek from 1747 to 1750, and again from 1753 to '56. But as the above extract from our county records show that he bought the 18-acre strip in 1750 and sold it in 1753, it seems fair to infer that he was there during that interval. And, indeed, Scharf in his " History of Baltimore City and County," says—without, however, giving his authority—" Father Neale officiated and said Mass near Deer Creek in 1752. He lived on a farm given him by Thomas Shea, and owned four or five negroes. Owing to the great opposition of the Protestants of the neighborhood and the trouble they gave him, he was compelled to leave after a residence of two or three years." If this was so, he afterwards returned, as we have already seen.

A record of the Society tells us that about this time, there being war with France, "there was an indictment against Father Neale for being in league with French against the English." Indeed, the Jesuits were always charged with treachery whenever England and France went to war, though probably without any very solid grounds. It was probably thought that the oppressive restrictions under which they labored were sufficient to drive almost any set of men to treachery, with the hope of bettering what could not well have been made worse.

Mr. Shea says in his letter before referred to, " I think the building mentioned in 1756 as a 'Mass House,' is that still standing. None of the kind were built after the revolutionary war. After the Jesuits sold the place they seem to have lost interest in it, and preserved nothing. One of their old houses at St. Inigoes was burnt forty or fifty years ago, and many of their papers. The register of baptisms kept at Deer Creek cannot be traced. It is not at Hickory, nor in the hands of the Jesuits at any of their repositories of old documents. Of this I am sure. The Mission was kept up till the early year of the present century. It was known at St. Joseph's, and in 1765 the farm gave the priest £24 a year for his support. It was abandoned between 1805 and 1814. The Hickory Chapel was built after that at Deer Creek was abandoned, but I do not know that the Jesuits ever attended it. I have a pretty detailed account of the condition of the Church in Maryland about 1805, but no mention is made of Deer Creek, or Hickory, or of any priest in Harford County."

Father Fowler, the resident priest at the Hickory,

writes me, " The Hickory Church was built about the time of the sale of the Deer Creek property, though I cannot find out exactly when. It was attended by the Jesuit Fathers until 1817, when Father Roger Smith, the first secular priest, was stationed here. The records previous to 1817 were taken by the Jesuits when they left the county, and I have not been able to find where they are—if they exist. It has always seemed a wonder to me that so little is known of the Catholic Mission in this county."

It would thus seem that both Mr. Shea and Father Fowler are of the opinion that the Deer Creek Chapel was attended by the Jesuits until it was sold. This, however, is contradicted by the following extract taken from the papers at Woodstock, the Jesuit study-house, in Howard County, and placed in my hands by George Archer, Architect, of Baltimore, who now owns the farm on which the Old Chapel stands. " Rev. Joseph Eden was a secular priest and a member of the "Corporated Body of Catholic Clergymen," an organization founded to preserve the properties of the Society of Jesus. He was stationed at Deer Creek about the year 1795, and again some time after 1811. Rev. Mr. Pasquet, a secular priest, and a member of the Corporated Body, was managing the Deer Creek estate in 1800. He had been sent there some years previously—when is uncertain." From these Woodstock extracts we learn further that "Father Neale died in St. Mary's County, March 20th, 1787," and that "he being a Jesuit, the property became vested in the Corporated Body " above referred to. At a meeting of that Body, held at Georgetown College, June 10th, 1811, it was resolved that the estate on Deer Creek be sold. Rev. Mr. Eden was authorized to receive the whole profits of the home place on Deer Creek. A writer for the *Cecil Whig*, a few years ago, signing himself " Quilf," stated that "some time during the 17th century two Capuchin Friars came to Maryland and went to Priest's Ford, in Harford County, and their names in some way became connected with Bald Friar Ferry, near " Conswingo." He does not give his authority for the statement.   Mr. Shea, the Catholic historian, says in the letter above cited, that there is no doubt that Franciscans were in Maryland about that time. He adds that he has ascertained that Franciscans labored in northern Maryland, during the 17th century, but he has not been able to find out exactly where—all his researches in England among old archives having failed to show the precise field of their labors.

From the records of our Circuit Court I have obtained some further information about the transfer of this property at various times during the closing years of the last century. The 18-acre strip, deeded by Beach to Father Neale in 1750, was conveyed by the latter to Benjamin Wheeler in 1753, and by Wheeler, in 1770, (most probably by deed of gift) to Rev. Ignatius Matthews, also a Jesuit, by whom it was devised, in 1790, to James Walton—the will being recorded in St. Mary's County—from which fact it would seem that Rev. Mr. Matthews died there.   The remainder, and much the larger portion of the farm which Shea conveyed to Father Neale in 1764, was devised by the latter in 1780 to James Walton, and by Walton by his declaration of trust in 1793, and by his will in 1798 (also recorded in St. Mary's County) to Robert Molyneux, and by Molyneux to Rev. Francis Neale in 1805—recorded in the same county. This frequent change of owners, as they all, except possibly the last named, seem to have been Jesuits, appears a little strange and is altogether confusing to the uninitiated.

In May, 1814, Rev. Francis Neale, as agent of the Corporated Body above referred to, sold the whole property and 36 additional acres, of which we have no previous mention (being in all 169 acres), to Dr. James Glasgow, of Baltimore, who soon afterwards removed to the farm, where he resided until his death, in 1823—his wife surviving him but three years.   Recently, their son, Mr. George R. Glasgow, conveyed it to his nephew, George Archer, of Baltimore, the present owner.

It appears that this was not the only property acquired

by the Jesuits in that vicinity. Our county records show that in Sep., 1786, James Calhoun (who by the way, was the first Mayor of Baltimore City), conveyed to Rev. John Ashton, of Prince George's County, for £645. common money, 344 acres of Arabia Petraea, and 25 acres of an adjoining tract called Conveniency. This land was on Deer Creek, bounding on the part of that stream which was then known as Bennett's Mill Dam, the precise locality of which I cannot as yet ascertain.* It is, however, described in the conveyance as being near the road leading from the Lebanon Forge to Deer Creek Chapel,† and near the intersection of the Forge road with the road leading from the Chapel to Samuel Webb's. Unfortunately, the exact whereabouts of Lebanon Forge and of Webb's residence seems to be lost to the present generation. In 1756, Rev. John Ashton—most probably the one above named—was the residing priest of Doughoregan Manor, the seat of the Carrolls, some fifteen miles from Baltimore Town, part of the mansion being used as a chapel, and he made monthly visits thence to the town, and doubtless other places to celebrate Mass in the private families of the faithful.

I will now present such facts (and they are by no means unimportant) as I have been able to glean from certain old ledgers in my possession. It is a little singular that the history of this old Chapel, which has baffled so many acute investigations, should, even in part, be dragged to light at this late day, from the musty ledgers of doctors, farmers, and storekeepers, for the edification of the faithful. These humble repositories of historical data, however, are by no means to be despised, in the great dearth of more regular ones, since they have this vast advantage over some other more pretentious records, namely, that the incidental facts which they present are, so far as they go, incontrovertible, the impartiality of the disinterested chroniclers being altogether above suspicion.

---

* Since ascertained to have been about one mile above the Old Chapel, directly on the north side of the creek.

† "The Chapel of Ease," of St. George's Parish."

In the ledger of my grandfather, Thomas Archer, who was a farmer, and had set up a skillful blacksmith on his premises, Thomas Shea is charged, from 1761 to '3, for some dozen items of work done by his smith on plows, which clearly shows that Shea was at that time engaged in farming. In 1766, Rev. Bennett Neale bought a plow from Thomas Archer, so that his Reverence had himself by that time undertaken to conduct the farm which he had recently bought of Shea. The plow being paid for by Henry McBride, we may perhaps safely infer that he was the manager, or overseer.

The ledger of Harris & McClure, who ran a store at the Tower X Roads (now Churchville), some two miles from the Chapel, shows that Thomas Shea dwelt there, and that among other purchases in Dec., 1764, soon after giving away his farm, he treated his wife to "one fine Hatt," at a cost of £2.10 (nearly $6, and equal to about twice or thrice that sum now), which may possibly have been designed to console her in part for the loss of the farm—a sort of peace-offering—showing that human nature was much the same then as now. From the same source we find "sundries," bought there in 1765, by Jenny Shea, entered to Thomas Shea's account, which seems to show that Jenny was his daughter.

We here get a glimpse even of domestic life at the Chapel. Mr. Shea had stipulated that Father Neale should board him during the remainder of his life—nothing being said about his family, which at first view seems a little strange. There can be little doubt, however, that there was an understanding, tacit or other, that Mrs. Shea was to have control of household matters, Jenny and whatever other children they may have had, being allowed their board as compensation for for the mother's services. And I, for one, make no doubt, that it was a happy family. But alas! like all human happiness, it was of very brief duration. In April, 1767, Thomas Archer's inexorable ledger enters "one plow" to the account of "Ann Shea, Widow"—so that, if she was the widow of Thomas Shea, as in all probability she was, he must have died between Sep., 1765, when Jenny purchased sundries," and April, 1767, when his widow bought the plow. The trouble is, to see what the widow would want with a plow, if Father Neale still ran the farm. The probability, however, is that, under the peculiar circumstances, she had thought it provident on the death of her husband to leave the Chapel ; and what could she better do than take up her residence on one of the other plantations which, as shown by old documents left by Judge Archer, Mr. Shea owned in the neighborhood—in which case she, of course, would want among other things, a plow.

The evidence offered by the ledgers of Dr. John Archer, brings matters down to a later period, and to a rather more interesting class of facts. I will note here, in justice to the Doctor, that although he carefully enters every visit and every prescription, he never makes any charges for them when the services are rendered to the priests themselves, as is often the case—his charges being only for attention to their negroes.

In 1773, '4, and '5, the Doctor enters to the account of Rev. Ignatius Matthews, charges for attending several negroes of both sexes. Now, as we have seen, Rev. Ignatius Matthews had, in 1770, obtained by conveyance from Wheeler, the long strip of eighteen acres contiguous to the property formerly held by Father Neale in the name of his Order, and it is fair to infer that Father Matthews, during these three years at least, was the resident priest and had charge of the farm, which he ran by the aid of slaves belonging to the Order of Jesuits—probably employing an overseer to manage them.

During the years 1774 and '5, the Doctor rendered professional services to Rev. Mr. Dedrick, which he enters on the account of Father Matthews, though he makes no charge. So that there can be little doubt that during that brief period at least, there were two priests at the Chapel.

It is quite likely, however, that Father Dedrick was an invalid, and had retreated temporarily from his field of labor to that beautiful spot, to rest and recuperate.

I will here explain that several of the Doctor's ledgers are missing. Before our Society was formed, I gave nearly all of them to the Medical and Chirurgical Faculty of Maryland, much now to my regret. This being the case we have to skip from ledger "B" to "F,', and then over two others "G" and "H," to "I." We find, however, that in 1786, he attended Rev. Sylvester Bowman, whom, as shown by a transfer from ledger "E," he had attended in former years. Now, I infer from the facts, that Rev. Mr. Bowman was a priest, and for the following reasons : 1. Although pretty familiar with the names of the ministers of all the other churches, I have never heard of that name in connection with any of them. 2. Although the Doctor was employed by him for some time before '86 until after '98, when the account is transferred to the missing ledger "L," and although during the twelve years and upwards he attended his Reverence himself and many of his negroes —seven being mentioned by name—there is not a single mention of wife or child throughout that long period. A Protestant minister who could live that long without a better half (be he bachelor or widower) would indeed be a rarity. Moreover, during two of his twelve years' attendance on Father Bowman's sable flock, namely, from 1795 to 1797, the Doctor has an account against Rev. Mr. Lusson for attendance upon sound negroes. And here, too, there is no mention of wife or child. The account of Rev. Mr. Lusson is transferred in the latter year ('97) to the account of Mr. Bowman, which certainly shows that the two ministers were in close alliance, like that existing between Jesuit priests; and I cannot thinking that they were both priests at the old Chapel, especially as Lusson is a name which I do not recollect ever to have seen on record.

I will now pass to the region of Tradition. Just ten

years ago, I conversed with Mr. George Lochary, Sr., who
said he had often heard that even before the Chapel at
Priest's Ford was established, there was a Priest's House
on the north side of Deer Creek, on the high hill back
from the old Nottingham Forge, which stood about a half
mile above the mouth of Thomas' Run.

Now, that forge was probably built about the year
1747, the time when Father Neale is said to have first
appeared on Deer Creek.   There were many Irish settlers in
that vicinity, which is fully proved by the numerous names
of that nationality to be found in the old ledgers of Thomas
Archer and of Harris & McClure.   I do not mean the
descendants of those Protestant English and Scotch who
had migrated to Northern Ireland in the long ago, (of
whom also there were some in this region—as the Archer
and Harrisses—who, like their ancestors, were still Protestants,) but the descendants of those genuine Celts who inhabited the Green Isle before St. Patrick drove out all the snakes
which are now replaced by the titled Englishmen fixed
there, gnawing at Ireland's vitals.   I mean the Flanigans,
Dougherty's, O'Neill's, Moriarty's, O'Hara's, and a hundred
other familiar good Catholics all, no doubt.   A majority,
too, of the workmen in the forge and wood-cutters appear
also, by the same authority, to have been genuine Irishmen; and if so, the greater part of them were, of course,
Catholics.   It is therefore quite likely that Father Neale on
his first coming to Deer Creek—and it is by no means impossible that he was in some measure drawn thither by
the presence of these forge people—would naturally establish himself within easy reach of the iron works.   And like
the zealous FatherWhite he may have used, at the very beginning of his mission, the first building that he could get, even
though it may have been as rude as the pioneer Father's
Indian hut.   This would, of course, be only a temporary arrangement; and he probably removed soon afterwards to
Priest's Ford.   Such traditions are not often entirely base-
less, and I can think of no better explanation of Mr. Locha-

ry's story.   The truth of this statement of Mr. Lochary is
greatly strengthened by the recent discovery of another old
Forge in the immediate vicinity.

Concerning the old building itself, Mr. Lochary said it
belonged to an Irishman who gave it to a priest. Long afterwards, money being needed to build the Church near the
Hickory, the property was sold and the money sent to Baltimore, When called for, to erect the new church, it could not
be found; and an exceedingly eccentric Mr. Toy [a Catholic,
I believe,] when he heard of the alleged defalcation [which
I think was afterwards made good] indignantly exclaimed :
" When the priests cheat each other, who's to do the cussin' ? "
Mr. Lochary further said that the Hickory Church was built
chiefly by one of the Wheelers, who were well-to-do at that
time. Mr. Wheeler bought, under the Redemptioner law,* a
German, who was a stone-mason, whom he put to work on
the walls, and when they were finished he was discharged
from all further service.

It is more than likely that the old chapel was visited
by some of Lafayette's army on the march through the county
in 1781. Mr. Angus Graeme, not long before his death, told
the late Dr. James M. Magraw, from whom I received the
statement, that his father, of the same name, who was a
Frenchman, and one of Lafayette's officers, marched with the
General through Harford; that on reaching the vicinity of
Priest's Ford, he, with a few of his comrades, went to the top
of some high hill thereabouts in order to get a good view of
of the country; that a wealthy French officer among them, an
intimate friend of Mr.Graeme's father, was so struck with the
beauty of the scenery that he afterwards bought the tract
known as Maiden's Bower, or Tobacco Run, in full view of
the Old Chapel, aud gave it in trust to his friend who had
decided to remain in the country.   At the end of the war,
the wealthy Frenchman returned to his native country and

---

* I confess that I had supposed this law had gone out of force before
the date above referred to.

to his family.   Mr. Graeme settled on the property and lived
there for many years.   When his friend died, his heirs sent
their attorney across the ocean to inquire about the property,
and Mr. Graeme delivered up his trust.   This account is, in
the main, confirmed by papers left by Judge Archer, who,
with his brother, Dr. Robert H. Archer, subsequently bought
the estate.   These papers further show that the French officer was Lt. Col. Gimat, who held at the end of the war a U.
S. Treasury certificate for $6,000 with which he bought the
property through Mr. Graeme.

It is not unlikely that the hill on which the Old Chapel
stood, and which presents one of the finest views in all
that region, was the one ascended by the Frenchmen; for
since they were no doubt good Catholics, it had the additional charm of presenting to them a sanctuary which they
would naturally wish to visit,—there being at that day a
great dearth of such consecrated places.   It is even possible
that the General himself would be likely to desire at least
a social interview with the priest of his own faith, if not
to seek spiritual ministration.

I was informed by the late Mrs. Thomas Archer, who was
a daughter of Dr. Glasgow and lived in the Old Chapel building for many years, that it was used for church purposes until
a short time before her father bought it, which was in 1814.
She also said she had often heard Mrs. Margaret Stump
who resided, in the early years of the present century, on
the farm just across the creek, now Mrs. Janney's, say,
that she had frequently attended services held in the
Chapel.

We next come to facts learned by an actual exploration. I visited the farm very recently and carefully examined the only two spots of interest except the building
itself, of which, having often been under its roof in time
past, I already knew about all that can be of much interest.   One of the spots which I explored is the old mill-site.
It is on the creek in a thicket of briers, saplings, and half-
grown trees, about a hundred yards below the bridge,

with very little more than the width of the road to Glen-
ville, between it and the creek.   The outline of the foundation, though easily traced, is quite buried in alluvial soil.
A large stump stands at one corner in such a position that,
even as a sapling, it could not have been there until the wall
had crumbled away. At a reasonable calculation it must have
sprung up nearly a century ago.   The two mill-stones, which
are the only remnants of the mill to be seen above ground,
lie partly overlapping each other and half covered with soil,
almost on the very spot to which they must have gradually
sunk, year by year, from the position in which the millwright
had placed them, as the wooden and iron fixtures that supported them rotted piecemeal away.   The deep pit in which
the main wheel revolved, and even the tail-race which leads
from it to the creek near at hand, are still plainly visible. So
far as I have been able to learn there were no more traces of
this old mill within the recollection of the oldest resident
thereabouts than there there are now.   When it began its
useful career, or when the great wheel made its last revolution cannot now be learned.   It is quite likely, however,
.that it was among the first, if not the very first, which
did duty for that region.   The race, which leaves the creek
some 300 yards above, can still be distinctly traced throughout its entire length, except, of course, where it crossed
the main road leading through the bridge.   I have seen
among our Circuit Court records, old deeds in which it is
referred to as "the Priest's Mill," and it may have been
erected by one of the priests of the Old Chapel; possibly
by Father Neale when he first settled there, or perhaps by
others even at an earlier date.   It stood so near the boundary of the Old Chapel tract that it is impossible to say
certainly, without running the line again, whether it was
on that tract or the next, which has since been added to
it—though, all things considered, there is but little doubt
that it was on the former.

The other spot which I explored is the graveyard. It
will be recollected that Shea's deed to Father Neale states

that the graveyard which he reserves was then (1764) in existence. How long it had already been used as such, there are now no means of knowing ; though, as we can learn of no other within many miles in which Catholics were interred, we may fairly suppose that it had been used at least from the time of the priest's first arrival on his mission—about 1747, if not earlier.

Uncleared as it is, and has been for many years, so far from having been encroached upon by the plow, as is the ill fate of so many abandoned burial places, it now extends considerably beyond its original specified limits of a half acre—being about 10 x 50 yards. Besides the many small trees which have sprung up from its surface, it is completely overrun with all those kinds of wild growth which usurp long neglected spots, insomuch that it is impossible to see what is there without forcing your way through the tangled maze. And, indeed, in view of what one finds there after effecting an entrance, (or rather does not find,) this almost impenetrable seclusion is perhaps preferable to the full glare of day. For although the graves are numerous, only about twenty are marked at all, and these have only common field-stones (a few of them white flint) at the head and foot, in the rough condition in which they have been turned out by the plow; while, so far from there being any inscriptions, there is not a word or letter to be seen, and on one only is there a token of any kind, that being a very small but neatly cut cross on a short rude stone almost as gray as the lichen that mottles it.

There are besides many sunken spots where evidently human ashes lie awaiting the last trump. These have no stones at all, unless they are so diminutive as to have been buried by accretions from the mould of the falling leaves of more than a century, and from the yearly decay of grass and wood. It may be that some—possibly many—of the bodies (or rather of their ashes) have been reverently removed by loving friends to spots better cared for. Of one and only one such removal I positively know—having heard of it many years ago and now seeing it verified. I found lying in the densest part of the thicket five fragments of what must have been, for the time of its erection, nearly ninety years ago, quite an elegant headstone of marble, though the grain is of the coarser sort. I gathered up the widely scattered fragments and laid them together on the dead leaves in a sombre sort of mosaic, and on brushing away the moss and mud which clung tenaciously to it, I had the melancholy satisfaction of reading as follows—the usual "I H S" and cross being at the top :

A small piece, including a portion of the cross, is missing from the top as is also a good deal of the lower end. What is left, when laid together, measured about 33 by 24 inches. James Cain was the father of the late Matthew Cain,

who lived on Thomas' Run, and the grandfather of James
Cain, now Chief Judge of our Orphan's Court. His remains
were removed many years ago to the burying-ground of the
Hickory Church. Whether or not the old stone was found
broken at the time I am unable to say; but a better one was
placed above his new resting-place. The mother of the late
Mr. James A. Fulton was buried here. It is probable, however, that her remains were removed. I do not know positively the names of any others of the silent sleepers here.
But among them there can be little doubt were Thomas
Shea and his family. Indeed, it is difficult to say where else
any Catholics of the vicinity who died prior to the establishment of the Hickory graveyard, could have been buried,
unless they were taken beyond the limits of the county. It
is by no means impossible that some of the first settlers
thereabouts at the very beginning of the last century are
resting in this neglected spot.*

PERMISSION TO BEG IN CANADA, FOR THE CHURCH IN ALBANY, IN 1797.

MESSIEURRS THE PARISH PRIESTS:

The bearer of the present is Mr. Barry, a Catholic from
the city of Albany, in the State of New York. He is appointed to collect funds to aid in the erection of a Church in
that place, an undertaking worthy of all encouragement; we
have accordingly promptly contributed to this work according
to our means. You are invited and solicited, gentlemen, to
co-operate likewise, and to afford Mr. Barry the opportunity
of collecting the donations which the zeal and the pious
liberality of your parishioners may secure him.

I am, etc.,

✠ JOHN FRANCIS, Bishop of Quebec.

Quebec, March 4, 1797.

---

* I have, since writing the above, seen the will of Michael Fay (who, 140
years ago ran the Ferry across the Susquehanna, 8 or 10 miles from Priest's
Ford) directing that his " body be buried at the Old Chapel according to the
rites of the Roman Catholic Church."

HISTORY OF THE ESTABLISHMENT OF THE
CARMELITES IN MARYLAND.

RESPECTED SIR:

As you requested to have some account of our establishment in this county, with pleasure we present this little history, which you can use as you think proper; if it should not be what you wished for, you can return it, or take out of it, what may suit your purpose.

The Rev. Charles Neale, brother to the late Archbishop Neale, was born the 10th of February, 1751, at the Mansion house of William and Ann Neale, near Port Tobacco, in Charles County, Maryland. At the age of ten years he was sent to Europe and commenced his studies at the Jesuit College at Bruges. He entered the Society in 1771, and was ordained priest at Liège a short time before the Suppression. Soon after that unhappy event, his cousin Mary Margaret Brent, Superior of the English Carmelite Convent at Antwerp, addressed him a letter in which she earnestly entreated him to take the direction of that Convent which invitation he humbly declined accepting, excusing himself on the plea of youth and inexperience. Satisfied with his superior merit and distinguished talents, this holy Superior urged him anew and at the same time wrote a pressing letter to Father John Howard who was then President of the English College at Liège. This truly great and good man, sensible of the happy effects which would result from their having so enlightened and pious a director, yielded to the wishes of the community. He was accordingly sent to Antwerp (which Mother house had been founded by Mother Ann of the Ascension, thirty-seven years after the death of Saint Teresa). Having arrived there he entered on the discharge of his duties in 1780. After a residence at Antwerp of ten years, a desire was expressed by a number of respectable and pious individuals residing in Maryland, who forwarded a petition to have a branch of the above holy order of St. Teresa established near Port Tobacco, Charles County. The pious Bishop of Antwerp willing to promote so desirable an undertaking, immediately conferred with Dr. Carroll on the subject, whose consent was soon obtained. The Rev. Charles Neale who was greatly charmed with the rules and regulations of St. Teresa, much wished to establish a house solely for prayer and for imploring the happy success of the American Missions and the propagation of the Catholic faith in this new world. He selected four nuns—one from the Mother house for that purpose—Clare J. Dickenson, and three from Hogstraet, Rev. Mother Bernandina, Superior of that house, sister to the Rev. Ignatius Mathews and her two nieces, Aloysia and Eleanora Mathews. They left Europe on the 9th of April, 1790, and after a dangerous and most stormy voyage, they landed at Mr. Robert Brent's, near Port Tobacco, on the 17th of July. On arriving, they were greatly embarrassed in getting a proper house to receive them, as the farm of the Rev. Charles Neale did not afford one. To remedy that defect, Mr. Baker Brook, who owned a farm a few miles distant, and had just erected a large house on it in addition to other buildings, offered to exchange with the Rev. Charles Neale, who, in addition to his farm, gave thirteen hundred and seventy pounds; he generously sacrificed the whole of his patrimony and devoted himself to the benefit of this foundation. They took possession of this place on the 15th of October. Here was established the first Convent ever erected in the United States of America, where from that time they flourished, increasing in numbers and in temporals owing to the prudence, zeal, and piety of so good a director. Rev. Mother Mathews was Superior of this new establishment until her death, which took place the 12th of June, 1800, leaving the community in great distress at being bereft of so valuable a

Superior whose eminent holiness made her qualified for the office which she discharged.

At that time. there were ten professed Sisters and three Novices.   Bishop Carroll being informed of her death, appointed S. Clare Dickenson, who was then Superioress, in her place, and whose virtues and talents as a religious made her capable every way of being a good Mother and Superior to the infant community.   Their rule required them to recite the Divine Office in the choir, and to fast eight months in the year; to abstain from meat except in cases of sickness; to wear woollen clothes and sleep on straw beds. This though apparently rigid and austere, yet persons in delicate health can undergo it, and many live to an advanced age.   They received a letter from Bishop Carroll in 1801, in which he said, " I have committed to my Rt. Rev. Coadjutor the general superintendence of that part of the diocese in which you are seated, but this must not hinder any one from having recourse to me in all things in which I can help them wishing always to be considered as their Father in Christ Jesus.

And from that time, Bishop Neale presided over them with the most fatherly solicitude and paternal affection. He had been their first extraordinary confessor.   In 1807, Sister Eleanora Mathews died; she was one of the four founders, and had been a fervent and exemplary Carmelite. The Rev. gentlemen who had manifested great interest and kindness for the community in its commencement were the Rev. John Boarman, Charles Sewall, R. Molyneux, John Bolton, Henry Pile, R. Plunkett, Francis Neale.   In 1827, a law suit was commenced which lasted ten years.   During this time, the community were sensibly afflicted by the loss of the Rev. Father and Founder, Rev. C. Neale, who sweetly and calmly expired on the 27th of April, 1823.   His holy example had animated them to the practice of every religious virtue which he had acquired in an eminent degree, especially his humility and charity, which will never be effaced from their most grateful recollection.   He was Superior of the Society of Jesus at the time of his death ; esteemed and venerated by all as a most cherished and distinguished member, beloved by every one who knew his worth.   He left his children of Mount Carmel deeply impressed by the strong lessons of solid piety his life constantly presented.   The successor of Rev. C. Neale was the Rev. B. Fenwick, for more than two years, when he was obliged to leave as the necessities of the college demanded his presence. His brother, Enoch Fenwick then took the direction of the Convent, whose charity and zeal for this establishment was unlimited until his death, in 1827.   His successor was the Rev. F. X. O'Brien.

The Most Rev. Archbishop Marechal, seeing how exceedingly the community were embarrassed on account of the law suit, having heavy fees to pay, kindly requested Roger B. Taney to undertake the cause, who cheerfully did so in a most friendly aud able manner, and by his endeavors it was favorably settled in 1821.   The 30th of March, 1830, dear Rev. Mother Clare Joseph Dickenson died, in the seventy-fifth year of her age and the fifty-eighth of her religious profession.   She was born in London and educated at an Ursuline Convent in France.   She had been Superior thirty years to the general satisfaction of her children, who revered her for her holiness of life and mortification, and loved her as a mother for her sweetness, meekness, and affability; her death was a source of great affliction, and the community sustained an irreparable loss.   The temporal losses increasing on account of the bad management of the farm, imposition of the overseers, the expenses of the law suit, and many other causes reduced them so low, that they could not be supported by the farm, nor could they rebuild their house which was falling over their heads.   The rain and snow beat in on all sides and they suffered exceedingly, for they had even to curtail their diet and live much lower than the rule prescribed. When the Most Rev. Archbishop Whitfield understood this he judged it better and more profitable for the Convent to remove to the city where they might support themselves by a day-school; he accordingly wrote to Rome and obtained from his Holiness a full confirmation of the dispensation to teach and instruct young ladies, which had been previously granted in the year 1793. The following is an extract from one of Bishop Carroll's letters : " I had letters lately from Rome. I had given in mine an account of your settlement, and of the sweet odor of your good example, and had taken the liberty to add, that, in order to render your usefulness still greater, I wished that it were consistent with your constitution to employ yourselves in the education of young persons of your own sex. The Cardinal Prefect of the Propaganda having laid my letter before his Holiness, informed me that it gave him incredible joy to find that you were come hither to diffuse the knowledge and practice of religious perfection, and adds, considering the great scarcity of laborers and the great defect of education in these States, you might sacrifice that part of your institntion to the promotion of the greater good and I am directed to encourage you to undertake it now. In obedience to this direction, I recommend to your reverence and your holy Community to take it into your consideration. I am considerably pleased at the increase of your most religious family; every addition to it I look upon as a safeguard for the preservation of the diocese. Praying Almighty God to grant His choicest blessings to yourself and your pious community, I am with fatherly affection and high esteem honored Mother,

Your most obedient servant in Christ,

✠ J., Bishop of Baltimore.

This leave was not acted upon until 1830, the nuns being unwilling to accept the dispensation until forced by extreme necessity. The 13th September, 1831, the community, twenty-four in number, with feelings of regret, bid a last adieu to that spot which had been so happy and sacred to them, and where so many had consecrated themselves to God. They were conducted by their kind friend Washington Young, Esq., to his residence Nonesuch, and their worthy chaplain, Mr. F. X. O'Brien, where they were most hospitably entertained. The next day, they proceeded to Baltimore and were cordially received by Archbishop Whitfield, who conducted them to the Cathedral, where after praying a short time in that sacred edifice, they hurried to take possession of their new abode. November 1st, 1832. Rev. Father O'Brien departed this life, who had done all in his power to promote the welfare of the community. He was succeeded by the Rev. H. Xaupi, but he soon afterwards retired to Mount St. Mary's, and the Rev. J. B. Gildea was appointed Confessor, who entered on the discharge of his duties November 27th, 1834. November, 1833, Sister Aloysia Mathews died. the last of their dear foundresses. She had been a fervent religious and an exact observer of her rule; she occupied the office of sub-Prioress 27 years.

The Abbé Hérard, during his residence in the city, hearing the Convent had no chaplain, kindly offered his services which were readily accepted by the Community and cordially sanctioned by the Most Rev. Archbishop Eccleston. Accordingly he took up his abode at the Convent, November 27, 1835. The Abbé soon discovered the great want the community were in of a chapel and choir, for the performances of their religious exercises. By his zealous endeavors, he induced the ladies of Baltimore to get up a fair for that purpose. Their success was crowned beyond expectation; the proceeds of which with his own liberal donation enabled them to accomplish their pious design and erect the additional building. This paternal solicitude continued long after he was obliged to leave for France, and he never ceased to promote the Community's interest and welfare though far from them. He is one of their most generous benefactors to whom they will ever owe the greatest gratitude, and to whose memory they must ever pay the tribute of their sincerest respect and affection, as he has since gone to that God who rewards with celestial glory the services rendered him on earth.

The number that have been professed in this country

is thirty-six choir nuns and seven lay-sisters and one out sister. At the present time there are twenty-six professed nuns, four of whom are lay sisters.

BOSTON, APRIL 3D, 1844.

DEAR SIR :

I do not know how it has happened that both on my way through Baltimore to Georgetown, after performing a very imposing and solemn ceremony in the Cathedral and on my return, I have had the misfortune to miss you each time. Well, it cannot be helped now.

The above was put in my hands by the good Mother of the Carmelites, while in Baltimore, for revision and correction, if I thought it needed it, and afterwards to hand it over to you. It appears she was applied to by Mr. Jno. Murphy, at your request, for information respecting her establishment. I have read the above, and find no cause for alteration in it, as I deem the entire perfectly correct. The use you may make of it in your multifarious writings must be left to yourself.

I remain, &c., &c.,

✠ BENEDICT, Bishop of Boston.

EARLY CATHOLICS IN ELIZABETH, N. J.

The Labadists, Danker and Sluyter, who visited New York and the neighboring colonies in 1679, found scattered Catholics. They say, (p. 359) the Papists believed we were priests and we could not get rid of them; they would have us confess them, baptize their children and perform mass; and they continued in this opinion;" but the only definite allusion to any Catholic family was at Elizabethtown Point, N. J. They say, (p. 147) "There was a tavern on it (i. e. the Point) kept by French papists, who at once took us to be priests, and so conducted themselves towards us in every respect accordingly, although we told them and protested otherwise. As there was nothing to be said further we remained so in their imaginations to the last, as shown both in their words and actions, the more certainly because we spoke French and they were French people."

THE PLUNDERING OF ST. INIGOES, ST. MARY'S COUNTY, MARYLAND.

Under date of October 31, 1814, a diary kept at Georgetown College, says :

" This day a barge from a British brig of war, named the Jason, Capt. Watts, landed at St. Inigoes Manor a captain and several men, plundered the private chapel of all its contents, even the Ciborium, Pixis, etc., containing the Blessed Sacrament, vestments, beds, clothing, etc., to the amount of $1,000. Fr. Rantzau, Bros. Mobberly, Barron and Redmond were present at the time, but could save nothing from the sacriligious wretches. Oh ! the goodness of our God, that permits Himself to be thus treated for the love of us. Fr. Rantzau prevailed all he could on them to return the most Blessed Sacrament, but in vain ; they rowed off their barge and were seen no more, leaving them without linen to change or clothes to defend them from the inclemency of the season. A list of the articles I have inserted on the next page with their prices annexed. We were obliged to send linen, clothes, etc., from the college for their relief—the letter containing the account was written by Bro. Mobberly, an extract from which was inserted in the National Intelligencer, and from thence copied into many other papers."

[The list unfortunately is not given in the diary, though a page is left blank for it.]

Nov. 20. Received information of the British having returned a great part of the articles plundered from St. Inigoes, and left some money to pay for the remainder.

THE DESTRUCTION OF NEW MEXICO SETTLEMENTS AND MISSIONS, AND THE RE-CONQUEST OF THE COUNTRY.

Told in a letter of Father Silvestre Velez de Escalante to Father Augustine Morfi.

Rev. Father Lector and Dear Sir :

1. As much in consequence of the urgent affairs of my office, which I have twice already vainly resigned, as of the journey made by me last winter to El Paso, I have been unable to seek or extract from the manuscript archives of this government anything except since 1680 (there are none older here) when this kingdom was lost, to 1692, the year in which Don Diego de Vargas began its recovery. I hope, nevertheless, to disengage myself and conclude an examination of the remaining documents in the coming May and June, and whatever I may then find of value I will send together where your reverence shall direct. And although I have not now the quiet proper for the labor, that your reverence may see that these reasons are not frivolous for delay, and that I earnestly desire to comply with your wishes, I will forward this epitome.

Notes taken from the papers of Don Antonio de Otermin, of Don Domingo Gironza Petris de Cruzate, who succeeded him in the government, in August, 1683, of Don Pedro Romero Posada, who succeeded Gironza in 1688, governing a year and some months; of Don Domingo Gironza, who returned to the government in 1689, and of Don Diego de Vargas who succeeded him in 1691, which remain in the archives. There are no acts or other papers of the predecessors of Otermin; even those belonging to the first years of his government are missing. In reports and petitions made to Otermin by inhabitants of this kingdom after the general insurrection, others are mentioned·incidentally; three whom Friar Francisco Farjan says, successively governed before Otermin. They are as follows : Don Fernando de Arguello governed in 1749; Don Hernando Ugarte y la Concha, in 1650; Don Fernando de Villanueva; Don Juan de Medrano; Don Juan de Miranda; and Don Juan Francisco Treviño, whom Otermin succeeded; this is the most of the early governors I have been able to find, from Don Juan de Oñate to Otermin.

1. This kingdom of New Mexico before it was lost by the general insurrection of the Indians, was composed of forty-six pueblos of Christian Indians, and one city of Spaniards, which was at San Gabriel del Yunque, and afterwards Santa Fé, which was then as now the capital of the kingdom; and also many settlements of Spaniards at different places on the banks of the Rio del Norte, which, although together they included a larger population than Santa Fé, yet, because of their being scattered and far apart could not properly be called a town. A few years before the insurrection, the Apache enemy destroyed by almost continual invasions seven of the forty-six pueblos; Tehuicu in the Province of Zuñi, and seven in the Valley of the Salinas: Chilili, Tagique, Quarac belonging to the Tejua Indians, Abo, Jumanas and Tabira belonging to the Tumpiros; all of them on the eastern slope of the Sierra Zandia, except two which were distant from the mountain in the direction of the Salinas. Nearly all the confines of the kingdom were at that time occupied by the infidel Apache nations, distinguished by different names according to the territory each inhabited; and only on the west of the Province of Moqui was it bounded otherwise, as it still is, by the Cojnina nation. At the beginning of the administration of Don Antonio de Otermin, the Yutas, of whom the Spaniards had not before heard, appeared and established relations with them. If there was any knowledge of the Comanche nation in the last century, they were not seen

until the present one, when the Yutas introduced them into the town of Taos. They now rule over all the plains and fields of Cibolo which were previously occupied by the Yutas and Apaches. The latter while occupying the plains were called such (Apache Vaqueros), and by other heathen nations. And thus the Comanches at this time bound this kingdom on the north-east, east and south-east; the Yutas on the north and north-west; and the Apaches from west north-west to south south-east.

3. In the year 1680, on the second administration of Otermin, on the tenth day of   , an Indian called El Popé of San Juan de los Caballeros, was a fugitive in the town of Taos. He was of the Tejua nation; and in the time of Don Juan Francisco Treviño was arrested with forty-six other Tejuas on various well attested charges of murder, idolatry and sorcery. He was now fleeing because of recent crimes of the like nature; and being in the town, he contrived the general insurrection. He sent messengers to all the pueblos of the kingdom, which had already before that time secretly obeyed him, as he had persuaded the people that the Fathers and Governors had no other aim in what they directed them to do than to enslave them more every day. They feared him because they were convinced that he had frequent and personal intercourse with the devil and could thus do them all the harm he pleased. All the pueblos came into his plans, except those of the Piros; for although the Queres of the town of Cienega and the Janos showed some repugnance, yet at the time of action they followed the rest. The thirteenth of August was fixed for the attack upon all the convents and houses of the Spaniards; but the treason was discovered on the ninth, although it could not be suppressed. The Janos of San Cristobal and San Lazaro disclosed it to Father Juan Bernal, then Custos, who promptly notified the Governor. The Pecos likewise made known the conspiracy to their missionary Friar Fernando de Velasco, who notified the Governor the same day. In consequence of this and of another notice received at the

same time from the Alcalde of Taos, Marcos de Eras, the Governor seized two Indians of the town of Tesuque who in the name of the Tejuas had gone to arouse the Janos and Queres. The Taos, Pecuris and Tejuas finding themselves discovered, arose by order of El Popé on the tenth day of the same month of August, and before sunrise attacked the convents and dwellings of the Spaniards, laying all in blood and ashes. All the other pueblos notified, as soon as they heard of this, did the like. The lives of the eighteen religious priests were taken (among with that of the Father Custos) and three religious lay brothers, and three hundred and eighty Spaniards, men, women, and children and servants; a few Spanish women being kept as prisoners. The rest of the Spaniards (that survived), and some friars who escaped slaughter were formed into two parties. In the town of Isleta were collected those that resided from San Felipe down; and, on the 14th, they began their retreat for El Paso, as the rebels had spread a report that the Governor and entire population of the city had already fallen. The inhabitants of the La Cañada assembled, and intrenched themselves in the house of the Chief Alcalde of the district, and though few held out together until Otermin sent them succor, when they joined those of the city.

On the nineteenth, the Taos of San Marcos, San Cristobal and Galisteo with the Queres of the Cienega, and the Pecos attacked Santa Fe on the south side; they took possession of the houses of the Tlascalteca Indians living in the suburb of Anlaco, and set fire to the chapel of San Miguel. They numbered nine hundred fighting men. The Spaniards of the place sallied out against them. A bloody battle ensued, which lasted more than six hours. Our people would have been victorious had not the Taos, Picuris and Tejuas arrived and attacked the city on the northern side; they began a violent assault on the public buildings in which were collected the families of the place as well as those of San Marcos, La Cañada, and the Tlascaltecas. At the end of five days they gained possession of the greater part of the houses, burning some and taking up their quarters in others. They set fire to the church and convent, leaving the Spaniards no more ground than the plaza and the public buildings. The Indians cut off the water, and reduced the besieged to the utmost extremity. The insurgents amounted by this time to about three thousand combatants, while our people, counting soldiers, inhabitants and servants, were less than one hundred and fifty; so that they had hardly courage to wield a weapon. The Governor, seeing that the only way was to break through the investing line, with the help of the three religious, who exerted themselves greatly to dispel the gloomy terror and despair, drew his force up in order. On the twentieth, with only one hundred men, the Governor, invoking the sweet name of Mary, charged upon the enemy, killing over three hundred of them, captured forty-three (whom he at once shot in the plaza), captured some arms and horses, and compelled them to raise the siege and flee. Of our party, five only were killed in the whole siege; but many were wounded, and among them, the Governor, by a ball received in the breast and a wound in the forehead, although neither injury proved dangerous. Otermin at once without delay marched with the three Fathers, Friar Francisco Gomez de la Cadena, now missionary at Santa Fé, Friar Andres Duran, Definitor of the Custodia, and Friar Francisco Farfan, and with the rest of the people retired towards El Paso. At Fray Cristobal, he met Lieutenant General Alonso Garcia, seven religious, and the residents of the lower part of the river. From there they went together to the town of Salineta, where they made an encampment and remained a short time. They next proceeded to another place which they called Real de San Lorenzo, where they underwent great suffering notwithstanding that Friar Ayeta, Procurator of this kingdom at the time, gave daily towards their support, in the name of his majesty, King Charles II., ten head of beeves and as many bushels of maize.

4. The rebels remained masters of the entire kingdom;

and as soon as the Spaniards were gone, El Popé commanded on pain of death that all the men, women and children should remove from their necks the crosses and rosaries they might have and break or burn them; that no one should call on the name of Jesus, or Mary, or invoke the Saints; that the men should leave the wives they had married in the Christian rite and take others as they might choose; that none should speak the Spanish tongue, or show love for the God of the Christians, for the Saints, or for the Fathers and Spaniards; and that, where they had not already done so, they should burn the churches and sacred images.   He went the round of the country, accompanied by a captain of the Taos insurgents named Ihaka, by another out of the Pecuris, formerly Governor of the tribe, called Don Luis Tupatu by a head-man of the Queres named Alonso Catiti, who had been interpreter to the town of Santo Domingo, and by a large number of lesser chiefs.   He took from the churches the vestments and sacred vessels he desired, and the remainder he distributed among the captains and inferior governors.   He fixed the quantities of wool, cotton and other things which the towns should contribute on occasions of his visiting them.   In the town of Santa Anna, he prepared a banquet from the stores which the religious and governors made use of, and set a great table in the Spanish style: he sat at the head, caused Alonso Catiti to take the opposite end, and seated the others in the remaining places. He ordered two chalices to be brought, one for himself another for Alonso; and the two began to pledge each other in scorn of the Spaniards and the Christian religion; and Popé taking his cup would say to Alonso, as if he were addressing the Father Custos: "To your Reverence's health," and Alonso taking his, would say, rising: "To your Lordship's, Sir Governor."   In fact, there remained no vestige of the Christian religion; every thing was profaned and destroyed.

  5. Otermin gave the Viceroy an account of the insur-

rection and succeeding disasters. Father Ayeta went to Mexico and made several representations to His Excellency, in order that all possible means should be used forthwith for reducing the apostate insurgents of New Mexico to the Catholic faith and to the obedience of His Majesty. This was done, with the sanction of the Royal Council: everything that was deemed necessary being provided for the subjurgation of the rebels and likewise for the subsistence of the Spanish families, with those of Piro, Jumpiro, Tijua, Geme and Jano Indians who refused to apostatize and fled with Otermin. Father Ayeta returned with these favorable orders and the royal means. At this time was built the presidio at El Paso, which is now in Carrizal, under the name of our Lady of Pilar and San José. He arranged a campaign into New Mexico, but some difficulties caused very mischivous delays. On the 18th of November, 1681, the force destined for the reduction of the rebels, consisting of one hundred and forty-six Spanish soldiers and one hundred and twelve Indian auxiliaries took up its march from the Ancon de Frai Garcia under Governor Otermin, attended by Father Ayeta and other friars. On the eve of the Immaculate Conception, the rebel Tihuas, in the town of Isteta were reduced. A part of the force was then detached by the Governor, which went to the pueblo of Cochiti, while Otermin marched with the remainder to the pueblo of Zandia, burning on the way the pueblos of Alameda and Poaray which he found without inhabitants, but with good store of cattle and vegetables. From Zandia, he returned to Isleta, but before reaching it he came up with the detachment sent to the towns above—San Felipe, Santo Domingo and Cochiti. No other incident of importance took place excepting the capture of three apostates, or rather one, for the other two voluntarily surrendered. Otermin desired to advance further; but the rigor of the winter, the extreme weakness of the horses, and the danger lest the newly converted at Isleta should relapse into infidelity, (for already in the course of a few days at

the instance of the rest of the rebels, they had again turned
from the faith, and one hundred and fifteen persons had
taken to flight), the Governor determined to return at once
to the town of El Paso, taking with him the inhabitants of
Isleta, recently subjugated, and the prisoners made by himself and by the detachment sent to Cochiti. The Isletans
taken away by him on the occasion numbered three hundred and eighty-five souls, and there were eight prisoners,
one of them a civilized Innian of the Queres, Pedro Nar-
anjo from the town of San Felipe, a famous sorcerer and
great upholder of idolatry, who in consequence was in the
highest esteem of El Popé. This man stated the reasons
of the insurrection and the plans of the chief with more full-
ness, intelligence, clearness and probability than any other.
The causes may be reduced to two heads only : first, the
attachment which many of the old people retained for the
ancient manner of living in idolatry, and for their estufas,
which had been destroyed in the time of Governor
Treviño; and secondly, the vexations and harsh treatment
that had been endured in many of the pueblos from some
of the Spaniards, and the persecution of Indians accused
of witchcraft, as well as the severe and capital punishments
inflicted on them by several of the predecessors of Otermin.

6. The force returning arrived at El Paso in January, 1682. The Governor then assigned places to the
Indians whom he had brought on the present and former
occasion from New Mexico, and settled the following pueblos : Senecu, two leagues below our Lady of the Guadalupe del Paso, with the Piro and Jumpiro Indians; Cor-
pus Christi de la Isleta, a league and a half to the east
of it, with Tijuas ; and the third pueblo, which was
founded under the name of our Lady of Socorro, twelve
leagues from El Paso and seven and a half from Isleta
following the course of the Rio del Norte, with Piros, a
few Janos, and some Jeme Indians.

In the year 1683, the inhabitants of Socorro attempted

the life of their missionary, Friar Antonio Guerra, and the lives of one or two Spanish families in the town; but they did not accomplish it, because the Yumas living with them made it known. The principal movers fled to New Mexico, and such as remained went by order of the Governor to another spot, much nearer the pueblo of Isleta, where at this time exists the second town they settled with the same name of Socorro. On the 24th day of October, of 1683, was established the first mission among the Yuma Indians, eight leagues south of El Paso, at the spot now called Ojito de Samalayuca ; but it did not last, as the Christian, civilized and pagan Indians revolted the next year with the Janos and (other) Yumas, and apostatized.

7. In December, 1683, Juan Sabeata, an Indian of the Jumana nation came to El Paso, saying that all his people desired to come to the faith, and asked for missionaries. He stated that not very far from his country were the Tejas, of whom he told so many things that the province was believed to be one of the most civilized, fertile and wealthy in America. In consequence of this relation, Friar Nicolas Lopez the Vice Custos, desirous of propagating the gospel, determined to go apostolically on this discovery with Friar Juan de Zaboleta and Friar Antonio de Acevedo without followers or protection. He made known his intention to Governor Don Domingo Gironza, who would however not consent that the fathers should proceed thus alone exposed to so many dangers. The Governor raised an expedition of volunteers from the people in the neighborhood, sending as commandant Don Juan Domingo de Mendoza, with directions for the safety of those religious in carrying out the end they proposed. They arrived at the junction of the rivers Del Norte and Conchos, and preached to the three nations of Indians there, the Conchos, Julimes and Chocolomos. The people appeared to be very docile; and Friar Antonio de Acevedo remained to teach them, while the others continued on

their journey up the River Pecos, at that time called Salado ; and after many days travel arrived at an Indian settlement then called Hediondos, where were some of the Jumana tribe to which Sabeata belonged. From this place they returned to the junction of the rivers by a more easterly route than that by which they set out. On the way a difficulty took place between the volunteers and the Commandant Mendoza, which caused great scandal among the accompanying heathens and mortification to the religious. So soon as they arrived, the Indians of La Junta asked Father Lopez for six missionaries to instruct them and administer the holy sacraments. He left with them Fathers Zaboleta and Acevedo, and proceeded with the remaining people by way of Tabalopa and Encenillas to El Paso. A short time after, there arrived at La Junta, (the junction of the rivers) certain Julime Indians, very resentful against the Spaniards, as they had seen two of their nation hanged in the Parral. They excited all the catechumens at La Junta, who arose, scourged the two friars, driving them out of the place naked, on foot and without food, killed several Tijua Indians who were in company with the friars, and profaned the vestments and sacred vessels that were there. With very great hardship, at the end of many days, the Fathers reached the pueblos of El Paso.

In the same year, 1684, as already noted, the Indians of the pueblo of Nuestra Señora of Guadalupe del Paso revolted, apostatized and departed to unite with the infidels of their nation then headed by Captain Chiquito, who, up to that time had been a very great friend of the Spaniards. The Yumas arose, and the Tanos, and, through the instrumentality of the domesticated heathens, took the life of their pastor, Friar Manuel Beltran, destroyed the church, and desecrated the vestments and holy vessels. The mission was called Our Lady of Soledad of the Tanos. All these nations persisted in their rebellion for two years, until unable to withstand the incessant war made upon them by Don Domingo Gonzales, who killed and captured many of them, they surrendered in the year 1686, suing for peace.

8. The rebel pueblos of New Mexico began to grow hostile to each other and to make cruel war among themselves. The Queres, Taos and Pecos fought against the Tehuas and Tanos; and these last deposed El Popé because, of his despotism, the rigor with which he enforced obedience, and the large contributions exacted in his frequent visits. Don Luis Tupatu was elected in his stead, who governed the Tehuas and Tanos until the year 1688, when El Popé was re-elected; but he dying soon after, Don Luis was again chosen. Alonso Catiti, principal person among the Queres, had died previously. While entering an estufa to sacrifice he suddenly burst asunder, his bowels all coming out in the presence of many Indians present. After this, each pueblo of the Queres governed itself. The Apaches were at peace with some of these towns, and to others they did all the injury in their power. The Yutas, from the time of their hearing of the disasters that befel the Spaniards, made incessant war on the Jemes, Taos and Picuris, and with even greater ardour on the Tehuas among whom they made formidable ravages.   Not only thus and by civil wars were all the apostates of the kingdom afflicted, but by hunger also and pestilence. The Queres and Jemes exterminated the Piros and Tihuas, who remained after the incursions of Otermin, because they considered them attached to the Spaniards. Of the Tihuas some families escaped, retiring to the Province of Moqui; but of the Piros, none.

9. In the year 1688, Don Pedro Reneros Pozada entered New Mexico; and having arrived at the pueblo of Zia, he took thence some horses, sheep and goats, and returned to El Paso without doing anything further. In September of the following year, Don Domingo Gironza also entered the country for the purpose of reducing the rebels, and had a bloody battle with them at the same pueblo of Zia, where they defended themselves with such valor and desperate resolution that many permitted themselves to be burned alive on the house-tops rather than

submit. The Queres left dead on the field after the fight, including those of Santa Anna and other places who came to succor the besieged, were as many as six hundred of both sexes and all ages. Only four old men were taken alive; they were shot in the public square. Nothing further appears to have been done during this invasion. Don Diego Gironza, had already prepared an expedition to enter New Mexico a second time, in 1690, but the converted Yumas, and the heathen, living at El Paso and in its neighborhoods revolted, and it became necessary to turn that force against them.

10. In the beginning of the year 1691, Don Diego de Vargas Zapata Lujan Ponce de Leon, entered upon the government. After quieting the Yumas, he contemplated the reduction of the rebels of New Mexico, upon which enterprise he consulted the Viceroy Count de Galvez. His Excellency acceded to the plan giving him fifty soldiers from the forts of the Parral. Before these could reach El Paso, Vargas marched for New Mexico, with the effective men that could be got together, accompanied by three religious of our order, Father Francisco Corvera, Father Miguel Muñiz and Father Cristobal Alonso Barroso. The Janos of the pueblo of Galisteo were entrenched at Santa Fé, and being besieged, they showed at first so great obstinacy, that upon the call of Vargas peacefully to surrender, they refused, adding that they would take the lives of all the Spaniards, allowing no chance for such escape as had been made at the time of the outbreak. To his second summons, they answered that they wished to fight until death, and never to yield. The religious preached, exhorting them as best they could to quiet submission, Don Diego de Vargas supporting them in this, regardless of insulting words and gestures, offering pardon for past offences, evincing in every particular a kind and parental regard, yet at the same time making every sort of disposition with great energy, for seizing the earliest favorable moment to reduce the Indians by force, in case there was no

other way, like a brave and prudent soldier, or a zealous and compassionate Christian. At last, the besieged surrendered, without the shedding of blood, on the 13th of September, (and the day following, being that of the Exaltation of the Holy Cross) in the year 1692, they gave their adhesion, and were absolved from apostacy by Friar Francisco Corvera. The City of Santa Fé having been gained, the fifty soldiers of the forts of the Parral came up, and Don Diego de Vargas marched to the pueblo of Pecos. The Indians abandoned it and retired to the table-lands and ridges near by, our people capturing at different places there twenty-three persons old and young of both sexes, being the last that had taken to flight. Vargas set them at liberty to influence the rest to return without hesitation to the pueblo, and their headmen to come to Santa Fe and make submission. The Governor returned with his force to the city, and thence set out on the 29th of September, for the towns on the upper Del Norte.

All the Tehuas submitted without resistance; the Janos, Picuris and Taos did the same, and were all absolved from their apostacy, giving the Fathers, for baptism, the children born during the rebellion. Those baptised in all the pueblos of the Tanos, Picuris and Taos, were nine hundred and twenty-six. Thus far extend the notes I have taken from the papers in these archives.

If not irrelevant, before concluding this letter, I desire to express my opinion touching the Tejuayo, and the Gran Quivira, the imaginary greatness of which has given rise to much speculation, from the beginning of the last century until the present time. Tehuayo, according to the diary of Oñate and other ancient narratives, may be considered to be at farthest two hundred leagues to the northwest of Santa Fé, and is no other than the country through which migrated the Tihuas, Tehuas, and other Indians on their migration to this kingdom, as is very clearly attested by the ruins of towns I have seen there, the style of which is the same as that afterwards given to the buildings erected in New Mexico ; and the fragments of pottery which I also saw at those ruins are very similar to the pottery which the Tehuas make at this day. To this may be added the tradition unvaryingly told by this people, which confirms it; besides which, I have myself traveled more than three hundred leagues in the same direction from Santa Fé to the forty-first degree and nineteenth minute of latitude, without having been able to gain any knowledge among the Indians who now occupy that country, of any other people living in pueblos.

12. The Gran Quivira, according to the place it has ever been considered to occupy, and according to what I have hitherto been able to make out, putting together all the accounts I have read and heard, is nothing more than the towns of the Panana (Pawnee) Indians, who have no other grandeur than that of dwelling in towns together, having the same civilization, a little more or less, as exists now among the Moquinos. Two things principally confirm my conjecture: one of them is, that the nearest towns to be found at the end of more than three hundred leagues to the north-east of Santa Fé, are those mentioned by the name of Panana, of which there was no knowledge in this kingdom until the nineteenth year of the present century, when it was brought by a Frenchman who came from that direction into New Mexico. In consequence, the Governor, at that time in power, sent a military force thither commanded by one Villazur, who arrived at the river on the opposite bank of which lay the towns. He was discovered by the Pananas, who crossed over by night with a large number of carbines, and the next morning at day light, they fired such a volley into the encampment that the greater part of the people were killed, among whom were Friar Juan Mingues, a missionary of this Custodia, the Commandant, and the Frenchman who served as guide. The other reason is, that about the middle of the last century some families of Christian Indians of the town and nation of

the Taos revolted, and retired to the plains of Cibolo, fortify-
ing themselves at a place which on this account was called
El Cuartelejo, where they remained until Juan de Archuleta
marched thither, by order of the Governor, with twenty soldiers and some Indian auxiliaries, and obliged them to return to their pueblo. He found in their possession, kettles
and other articles of copper and tin, and asking them
whence these had been obtained; they said, from the Quivira towns to which they had made a journey from Cuartelejo. This statement caused universal astonishment and
satisfaction to the Spaniards and religious in the kingdom,
as they supposed these kettles and other utensils to have
been made in Quivira, which they believed must be a very
civilized and wealthy kingdom. From El Cuartelejo by that
route is the way to the Panana; and it is evident at this
day that there are no other towns in that direction, and
the French already trafficked with them at that time. Moreover, in all the towns that have been seen by French
and English in a course from the Jumanas towards the
north and north-east, we have never heard of their finding
any of the civilization and opulence that were imagined of
the grand Quivira.

   13. In the same way, from the accounts of the heathen
Indians misunderstood, many persons were persuaded that
on the farther side of the Colorado River, (which enters
with the Gila into the Gulf of California), there dwells a
people having the appearance of the Spaniards, with long
beards, and arms like our ancient ones of breast-plate, helmet and back-piece, who were doubtless the Yutas Barbones,
(bearded Yutas), of whom the Rev. Father Custos and I
speak in the diary of the journey we performed into those
parts in the year seventy-six.* They live in ranches, not
in towns, are very poor, bearing no other arms than bows

---

* Diario y Derrotero de los nuevos descubrimientos de tierras a los rbos.
N. N. Œ. Œ. del Nuevo Mexico, por los RR. PP. Fr. SILVESTRE VELEZ
ESCALANTE, y Fr. FRANCISCO ATANACIO DOMINOUEZ.

and arrows and some lances pointed with stone; but as for breast-plate, helmet or back-piece, they have none other than they brought with them from their mothers' womb.

This is as much as I am now enabled to say, and as the brevity of a letter will allow. May our Lord God preserve your reverence many years in His grace.

Santa Fé, April 2d' 1778.

Your affectionate servant, brother and chaplain kisses your Reverence's hand.

FRAI SILVESTRE VELEZ DE ESCALANTE.

REV. FATHER LECTOR, FRAI JUAN AGUSTIN MORFI.

GENERAL HALDIMAND'S ORDER EXPELLING MR. LAVILINIERE FROM CANADA FOR SYMPATHIZING WITH THE AMERICANS.

To MGR. BRIAND, Bishop of Quebec :

MGR.,

You will have the kindness to order Mr. de la Valiniére, parish priest of Ste. Anne du Sud, to repair at once to this city with all his baggage, and to take up his residence during his stay here, at the Seminary, or with the Jesuit Fathers, as you deem proper. I leave you at liberty to tell him, if you deem proper, that he must sail to Europe with the fleet which clears on the 25th inst., and care will be taken to provide him refreshments and all possible conveniences for his voyage. You will take care especially to recommend him, not to give way to his ordinary vivacity, and be careful of his manner of acting and speaking till his departure. Mr. de la Valinière may give a power of attorney to any one he chooses, provided it be some one with whom the government has reason to be satisfied, in order to arrange the affairs he leaves in this province.

I have the honor to be, etc.,

FRED. HALDIMAND.

Quebec, October 14, 1779.

PASTORAL LETTER OF V. REV. PATRICK WALSH, ADMINISTRATOR OF THE DIOCESE OF NEW ORLEANS.

The diocese of Louisiana and the Floridas was erected by Pope Pius VI., April 25, 1793, the territory it embraced having from 1789 formed part of the diocese of St. Christopher of Havana. The first Bishop, Rt. Rev. Luis Peñalver y Cardenas, had held positions which made him familiar with the new diocese and its wants. Before coming to Louisiana he obtained from the Propaganda a rescript, authorizing him to appoint one or more Vicars General, who might replace him in case of vacancy in the bishopric. He reached New Orleans, July 17, 1795, and appointed as his Vicars General two Irish priests, Thomas Canon Hassett, formerly parish priest of St. Augustine and Rev. Patrick Walsh. When Bishop Peñalver was promoted to the see of Guatemala in July, 1801, the Vicars General became Administrators or as the Spaniards term it, Governors of the Diocese. They were fully recognized by the Spanish government, the clergy and people, Canon Hassett taking the main part in the management of affairs till his death, in April, 1804.

Meanwhile, Spain (Nov. 30, 1803) gave up Louisiana to France, which soon after, on 20th Dec. transferred it to the United States. These changes made many regard themselves as free from ecclesiastical control.

Rev. Anthony Sedella, rector of the Cathedral, refused to recognize V. Rev. Mr. Walsh, to admit him to that edifice or allow him any income. He was thereupon suspended. A public meeting called under the auspices of the City Council elected marguillers or wardens, who in turn elected Sedella parish priest of New Orleans. After a show of resistance, this priest resumed his position sacreligiously officiated and began a schism which lasted for years. The Administrator thereupon issued the following Pastoral Letter, which has been carefully translated from the French.

Vicar General Walsh, died Aug. 22, 1806, and Bishop Carroll who had been appointed by the Holy See Administrator of Louisiana and the Floridas appointed Rev. John Olivier his Vicar General, but Sedella refused to recognize his authority and persevered in his schism.

PASTORAL LETEER.

Patrick Walsh, Vicar General, Provisor and Spiritual Governor of the Diocese of Louisiana, to all the Faithful, Apostolic and Roman Catholics of the City of New Orleans, health in our Lord Jesus Christ:

DEARLY BELOVED BRETHREN,

By virtue of the powers granted to us, on the 3d of November, 1801, by the most Illustrious and most Reverend Monsigneur de Peñalver y Cardenas, lately Bishop of this Diocese, duly authorized to appoint one or more Vicars General, who might replace him in case of a vacancy of the See till the Sovereign Pontiff otherwise provided, all in the terms of a rescript from Rome, dated September 14, 1794, which rescript signed by Cardinal Antonellus, Prefect of the Sacred Congregation de Propaganda Fide, is countersigned by the most Illustrious Archbishop Aduneno, Secretary of the same Congregation; by virtue, I say, of these powers, emanating from the Holy See, and which have been lawfully and canonically transmitted to us by the said Most Illustrious de Peñalver y Cardenas,

We, finding ourselves charged with the government of this diocese, under the weight whereof we groan before God, believe that it is our solicitude and duty to labor, in these evil days, to strengthen you in the faith. Meanwhile, my brethren, I know, and I say it, in the joy of my soul; there are some of you, who have never belied their baptismal promises, and who gladen heaven and earth by their fidelity and their attachment to the dogmas of our holy religion; but I know also that many have wavered and disappointed our expectations. God forbid that I should ascribe to the stubborness of your minds or the hardness of your hearts, the opposition recently manifested among you against the dogmas and discipline of the Church. Do I not know in Faith as in morals, there are falls, temptations, vicissitudes?

Dear brethren, if as I am happy to believe, you do not wish to renounce the religion of your fathers, if in a word you wish to live and die in the bosom of the Church, our Common Mother, of whom, notwithstanding my unworthiness, I am here the chief minister, hear me : I am about to expose what She herself teaches on the points which seem already to have divided you.

No priest can enter upon the pastoral functions, unless he is authorized and sent by Ecclesiastical Power. This mission which Jesus Christ Himself received from God the His Father, and transmitted to His apostles, and which, by apostolical succession has come to us, is so necessary that a priest who has not received it, or who after receiving it, is is deprived of it, cannot be considered as a lawful minister of the Word and of the Sacraments. This, my dear brethren, is of faith, and has been decided by the Council of Trent.

"If any one," says the Holy Council, "saith that those . . . not sent by Ecclesiastical and Canonical power, but come from elsewhere, are lawful ministers of the Word and the Sacraments, let him be Anathema." Sess. 23, can. 7.

In chap. 4, of the same session, it is said : "The Holy Council decrees that all those who being called and instituted by the people only, or by the civil power, and magistrate, ascend to the exercise of these ministrations, and those who of their own rashness assume them to themselves, are not ministers of the Church, but are to be looked upon as thieves and robbers who have not entered by the door."

In the decree on Reformation of Marriage on the 1st chapter of the 24th Session, the Fathers of the same Couucil declare null all marriages made in the presence of any priest but the true pastor, unless the priest who blesses them, is approved, either by the true pastor or by the Ordinary, that is to say, the Bishop or his Vicar General.

Finally, the same Council orders absolution given by a priest who has not ordinary jurisdiction or delegated jurisdiction to be regarded as null.

You must not forget, my brethren, that an Œcumenical Council, like that of Trent, whose decrees you have just heard, is a holy assembly, in which the Church by the mouth of its first pastors, forms decisions and proposes to all the faithful the infallible rules of Catholic worship and doctrine. Not to believe and not to submit to these Councils, is to renounce the character of child of the Church, is to excommunicate one's self and take a place in the ranks of infidels, as Jesus Christ Himself warns us. Si Ecclesiam non audierit, sit tibi sicut ethnicus et publtcanus. St. Matt. ch. 18, v. 17.

Hence I conclude, my dear brethren, and if you wish to be Catholics, you must conclude with me : 1st. That a priest cannot lawfully announce the word of God and administer the sacraments without ecclesiastical or canonical mission or approbation. 2nd. That the acts of authority or jurisdiction, which he shall undertake to do, such as absolving penitents or blessing marriages, are acts null in the eyes of the Church. 3d. Finally, that all the sacraments he administers, are so many profanations, both on the part of him who administers them, and on the part of those who receive them. I cannot, without rendering myself grievously culpable before God and before you, my brethren, leave you in ignorance that a priest interdicted from all ecclesiastical functions, by his lawful superior, and who despising Divine and ecclesiastical laws, is bold enough to break through, by his own authority, the interdict notified to

him, and to which he has promised in writing to submit, falls *ipsofacto* into schism and irregularity. Schism is a
culpable and voluntary separation from the Church. Irregularity, here in question, is a disability, an impotence to
hold any position, receive any order, any ecclesiastical dignity. Only the Sovereign Pontiff can absolve from schism
and dispense from this irregularity.

Such is the unvariable doctrine of the Catholic Apostolic and Roman Church, of which by Apostolical and uninterrupted succession, I am here the ordinary minister, and of
whom, undoubtedly, you do not wish to cease to be children.

Meanwhile, my brethren, such of you as may still have
difficulties and doubts as to the reality of my powers, which
being entirely spiritual, cannot depend either on change of
times, nor on that of government, or in fine on any other
point; let them come to us with with all confidence. Always
ready to answer and instruct you, we will destroy your doubts,
and convince you of our faith, and we shall endeavor to
edify yours. We owe you instruction and our assistance.
We owe ourselves to the strong and to the weak, to the
learned and to the simple. Providence has established me
your pastor. Wo to me, if I do not instruct you, but wo also
to you, if you shall not hear my voice. God is witness that
I bear you all in my heart and in my bowels. Phil. v. 8.

Meekness, persuasion, charity, condescension, but only
lawful condescension, shall always be the objects of my ministry, and this conduct is not less conformable to my inclination than proper to my duties.

I shall mourn incessantly till Jesus Christ, who is the
Life, the Way and the Truth is formed in you, and peace
dwells forever in your hearts.

Do not hearken, my dear brethren, to the counsels of
certain men, enemies of your repose and of your salvation.
I address you, in conclusion these words of the Apostle St.
Paul, in his Epistle to the Galatians, chap. 1, v. 7, 8. " There
are some that trouble you, and would pervert the Gospel

of Christ, but if any any one preach a gospel to you, beside that which we have preached to you, let him be anathema."

Return then sincerely to the Church, which urges you, which desires you and calls you.

How beautiful, how consoling would it be, to see our holy religion maintained pure and spotless among us, pass from parents to children, and triumph over the efforts of a world, always conspiring against the Lord and against his Christ.

What other doctrine than ours, has better regulated the duties of men. It teaches us, it forces us to obey lawful authorities, as established by God, not only through a sentiment of fear, but what is surer, through an obligation of conscience. It teaches us to respect our superiors, to be affable to our equals, to love all men as ourselves. It alone forms faithful citizens, patient servants, incorruptible magistrates, true friends. It alone can render inviolable fidelity in marriage, assure peace in families, maintain the tranquility of States, and in a word present to us the picture of heaven on earth.

After having succinctly exposed, my brethren, those dogmas of the Catholic religion, which seem to have been unknown or misunderstood, after making known to you the spirit of that holy religion, of which I am the minister; as the American Government does not interfere at all in religious affairs, and we can freely profess ours, in all its purity, and also, in order that, especially in this holy time, nothing can hamper you in accomplishing your religious duties and in the exercise of the Catholic Apostolic and Roman worship, of which I am, *pro tempore*, the ordinary superior, I declare to the faithful of my religion:

Art. 1. I appoint the Church of our most holy and beloved daughters, the Ursuline nuns of New Orleans, to be the only one in this city, where, till otherwise ordered, the sacraments shall be solemnly administered, and where the offices shall be celebrated, conformably to the laws and usages of our Mother the Holy Catholic Apostolic and Roman Church.

Art. 2. Every Sunday three masses will be celebrated, viz: the Community mass at a quarter past six; a low mass at half past seven, and a high mass at half past nine. A homily and instruction will be given high mass. There will be catechism at three o'clock in the afternoon, and vespers will be sung immediately after.

Art. 3. On holidays of obligation, the masses and offices will be celebrated at the same hours as on Sundays.

Art. 4. I declare that I put myself immediately at the head of the Catholic Apostolic and Roman worship, which I shall exercise in the church above appointed with the assistance of Messrs. John Baptist Olivier, formerly parish priest of Sauteron in the diocese of Nantes, and now chaplain of the Religious Ladies of this city, Peter Francis de l'Espinasse, formerly canon of the Cathedral Church of Mans, and one of my vicars, the Reverend Fathers John Kouane and Charles Lusson, formerly parish priest of St. Charles, in Missouri of the Illinois, and both my vicars. My four co-operators are canonically approved and authorized, in order, conjointly with me, and to the exclusion of any other priest. whether secular or regular, to exercise the functions of the holy ministry, in the whole extent of the city and the Catholic Apostolic and Roman parish of New Orleans.

Art. 5. The present regulation shall be in vigor from this day, and it shall be read, as well as the annexed pastoral letter, at the homily during the parochial high mass for three consecutive Sundays.

Given at New Orleans, the 27th day of March, in the year of Grace eighteen hundred and five. ·

PATRICK WALSH, Vicar General.
By the Vicar General,
OLIVIER, Secretary of the Diocese.

CATHOLIC BIBLIOGRAPHY.

A Preliminary Catalogue of Councils, Synods and Statutes which have obtained force in any part of the United States.

COUNCILS.

Concilio Provincial celebrado en la muy noble y leal ciudad de Mexico, presidiendo el Illmo y Rmo Señor D. Fray Alonso de Montufar en el año 1555.

Mexico Juan P. Lombardo. 1556.

Sanctum Provinciale Conciliam Mexici celebratum.

Mexico; J. Ruiz, 1622.

Sanctum Provinciale Concilium Mexici celebratum, Paris.

Concilios Provinciales Primero, y Segundo, celebrados en la muy noble, y muy leal ciudad de Mexico, presidiendo el illmo, y rmo Señor D. Fr. Alonso de Montufar, en los años de 1555, y 1565. Da los a luz el Illmo Sr. D. Francisco Antonio Lorenzana, Arzobispo de esta santa Metropolitana Iglesia. Folio. 408 pp.   Mexico, Hogal, 1769.

Concilium Mexicanum Provinciale III. celebratum Mexici año MDLXXXV. Preside D.D. Petro Moya, et Contreras, Archipiscopo ejusdem urbis. Confirmatum Romæ die xxvij Octobris anno MDLXXXIX. Postea jussu regio editum Mexici año MDCXXII sumptibus D.D. Joannis Perez de la Serna, Archiépiscopi. Demum typis mandatum cura, et expensis D. D. Francisci Antonii a Lorenzana, Archipraesulis. Folio. 332 pp.   Mexico, Hogal, 1770.

Statuta ordinata a Sancto Concilio Provinciali Mexicano III. anno Domini MDLXXXV. ex prescripto Sacrosancti Concilu Tridentini Decreto sess. cap 52 de Reform. verbo Cætera.

Revisa a Catholica Majestate, et a Sacrosancta sede Apostolica confirmata anno Domini millesimo quingentesimo octua-
gesimo nono.

Folio.   145 pp.   n. p. n. d.

Statuta Ecclesiæ Mexicanæ necnon ordo in choro servan-
dus curante Vallisoletanæ Ecclesiæ capitulo sumptus sup-
peditante Illmo. ac Rmo D. M. D. F. Antonio a Sancto
Michaele Episcopo Mechoacanensi, Regis a Consilus, etc.,
etc., denuo in lucem edita

Folio.   143 pp.   Mexica, Znñiga, 1797.*

PLENARY COUNCILS HELD IN THE
UNITED STATES.

Concilium Plenarium Totius Americæ Septentrionalis
Fœderatæ, Baltimori habitum anno 1852.

80 pp 72.   Baltimore, John Murphy & Co., 1853.

Concilii Plenarii Baltimorensis II, en Ecclesia Metropoli-
tana Baltimorensi a die vii ad diem xxi Octobris, A. D.
MDCCCLXVI habiti et a Sede Apostolica recogniti Acta et
Decreta, Preside Illustrissimo et Reverendissimo Martino
Joanne Spalding, Archiepiscopo Baltimorensi et Delegato
Apostolico.

8vo. iv. 346 xxviii, xxvi pp.   J. Murphy & Co., Balt. 1867.

Title as above omitting " Acta et."

8vo viii, 274, xxviii,   John Murphy, Baltimore, 1868.

Title as above omitting"Acta et" but ending with "secun-
dis curis editum."

8vo. viii, 274, xxviii pp.   John Murphy & Co., Balt., 1868.

Decreta Conciliorum Provincialium et Plenarii Baltimorensium, pro majori cleri Americani commoditate simul collecta..

8vo. pp. 43.   John Murphy & Co., Baltimore, 1853.

Acta et Decreta Concilii Plenarii Baltimorensis Tertii A.
D. MDCCCLXXXIV.   Preside Illmo. ac Revmo. Jacobo Gib-

---

* The preceding were in force in Texas, New Mexico, Arizona and California.

bons, Archiepiscopo Balt. et Delegato Apostolico.
8vo. cix, 329 pp.   Baltimore, John Murphy & Co., 1886.

PROVINCIAL COUNCILS.

Baltimore Concilium Baltimorense Provinciale Primum, habitum Baltimori anno reparatæ Salutis 1829, meuse Octobri.
8vo. 30 pp.   Baltimore, J. D. Toy, 1831.

Concilium Baltimorense Provinciale Secundum : Habitum Baltimori a die 20ª a diem usque 27am Octobris A. R. S. 1833.
8vo. 18 pp.   Baltimore, J. D. Toy, n. d.

Concilia Provincialia Baltimori habita ab anno 1829, usque ad annum 1840.
8vo. 221 pp.   Baltimore, John Murphy, 1842.

Fasciculus quo recensentur Acta ac Decreta Synodorum Provincialium Baltimori habitarum ab anno MDCCCXXIX usque ad annum MDCCCXL quæ Sacri Consilii Christiano nomine propagando judicio subjecta, et ab Apostolica Sede confirmata sunt.
8vo. 162 pp., paper.   n. p. n. d. (Rome).

Same in Bullarium Pontificium Sacræ Congregationis de Propaganda Fide, Rome, 1841, vol. 5, 86 pp 4to.

Acta et Decreta Synodorum Provincialium Baltimori habitarum ab anno MDCCCXXIX usque ad annum MDCCCXL, que Sacri Concilii Christiano nomine propagando judicio subjecta et ab Apostolica Sede confirmata sunt; Referuntur simul Sacri Consilii Decreta et Responsa de rebus in qualibet Synodo pertractatis. Editio Secunda.
8vo 160 pp,   Rome, Propaganda, 1841.

Concilium Provinciale Baltimorense V. Habitum anno 1843.
8vo. 30 pp.   Baltimore John Murphy, 1844.

Concilium Baltimorense Provinciale VI. Habitum anno 1846.
8vo. 36 pp.   Baltimore, John Murphy, 1847.

Concilium Baltimorense Provinciale VII.   Habitum anno 1849.

8vo. 33 pp.   Baltimore, John Murphy & Co., 1851.
Concilium Baltimorense Provinciale VIII., Habitum anno 1855.

8vo. 40 pp.   Baltimore, John Murphy & Co., 1857.
Concilium Baltimorense Provinciale IX, Habitum anno 1858.

8vo. 42 pp.   Baltimore, John Murphy & Co., n. d.

Concilii Provincialis Baltimorensis X. in Metropolitana Baltimorensi Ecclesia, Dominica quarta post Pascha, quæ festo S. Marci Evangelistæ incidit A. R. S. 1869 inchoati, et insequenti Dominica absoluti, Acta et Decreta, Præside Illmo ac Revmo. Martino Joanne Spalding, Archiepiscopo Baltimorensi.

8vo. 78 pp.   Baltimore, John Murphy 1870.

CINCINNATI. — Concilium Cincinnatense Provinciale I. Habitum. anno 1855.

8vo. pp 50.   Cincinnati, John P. Walsh, n. d:

Concilium Cincinnatense Provinciale II. · Habitum anno 1858. 8vo. pp 32.   Cincinnati, J. P. Walsh, n. d.

Concilium Cincinnatense Provinciale III. Habitum anno 1861. 8vo. pp 48. Cincinnati and N.Y. Benziger Bros. n.d.

Acta et Decreta Quatuor Conciliorum Provincialium Cincinnatensium, 1855—1882 Adjectis pluribus Decretis, Rescriptis, aliisque Documentis.

8vo. pp vii 319.   Cincinnati, Benziger Bros., 1886.

MILWAUKEE.—Acta et Decreta Concilii Provincialis Milwaukiensis Primi. A. D. MDCCCLXXXVI. Præside Illmo. ac Revmo. Michaele Heiss, Archiepiscopo Milwaukiensi.

8vo. 53 pp.   Milwaukee, Hoffman Bros., 1888.

NEW ORLEANS.—Concilium Neo-Aurelianense Provinciale Primum, Habitum anno 1856.

8vo. pp 35.   New Orleans, H. Meridier, 1857.

Concilium Neo-Aurelianense Tertium, Habitum mense

Januario, A. D. 1873, cui addita sunt in appendice Duæ Constitutiones Vaticanæ—Epistola Encyclica Quanta Cura—Syllabus et Formula Juramenti pro ordinandis ad subdiaconatum sub titulo Missionis.

8vo. pp 69. New Orleans, Propagateur Catholique, 1875.

NEW YORK.—Concilium Neo-Eboracense Primum. Habitum anno MDCCCLIV.

8vo. pp 32.   New York, E. Dunigan & Bro. 1855.

Concilium Neo- Eboracense III. mense Junii anno MDCCCLXI. celebratum.

8vo. pp 37.   New York, E. Dunigan & Bro., 1862.

OREGON.—Decreta Concilii Provincialis Oregonensis I. Sancti Pauli habiti diebus 28, 29 Februarii et 1 Martii 1848.

8vo. pp 7.   New York, 1887.

Reprinted from the U. S. Catholic Historical Magazine, Vol. I.]

PHILADELPHIA.—Decreta Concilii Provincialis Philadelphiensis I. anno MDCCCLXXX habiti.

8vo 36 pp,   n. p. n. d.

SAN FRANCISCO.—Concilii Provincialis S. Francisci I. in Ecclesia Metropolitana Sancti Francisci A.D. MDCCCLXXIV. habiti, et a Sede Apostolica recogniti, Acta et Decreta.

8vo. pp 91.   San Francisco, Thomas & Co., 1875.

Concilii Provincialis S. Francisci II. in Ecclesia Metropolitana Sancti Francisci, A. D. MDCCCLXXXII. habiti, et a Sede Apostolica recogniti, Acta et Decreta.

8vo. pp 36.   San Francisco, P. J. Thomas, 1888.

ST. LOUIS.—Concilium Provinciale Secundum. Mense Septembris, A. D. 1858. Sancti Ludovici, habitum.

8vo. pp 16.   St. Louis, G. Knapp & Co., 1859.

DIOCESAN SYNODS AND STATUTES.

ALBANY.—Diœceseos Albanensis Statuta quæ in Synodo Albanensi II A.D. 1869 lata ac promulgata fuere al Illustrisso. et Reverendisso. Joanne Josepho Conroy, Episcopo Albanensi.

8vo 28 pp.　　　Troy, N.Y., A. W. Scribner & Co., 1869.

Synodus Diœcesana Albanensis Tertia quæ antecedentium etiam complectitur constitutiones, diebus 6 et 7 Februarii, A. D. 1884 in Seminario S. Josephi, Trojæ habita ab Illustrissimo et Reverendissimo Francisco McNeirny, Episcopo Albanensi.

8vo. 85 pp. New York Catholic Publication Society, 1884.

BALTIMORE.—[Statuta Synodi anno 1791 celebratæ—II Quidam ex articulis ecclesiasticæ disciplinæ quos Ill. DD. Archiepiscopus Baltimorensis et Episcopi Americæ Fœderatæ communi consilio, anno 1810, sanxerunt—III Regulæ ab Illo. et Revmo. Ambrosio Maréchal conditæ.]

No title page. 8vo. pp 34.　　apparently Baltimore, 1817.

Synodus Diœcesana Baltimorensis II. habita ab illustrissimo ac Reverendissimo Jacobo, Archiepiscopo Baltimorensi. Anno reparatæ Salutio 1831.　Mense Novembri.

8vo. 10 pp.　　　　　　　Baltimore, J. D. Toy, 1831.

Synodus Diœcesana Baltimorensis, mense Junio, 1852 habita.

8vo. 18 pp.　　　Baltimore, John Murphy & Co., 1853.

Synodus Diœcesana Baltimorensis, mense Junio, 1857 habita.

8vo. 14 pp.　　　Baltimore, John Murphy & Co., 1857.

Synodus Diœcesana Baltimorensis, mense Maii, 1863 habita.

8vo. 18 pp.　　　Baltimore, John Murphy & Co., 1863.

Acta Synodi Diœcesanæ Baltimorensis Sextæ: una cum constitutionibus ab illustrissimo ac reverendissimo Martino Joanne Spalding, Archiepiscopo Baltimorensi latis ac promulgatis; in feria quarta Rogationum, Die 24 Maii, A. D. MDCCCLXV.

8v. 22 pp.　　　　　Baltimore, Kelly & Piet, 1865.

Synodus Diœcesana Baltimorensis Septima; quæ antecedentium etiam complectitur constitutiones; die III Septembris. A. D. 1868 in Ecclesia Collegiali S. Mariæ ad Seminarium S. Sulpitii, Baltimoræ habita: ab Illustrissimo ac

Reverendissimo Martino Joanne Spalding, Archiepiscopo Baltimorensi.

8vo. 28 pp.   Baltimore, John Murphy, 1868.

Synodus Diœcesana Baltimorensis Octava, quæ antecedentium etiam complectitur Constitutiones, die xxvii Augusto, A. D. 1875 ad B. M. V. en Seminario S. Sulpitii Baltimoræ habita, ab Illustrissimo ac Reverendissimo Jacobo Roosevelt Bayley, Archiepiscopo Baltimorensi.

12mo. 134 pp.   Baltimore, John Murphy & Co., 1876.

Synodus Diœcesana Baltimorensis nona quæ antecedentium etiam complectitur Constitutiones; die xxiv Septembris, A. D. 1886 ad B. V M. in Seminario S. Sulpitii Baltimoræ habitea ab Eminentissimo ac Reverendissimo Jacobo Cardinale Gibbons, Archiepiscopo Baltimorensi.

12mo. 136 pp.   Baltimore, Foley Brothers, 1886.

BOSTON.—Synodus Diœcesana Bostoniensis I habita anno 1842. 8vo 11 pp., no place, no date.

(2d ed.) 8vo 11 pp.   Boston, P. Donahoe, n.d.

Constitutiones Diœcesanæ ab Illmo. ac Revmo. Domino Joanne Josepho Williams, Episcopo Bostoniensi in Synodo Diœcesana Secunda habita Bostoniæ, A. D. 1868, latæ et promulgatæ.

8vo. 59 pp.   n. p. n. d.

BUFFALO.—Synodus Diœcesana Buffalensis Secunda, habita anno MDCCCXLIX.

8vo.   Buffalo, Brunck & Domediou, 1850.

Synodus Diœcesana Buffalensis Decima Septima, quæ complectitur etiam Statuta lata in Synodis ab A.D. 1847 usque ad 1886, die 13ª Augusti, A. D. 1871 in Ecclesia Cathedrali Sancti Josephi in Civitate Buffalensi habita, ab Illustrissimo ac Reverendissimo Stephano Vincentio Ryan, D. D., Episcopo Buffalensi.

8vo. 50 pp.   Buffalo, 1871.

BURLINGTON — Statuta Diœcesis Burlingtoniensis. Deus providebit.

8vo 11 pp.   St, Albans, 1878.

CHARLESTON—Statuta quœ in Synodo Carolopolitana XVI lata et promulgata fuere ab Illmo. ac Revmo. Dominio, Henrico P. Northrop, Episcopo Carolopolitano.

12mo 47 pp Charleston, Walker, Evans & Cogswell & Co., n. d.

CINCINNATI—Statuta Diœcesana ab Illustrissimo ac Reverendissimo P. D. Joanne Baptista Purcell, Archiepiscopo Cincinnatensi in variis synodis, quæ hucusque in Ecclesia sua Cathedrali, vel in Sacello Seminarii, celebratæ sunt, lata et promulgata. Una cum Decretis Conciliorum Provincialium et Plenarii Baltimorensium, quibus interfuerunt omnes Statuum Fœderatorum Episcopi, et decretis Conciliorum trium Cincinnatensium, nunc primum in unum collecta et publici juris facta. '

8vo 69, x, 15, 44, 14 pp.   Cincinnati, 1865.

Synodus Diœcesana Cincinnatensis Secunda, diebus 19, 20, 21 Octobris A. D. 1868, in Ecclesia Metropolitana St. Petri in Vinculis, Cincinnati habita, ab Illmo. ac Revmo. Gulielmo Henrico Elder, Archiepiscopo Cincinnatensi.

8vo 82 pp.   n. p. n. d.

CLEVELAND — Statuta Diœcesis Clevelandensis lata in Synodo Diœcesana habita A. D. 1852, et in aliis Synodis A. D. 1854 et A. D. 1857 aucta et emendata.

80 pp.   Cleveland, H. Kramer, 1857.

DENVER—Synodus Diœcesana Denveriensis Prima juxta norman a Conc. Balt. III præstitutam habita in Collegio S. S. Cordis, Highlands, a Reverendissimo Nicolao Chryosostomo Matz, Episcopo Denveriensi die ii Augusti MDCCCLXXXIX

8vo 59 pp.   Las Vegas, 1889.

DETROIT—[Statuta, Dec. 25, 1851].

8vo 15 pp.   n. p. n. d.

Constitutiones Synodi Diœcesanæ Detroitensis Primæ, habitæ mense Octobri, A.D. 1859.

8vo 44 pp.   Detroit, John Slater, 1859.

Synodus Diœcesana Detroitensis Secunda, habita mense Septembri A. D. MDCCCLXII.

104 *United States Catholic* (No. 9.

8vo pp 9. Detroit, John Slater, 1862.

Acta et Constitutiones Synodi Diœcesanæ Detroitensis Sextæ, habita in Collegio Assumptionis BMV. Sandwichensi, diebus 20 et 21 mensis Julii A. D. 1885 Præside Reverendissimo et Illustrissimo Casparo Henrico Borgess, Episcopo Detroitensis.

8vo 17 pp. Detroit, Kilroy & Brennan, 1881.

A. M. D. G. Synodus Diœcesana Detroitensis Septima; antecedentium etiam complectitur Constitutiones, die XIX M. Augusti, A. D. 1886 in Collegio Assumptionis B. M. V. Sandwichensi, habita; ab Illustrissimo ac Reverendissimo Casparo Henrico Borgess, Episcopo Detroitensi II.

8vo x, 24, 11 pp paper. Marshall, Mich., 1886.

DUBUQUE—Statuta lata et promulgata ab Illmo ac Revmo D. Clementi Smyth, Episcopo Dubuquensi in Synodo Primo Diœcesana, Dubuquii, mense Maii 1871 habita.

8vo 19 pp. Dubuque, Rich & Ryan, 1871.

FORT WAYNE—Statuta Diœcesis Wayne Castrensis in Synodo Diœcesana 1874 promulgata ab Illustrissimo ac Reverndissimo Joseph Dwenger.

8vo 23 pp. Fort Wayne, Sentinel, 1875.

GREEN BAY—Constitutiones Diœcesos Sinus Viridis.

12mo 12 pp. Milwaukee, P. V. Deuster, 1869.

Decreta edita in Synodo Diœcesana 1ma celebrata Sinu Viridi a Revmo, ac Illustrissimo D. Domino Francisco Xaverio Krautbauer, diebus 11mo et 12mo Julii A. D. 1876.

12mo 30 pp. Green Bay, Robinson Brothers & Clark, 1877.

HARTFORD—Decreta Synodi Hartfordensis Primæ, mense Octobris, anno MDCCCLIV celebratæ.

8vo 20 pp. Providence : B. T. Albro, 1855.

Constitutiones Synodi Hartfordensis II, mense Septembri anno MDCCCLXXVIII habitæ.

8vo 40 pp. Hartford: Case, Lockwood & Brainard Co., 1878.

Constitutiones Synodi Hartfordiensis IV. ab Illmo. et Revmo. Domino Laurentio Stephano McMahon, Episcopo Hartfordiensi. mensi Augusti anno MDCCCLXXXVI habitæ.

8vo 61 pp. Hartford: Case, Lockwood & Brainard Co., 1887.

LOUISIANA—Statutes of the Diocese of Louisiana and the Floridas, issued by the Rt. Rev. Luis Peñalver y Cardenas, 1795, with a translation by John Gilmary Shea, [Spanish and English.] 8vo 29 pp. New York, 1887.

Reprinted from U. S. Historical Magazine for Oct. '87.

LOUISVILLE—Constitutiones Diœcesis Ludovicopolitanæ, a Reverendissimo ac Illustrissimo Domino Martino Joanne Spalding, Episcopo Ludovicopolitano, in Synodo Diœcesana prima, habita mense Julii 1850 en Ecclesiao St. Josephi, Bardpoli, latæ et promulgatæ.

8vo 20 pp.   Louisville: Webb, McGill & Levering, 1850
[2d ed.] 8vo 16 pp.   Louisville : Joseph F. Brennan, 1857.

Synodus Tertia Diœcesana Ludovicopolitana, habita die 27 Augusti 1862, in ecclesia Sancti Joseph Bardensi.

8vo 28 pp.   Louisville : Bradley & Gilbert, 1862.

Synodus Diœcesana Ludovicopolitana IV. in Ecclesia Cathedrali, die 21 Julii A. R. S. 1874 ab Illustrissimo ac Reverendissimo D. Gulielmo McCloskey, Episcopo Ludovicopolitano, habita.

8vo 24 pp.   Louisville: Bradley & Gilbert, 1874.

MOBILE—Statuta Synodi Mobiliensis Primæ mense Novembris, anno Domini 1861 celebrata.

16mo 16 pp.   Montgomery, 1862.

NATCHEZ—Synodus Diœcesana Natchetensis Prima, habita ab Illmo et Rmo Gulielmo Henrico Elder, Episcopo Natchetensi, hebdomada secunda post Pascha anno 1858.

8vo 14 pp. New Orleans: Propagateur Catholique, 1858.

Synodus Diœcesana Natchetensis mense Januarii 1862, habita.

8vo 12 pp. New Orleans : Propagateur Catholique, 1862.

Synodus Diœcesana Natchetensis Quarta, habita diebus 19a, 20a et 21a mense Januarii A. D. 1874 a Rev^{mo} Gulielmo Henrico Elder, Episcopo Natchetensi, in Monasterio cui nomen "St. Theresa's Retreat" Patrum Congregationis SS. Redemptoris, apud Chatawa, Mississippi.

16mo 26 pp.   n. p. n, d

NEWARK—Statuta Novarcensis Diœceseos a Reverendissimo Domino Jacobo Roosevelt Bayley, Novarcensi Episcopo, in Synodo Diœcesana Prima habita mense Augusto, 1856, in Collegio Seton Hall. Madison, N. J.. lata et promulgata.

16mo 52 pp.   New York : E. Dunigan & Brother, 1857.

Statuta Diœcesis Novarcensis quæ post Synodum I[um] A.D. A. D. 1853, et II[a] A. D. 1868 a Rev[mo] Jacobo Roosevelt Bayley, fe. me., celebratas, in Synodo Diœcesana Tertia, diebus 8 et 9 Maji 1878 habita, tulit et promulgavit Illustr[mus] et Rev[mus] Michael Augustinus Corrigan, Episcopus.

16mo 161 pp.   New York, Benziger Brothers, 1878.

Synodus Diœcesana Novarcensis Quinta, A. D. 1886 celebrata ab Illustr[mo] et Rev • Michael Venantio Wigger, Episcopo.

8vo 45 pp.   Arlington, N. J., 1887.

NEW ORLEANS—Synodus Diœcesana Neo-Aurelianensis Secunda, habita mense Aprili anno 1844.

8vo 22 pp.   New Orleans: H. Meridier, 1844.

NEW YORK—Synodus Diœcesana Neo-Eboracensis Prima, Habita anno 1842.

8vo 22 pp.   New York, George Mitchell, 1842.

Synodus Diœcesana Neo-Eboracensis Tertia, quæ antecedentium etiam complectitur Constitutiones, die 29 et die 30 Septembris, A. D. 1868 in ecclesia Metropolitana S. Patritii, Neo-Eboraci habita ab Illustrissimo et Reverendissimo Joanne McCloskey, Archiepiscopo Neo-Eboracensi.

8vo 23 pp. New York, Catholic Publication Society, 1868.

Synodus Diœcesana Neo-Eboracensis Quarta, quæ antecedentium etiam complectitur Constitutiones diebus 8 et 9 Novembris A. D. 1882, in Ecclesia Metropolitana S. Patritii, Neo-Eboraci habita ab Eminentissimo et Reverendissimo Joanne Cardinali McCloskey, Archiepiscopo Neo-Eboracensis.

8vo 51 pp. New York, Catholic Publication Society, 1882.

MEETING OF THE UNITED STATES CATHOLIC
HISTORICAL SOCIETY.

A public meeting of the United States Catholic Historical Society was held on Monday evening, November 25. 1889, at the Hall of De La Salle Institute, West 59th street. Hon. Morgan J. O'Brien, President, presided. There were present the Vice-President, Charles Carroll Lee, M. D., the Corresponding Secretary, the Recording Secretary, the Librarian, a large uumber of the Trustees, Councillors and members, Judge Daly, Register James Slavin, Brothers Justin, James. Azarias and a goodly number of Christian Brothers, and quite a gathering of ladies and gentlemen.

The exercises opened with an address from the President, in the course of which he made a very strong and eloquent appeal to the intelligent and wealthy Catholics of New York and elsewhere to assist, by their talents and means, in collecting and preserving the past and securing the present history of the Catholic Church in America.

The Historical Paper of the evening was on the "Early History of the Redemptorists in the United States, 1832–1850." It was prepared by the Rev. Charles Warren Currier, C.SS.R., of Boston, Mass., and, in his absence was read by Marc F. Vallette, the Corresponding Secretary.

On motion by Dr. Charles Carroll Lee, a vote of thanks was tendered to the Rev. author of the paper.

A vote of thanks also tendered to the Christian Brothers for their kindness in granting the use of their beautiful Hall for the occasion, and to the young gentlemen of De La Salle Institute for the vocal and instrumental selections which added so much to the enjoyment of the evening.

NOTES.

Bricknell's Alleged Catholic Settlement in North Carolina.

In a work by John Bricknell, "The Natural History of North Carolina," Dublin, 1737, the statement is made that there was then a settlement of Irish Catholics with a priest near Bathtown, N. C. The work is mainly a plagiarism from Lawson's work which appeared in 1718, but there is nothing of the kind in Lawson. Judge M. E. Manly, the most eminent Catholic of the North State after Gaston, when addressed more than thirty years ago to ascertain whether there was any documentary or traditionary support to Brickell's assertion, wrote :

"My enquiries in respect to the point you make in the early settlement of North Carolina, about Bathtown, have not resulted in anything satisfactory. President Main, of our University suggests that Brickell was interested in the land sales in the colony, and magnified a few Irish settlers and an occasional visit from a priest into a settlement of Catholics and a resident priest, for selfish purposes. This is probable, as there are evidences about the work of untrustworthiness to justify unfavorable inferences in other respects. He copies, for instance, from Lawson, a book with the same title a few years before without acknowledgement.

His paragraphs upon the subject of religious character of the settlers are original, and in many respects are now known to be truthful, and that therefore touching Roman Catholics, merits enquiry.

I will keep the matter in mind, and if anything transpires to throw light upon it, I will communicate it." (Letter Feb. 17. 1857.) Researches for a third of a century fail to give sny data substantiating Bricknell's statements, and it is not easy to see from what point a few straggling Catholics in North Carolina, between 1718 and 1737 could have been visited. There is no trace of any of the Jesuit Fathers in Maryland having penetrated so far south. The whole matter remains one of the mysteries.

A Catholic Centenarian of Colonial Days. — " The Patriarch of Baltimore, on Wednesday, 14th February, died at his dwelling in Wagon alley, Jacob Nurser, in his 114th year and was buried on the 16th following, in the burial ground of the German Catholic Church of St. John's, in Saratoga street, of which he was a member. He was 27 years old when he came to this country from Germany. He then served five years in the military service, and was at the battle and surrender of Lewisbourg in the year 1745, after which he came to Baltimore, and remained till his death. At his arrival, he found but two houses on the west side of Market street bridge, one belonging to Alexander Lawson, the other to Daniel Bernard, who kept a tavern and made soap. Soon after came a singleman by the name of Andrew Steiger, a butcher. On the other side of the bridge, there was a little village, he believed of seven houses. He always lived honorably though rather poor. The late Archbishop Carroll often visited him, and treated him as a friend, and was delighted to enjoy his company. Before he entered the British service he had been in the service of Austria.

May he rest in peace, Amen.

"U. S. Catholic Miscellany," March 3, 1827.

REPLIES.

What College in the United States did the Holy Man of Tours attend? (U. S. C. H. M. ii p 106). There is no trace of the name of Leon Duprat among the students of Georgetown College, our oldest Catholic institution, so that his name must in all probability be sought among the pupils of St. Mary's College, Baltimore.   F. J. G.

Rev. Pierre Gibault (U. S. C. H. M. 1 p 115). This patriotic clergyman died at New Madrid, Mo., in 1804. Letter of V. Rev. John Olivier cited in Life and Times of Archbishop Carroll, p. 56.   '

Capt. Bentalou. (U. S. C. H. M. i p 230). This aide and advocate of Count Pulaski died at Baltimore in 1826. He had resided for many years in that city.

BOOK NOTICES.

THE PRE COLUMBIAN DISCOVERY OF AMERICA BY THE NORTHMEN, with Translations from the Icelandic Sagas. By B. F. DeCosta. Second Edition: Munsell, 1890. 196 pp.

Some years ago any recognition of the claims of the Northmen to an early discovery of a portion of our coast was treated by a class of American scholars with contempt and disdain. Rev. Mr. DeCosta was one of the first to take up the matter seriously, and to present to English readers the evidence of the old Sagas with illustrative notes. He now presents a second edition with all the ripe knowledge acquired by his patient study of early American cartography and of the first known voyages to our coast. Few scholars can be found better equipped than DeCosta to give a work that will be a real aid to a student of the subject. He well takes the position that there is no real question of priority between the Northmen and Columbus. Their objects were essentially different. The Northmen extended their discoveries from the Faroe Islands to Iceland, then to Greenland, then to Vinland. In this they were merely bringing within the range of knowledge outlying parts of Europe. The successive editions of Ptolemy after the invention of printing show Iceland and Greenland as part of Europe. Columbus on the other hand had a definite object. It was not to discover new lands, but to reach India and the Coast of Asia generally, old and well known lands, by sailing west. That he became the discoverer of a new continent was not suspected by him after his first voyage, for the earliest printed account in 1493 describes the islands as part of India beyond the Ganges.

Mr. DeCosta's introduction treats of the early historic fancies as to the Sea of Darkness, the voyages of the Phoenicians, Juba's expedition, and early traditions. Then he takes up the Northmen, traces the discovery and colonization of Iceland and of Greenland, the Greenland settlements, the organization of the Church there; the movements and ruins discovered there in recent times, as well as the decline and final abandonment of the colony. After a discussion of the vessels used by the Northmen, he treats of the Sagas and of

Islandic literature, estimates their value, and shows how English records corroborate them. He justly ridicules the lunatic idea that the Catholic Church seeks to depreciate the Northmen in order to exalt Columbus, when in fact, Catholics claim both. The last man who endeavored to reopen communication with Greenland was Eric Walkendorf, one of the last Archbishops of Drontheim, who died in exile at Rome.

He then gives translations from the Landamanna Book (1100-1300); of the Sagas relating to the discovery of Greenland; then all known of the voyages of Leif Ericson, Thowald Ericson, Thorstein Ericson, Thorfinn Karlsefne and Freydis to Vinland, with minor narratives and fragments. Without attempting to determine positively every locality mentioned, he establishes in a convincing manner the identity of Vinland with Massachusetts and Rhode Island. Master of all the discussions of the question, his notes, full and clear, make his volume one of remarkable value to the student, and full of interest to the general reader.

THE STORY OF TONTY. By MARY HARTWELL CATHERWOOD, Chicago. A. C. McClurg & Co.

The indifferenc of Catholics to the early Catholic History of our Northern continent is something incomprehensible. It is not dull or repulsive like the annals of New England; it is full of all that is grand, heroic, devoted, dramatic. Longfellow found in it the theme of his Evangeline, and borrowed from some of the noblest episodes of of Hiawatha. Our author took the plot of one story from the heroic fight of Dollard at Long Sault, which saved Canada, and now makes Tonty of the Iron Hand the central figure of a story .of the days of La Salle. The main incidents are woven into a love story, but the result is scarcely as attractive as the " Romance of Dollard." Yet many will read it with interest, and it is worthy a place as recalling the heroic days of old.

GESCHICHTE DER KATHOL KIRCHE. Chicago's mit besonderer Beruckt sichtizung des Kathol ischen Deutschthumo Von H. Burgler Wilhelm Kuhlmann: Chicago, 1889, 8vo, pp. 222.

This is a useful and apparently accurate little work on the Catholic Churches and institutions of Chicago, amply though not expensively illustrated. It will be found extremely useful as a contribution to the history of the Church in this country, especially as embodying the Ger-

man view. Our German Catholics are doing not a little
for the history of the Church in this country, and should
stimulate others. Father Oswald Moosmuller's "St. Vin-
centz," has been followed by lives of Bp. Neumann, Father Seelos, the Life of Bishop Henni, an account of
The Redemptorists in Pittsburg, the Life of Rev. F. Sales
Brunner. Their activity make us blush to see so little
interest generally manifested in the glorious annals of
our Church. Others find themes for history, poetry, and
romance in what we neglect.

OLD CALIFORNIA DAYS. James Steele. Illustrated; Chicago.
BELFORD, CLARKE & Co., 1889.

A bright lively book for a stray moment, that makes a
Catholic, and a historian especially, sigh over the ruin wrought
in a land of peace and plenty by men who in their self-satis-
fied vanity boasted of a higher civilization The author could
not write without telling of the wonderful California missions
created by Fr. Juniper Serra, which scattered along the coast
seven hundred miles, brought the Indians to industry, agriculture, the various trades, plenty and happiness. Those who
reviled the Francicians and were going to show what superior
intelligence could do, have squandered the means of the
Missions and exterminated the Indians. A mere handful of
Mission Indians now remain, and the whole power of the great
Republic is wielded to prevent the influence which civilized the
ancestors from reaching the descendants. Our author well
says of Father Serra, "It would not only be no impropriety,
but would be a fitting and proper thing, if his statue should
be set by Protestant hands in every Californian town, and his
heroic story told in every public school." Will any one believe it—the name of Juniper Serra, founder of the great
California Missions, cannot be found in Appleton's Cyclopæ-
dia of American Biography !

Our author writes interestingly and gives an attractive volume, but why did he take from that wretched charlatan Bancroft the list he gives on p. 184. Bancroft put it in his work
only to traduce and misrepresent Catholic matters and expose
them to the ridicule of people of little brain. Bancroft knew
well enough the proper English terms for Catholic articles,
but strained his wits to employ in derision terms that are little
better than insults.

MEETING OF REV. D. A. GILLITZIN AND FATHER LEMCKE.

UNITED STATES CATHOLIC

HISTORICAL MAGAZINE.

Vol. III.)   (No. 10.

WHY IS CANADA NOT A PART OF THE UNITED STATES?

Read before the U. S. Catholic Historical Society, Nov. 25th
1889, by John Gilmary Shea.

Six score years ago England ruled supreme over all
the northern part of this continent. From Hudson Bay to
the Gulf of Mexico no flag but hers fluttered in the breeze.
From the region of perpetual snow to the region of Spring
in North America, no rule was recognized but George's
of England.

All, however, was not peace and calm. Discontent
pervaded the land.   Men clamored for rights which they
claimed as the inalienable birthright of British subjects.
Delegates at last met from the various colonies. This body
assumed the title of Continental Congress, for it proposed
to represent not a few colonies only, but the Continent.
As the Continental Congress it finally met England in
battle and carried on a seven years' war.   Nothing less
than the Continent satisfied the aspirations of the grand and
noble minds who planned the union of the colonies into a vast
republic.   Why then did the close of the war find their plan
defeated, the republic dwarfed, confined between the northern lakes and shut off from the Gulf of Mexico, with England holding Canada as a perpetual menace to her peace
and prosperity ?

Perhaps Canada was settled by men full of devotion to
the house of Hanover, grateful for favors, eager to show
her their loyalty. On the contrary, it was a colony where
England was hated as a power, alien in blood, alien in

language, alien In religion; a power submitted to only after a struggle in which the Canadians, left almost unaided by France, had tested the resources of England to crush them, and after being beaten to the earth had in a last desperate effort, almost regained the day.

Canada was writhing under the yoke, her people were too numerous to be torn from their homes by England and scattered far and wide like the unhappy Acadians of Nova Scotia: but if England made concessions, she was only biding her time, to crush them utterly.

Canada was ripe for revolt. The Continental Congress and its wise leaders counted surely on the adhesión of the Canadians in their struggle with England, at first simply a struggle for the right to govern and tax themselves, a right as essential to the prosperity of Canada as to that of any other colony.

The Continental Congress issued "an address to the inhabitants of the province of Quebec," inviting them to act in concert with the other colonies. "We are too well acquainted," says this address drawn up by John Dickinson, "we are too well acquainted with the liberality of sentiment distinguishing your nation, to imagine that difference of religion will prejudice you against a hearty amity with us. You know that the transcendant nature of freedom elevates those who unite in her cause above all such low minded infirmities. The Swiss cantons furnish a memorable proof of this truth. Their union is composed of Roman Catholic and Protestant States, living in the utmost concord and peace with one another, and thereby enabled, ever since they brave- ly vindicated their freedom to defy and defeat every tyrant that has invaded them." *

---

* See address of Congress to the Oppressed Inhabitants of Canada. Pennsylvania Packet. June 19, 1775. " We perceive the fate of the Catholic Colonies to be linked together." Evidences teem in the papers of the day of the active sympathy of the Canadians. "There is advice from Canada that Governor Carlton having in vain endeavored by fair means to engage the Canadians in the service against the Colonies, he attempted to compel them

Among the Canadian clergy many were openly in favor of the Colonies. One * was driven out of the province by the British officials, others were kept under strict watch, one a man of high social position, and member of a religious order, threw himself into the movement, and when Canadian regiments were raised for the Continental service this priest, the Rev. Mr. Lotbinière was commissioned by Congress as chaplain, and served during the whole war of the Revolution.†

The two Canadian regiments were constantly kept up by recruits, and maintained their organization till the army was disbanded at the peace.

Canada evidently was ready to join the cause of American freedom. Jesuit and Recollect and Secular priest favored it; the Canadians themselves shouldered the musket as the best proof.

In the outlying parts of the old French province the same feeling prevailed. The Indians in the province of Maine, who had been converted to Christianity by the French missionaries from Canada, at once sided with the colonies, and their Catholic Chief Orono had a commission from Congress.

In the west, the French in Indiana and Illinois, with

---

by force, in which there was an insurrection of 3,000 men to oppose that force. . . . It is said they are determined to observe a strict neutrality." Pennsylvania Packet, Aug. 14, 1775 "A party of regulars went out in a floating battery" (near Ticonderoga,) " to drive off our Canadians about 500 in number, who were at work on the east battery but were repulsed three days successively." Pennsylvania Packet, Oct. 30, 1775. " A party of our troops with the Canadians took possession of Chambly." Letter of Oct. 23d in Pennsylvania Packet, Nov. 18, 1775, " The Canadians in general, on this side of the St. Lawrence are very friendly to us, almost unanimously so along the river Sorel, where they are actually embodied and in arms, altogether to the number of more than 1,000." Pen. Packet, Nov. 20, 1775.

     * Rev. Peter H. de la Valiniére. See Gen. Haldimand's order expelling him. U. S. Catholic Hist. Mag. III. p. 88.

     † Hamersly " Army Register," Washington, 1881, p. 82. "Life and Times of Archbishop Carroll," New York, 1888, p. 144.

their priest, Rev. Pierre Gibault, received Clark with open arms and aided him to drive the English out of that part of the country. The flower of the young Frenchmen of the West perished in gallant attempt to drive the English beyond the lakes.* Even in the heart of Canada, the Indians, converted by the French priests, were so friendly to the Americans, that Burgoyne, who could use Brant to massacre the settlers of Cherry Valley, Wyoming and Esopus, failed to enlist these Catholic Indians in his work of blood, and in an address of reproach he loaded them with abuse.

Why then, if the Continental Congress wished the co-operation of Canada, if Canada and her French and Indian population were full of sympathy for the cause, why is it that England was able to secure that province and so gain its discontented people as to make it a stronghold against us, the base of constant operations?

The answer of history must be, that this great blow to American hopes, this disastrous result was due to an anti-Catholic bigotry fostered in New York, of which John Jay was the prime mover and instigator, and which as a delegate to the Continental Congress he succeeded in foisting into some of the acts of that body. That man stands out in history as the embodiment of narrow and short sighted views, who was willing to sacrifice to their unholy gratification, the best interests of America.

To see the man as he really was, we need only open the Journal of the Convention which framed the first Constitution for the State of New York in 1777, and follow the actions of Jay.

There was bigotry in New York. Public policy demanded that in the struggle with England all such feelings should be buried. Real statesmen sought to dispel this feeling, but Jay fostered and stimulated it. He was in full accord with those who ran up a flag in New York with "No Popery" inscribed upon it. He was in full accord with those whose anti-Catholic feeling led them to drive the

---

* In the Expedition of Mottin de la Balme.

Catholic MacDonalds from the Mohawk and force them to place themselves under the flag they hated, the flag of the Hanoverian—in full accord with those who sent those stalwart Highlanders within the British lines when they would gladly have avenged Culloden !

In the Constitutional Convention of 1777, Jay appears as the advocate of blind unreasoning bigotry, as Governeur Morris was the champion of toleration, liberality and all that is broad and farseeing in statesmanship. The County of Westchester gave the leaders of the two policies.

When the question of naturalization came up, the paragraph in the proposed Constitution excited the wrath of Jay. He sprang to his feet at once to offer an amendment requiring the applicant "to abjure and renounce all allegiance and subjection to all and every foreign king, prince, potentate and State in all matters ecclesiastical and civil."

Morris opposed the amendment with all his eloquence and proposed a substitute committing naturalization to the legislature : but Jay had evoked the hostile feeling, and his amendment was carried. In vain did Morris, battling in the cause of human freedom, endeavor to alter the clause, the amended section was carried, and though Livingston appealed for a reconsideration, the Constitution was adopted with Jay's amendment, and till the Constitution of the United States vested the entire control of naturalization in the Federal government, no Catholic immigrant could become a citizen in the State of New York—though he might show wounds received in battle against England, for he could not on oath renounce allegiance to the Pope, as head of the Church.

When the clause of the proposed Constitution came up for debate, in which it was declared "that the free toleration of religious profession and worship shall forever hereafter be allowed to all mankind," Jay found it too broad. He introduced an amendment giving the legislature power at any time to deny toleration to any denomination at its option.

Debates followed, and a majority seemed loth to con-

cede such a power; but Jay dropped the mask and proposed
a new amendment showing his real object: " Except the
professors of the religion of the Church of Rome, who ought
not to hold lands in or be admitted to a participation of
the civil rights enjoyed by the members of this State,
until such time as the said professors shall appear in the Supreme Court of this State, and there most solemnly swear
that they verily believe in their consciences that no pope,
priest, or foreign authority on earth hath power to absolve
the subjects of this State from their allegiance to the same.
And further, that they renounce and believe to be false and
wicked, the dangerous and damnable doctrine that the Pope
or any other earthly authority hath power to absolve men
from their sins, described in and prohibited by the Gospel of
Jesus Christ : and particularly that no Pope, priest or foreign
authority on earth hath power to absolve them from the obligation of this oath."

We can almost picture him to ourselves in wild frenzy,
with bloodshot eyes, foaming at the mouth and gesticulating
like a madman, as he read this proposed amendment, the rig-
marole of stupid ignorance.

The amendment found advocates in the body, such
anti-Catholic feeling had Jay evoked, and it was lost by a vote
of 19 to 10, not two-thirds voting for it.

Still unappeased, Jay moved another amendment; Livingston insisted that it was virtually the same as the last; but
the house held otherwise, and though modified by an amendment of Morris, it was passed in a form which gave Jay
hope that Catholicity could never gain a foothold in this
State. The grand, broad charter of toleration as proposed at
first was blotted from the Constitution of New York.

When we consider that at this moment men, as Bancroft
drily remarks, had outgrown the silly anti-catholic raving
about the Quebec Act;* that the United States were using

---

* As soon as the Quebec Act was proposed in Parliament protests against
it appeared in the American papers. It was after the Boston Port Bill con-

every effort to gain Catholic France as an ally, and that a show of amity to professors of the faith of Rome in the several States would have aided the cause of Independence, we can imagine what bitter hatred of Catholicity seethed in the heart of John Jay, where no consideration of public policy could whisper a counsel of moderation.

If his spirit showed itself in this shape in 1777, we can imagine what it was three years earlier. And yet, unfortunately, it was to this man that Congress gave a fatal power by confiding to him the preparation of the " Address to the People of Great Britain," and this at the very time when the wise and judicious Dickinson framed the conciliatory address to the Canadian people, and Congress sent Commissioners with a Catholic priest to influence Canadian adhesion to the common cause.

A man of Jay's temper could not lose the opportunity of introducing his favorite topic. The Quebec Act, by which the Canadian French were left in the enjoyment of their religion and their former laws, in Canada, and at the feeble set-

---

sidered as the greatest of their wrongs. See Postscript to Philadelphia Packet, Aug. 15, 1774.

The following stanza from a song shows the temper of the times, to the tune of " O my Kitten, my Kitten :

> " Then heigh for the penance and pardons,
>   And heigh for the faggots and fires ;
> And heigh for the Popish church wardens,
>   And heigh for the priests and the friars;
> And heigh for the rare-e show relics
>   To follow my Canada Bill-e
> With all the Pope's mountebank tricks ;
>   So prithee, my baby, be still-e
>   Then up with the papists, up, up,
> And down with the Protestants down-e
>   Here we go backwards and forwards
> And all for the good of the Crown-e,"
>   *Philadelphia Packet, Aug. 29, 1774.*

The Act was given in full in the same paper in the Supplement to No. 150, Sep. 5, 1774 and in the paper itself, the violent Protest of the City of London.

tlements of Detroit, Vincennes and Kaskaskia, afforded Jay
the means of counteracting the whole beneficent policy
of Congress.

He was one of these who pretended that the act of
justice to the conquered French by which they were al-
allowed to enjoy religious freedom, and live at least for a
time under their own system of laws, was a subtle scheme
of Great Britain to compass the ruin of her old colonies.*
The experience of more than a century shows that England
acted wisely.

But Jay, then a young fanatic of twenty-nine, could see
nothing but the triumph of the Catholic religion. As to
his authorship of the Address there is no doubt. "The
Address to the People of Great Britain," says his biogra-
phers, "was assigned to Mr. Jay. To secure himself from
interruption, he left his lodgings and shut himself up in a
room in a tavern, and there composed that celebrated
state paper, not less distinguished for its lofty sentiments,
than for the glowing language in which they are expressed."

Unfortunately, we cannot agree with this opinion. The
Address is narrow-minded, bigoted, fanatical and short-
sighted. Congress was at first led away by the silly prejudice aroused by the Quebec Act, and it took some time
before it outgrew the feeling. Though Congress did at
last, Jay never did.   •

In this address, unfortunately issued in the name of
Congress, Catholicity is branded as "a religion fraught
with sanguinary and impious tenets." Then developing

---

* Influenced by men like him, Congress in Sept. 1774, said: "The late Act of
Parliament for establishing the Roman Catholic religion . . . . is dangerous in an extreme degree." *Philadelphia Packet Sept. 19, 1774.* The paper
of the 12th, contained a contribution against the Act addressed to the King.
But the subject was soon dropped with only an occasional reference to it, and
in the papers of June 10, 1775, we find an address of Congress to the oppressed inhabitants of Canada, and that of July 10, gives a bill introduced into the
House of Lords by Lord Camden for the repeal of the Quebec Act.

his idea, Jay adds : "By another act the Dominion of Canada is to be so extended, modelled and governed, as that by being disunited from us, detached from our interests, by civil as well as religious prejudice, by their numbers daily swelling with Catholic emigrants from Europe, and by their devotion to administration, so friendly to their religion, they might become formidable to us, and on occasion be fit instruments in the hands of power to reduce the ancient free Protestant colonies to the same state of slavery with themselves. . . . . "Nor (the address continues) can we suppress our astonishment that a British parliament should ever consent to establish in that country a religion that has deluged your island in blood, and dispersed impiety, bigotry, persecution, murder and rebellion through every part of the world."

"This being a true state of facts, let us beseech you to consider to what end they lead.

"Admit that the Ministry by the powers of Britain, and the aid of our Roman Catholic neighbors should be able to carry the point of taxation, and reduce us to a state of perfect humiliation and slavery. Such an enterprise would doubtless make some addition to your national debt," etc.

In a few words : nothing would satisfy John Jay but penal laws against the Catholics in Canada, and the establishment of English laws there. He wished no part or fellowship with them, and would rather see the Canadians remain under English rule, than have Catholics on our side.

Such was not the view of Congress. On the 15th of February, 1776, it was—"Resolved that a committee of three—two of whom be members of Congress—be appointed to repair to Canada, there to pursue such instructions as shall be given them by that body."

Benjamin Franklin, Samuel Chase and Charles Carroll, of Carrollton were chosen, and the last named was desired by Congress " to prevail on Mr. John Carroll to assist them in such matters as they shall think useful."

The Catholic priest responded to the call and accompanied the Commissioners to aid them "to promote or to
form a union between the colonies and the people of Canada."

The instructions to the Commissioners all tended to
this. "To convince the Canadians of the uprightness of
our intentions towards them, they were to declare that
it was the inclination of Congress that the people of
Canada should set up such a form of government as
would be most likely in their judgment, to promote their
happiness. And the commissioners were, in the strongest
terms to assure them, that it was our earnest desire to
adopt them into our union as a sister colony and to secure
the same system of mild and equal laws for them and
for ourselves, with only such local differences as might
be agreeable to each colony respectively."

"They were directed further to declare that that we
held sacred the rights of conscience; and should promise
to the whole people solemnly, in the name of Congress,
the free and undisturbed exercise of their religion; and
to the clergy the full, perfect and peaceable possession
and enjoyment of all their estates; that the government
of everything relative to their creed and clergy should be
left entirely in the hands of the good people of that
province, and such legislature as they should constitute ;
provided however, that all other denominations of Christians should be equally entitled to hold offices and enjoy civil privileges, and the free exercise of their religion
as well as be totally exempt from the payment of any
titles or taxes for the support of religion." *

Congress had been forced by the bigotry of a few to
denounce the Quebec Act in terms which showed more
religious hate than sound political wisdom, but good sense

---

* This was asking Canada to give Protestants greater rights than Massachusetts or New York gave Catholics in 1800 ; or New Hampshire did in
1876.

was gaining the day, and the allusion to the Quebec Act in the Declaration of Independence of 1776 is so obscure that few now understand it, and on the point of religion it is silent.

At the time of the appointment of the Commissioners everything indicated the possibility of securing the co-operation or at least the neutrality of the Canadians. At Montreal, the King's statue was smeared over and decorated with a necklace of potatoes; a leading Canadian gentleman was insulted and struck; and the feelings of the people in favor of Congress was so clearly shown that the British Colonel stationed there threatened to use the powder he had to blow up the city.

The parishes around Chambly, openly joined the American cause ; those in the government of Three Rivers, Nicolet, Becancour, Gentilly and St. Pierre refused to send a man in response to the call for militia to fight against the Americans. Carleton's proclamation was disregarded.† The Caughnawaga Indians sent all their warriors to the American camp, and the British agent appointed to that tribe confesses that he could find no one to side with him, except one miscreant who had been expelled from the village for his notorious vices.

It might be thought that as the Canadians and colonists to the South had more than once served in arms against each other, there must have been a feeling of hostility. But it should be remembered that they never took up arms for any quarrel of their own, they had both been forced to expend their blood and their means, because France and England chose to go to war, and America became the scene of hostility for disputes in which it had no interest, and when it really needed peace.

The colonists, whether of French or English origin,

† "This Proclamation so far from compelling the Canadians to take up arms, only produced the greatest aversion and repugnance to his orders." Smith, " History of Canada," Quebec, 1815, p. 76.

whether in Canadian or the old British colonies had common interests, and had a common history. They had re-
claimed the wilderness by their sturdy labor, reared their
modest homes, and spread their rich fields of grain, their
fisheries, their manufactures crippled only by the policy of
the home government. Both trained in the same hard nur-
sery of frugal industry had been compelled to defend their
hard bought property against Indian foes; both saw advantages in peaceful trade and free intercourse.

From the first, Canada had sought to bind herself
closely to the English colonies by the bonds of commerce, and amity; she had proposed a plan of neutrality
so that, though France and England might in the ambi-
tious projects of their state-craft, make Europe one vast
charnel house, peace should reign amid the settlements in
America, and each man pursue his avocations undisturbed
by the sound or even the thought of war. Canada asked
that Indians should not be employed in war; and not till
the streets of her thriving town of Lachine were lighted
by the flames of the burning houses, and strewn with
the mangled corpses of men, women and children slaugh-
tered by Indians sent from New York by the bigotry
roused by the English Revolution of 1688, did Canada
summon to her standard the multitudinous tribes to which
her influence reached.

Between Canada and the Colonies there was and never
had been but one bar, an insensate anti-Catholic feeling.

When the Commissioners appointed by Congress to
undo the mistakes of the past and form a close union reached
Canada, General Arnold was in command of Montreal; Canadians were flocking to the American standard, and all seemed
to promise the speedy union of Canada with the other colonies, but just then Jay's handiwork, the Address of Congress
to the people of Great Britain, was translated and scattered
among the people of Canada.   •

There instead of flattering words of harmony, toleration
and union, they found themselves denounced, their religion

execrated, the very idea of union with them scouted. A general burst of indignation followed. "O the perfidious double faced Congress!" cried the people. "Let us bless and obey our benevolent prince, whose humanity is consistent, and extends to all religions; let us abhor all who would seduce us from our loyalty." From that moment the tide of opinion changed. Doubt and suspicion prevailed; the leaders of the Canadians threw their influence in the British scale, and Canada was lost. In vain did the Commissioners labor to efface the impression produced by the spirit which dictated the Address to the People of Great Britain.

The Canadians as a body could not be induced to send delegates to a Congress which could put forward two doctrines so utterly irreconcileable, one all friendship and brotherhood; the other unjust, vindictive, oppressive and malignant. Events soon occurred which made their conviction deeper, that the colonies as a whole were imbued with bitter hatred of Canada and her religion. The fugitive Scots from the Mohawk told their tale; the debates in New York convention became known. Gradually all or nearly all Canada became alienated, indifferent to our cause. Yet never had there been a greater opportunity. As Colonel Barré declared on the floor of Parliament reading from a letter written by a military friend in Canada, the French there would not fight against the Americans. When the British authority summoned them to train as militia, they hid their guns in the woods and came with sticks, declaring that if they must fight, it would be against the English, and not for them.

Down to the Battle at the Cedars, the Caughnwagas fought under the Continental flag, at severe loss.

Canada was assured to England. It became the basis for operations against this country in the East and West. Burgoyne was sent over with an army : the Canadians, overawed and overpowered, were forced into service ; the hostile Indians in New York and the West were organized against our frontiers, and went forth to destruction led by white men in English pay. From Quebec to Green Bay every post was

a fomenter of Indian raids on the homes of the hardy settlers.

A broad belt of fire and blood marks the scene of
their inhuman warfare, and all this misery and woe
were brought upon the country by the hostility to the
Catholic Church, a hostility which deprived us of Canada, and
esteemed the welfare of America, as of no account. when
weighed against the gratification of religious hatred.

When, by the aid of the army and fleet of a Catholic
ally, an English army was forced to yield at Yorktown and
Great Britain lost all hope of reducing the United States
to their old colonial condition, Canada might still have
been secured, and would have been, but for John Jay, who
was unfortunately one of those appointed by Congress to
negotiate with England.

Franklin and Adams were fully alive to the necessity
of securing Canada, for Americans ever to have a real
peace with England. This too, was the feeling in the Continental Congress, which wrote. to its envoys in August,
1779, " It is of the utmost importance to the peace and
commerce of the United States, that Canada and Nova
Scotia should be ceded." To secure Canada, Franklin
even proposed to indemnify the loyalists for their losses,
but when John Jay joined the others in Paris, he threw
his whole weight on the English side. He was opposed to
the annexation of Canada, true to his old anti-Catholic in-
stincts rather than to the welfare of America. He opened
correspondence with the English ministry without the
knowledge of his fellow negotiators, and he was not only
willing to give up Canada to England, but offered her an
equal right to the navigation of the Mississippi River, and
insisted on making the new republic assume the payment
of debts due by persons residing in the colonies to credi-
tors in England before the war, although he was well aware
that the Continental Congress was utterly powerless under
the Articles of Confederation to compel the payment of
such claims. The very failure of the United States on this

point was made by England a pretext, for maintaining a hold on our western country, which cost thousands of lives, checked settlements, and desolated the homes of the brave frontiersmen.*

The result was soon seen. England held Canada, and not only that, but from Canada maintained posts at Niagara, Detroit, on the Maumee and on Lake Michigan, which by the treaty of peace were territory of the United States. Her Indian agents gained the Western chiefs and supplied the tribes with arms, while constantly fostering their hostility to the United States. The defeats of Harmar and St. Clair were due to English arms and English guidance. And if Wayne defeated the Indians on the soil of Indiana, it was under the very guns of a fort which England had planted on our soil.

At last John Jay, one of the most prominent among those who caused this terrible and lasting scourge to America was sent to England, and he, in order to induce England to retire within her own Canadian boundaries, signed a treaty which excited universal execration.

Thirty-six years passed, and we were again at war with England : Canada had become thoroughly submissive under the British yoke. Her increasing population gave soldiers and officers to maintain English supremacy, and to aid in repelling the forces we sent to reduce the province. England still exercised an influence over our Western Indians and again incited them to massacre and arson, while Tecumseh, with a royal commission, fought with his Indian braves beside the British regulars.

Deeply, deeply has the country atoned in blood, for the error of 1774. Had the liberal and Christian spirit of a Morris and a Livingston been able to counteract the malignant purblindness of Jay, the flag of the United States would have floated for the last century over the Continent.

---

* Bancroft, History of the United States, v. pp. 537, 568, 371, 575.

CHRISTOPHER TALBOT, BOOKSELLER, PHILADELPHIA.—The following letter of Rev. Robert Molyneux is interesting as throwing some light on Christopher Talbot, who seems to have been the first publisher of Catholic books in this country.

NEWTOWN, JULY 25th, 1797.

REV. DEAR SIR:

I received lately a box of sweet oil, which I suppose was intended for the use of this house. I must beg you would inform me of the cost, and charge the same against my account on the College books. Mr. Robert Brent has promised to pay your order, and I doubt not his word. Can you inform me of the fate of my lottery tickets? I left them in the care of ye steward, Mr. Greenwell. My money is all spent and our house has none.

I have heard little concerning the College since my arrival here; I hope however, you are well and happy, and that you may so continue is my sincerest wish. When the fatigue of ye Examination is over, if I cannot be honoured by a personal visit, a line from yr. pen will be acceptable.

I have the honor to be Rev. dear sir,

My best compliments and good wishes to all.

Yr. most obedient servant,

ROBT. MOLYNEUX.

P. S.—I intend sending you by the first safe conveyance 37 histories of the Bible and seventy Catholic Christian Instructed, the property of Christopher Talbot's heirs, and which are for sale for their benefit. N. B.—A deduction in what is due or to become due to them should be made in yr. favor for the various charges incurred; first, for freight of three similar trunks from Philadelphia to Baltimore, from thence of one of the three to Georgetown, of one to Port Tobacco, of another to Newtown, and of the two latter again to Georgetown, besides losses in bad payments, cost of postage, carriage and wharfage, etc., all with trouble in selling, collecting, etc., cannot be less than five or six per cent. I send you the information for your guide in settling that very troublesome account.

REV. MR. WM. DUBURG.　　　　　　　　　　　　　　R. MOLYNEUX.
President of Georgetown College.

REV. FRANCIS A. MATIGNON, D.D., FIRST PASTOR OF THE CHURCH OF THE HOLY CROSS, BOSTON, MASS.

Read before the U. S. Catholic Historical Society, April 1890,
by Rev. Arthur J. Connolly, of Roxbury, Mass.

In memoria aeterna erit justus.   Psal. CXI.

Rev. Francis Anthony Matignon, D.D., was born in Paris, on the 10th of November, 1753. From his earliest years he evinced a pre-dilection for the altar, and after a youth of exemplary innocence and close application to preparatory studies, he commenced his academical course. Gifted with talents of the first order, and possessing in the constitution of his mind that steadiness of purpose and pursuit which gives to genius all its power and efficiency, he soon enriched a capacious mind with almost all that was valuable in literature and science. The attainment of mere human learning however, was secondary with him to the formation of an ecclesiastical spirit. He studied deeply and embodied in his life and practice "the science of the saints," and seizing at once the full conception of the sacerdotal character, he soon exhibited in himself the noblest specimen of what that character was designed by God to be—pure, holy, unearthly, forgetful of self, and living only for God and others.

Having completed his theological studies, he took the degree of Bachelor of. Divinity, and was ordained a priest, on Saturday, 19th of September, in the year 1778, the very day of the month and week which forty years afterwards was to be his last.

In the year 1782, he was admitted a licentiate, and in 1785, received from the Sorbonne the degree of Doctor of Divinity. Owing to his scholarly attainments he was soon afterwards appointed Regius Professor of Divinity in the College of Navarre, and for several years fulfilled the

duties of this important position with honor to himself
and to the entire satisfaction of his ecclesiastical superiors.

About the year 1789, his health began to fail, and as
a mark of his appreciation for his piety and talents,
Cardinal de Brienne, then high in favor at the court of
Louis the XVI. obtained for him an annuity, which was sufficient to meet all his wants, establish him in independence, and secure his future needs. Unfortunately for Dr.
Matignon, France was at this time on the verge of that
terrible revolution which destroyed in an hour the fortunes,
the happiness and the lives of so many of her children. To
escape the fury of the revolutionists, he fled to England,
and for several months remained there with many of his
fellow priests in exile.

While we may justly suppose that his heart ached
at the frightful condition of his beloved country, and that he
mourned the sad necessity that drove him into exile,
still his own words proclaim that the kindness he received
at the hands of England's charitable children did much
to lighten his sorrow. In referring to these days of
his eventful life, he always spoke of England as a great
nation in which there was so much to admire and imitate, and
his gratitude kindled at the remembrance of British muni-
ficence and generosity to exiled priests, of a nation not only
hostile but of a different religious creed.

When the fury of the revolution began to spend itself he
hastened back to France, but not with the intention of remaining. During the months of his exile he had made up his
mind to devote the remainder of his life to missionary
work in the infant church of the United States of America.

In company with three members of the famous Society of St. Sulpice, Revs. Gabriel Richard, Francis Ciquard,
and Ambrose Maréchal, all of whom had taken the same
resolution, he set sail from France and arrived in Baltimore on the 24th of June, 1792. Immediately on his arrival
he offered his services to Bishop Carroll, who at this time

was the only Bishop in the United States.

It is needless to state that his services were thankfully accepted, the more so as Bishop Carroll had for some time past felt the necessity of obtaining a prudent director for the little congregation at Boston, in New England.

On the 4th of Jan., 1790, Rev. John Thayer, by appointment of Bishop Carroll, began his priestly duties as the first Missionary Rector of the Holy Cross in Boston, but, owing to the want of prudence or the inordinate zeal of this otherwise good priest, but little progress had been made. It often happens, especially with people recently converted, that they fancy that nothing on earth is wanted to convert this or that person among their friends than that he should just hear what is to be said in defence of Catholicity and against Protestantism.

He sees the argument to be so irresistible that he conceives everybody whom he loves or regards must find it the same, and so he is disappointed that Catholic sermons are not like so many " cannons loaded to the mouth with logic, to be shot forth week after week to blow the head off from every stray heretic who may chance to come within their range." Such undoubtedly were the sentiments of honest Father Thayer, for a few months after his arrival, he began a series of controversial discourses, and publicly challenged the ministers of New England to answer him if they could. The gauntlet thus publicly thrown down had to be taken up, and a Rev. Mr. Lesslie of New Hampshire, attempted to answer Father Thayer, but failed most ignominiously. His failure while stimulating the imprudent zeal of Father Thayer, naturally embittered but more and more the minds of the enemies of Catholicism. Father Thayer forgot that papists, as New Englanders then openly designated Catholics, were simply tolerated, and priests were to be left undisturbed as long as, according to the Protestant criterion of behavior, they behaved themselves.

His well meant zeal in furthering the interests of Catholicism was anything but good behavior, in the estimation of Bostonians. Bishop Carroll, who well understood the character and deep rooted prejudices of New England Congregationalists for everything connected with the Catholic Church, determined to withdraw Father Thayer from Boston and send Dr. Matignon to take his place. Leaving Baltimore with the best wishes of his Superior for his success, Dr. Matignon started for Boston, where he arrived in the month of July. Immediately on his arrival, he communicated the wishes of Bishop Carroll to Father Thayer. and after spending a few weeks in the study of English, entered upon his public ministry on the 20th of August, 1792.

The germ of a church had been started, but he found it on the point of being crushed and ruined by prejudice and suspicion. He saw at a glance that it would require on his part the wisest policy to stem the tide of opposition that confronted him. " The good people of New England were something more than suspicious on the subject of his success; they were suspicious of the Catholic doctrine.

" Their ancestors from the beginning of the settlement of the country had been preaching against the Church of Rome, and their descendants, even the most enlightened, felt a strong impression of undefined and undefinable dislike, if not hatred, towards every papal relation.

Absurd and foolish legends of the Pope and his religion were in common circulation, and the prejudice was too deeply rooted to be suddenly eradicated or even opposed."

To New Englanders, Catholicity was a religion of priestcraft, formalism and unscriptural display. Prelatic magnificence was identified only with worldliness and humbug.

" It required a thorough acquaintance with the world to know how to meet these sentiments of a whole people."

" Dr. Matignon, saw at a glance, that it would not do to make direct and open attacks upon people's consciences any more than on their consistency. He saw that he was not to tell New Englanders that they were knaves any more than to tell them that they were fools. "Violence and indiscretion would have destroyed all hopes of

success. Ignorance would have exposed the cause to sar-
casm and contempt ; and enthusiasm too manifest, would
have produced a reaction that would have plunged the infant church into absolute ruin."

"Dr. Matignon was exactly fitted to grapple with all
these difficulties. His first study was to enter thoroughly
into the Protestant character as it existed living around him,
for he was well aware that the great secret of conviction and
persuasion lay in a knowledge of an opponent's state of mind.
He felt that he must show those who lived around him what
Catholicism really was, and he was persuaded that this was
not to be effected by abstract statements of doctrine or history, but by a life of true apostolic poverty. To the person who has the slightest knowledge of human nature in
general, and the early New Englander in particular, it is
easy to see that in this apostolic poverty of Dr. Matignon
all his strength consisted.

Thus clearly seeing his way towards the end, he aimed
at, and inspired with a love for his fellow man, and
guided by delicacy of feeling, modesty and charity, he
labored to let Protestants know what Catholicity was, without giving unnecessary offence. One of his admirers thus
speaks of him : "With kindness and humility, he disarmed
the proud ; with prudence, learning and wisdom. he met
the captious and slanderous, and so gentle and just was
his course that even the censorious forgot to watch him,
and the malicious were too cunning to attack one armed so
strong in poverty." Blending at once the strength and
severity which is required for the guidance of others and
for self-respect, with that mild and conciliatory demean-
or which attacks and attaches all within the sphere of its
action, piety without rigor, humility without weakness, labor
without noise, pretension or calculation, he soon proved
himself eminently fitted for the confidence that Bishop
Carroll reposed in him.

In the words of the poet we can say of him :—

" Earnest he toil'd his mission to fulfill,
And strove those heavenly doctrines to instil,
That brightly shine in Truth's inspired page,
Unchanged and pure from age to age.

These ancient truths so strenuous he impressed,
As flash'd conviction o'er the conquer'd breast;
Resistless truth pour'd in the brilliant ray,
Dispell'd the gloom and showed the unclouded day.

The bright'ning impulse ran through every heart,
And dark entangling Falsehood bore a part,
Which came to hear, with subtle close intent,
Astonished heard and grimly frowned assent."

Surely but steadily Dr. Matignon disarmed by his humility, gentleness, learning and tact, the overt hostility of the enemies of Catholicity.

Without assistance, in his quiet unassuming manner, he continued for four years after his arrival in Boston, to minister to the spiritual wants of his little congregation. Owing to his unremitting labors and saintly life, many who had almost lost the faith returned to the practice of their religion, and the little congregation of one hundred that Father Thayer had gathered together soon became noticeably larger. About this time it became evident to Father Matignon, that the requirements of his now rapidly growing congregation were greater than his unaided labors could meet.

While in England, he had as a fellow-exile, a priest, for whom he had conceived the greatest attachment and affection. This priest was Rev. John Cheverus. Knowing him to be a man of noble disinterestedness, gentle in character, and of a cultivated mind, all of which qualifications were requisite to overcome the prejudices, to secure the affections, and gain the esteem and respect of New Englanders; he immediately wrote a letter entreating Cheverus to join him on the mission in Boston. In his letter, he represented to Rev. Mr. Cheverus the great importance of this destitute station, set before his view a new church to be formed in a new country; Catholics without teachers scattered over an immense tract and exposed to the loss of their faith; savage tribes to be evangelized, and all the duties of an apostle to be fulfilled. Is not this vast field, said he, worthy of your zeal and devotion, or in what part of the world can your services be more useful to the church? Vividly impressed' with the contents of Dr. Matignon's letter, Fr. Cheverus resolved to accept the earnest invitation extended to him, and after settling his affairs in France, took passage on a vessel about to sail for Boston.

While on shipboard he so impressed his fellow passengers with respect and interest, that notwithstanding the prejudice existing against Catholic priests, no one presumed to indulge in the least unkind reflection, and the captain of the ship, in testimony of his admiration, ordered every Friday and Saturday a dinner of fish to be prepared for the Catholic Missionary. On the 3d of October, 1796, the vessel on which he set sail anchored safely in Boston harbor. Dr. Matignon received him as an angel sent by heaven to his aid, tenderly embraced him with tears of joy, and declared it was the happiest day of his life.

He wrote immediately to Bishop Carroll announcing the happy news, and requesting at the same time full powers for the new missionary whose credentials he forwarded at the same time.

Bishop Carroll gave thanks to heaven for the precious intelligence, and without delay, invested Father Cheverus with full powers for entering on his ministry.

Rev. Francis Ciquard who, on his arrival in 1792, had been sent by Bishop Carroll to the Indian Mission in the State of Maine, had prior to the advent of Cheverus earnestly besought an assignment to another mission. Father Cheverus in a letter to Bishop Carroll shortly after his arrival, expressed himself thus: "Send me where you think I am most needed without making yourself anxious about the means of supporting me. I am willing to work with my hands, if need be, and I believe I have strength enough to do it."

·   Rejoicing at the thought that he might now comply with the request of Fr. Ciquard without depriving the Indians of a spiritual guide, he assigned Fr. Cheverus to this important mission.   .

Dr. Matignon who had hoped by the arrival of his friend to lighten the now rapidly increasing duties of the ministry, could not but feel disappointed at this news. In the will of his superior however, he saw only the will of God, and without expressing a single word of complaint simply besought, that he might retain Fr. Cheverus in Boston until the following Autumn. His request was granted, and thus his labors were lightened and his solitary home made brighter by his friend's loving companionship.

"A new and touching sight was then witnessed in Boston," says the memorialist of Cheverus; "two men, examples of every virtue, living together as brothers, without distinction of property, with no difference of purpose or will; always ready to yield to each other, to anticipate each other in rendering the most polite and delicate attentions, possessing in truth, but one heart, and one soul, filled with the same desire, that of doing good, the same inclinations those which pointed to virtue; and the same love of whatever is good, upright and charitable.

Such indeed was the respect and admiration that Matignon and Cheverus insensibly secured for themselves that we find even a Protestant paper thus constrained to speak of them. "Those who witnessed the manner in which they lived together, will never forget the refinement and elevation of their friendship; it surpassed those attachments which delight us in classical story, and equalled the lovely union of the son of Saul and the Minstrel of Israel."

"To the example of a union which religion alone could render so perfect, they added that of a life of poverty and privation, but honorable and dignified, pursued wholly in prayer, in study or the labors of the ministry; that is to say, in perfecting themselves or rendering mankind wiser and better.   They did good whenever an occasion presented itself, and "blushed to find it fame," they exhausted their strength in journeyings and toils ; travelling on foot at all hours of the day and night, and at all seasons of the year to carry, often many miles distance, consolation to the afflicted, secret assistance to the indigent, words of reconciliation to families at variance.   In short, they sacrificed themselves without reserve for their fellow men, and regarded all their sacrifices as nothing."

In the month of July, 1797, this happy companionship of Father Matignon and Cheverus was interrupted, and Fr. Cheverus in compliance with the expressed wish of Bishop Carroll left Boston and proceeded to the Indian missions of Maine.

Left once again alone, Fr. Matignon continued to minister to the congregation of Boston, making from time to time as opportunity permitted, missionary visits to the adjacent towns and villages.   Thus engaged in confessing, teaching, baptizing, and endeavoring above all to restore piety and the love of religion in the hearts of Catholics he fulfilled his duty as a faithful servant of God.

What joy and consolation these visits brought to many a poor exile who perhaps for years had been denied the consolations of religion, God alone knows.   Certain it is, that to the New England shores hundreds of Irish Catholics had been brought and sold as indentured slaves from the earliest colonial days. That this assertion cannot be denied, ample proof is furnished by the files of the colonial State papers.   Among the many that might be cited, let the following suffice :

"April 1st, 1653.   Order of the Council of State.

For a license to Sir John Clotworthy to transport to America 500 natural Irishmen."

"Order of the Council of the State. Sep. 6, 1653.

Upon petition of David Sellick, of Boston, New England, merchant, for a license for the Good Fellow of Boston, Geo.

Dalle, Master and the Providence of London, Thomas Swanlly, Master, to pass to New England and Virginia, where they intend to carry 400 Irish children, directing a warrant to be granted, provided security is given to pass to Ireland, and within two months to take in 400 Irish children and transport them to these plantations."

Mr. Pendergast in his Cromwellian Settlement of Ireland, quotes the following from Thurloe's State Papers: " Captain John Vernon was employed for the Commissioners for Ireland in England, and contracted in their behalf with Mr. David Sellick and Mr. Lander, under his hand, bearing date the 14th of Sept., 1653, to supply them with 250 women of the Irish nation above 12 years and under the age 45, also 300 men above 12 years and under 50, to be found in the country within twenty miles of Cork, Youghal, and Kinsale, Waterford and Wexford, to transport them into New England." All these were Catholics who were rendered penniless and outlaws by the thirteen years bitter persecution that they had endured during the war from 1641 to 1654.

Later on, when the Acadians were ruthlessly driven from their peaceful homes, more than 2,000 were cast upon the shores of New England. Finally, between the years 1780 and 1790 the new prison in Dublin was emptied by forced emigration or temporary slavery.

" In 1785 and 1786, the Snow Despatch took over 183 and tried to land them at the loyalist settlement in Shelburne, Nova Scotia, but was prevented, and induced to land them in a remote and unsettled part of the Bay of Machias, where the survivors begged their way into the more southern and distant part of the United States, saying, (which was true) that they were indentured servants from Ireland who had been put on shore from suffering a want of provision on shipboard."

" The brig Chance landed upwards of 100 on the Island of Antigua, one of the Bermudas, totally desolate. After suffering extreme hardships, 49 were taken by a humane captain of a New England vessel and landed in Massachusetts "

"The brig Nancy, Captain Robert Winthrop, of New London, Conn., sailed from Dublin, in June, 1788, having the convicts indentured in New-Prison, and took out 201. The vessel arrived in the middle of the month at New London. He disposed of some there by sale as indentured servants, and sent the remainder to market in the ports to the southward."

From these few examples it can be readily concluded that the hundreds of Irishmen and women had already landed upon the shores of New England from the Mother Country. With few exceptions all those brought by force were Catholics. They were shipped by the wholesale to British Colonies, because forsooth they had no visible means of livelihood and were reputed as convicts and slaves. They had no visible means of livelihood and why? Because cruelty had confiscated the ancient possessions of their race.

They were convicts and slaves, yes, but again why? Because they clung to the faith of their forefathers and preferred prison walls and slavery to apostacy. That Dr. Matignon notwithstanding this undeniable fact that hundreds of Catholics landed in New England, found comparatively few who were such on his arrival, is not to be wondered at.

We must not forget that until the beginning of the trouble between New England and Old England, their most bitter enemy, in the estimation of New Englanders was Catholicism.

The poor Irish Catholics who had been brought over at an early day had gone long since, down to their graves without, it is true, the consolations of their holy religion, but we can believe steadfast in their faith and strong in the hope of a future happiness. Their children and childrens' children left without religious instruction or with instruction such as was worse than none, as far as Catholicity was concerned; without priests to minister to their spiritual wants, grew up in ignorance of Catholic truths and were forever lost to the faith.

It is not then much to be wondered at that Dr. Matignon found but a small number of Catholics in New England.' When however we think of the hundreds of Irish Catholic fathers and mothers, young men and maidens who were brought to New England, we can feel safe in asserting that had God given Dr. Matignon the gift of prophetic vision he would have seen in hundreds who walked the streets of Boston with him in his lifetime, the children and children's children of Irish Catholics.

Would God grant to us a like prophetic vision. I am firmly persuaded, that many a proud New Englander of the present day who vauntingly boasts of the Puritan blood that courses through his veins, would be compelled to acknowledge as a maternal ancestor one of the poor, but pure and virtuous Catholic maidens whom Cromwell's mancatchers had shipped in servitude to New England shores.

Deprived of assistance at least for the time being, by the departure of Fr. Cheverus to the Indian missions of Maine, Fr. Matignon redoubled his labors, and hours of the day and night found him planning and working in the interest of the little congregation of the Church of the Holy Cross.

From the time of his arrival in Boston until the year 1798, the general health of the community had been good, and as a consequence there had been but few deaths among the Catholics. In this year, the yellow fever broke out, and in a few months brought sorrow and mourning to many a home. By a careful examination of the records of Baptisms and marriages and deaths from 1790 to 1798, I find that during the year 1798, there were twice as many deaths as in any former year.

From 1790 until the beginning of the year 1798, the number of deaths ranged annually from two to eighteen, while in 1798 there were thirty-four.

During the prevalence of the fever, Dr. Matignon by his charity and zeal, exhibited to Protestants what a soul inspired by religion could do.

When everyone in the city was in momentary fear of being attacked by the dread scourge, and many in panic abandoned their nearest and dearest relatives the moment they were affected, Dr. Matignon fearlessly sought the fever stricken victims, and hastened from house to house to render assistance and consolation. In the exercise of his charity he made no distinction between Catholics and non-Catholics. All, without exception, became when in suffering and affliction the objects of his truly Christian charity.

Just as the epidemic was at its height, Fr. Cheverus providentially returned to Boston from his mission among the Indians of Maine, and following the example of his friend and superior, devoted all his time, day and night to the care of his fever-stricken fellow citizens. " The ministers of the sect fled, or with their families kept themselves aloof. Frs. Matignon and Cheverus alone were among the dead and dying, braving death for their brethren with a calmness and equanimity which seemed to suspect no danger, as well as with a modesty and a humility which were hardly aware of any sacrifice in that which all the world admires as the most beautiful example of self-devotion.

Such a noble exhibition of disinterested charity could not fail to strike the inhabitants of Boston with astonishment and even those most prejudiced against Catholics were forced to exclaim, "Are these then, the *Catholic priests* about whom we have heard so many evil things? Are these the *Papists*, who have been depicted to us in such dark colors ?"

As much of the prejudice that had thus far existed against Catholicism was now happily removed, Dr. Matignon felt that the time had arrived for putting into execution a long cherished wish.

Year by year, as he saw his little congregation growing larger and larger, the constantly cherished hope of his heart was that one day he would behold a suitable church building erected for the accommodation of the Catholics of Boston.

This hope long and ardently cherished, he now felt could and would be realized, for a communication that he received from Bishop Carroll settled for good all doubts that he had entertained with regard to the success of his plans. This great and ever to be remembered father of the American Episcopacy, fully realizing the increasing wants of the New England Church, and firmly convinced of the great good that could be accomplished by the united labors of two such zealous and prudent priests as Frs. Matignon and Cheverus, resolved to withdraw the latter from the Indian Missions and station him as a permanent assistant in Boston. This decision Bishop Carroll the more readily arrived at, owing to the very opportune arrival from France of the Rev. James Romagné whom he immediately assigned to the Indian Missions about to be made vacant by the withdrawal of Fr. Cheverus. Encouraged by this evident indication of Bishop Carroll's solicitude for the prosperity of the Church at Boston, Dr. Matignon communicated his plans to Father Cheverus, and on the 31st of March, 1799, called a meeting of his parishoners. The little French Chapel on School Street, which the Catholics had leased and fitted up for Divine Service measured only thirty-five by thirty feet, and when Dr. Matignon proposed the erection of a more suitable and commodious church building there were no dissenting voices heard. At this first meeting a committee consisting of seven persons was appointed to consider the matter and report the following Sunday. The members of this committee were the Spanish Consul, then residing in Boston, Don Juan Stoughton, John Magner, Michael Burns, John Duggan, Patrick Campbell, Owen Callaghan and Edmund Connor. On Sunday, April 7th, a report was made declaring the great need of a new place of worship, and the consequent necessity of subscribing for the same.

Of the exact number of Catholics in Boston at this period we have no record, except only in so far as it may be computed from the number of marriages and baptisms. In the year 1800, there were but fifty-four baptisms and nine marriages in the whole city. The Catholics then could not have numbered even in the year 1800 more than 1,000 or 1200.

Within a short time after subscriptions had been solicited 212 persons had subscribed the sum of $3,202, and in the space of four years, the little congregation had subscribed the grand sum of $10,771.00.

On October 28, 1799, the amount subscribed being sufficient at least for the purchase of a site, Dr. Matignon called a meeting to consider a location. The committee recommended a site in Franklin Square, owned by the Boston Theatre Corporation. It seems that this Corporation was actuated by the most liberal and generous sentiment towards Catholics, for it publicly acknowledged at the time that it preferred to sell the property at a lower rate for a Church and a Catholic Chnrch, than to have erected there any other kind of building. In the deed by which the ownership of the lot was transferred to Bishop Carroll and Dr. Matignon as trustees, it is expressly stipulated that it is to be held for the purpose and use of a place of worship by the Catholic Society of Boston.

· The price paid for the lot was $2500, and in passing, it may not be out of place to state that just sixty years afterwards, the same lot sold for $115,000. Immediately after the purchase of the site, Fr. Matignon started a subscription for a building fund, and the best and surest indication of the esteem in which he and his co-laborer Fr. Cheverus were held in Boston, is the fact that several Protestants contributed most generously to it. Among these was no less a personage than John Adams, at that very time occupying the exalted position of President of the United States.

By an appeal to Catholic friends in the South, Dr. Matigdon added materially to the amount subscribed, until $16,153 was collected. Of this amount, $3,433 was contributed by Protestants friendly to Dr. Matignon and Catholics. Ground was broken on St. Patrick's day, the 17th of March, 1800, but the work was advanced only as the means for paying for the same was subscribed. Mr. James Bulfinch, Esq., drew the plans and superintended the execution of the work gratis. The Church was of the Ionic style of architecture, and measured 80 by 60 feet. It was built of brick with a stone foundation, by Johnathan Hunnewell. having under its whole length a commodious basement, nine feet high.   The timber used in the construction was principally furnished by Messrs. Kavanagh and Cottrell, two Catholic gentlemen living at Damariscotta, Maine, and the carpenter work was performed by Oliver Miscal. In the year 1803. the Church, which if we except the ancient Chapels in the Indian Missions of Maine, was the first in all New England was completed and ready for dedication. Dr. Matignon's joy was great indeed when he saw the cherished hopes of years realized.

He immediately wrote to Bishop Carroll, and after informing him of the completion of the Church, invited him to come to Boston and consecrate the new temple to the service of God, on St. Michael's day, the 29th of September, 1803. Realizing how important an event the dedication of the first Catholic Church in a city like Boston would be, he cheerfully consented to Dr. Matignon's request, and reaching Boston shortly before the day fixed for the ceremony, dedicated the Church under the title of the Holy Cross, on the 29th of September, 1803. On the day of the dedication, a solemn procession issued from the house of Don Juan Stoughton, in Franklin Street, nearly opposite the new edifice.

Bishop Carroll, of Baltimore, Dr. Matignon, Rev. John Cheverus and two other priests whose names are not mentioned, were the clergy; a few altar boys made up the rest of the procession.

Bishop Carroll officiated pontifically, assisted by the clergy present. Father Cheverus preached on the occasion to a curious but respectful assemblage who crowded the Church to its utmost capacity. On the evening of the same day, the exterior of the Church was illuminated. " The

whole front was resplendent with light, and the richly gilded
cross, which surmounted the edifice sparkling with a thousand lamps, seemed from that day to assert its sway over
Boston and to plant there its empire." Thus was the
the great work that Dr. Matignon so often prayed to
see accomplished completed, and the Catholics beheld with
infinite satisfaction a Church belonging to themselves,
crowned by no changing weathercock, but surmounted by
the unvarying cross, strong in its repose, fit symbol of a
Church which never changes its doctrine.

Cheered by the thought that the good people of Boston now possessed a suitable Church edifice, and that not
one penny of indebtedness rested upon it, Dr. Matignon gave
himself up entirely to the work of rearing a spiritual edifice in the piety and faith of his beloved people that would
far outstrip in splendor the material building that he had
so successfully completed.

While thus engaged, he was far from suspecting that
Bishop Carroll, ever occupied with the thought of pro-
moting the progress of the Catholic religion in the United
States, was planning for him the honors of the Episcopal
office. Deeming it expedient to establish four new Bishop-
rics in the United States, one of which should be in
Boston extending its jurisdiction over New England, Bishop
Carroll had fixed upon Dr. Matignon as Bishop of that
city, thinking that on account of this years, his ability and
his reputation of both Doctor and Professor of the Sorbonne, this good priest had claims upon the office prior
to those of Dr. Cheverus who was still young and only
his curate. When he was about to send his petition to
Rome, Dr. Matignon heard it, and greatly troubled and
alarmed, he remonstrated with him and formally refused
the great honor, suggesting in his stead the nomination
of his worthy friend Mr. Cheverus. In deference to the
wishes of Dr. Matignon, Bishop Carroll wrote to Rome to
that effect, and his request being favorably received, Pius
the VII. issued a brief, on the 8th day of April, 1808,

which elevated Boston to the rank of an Episcopal See, with Dr. John Cheverus as its first Bishop. Owing however to the troubled state of Europe, the Bulls did not arrive until 1810, and on All Saints Day, of the year, Dr. Cheverus was consecrated in the Cathedral Church of Baltimore, by Bishop Carroll. Although raised by virtue of his consecration above his aged and esteemed friend, Bishop Cheverus insisted on his return to Boston, that Dr. Matignon should continue to be the Pastor of the Church of the Holy Cross. This honored position he continued to hold to the great joy of Bishop Cheverus and the edification of the Catholics of Boston until the hour of his death.

About the year 1818, Dr. Matignon's health began to fail, and day by day as he grew weaker and weaker, Bishop Cheverus clearly saw that this venerable priest whom he honored as his guide and loved as a father, was rapidly drawing near the tomb. The thought of losing so dear a friend caused him many days of sadness and hours of grief, and this sadness and grief increased daily with the progress of his friend's illness. On Friday evening, the 18th of September, 1818, says Bishop Cheverus in his diary, as I was about retiring for the night, Dr. Matignon said to me, " my dear Bishop, to-morrow will be the anniversary of my ordination; it is forty years since I received sacred orders. Alas. how many have been my faults and omissions during my ministry." "And how many have been your good works," I replied. He forbade me to speak of them, saying at the same time, that he was an unworthy sinner, but that God was so good that he dared to hope in Him. My tears and sobs, continues Bishop Cheverus, choked my voice, and as he drew me nearer to him, he said : " I regret one thing only, and that is my separation from you, but we shall one day be united again." When parting with him for the night, he requested me to bring the Blessed Sacrament at an early hour in the morning.

" On Saturday morning, the 19th, I brought him Holy Communion, about half-past five. He was fasting and gave no signs of his immediate dissolution. His eyes were brilliant with hope and pious fervor when he received Jesus Christ in the Sacrament of the Altar. At half-past six he was brought a cup of coffee, but took only a few mouthfuls. Suddenly a deathly pallor announced the approach of death. I said to him, my dear friend do you wish to receive Extreme Unction, you seem very ill? He appeared somewhat surprised, fixed his eyes upon me, and taking hold of my hand said "yes," in a hoarse and trembling voice. I administered the last Sacrament to him, and read the prayers for obtaining the indulgence at the hour of death. Choked by my sobs, I requested an ecclesiastic who was present to read the prayers for the dying. Dr. Matignon held the Crucifix attached to his beads in his hand, he kissed it repeatedly, and pressing my hand, made a sign that I should approach and embrace him for the last time. At half-past nine he appeared exhausted, and at ten o'clock his soul had fled. As he died without a struggle, I could not say just when he breathed his last. His death like his life was calm and holy."

As soon as the sad tidings of Dr. Matignon's death were announced, the inhabitants of Boston, Protestant as well as Catholic, expressed but one sentiment, that of sincere regret and sorrow.

On Sunday, the 20th of September, his body clothed in his priestly vestments was borne by loving hands to the Church that he so dearly loved. The wall and windows of the building were draped in black, and the coffin containing the body was placed on a platform in the centre of the choir. Throughout the day the Church was crowded by a vast throng of people who came to take a last look at the face of the one whom they knew only to love and admire.

On Monday, the 21st, a Solemn Mass of Requiem was sung by Bishop Cheverus. The galleries and other parts of the building were filled with Boston's most respected citizens, Protestants as well as Catholics, who took this opportunity to testify their appreciation of the merits and character of the deceased. The solemn chant of the choir, the presence of the remains of one so dearly beloved, the serious tone of mind which manifested itself in every look and action of the assemblage, the peculiar nature of the solemn service, which had collected so many together in the living God, and the silent tears that occasionally gushed from every eye, all tended to render the spectacle at once most solemn and affecting. Bishop Cheverus delivered a most touching eulogy, and when tears choked his voice, his audience wept with him. At the conclusion of the services in the Church, the solemn procession began to move towards the Granary Burying-ground, on Tremont Street, and seldom, perhaps never, within the memory of Bostonians of that day, was witnessed so numerous and respectable a body of persons assembled to pay the last sad tribute to departed worth

Bishop Cheverus clothed in the insignia of his Episcopal office, with the mitre on his head, marched in the procession of mourners which numbered fully one thousand. It must not be supposed that all those who made up the procession were Catholics, for the following notifications to well known Societies, composed alike of Protestants and Catholics, clearly prove the contrary.

In the Boston Commercial Gazette. Sept. 28, 1818. I find the following :

Boston. Sept. 21st, 1818. "Notice. The members of the Massachusetts Charitable Fire Society, are requested to attend the funeral of the Rev. Fràncis A. Matignon this day, at three o'clock. Per order

WM. ALLINE, JR., Rec. Sec

And again. "The members of the Charitable Irish Society are requested to attend the funeral of the Rev. Francis Matignon, at the Catholic Church, this day, at three o'clock, per order of the President.

JOHN BEAN, Sec'y."

"The inhabitants of Boston respected the funeral ceremonies unwonted as they were, and by their silence and orderly demeanor, showed that they honored the grief of Bishop Cheverus and the memory of his friend."

There was nowhere visible curiosity, indifference or noise, the entire mass of people seemed actuated by one single feeling, deep and intense regret. The shops in the streets through which the funeral moved were as if closed, and the windows were filled with persons whose looks bespoke their awakened sensibilities to be in perfect unison with the solemn spectacle which they witnessed. On the arrival of the body at the burying ground, the last absolution was pronounced by Bishop Cheverus with a solemnity and feeling which excited the sympathies and called forth the tears of most of the persons present. The coffin was placed in the tomb of Mr. John Magner, where it was to rest until the completion of the St. Augustine's Cemetery in South Boston would admit of its removal thereto.

Thus closed the public tribute of respect to as valuable and regretted an individual as was ever to exist among the clergy of Boston. While most men do little more in life than to labor for themselves or their dependants, there are some in every age and country who seem born for mankind, and whose habits, reasonings and feelings separate them from the rest of the world, and whose actions prove that the true philanthropist is not an ideal character created in the dreams of fancy and fiction. Of the latter, was Dr. Matignon, the quiet pious man, who asked nothing of human glory, and who did good "and blushed to find it fame." He possessed talents of a very superior order, acquirements profound and varied; a mind noble and disinterested; a heart the very temple of honor, sincerity and truth; a benevolence worthy of his sacred calling as a minister of the Christian Religion, and these and every other qualification that could ennoble or adorn human nature were his characteristic traits.

When the Cemetery at South Boston was opened, Bishop Cheverus had the remains of his dear friend lovingly borne thither, and there they rest until the present day awaiting the summoning angel's final trumpet call.

On the epistle side of the altar in the little Mortuary Chapel in the Cemetery at South Boston to-day may be seen the marble slab that Bishop Cheverus erected to Dr. Matignon's memory.

The following is the epitaph inscribed thereon in gilt letters :

HERE LIE THE REMAINS OF

FRANCIS ANTHONY MATIGNON, D. D.

AND FOR 26 YEARS

PASTOR OF THE CHURCH OF THE

HOLY CROSS

IN THIS TOWN

OB. SEPTEMBER 19,

1818.

AET. 65.

" Beloved of God and men, whose memory is in benediction."

Eccl. XIX.

" The law of truth was in his mouth, and iniquity was not found in his lips; he walked with me in peace and equity, and turned many away from iniquity; for the lips of the priest shall keep knowledge, and they shall seek the law at his mouth; because he is the angel of the Lord of Hosts.

Mal. 2: 6, 7."

" Far from the sepulchre of his fathers repose the ashes of the good and great Dr. Matignon; but his grave is not as among strangers for it was and will be watered by the tears of an affectionate flock, and his memory is cherished by all who value learning, honor, genius, or love devotion.

The Bishop and Congregation, in tears, have erected this monument of their veneration and gratitude."

R. I. P.

DIOCESAN SYNODS AND STATUTES—Concluded.

PHILADELPHIA—Acta Synodi Diœcesanæ Philadelphiensis Primæ, habitæ in Ecclesia Cathedrali S. Mariæ Philadelphiæ, anno Domini 1832, mense Maji a Reverendissimo Francisco Patritio Kenrick, Episcopo Arathensi et Coadjutore Episcopi Philadelphiensis.

8vo 16 pp.   Philadelphia, E. Cummiskey, 1832.

Constitutiones Diœcesanæ in Synodis Philadelphiensibus, annis 1832 et 1842 latæ et promulgatæ.

8vo 18 pp.   Philadelphia, M. Fithian, 1842.

Constitutiones Diœcesanæ in Synodis Philadelphiensibus, annis 1832, 1842, 1847, 1853 et 1855 latæ et promulgatæ.

8vo 50 pp.   Philadelphia; J. B. Chandler, 1855.

Acta Synodi Diœcesanæ Philadelphiensis Sextæ, habitæ a Revmo. Joanne Nepomuceno, Episcopo Philadelphiensi, diebus 28 et 29 Octobris A. D. 1857.

8vo.   Philadelphia.

PITTSBURGH.—Statuta Diœcesis Pittsburgensis, lata in Synodo Diœcesana habita A. D. 1844 et in aliis Synodis A. D. 1846 et A. D. 1854 emendata.

8vo 26 pp.   Pittsburgh; George Quigley, 1854.

Statuta Diœcesis Pittsburgensis lata in Synodo Diœcesana habita A. D. 1844 cum decretis in aliis Synodis A.D.1846, 1854, 1858 et 1869 promulgatis.

8vo 43 pp.   Pittsburgh: James Porter, 1870.

PROVIDENCE.—Acta et Decreta Synodi Diœcesanæ Providentiensis Tertiæ habitæ in Ecclesia Cathedrali ab Illᵐ⁰ et Revᵐᵒ Matthæo Harkins, Episcopo Providentiensi die 21 Decembris, 1887.

8vo 64 pp.   Woodstock College, 1888.

QUEBEC.*—Statuts publiés dans le premier Synode, tenu à Québec le 9 Novembre, 1690.

Avis et Reglements publiés dans l'Assemblée tenue à Ville Marie le 10 de Mars, 1694.

Statuts publiés dans le troisième Synode tenue à Quebec le 27e Fevrier de l'anné 1698.

Statuts publiés dans le quatrième Synode tenu à Quebec, le 8 Octobre, 1700.

" In Mandements, Lettres Pastorales et Circulaires des Evêques de Quebec," Quebec 1887, i p. 270, 325, 368.

RICHMOND.—Statuta Synodi Richmondensis primæ mense Octobris Anno Domini 1856 celebratæ.

8vo 39 pp.   Baltimore: John Murphy & Co., 1857.

ROCHESTER.—Acta & Statuta Synodi Diœcesanæ Roffensis Primæ habitæ diebus 13 and 14 Octobris.   A. D. 1875.

8vo 36 pp.   Rochester: Union and Advertiser Co., 1875.

SAN FRANCISCO.—Synodus Diœcesana Sancti Francisci habita mense Julii 1862.

8vo 16 pp.   San Francisco : Towne & Bacon, 1862; [2d edition]. 8vo 19 pp. San Francisco: Smyth & Shoaff, '72.

SANTIAGO DE CUBA.—Constituciones Synodales de la Iglesia de Cuba.   Folio.   1682.

Constitutiones Synodales de la Iglesia de Cuba. 2d edition.

Synodo Diœcesano que de orden de S. M. celebro el Ilustrisimo Señor Doctor Don Juan Garcia de Palacios, obispo de Cuba en Junio de 1684, Reimpreso por orden del Ilustrisimo Señor Doctor Don Juan Jose Diaz de Espada y Landa, Segundo Obispo de la Habana, y anotado conforme à las ultimas disposiciones eclesiasticas y civiles.   Reimpreso.

8vo 229 pp.   Habana, Imprenta del Gobierno, 1844.†

---

* These Synods were in force in Michigan, Indiana, Illinois, Wisconsin, etc., before the creation of the See of Baltimore.

† The Synod was in force in Florida till 1820.   The Florida Constitutions have been published in the U. S. Catholic Hist. Mag.

SANTA FE.—Constituciones Eclesiasticas para la Diocesis de Santa Fé N. M. Publicadas por el Il* Sr. Obispo D. Juan B. Lamy.

8vo 37 pp. Albuquerque, N.M., Rio Grande Press, 1874.

ST. PAUL.—Decreta Synodalia Diœceseos Sti Pauli de Minnesota.

8vo 36, 8 pp.   St. Paul, Pioneer Co., 1874.

ST. LOUIS. — Statuta lata et promulgata ab Ill**. ac Rev**. D. Petro Ricardo Kenrick, Archiepiscopo S. Ludovici, in Synodo Diœcesana mense Augusti. A. D. 1850 habita.

8vo 19 pp.   St. Louis: Richard Phillips, 1850.

Statuta Diœcesis S. Ludovici, promulgata ab Ill⁻. ac R**. D.D. Joseph Rosati, Congregationis Missionis, Episcopo S. Ludovici, in Synodo Diœcesana habita in Ecclesia Cathedrali. mense Aprili 1839.

8vo. St. Louis: C. Keemle, 1839. [2d ed.] 8vo Rome, 1839.

SAULT ST. MARY.—Statuta Diœcesis Marianopolitanæ in Michigan.

8vo 84 pp.   Detroit: John Slater, 1863.

SYRACUSE.—Synodus Diœcesana Syracusana Prima, die xiv Septembris A.D. 1887 in Ecclesia Sanctæ Mariæ in Cœlos Assumptæ. Syracusis habita ab Illustrissimo ac Reverendissimo Patritio A. Ludden. Episcopo Syracusano.

8vo 113 pp. NewYork Catholic Publication Society, 1887.

WHEELING.—Statuta ab Ill**. ac Rev**. Dom. Richardo Vinc. Whelan Episcopo Wheelingensi, in Synodo Diœcesana, in Cathedrali, diebus 28 ac 29 Octobris an. 1873, habita, lata .et promulgata.

8vo 15 pp.   Wheeling: James F. Carroll, 1873.

CATHOLIC SCHOOLS IN COLONIAL MARYLAND —Soon after 1752, Daniel Connelly and Patrick Cavanagh established a Catholic School near My Lady's Manor. When Mary Anne March opened a Catholic school in Baltimore, in 1757, the Rev. Thomas Chase of St. Paul's parish complained to the Assembly. The Protestant schoolmaster said "he had lost many of his scholars which were immediately put to the Popish school." On the 25th of April, 1757, the Magistrates were ordered to call all persons before them who were keeping public and private schools, and to administer to them the oaths to the Government required by law, which oaths, if any refused to take, and afterwards kept school, they were to prosecute them accordiug to law. Scharf, "History of Baltimore City and County." Philadelphia, 1881, p. 526.

REV. DEMETRIUS A. GALLITZIN,
"THE PASTOR OF THE ALLEGHANIES."

By CHARLES CONSTANTINE PISE, D. D.

[From the Biographical Annual for 1841.]

The career of this venerable ecclesiastic has been characterized by traits of a very extraordinary nature. Destined, by birth, for the highest honors in his own country, he abandoned it, and sacrificed all his brightest anticipations, in order to devote himself to the cause of religion in the New World. Nor did he select, even here, a conspicuous theatre on which to figure; but preferred the retired and rugged fastnesses of the Alleghany mountains, for the exercise of his zeal, and other eminent virtues. It was amid those solitary retreats, surrounded with a colony of poor settlers that he erected a church, and made the "desert to blossom as the rose." During forty-one years, he devoted his fortune, his fine mind, his literary and theological attainments, to the service of the poor, amid the wilds of Penn-. sylvania. And he cherished this voluntary obscurity beyond the glare of the court, and the purple of the church—either, or both of which he might have enjoyed, had he embraced the ecclesiastical state in Europe, or chosen for his abode the metropolis, where Pontiffs love to cover with merited digni-. ties the princes of the earth, who choose "the Lord as their portion and heritage."

The Rev. Demetrius A. Gallitzin was the son of the most noble Prince Gallitzin; a name in which Russia prides herself, as among her widest and most renowned, and all Europe recognizes as most distinguished and illustrious. Having filled some of the highest offices in the empire, the Prince was sent to represent the Czar, as minister plenipotentiary to the Court of Holland. It was whilst in the discharge of this high function, that was born to him, at the

Hague, the subject of this brief memoir. The 22d of December, A. D. 1770, ushered into life the young Gallitzin, the flower of his family—the future "pastor of the Alleghanies."

His boyhood was spent in acquiring all the accomplishments proper for a youth of his noble condition : and possessing great talents and a natural enthusiasm of character, he did not fail to turn to the best advantage the opportunities which he enjoyed. Having arrived at his 22d year, adorned with an elegant person and captivating manners, but still more with an ingenuous and inquiring disposition, he determined to travel, in order to prepare himself still more thoroughly for the elevated station for which he was intended. He crossed the Atlantic, with the view of observing the progress of civilization and human liberty in the republic of the United States.

It is no difficult matter to imagine with what distinguished and cordial welcome the hope of the princely family of Gallitzin was received on these shores; and with what exciting emotions his parents looked forward to the realization of all their designs in his regard.

But Providence, who disposes all things "strongly and sweetly," had other views: in the midst of his career, when courted by all the world, on account of his immense fortune and illustrious birth, the convictions of religion came upon his spirit with irresistible energy. He had been born and educated in the Greek Church, which, ever since the seventeeenth century, had separated from the See of Rome, and, under an Œcumenical patriarch of its own choice, erected an ecclesiastical polity independent of the ancient Church. The great controversy which agitated the east and west on the subject of the Holy Ghost from the Father and the Son, and the violent usurpation of authority grasped by the Greek patriarch in opposition to the rightful supremacy of the Roman Pontiff, are familiar to every reader of ecclesiastical history. It may be, however, added, that, although most of the dogmata of the Greek Church are orthodox—although the mass, transubstantiation, auricular confession, purgatory, etc., are strictly believed and adhered to, by its members, still no schismatics are more hostile to the western or Roman Catholic Church, than the Russians, and other partisans of the Oriental usurpation. The conduct of the reigning autocrat towards his Catholic subjects, as well in Russia as in Poland, sufficiently attests the truth of this assertion. Hence it is, that the Russians are taught, from their cradle, to abhor the Roman supremacy—and to cleave with superstitious and national tenacity to their own Œcumenical patriarchs, as to the source of all orthodox doctrine and legitimate discipline. The nobility and gentry are nurtured, with peculiar care, in all these prejudices and hostile feelings against Rome. The reader may, therefore, easily conceive how profound must have been the investigations—how since the convictions—how great the triumph over prejudice—of young Gallitzin, when, amid all the dissipating scenes into which, as a gay traveller, he was thrown, he became a convert to the doctrines and supremacy of the Roman Church. By taking this step, he was fully aware that he was blasting, at one stroke, all his future worldly hopes—that he was incurring the inexorable displeasure of a father, who before had doted on him, and was closing the doors of imperial favor forever.

But his generous heart had resolved to make sacrifice. He was in quest of truth; and once convinced where it was to be found, he made up his mind to obtain it, at the peril of all things else. This was, for him, that "precious stone" of which the Scripture speaks: to purchase which he he was prepared to "sell all things he possessed." He had paused from the hurry of his travels, to search into the question which divided the Greek from the Roman Church. He consulted the oracle of the American Catholic Church—John Carroll—at that time Bishop of Baltimore, a prelate, whose memory is as dear to our country as it is sacred to our religion; a prelate, whose patriotism and virtues were well known to the first Congress which deputed him on a most important mission to Canada, in company with his cousin Carroll of Carrollton, Benjamin Franklin, and Samuel Chase; a prelate, who combined the deepest convictions of religion with the blandest manners and most tolerant disposition. It was this immortal Bishop, in whom Gallitzin found an instructor—as Augustine found in Ambrose, at Milan—to whom he unbosomed his inmost feelings—by whom he was instructed—and through whom he was admitted into the pale of the Catholic Communion.

Having taken this step, he now formed the resolution not to return to his native country, but to embrace the ecclesiastical state, and spend his life in spreading through the NewWorld the doctrines which he believed to be revealed from heaven. To this end, he withdrew altogether from society, and retired into the Theological Seminary at Baltimore, in order to prepare himself for the work of the holy ministry. His course in that venerable institution, which had been founded by eminent divines exiled from France by the horrors of the Revolution, was edifying and exemplary; and, on the festival of Saint Joseph, the 19th of March, anno 1795, he received the order of priesthood from the hands of Bishop Carroll.

Had he, then, betaken himself to the "Eternal City," it is more than probable that he would, in a very short time, have been invested with the highest honors of the Church. His name, his fortune, his accomplishments, his piety, would have richly entitled him to them. But, instead of seeking for such distinctions, he courted obscurity; and, under the anonyme, as it may be termed, of "Rev. Mr. Smith," he retired into the interior of Pennsylvania, and commenced the exercise of the ministry on one of the farms belonging to Georgetown College, called Conewago.

But, not satisfied with bounding his labors within the district of that mission, he extended them into the bosom of the Alleghanies; in which, as if to bury himself still

more deeply in solitude and oblivion, he, at length, determined to fix his residence. There, in the midst of a few
poor families, he began his apostolic labors in the year 1795;
and continued in that wild retreat, round which, however, ·
he gradually drew large congregations, until the period of
his death.

They only who have witnessed it, can form an idea of
his boundless charity. Thousands now live to proclaim it,
and bitterly to bewail the loss of it, by his departure into another world. His ample fortune was spent in affording them
temporal comfort, while his life was exhausted in conferring
on them spiritual consolations.

The Reverend Demetrius Gallitzin was gifted with rare
intellectual endowments—and, as an author, occupies a conspicuous rank among the ecclesiastical writers of America.
He had become a perfect master of the English language,
which he spoke and wrote almost without any foreign
idiom or accent. His "defence of Catholic principles,"
holds a place among the standard polemical works of our
country; and the number of editions through which it has
gone, both here and in England, vindicates his claim to
the position which it now holds, and is likely to hold among
future generations. His manner of writing is vigorous;
and a spirit of candor and a tone of high breeding preside over his most earnest and ardent works of controversy. He is keen, it must be admitted; but he cuts with
a polished razor : and when he meets his antagonist in
the theological arena, he encounters him according to the
tactics of honorable warfare; and in his victory, he is calm,
forbearing, and just.

Full of merits and good works, this venerable priest
expired, in the 71st year of his age, on the 6th of May,
1840. In his demise, the Church has been deprived of
one of her most eminent divines—the sanctuary, of one of
its brightest luminaries—the community, of one of its most
accomplished ornaments—the poor, of their best benefactor

—and a numerous congregation, of their devoted pastor and father.

Multis ille quidem fiebilis occidit ! *

His grave is made in the solitude wheie his life was spent: and better rest, in peace, under the green turf watered by the tears of the poor, than lie neglected and forgotten beneath the stately mausoleums of the great. He has gone to receive the reward promised to the good and faithful servant—and his memory, as " Pastor of the Alleghenies," will be in benediction in the annals of the Church.

CATHOLIC SCHOOLS IN ENGLAND, AND AMERICAN PUPILS.—"Father Harvey is another very considerable missionary.". . "He has also set up a school for the benefit of Catholic children, where he instructs them in all the principles of our holy religion; and though the laws are very severe against us on this head, yet . . . he practices in this double capacity without any disturbance. The success this pious Father's undertakings have been attended with, and the applause so deservedly given him by our zealous Catholics, induced several other missionaries to set up schools also." . . . " The Catholic merchants of Maryland, Barbadoes & Co., send their sons to England to be educated by those Fathers." Letter of a Catholic priest in London, Jan. 1, 1732–33, to a Cardinal at Rome, in "The Present State of Popery in England," etc., London, 1733, p. 19.

STATISTICS OF ST. ANNE'S CHURCH, DETROIT.

	BAPTISIMS.	MARRIAGES.	DEATHS.
1703—1710	94	3	13
1711—1720	43	7	15
1721—1730	106	16	44
1731—1740	156	27	73
1741—1750	235	24	114
1751—1760	363	70	216
1761—1770	351	80	217
1771—1780	476	60	182
1781—1790	551	80	219
1791—1800	914	167	367
	3,289	534	1,460

* The tears of many will bewail his loss.

ILLINOIS, OSAGE AND OTOPTATA CHIEFS

IN PARIS, IN 1725.

Since our last came in the Mail due from Holland with a farther Account from Paris of the four Savages of Mississippi:

On the 28th of November, the four Chiefs, and the Savage Maid were again presented to the Company, when the Chief of the Illinois, as a Christian, and an ancient Ally of the French, presented his Speech to the Comptroller General, and the three other Chiefs also presented theirs in the name of their Three Nations, which were read by the Company's Secretary.

The speech of the Illinois to the India Company, was as follows:

"The Black Gown* tells me that you are some of the
" most eminent Men of the French Nation, whom the King
" has made Chiefs of Mississippi. I am ashamed to be so lit-
" tle in comparison of you. Tho' I am Chief of my Village,
" and esteemed in my own Country, I am nothing; but I
" love Prayer and the French. Therefore, you ought to
" love me and to love my Nation, which has always been
" allied to the French.

"The French are with us. We have yielded them the
" Country which we possess in Cassakias. We are very
" well pleased with them, but we don't like to see them
" come and mingle themselves with us, and to take up their
" Habitations in the midst of our Village and our Deserts.
" 'Tis my Opinion that you who are the great Chiefs, should
" leave us Masters of the country where we have placed
" our Fire.

---

* This is the name which the Savages gave the Jesuits. The person here meant is Father Beaubois.

" I am come hither to see the King in the Name of my
" Nation and my young People. When shall I see him? All
" the fine Things I see are nothing if I do not see the King,
" our true Father and yours, and if I do not hear His
" Word to report them to my young people.

" I was dead some Days ago, but now I am reviv'd,
" because great Care has been taken of me. I thank you
" for it, and hope that you will continue it. In short, be-
" cause you are our Chiefs, speak kindly to me that my
" young People may be pleas'd when I see them again,
" and that they may perceive that you are well disposed
" towards us. This is what I had to say to you, who am
" your Son, and a Friend of the French.

CHICAGOU.

The following Speech was made to the India Company,
by the Chiefs of the Indian Nations call'd Missoury, Osages,
and Otoptata.

"'Tis now Twelve entire Moons since we set out from
" our lands to the Country. One of our Chiefs dy'd by the
" way, the others were left on the Sea Shore.

"We were given to understand that the King and
" Company demanded some of each of our Nations. We
" are here now before you, but still ignorant of what you
" want with us.

" We are asham'd to see that we have nothing worth
" your acceptance. We brought with us some Skins and
" the Workmanship of our Wives, which you that have
" abundance of fine things of more importance would not
" have valued, but all was lost in the first Ship that was
" to have carry'd us

" We can't sufficiently admire the fine things which
" we see every day, Things which we shall never forget,
" and which will rejoyce all to whom we relate them.

" We are very well pleas'd with the Treatment we have
" met with since we came to this Country, but were uneasy
" till we arrived.

" Our Seniors each for his Nation, have enjoyn'd and
" charged us to lay their Demands before you.

   1. 'They desire you not to abandon them, and hope
" the French will not only furnish their necessities, but
" maintain their union

   2. "They complain that they never had any Body among
" them to instruct them to pray, but one White Band* lately
" come thither, with whom they are well pleased.

   3. " They desire you to send us back furnish'd with
" your Promise. They are all looking this way to see us
" again.

   4. " The French have told us that you consider well
" in all this Country, and that the Magazines there are yours.
" We are in your power. Consider how to dispose of your
" Bodies.

After the reading these Speeches, the Comptroller General ordered his Answer to be read to all of them, which was composed with that Spirit proper for conversing with that People, and the better to be understood by means of their Interpreters. He gave a Copy of it to each of their Chiefs.

Then he caused the presents of the Company to be delivered to them, consisting of a Habit compleatly French, being a blue Coat with Silver Buttons and Buttonholes, scarlet Waste coats, embroider'd with Silver, red Breeches and Hose, Silver Lac'd Hats, some with red and others with blue Feathers, six ruffled Shirts, six Necks, etc. A Savage Habit, consisting of a Cloth Wrapper, five Quarters wide, with Silver Lace two Inches above the List, which is left there, because the Savages reckon it an Ornament, a Braguet, which is a quarter of an Ell of scarlet Cloth adorned with silver Lace above the Selvage. This they make use of to cover their Nudities. And a pair of Mitase, which are Cloth Stockings half blue and half red, which come up to the Thighs, and are ty'd with Ribbonds to their Sashes.

The Dress presented to the Savage Girl, was a Damask

_____
* They call a Foreign Missionary by the name of White Band.

Gown of Flame Colour, with Gold Flowers, an under Petticoat
of the same, a Panier, two pair of Boddice, six lac'd Shifts,
and Ribbonds of Gold and Silver,and a pair of Silk Stockings.

THE ANSWER OF THE COMPTROLLER GENERAL OF THE FRENCH
   INDIA COMPANY, TO THE SPEECH OF THE FOUR SAVAGES
   INSERTED IN OUR LAST, WHICH ANSWER WAS PRONOUNCED
   BY THE COMPANY'S SECRETARY.

Hear Illlnois, Missoury, Ozages and Otoptata :
    " I am very glad that you have heard the Speech of
" the Company, I see you here with Pleasure. The Com-
" pany will always think of you, and can never forget your
" saying.
    " They know, Illinois, that you are a Man of Prayer.
" They conjecture that you Missoury, you Ozages, you Opta-
" ta will hear the Words of the Missionaries that shall be sent
" unto you.
    " You have seen how many People the great Onon╪
" tio [King] commands. You cannot but know his Riches
" and Magnificence by his Palaces and Gardens where you
" have been.
    " This great Onontio is he whom we all obey. He is
" our Father and the Governor of Louisiana is his Interpre-
" ter. He has kindled the Fire of his Council at New
" Orleans. 'Tis from thence all our Thoughts ought to
" proceed. Hearken not to any other Words but such as
" shall be deliver'd to you from the place. They will be
" the Words of the great Onontio. If you hear them, the
" Roads will be free, and you will have very good Hunt-
" ing.
    " The Company, who loves you, and takes you into
" their very Bosom, gives you Tobacco to made your hearts
" merry, to disperse any clouds that might overcast your
" Minds, and to keep you in good Humour till you depart.
" They also give you Cloaths for you to wear here, and
" others, after the Fashion of your own Nation. They have

" made the like provision for the good Woman that is come
" with you.

On the 22d of November these Savages set out for
Fountainbleau. On the 24th, they were carried about to all
the Princes and Princesses and other Lords and Ladies of
the Court, who were fond to see Savages whom to their
Surprize they found to have as much Spirit and good Sense
as other Men. At night, the Comptroller General carried
them to the Duke of Bourbon, to whom the Illinois made
the following Speech :

GREAT CHIEF, MY FATHER,

" I know that your Ancestors were mighty Men and
" great Warriours, who have often dy'd their Helmets with
" the Blood of the Enemies of the French. At this Day
" you are without your Helmet because there are no En-
" emies; but you have given to the French their true
" Mother, who is above all the great women in the World.
" This is more than beating an Enemy. I know also that
" the Father of the French loves you, and that he com-
" mits his Children to your care, and that he hears
" your Words. Learn therefore of him to be always truly
" the Father of the French and ours; cause him to think of
" us, and to love me and my Nation. May you also love
" us as much as I admire you, and may you be of Opinion
" that you can never love us too much."

The Duke of Bourbon answer'd the Illinois, That he
was much obliged for the advantageous Idea he had of
him, and that he could not return a better Answer to his
Compliment than by assuring him that he looked upon as a
Chief and a great Warriour, and by promising to take Care
that he returns away contented, and more attached than
ever to the French nation.

His Serene Highness afterwards received the compliments of Missoury, Ozages and Otoptata, and when he had
return'd a civil answer to each, promised to present them
next Day to the King as he came from hunting, which he

accordingly did, and introduced them all dress'd in their Savage Habits into the King's Cabinet, when Father Beaubois presented his Majesty the Illinois and a letter from the Grand Chief, and made the following speech :

SIRE,

. "This Savage, who has the honor to appear before
" your Majesty, is no ordinary Man. Yet tho' the Chief of
" his Village, and one of the most considerable of his Nation,
" he has nothing of . that Pomp and Grandeur which sur-
" round Princes, and which render them so venerable to
" the people who are under 'em, these being things unknown
" in America. But what your Majesty will no doubt value
" him for is, that this Indian, born as one may say in an-
" other World, and brought up in the middle of Forests, could
" conceive so high an Idea of your Grandeur, as so earnestly
" to desire to see it nearer, and to come and pay you Homage.
" An unhappy Shipwreck, which chang'd the minds of those
" who accompanied him, did not intimidate him, and since
" he has been in France, the sight of what has been the
" Astonishment of all Foreigners, has still made him the more
" eager of seeing the Monarch of so potent an Empire.
" The most considerable Chief of all the Illinois nation
" has a thousand times enjoy'd the happiness of this, as
" himself ingenuously owns to your Majesty, and has, as
" one may say, a thousand times regretted that he is so
" necessary to the French nation in his own country. Vouch-
" safe, Sire, kindly to receive the Letter which he presumes to
" send to your Majesty, and be pleased to return a favor-
" able Answer.

    " For my Part, Sire, I think myself very happy, that I
" have this Day the Honour of approaching your Throne, there
" to be Witness of the Wonders which France admires in your
" Sacred person. Permit me, Sire, to beg your Majesty's
" Royal Protection for the Missions of Louisiana, that vast
" Province, where there cannot be too many for the welfare
" of yonr Colony, and to procure to the many Savage na-

" tions that inhabit it, the Knowledge of the True God. Lewis
" le Grand of Glorious Memory, always made it his delight
" to protect those whom Providence honours with so holy a
" Ministry, and thereby to demonstrate that Zeal he had
" for the Propagation of the Faith. Being Heir, Sire, of his
" HeroickVirtues, as you are of his rich Diadem, do you show
" the same Zeal, which cannot but be infinitely glorious to
" you. We have a Right it seems to expect it from your
" Piety, which appeared so eminently in the Choice you have
" made of the most virtuous Princess of the world, to place
" her by you on the most August Throne in the Universe.

[The Post Man, London, Jan. 27, 1726. Upcott Coll. I p.
33. New York Historical Society.]

TRUSTEES OF ST. PETER'S, NEW YORK, TO BISHOP CARROLL :

New York, June 11, 1806.

" Rt. Rev. Dear Sir—If to be impressed with the highest respect and
warmest affection for the venerable prelate, whose pious zeal watches with
paternal solicitude over the concerns of our most holy religion in this country, and whose virtues display its purity, be a criterion of attachment to
religion itself, we, the undersigned Trustees of this Church, feel a con-
sciousness of that attachment in the sincerity with which we offer our good
Bishop our expression of those sentiments towards his revered and beloved
person Actuated by that attachment, and divested of all prejudice and
partiality with respect to persons but what result from it, we beg, Sir, you
will also accept the assurances of our zealous co-operation, to the extent
of our power and duties both as individual members of the Congregation
and in our corporate capacity, in carrying into beneficial effect every measure your wisdom and piety may suggest for the promotion and respecta-
bility of Catholicity here, and the fostering those virtues both in the clergy
and laity, the want of which in either must be productive of injury and
disgrace to the most sacred institutions.

We pray the Almighty to prolong a life so eminently directed to the
advancement of his glory and the promotion of his holy religion, and that
the remainder of your mortal journey may be comfortable and happy, till
it shall please Him to reward your pious labors with a crown of never-
ending fidelity. We beg your benediction and remain, Rt. Rev. Sir, your
affecty. respectful servants,

THOMAS STOUGHTON.   CORN. HEENEY,   JOHN HOES,   JOHN BYRNE,
      AND. MORRIS,   MICHAEL ROTH,   JOHN HINTON.

GERMAN MISSIONS IN EASTERN PENNSYLVANIA.

By Marc F. Vallette.

Although Pennsylvania was the last of the American Colonies settled, with the exception of Georgia, it was not long in becoming one of the richest and most populous, and at the time of the Revolutionary War Philadelphia had become the largest town in the colonies. This was due, in a large measure, to the liberal spirit of its founder, William Penn. English, Welsh and Irish people attracted by the peaceful relations existing between Penn and the Indians, felt a sense of security when they set foot in the colony. People in moderate circumstances found another attraction in the fact that both in Pennsylvania and New Jersey, the land was not taken up in large bodies, as in some of the other colonies, and the poor man could get a farm of his own.

The first large accession to the population, next to the Friends or Quakers, was a German immigration which begun in 1730, and which peopled several counties in the vicinity of Philadelphia. Among these were a number of Catholics who must have been for a long time without the ministrations of a priest. The Rev. Leonard Neale (afterwards Archbishop of Baltimore) in an account he gives of the visit of a priest to Philadelphia, says that, "a considerable number of persons assembled to hear him, most of whom were Germans." These people were overjoyed at the sight of a priest after being for so many years deprived of the consolations of their religion.

In 1741, the German Catholics of Philadelphia and vicinity were rejoiced by the arrival of two Jesuit Fathers of their own nationality, Rev. Theodore Schneider and Rev. William Wappeler. The latter, though a zealous and hard working priest remained only a few years in America, his health compelling him to return to Germany. Before doing so, however, he founded the missions of Conewago and Lancaster. Father

Schneider was more robust, and consequently succeeded in laying the foundation of a number of important missions, the chief of which was Goshenhoppen. Some time after, the Rev. Rev. Ferdinand Farmer came out from Germany. He assisted the Rev. Robert Harding, at Philadelphia, for a time, and later on, joined the Rev. Robert Molyneux, S.J., Rev. James Pellentz, S. J., Rev. Luke Geisler, and Rev. Joseph Ritter, S. J., who appear to have attended to the spiritual wants of the Catholics within the limits of the present Dioceses of Philadelphia, Harrisburg, Trenton, and Newark. Father Farmer sometimes went as far as New York. Father Schneider visited New Jersey in 1744, to say Mass at Iron Furnaces. The Jerseymen of that day do not seem to have had much love for the Catholic priest, for Father Schneider was subjected to persecutions of various kinds and was shot at several several times. His medical knowledge enabled him cure many sick poor, and he sometimes availed himself of this fact to travel under the name of Dr. Schneider.

The Church of the Blessed Sacrament at Goshenhoppen was founded in 1741, thirty-five years before the reading the Declaration of Independence. It seems to have been a sort of Mother-House for the country missions for many miles around. In 1745, Father Schneider built the original chapel. It is worthy of note that while this mission was never considered as distinctively German, all its pastors have been of that nationality. Father Schneider was succeeded in 1764, by the Rev. Joseph Ritter, S. J., and he, by a Livonian Jesuit, tne Rev. Father Krakowski. In 1836, the Rev Augustine Bally, S. J., became Superior of this Mission, and for forty-five years he ministered to the wants of the people of that region. The name of Goshenhoppen was afterwards changed to Churchville and still later to Bally, in honor of the good priest just named. Within a few miles of Goshenhoppen there once stood, and perhaps, still stands, a house which was pointed out by the people of the neighborhood, and which their ancestors had told them had been the residence of the first priests in that vicinity. .Father Bally, died January 30,

1882, and was succeeded by the Rev. John B. Meurers, S. J. In 1889, the mission was abandoned by the Jesuits and is now, (1890) under the pastoral charge of Rev. Aloysius Misteli, a German secular priest.

The German Catholic population in Pennsylvania up to 1757 has been variously estimated. Father Schneider in his report of that year gives the following estimate of the number under his charge :

		MEN.	WOMEN.
In and around Philadelphia, all Germans,		107	121
" Philadelphia County, but up the country,		15	10
" Berks County, - · · - ·		62	55
" Northampton County, · · -		68	52
" Bucks County, - · · -		40	12
" Chester County, - · · -		13	9

Father Farmer's report of the Catholics under his charge, all Germans, gives the following figures :

In Lancaster County, 108 men, 94 women; in Berks County, 41 men and 39 women, and 3 men in Chester County.

Father Mathias Manners had under his care, in York County, 54 men and 62 women.

In 1788, the number of German Catholics in Philadelphia was sufficiently large to warrant their building a Church for themselves. An association had been organized the year before and on February 21, 1788, Adam Premir bought from the Supreme Executive Council of Pennsylvania, the lots on the northwest corner of Sixth and Spruce Streets with money contributed by the members.

The act of incorporation was gtanted to the " Trustees of the German Religious Society of Roman Catholics, called the Church of the Holy Trinity, in the City of Philadelphia." The Church was rather quaint in shape, being what might be called a half-hexagon. It was built of old-fashioned red and black glazed brick. Its original dimensions were 100x61 feet, and there were no galleries; those now in it were added subsequently. Rev. John Charles Helbron was the first pastor, he having been named in the deed of Adam Premir, Nov.

13, 1790, conveying the Church to the Trustees. The irregular manner of his appointment gave rise to untold difficulties between the Trustees and the Bishop which existed for nearly three-quarters of a century. The conduct of some of these trustees was, at times, anything but edifying, and on more than one occasion, the Bishop was obliged to close the doors, and the people were obliged to go to some other church for spiritual consolation and ministrations.

In 1831, during the pastorate of the Rev. J. Vanderback, there was another great excitement at the Church of the Holy Trinity. Stephen Girard, the founder of Girard College died, and in his will directed that he should be buried in the grave-yard adjoining the Church. Mr. Girard had not been a practical Catholic, and by his will no clergyman of any kind, is permitted, even as an ordinary visitor to enter Girard College; yet, on his death-bed his sister, who was a good Catholic, asked him whether he would be willing to see a priest. He replied in the affirmative, but before the priest arrived, Stephen Girard had passed away. The sister made certain representations to Bishop Kenrick concerning her brother's desire to be reconciled to the Church, which the Bishop thought would justify his burial in accordance with her wishes. But, as the Bishop with attending clergy was about to enter the sanctuary, he noticed that the Free Masons had turned out in force and in full regalia. He immediately withdrew and the only services performed were at the grave and, in accordance with the Masonic Ritual.

But, the trouble did not end here. Twenty years later, in 1851, the executors of the will desired to remove the remains to Girard College. No opposition was made to the removal by the Bishop, but the heirs entered a most solemn protest, declaring that the deceased had expressed, in his will, a desire to be buried in consecrated grouud, and they appealed to the Courts for an injunction. Judge King, before whom the case was brought declared that " an injunction would probably not lie after the actual removal of the body, but that pending the hearing, the corpse having already been removed from the ground, it could do no harm to permit the ceremonies to proceed, especially as the preparations having been on such a magnitude, much inconvenience would result from any interference." It must be borne in mind, that this was the first public demonstration of the Free Masons since the anti-masonic excitement caused throughout the country by the murder of Morgan, who it is said, had been done away with for revealing the secrets of the Order. The procession took place, and the remains of Stephen Girard are deposited in the vault prepared for him at the College.

One of the first, if not the first, asylumns for boys, in Philadelphia was opened in the early thirties, on Sixth Street, adjoining the Church, during the pastorate of the Rev. Michael Guth, an Alsatian priest. But the good man was not permitted to remain long with the orphans for whom his charity had provided. There was, at that time in Philadelphia, a large number of colored people. They had followed their masters who had been driven out of St. Domingo by the Revolution. These poor people occupied seats in the galleries, and Father Guth was anxious to give them the benefit of his ministrations. He was in the habit of preaching in German on three Sundays in the month, and it occurred to him that on the fourth Sunday he would preach in French for the benefit of those of his flock speaking that language and not understanding German or English. But the German trustees would not listen to this, and Father Guth asked to be transferred to another mission. He went to Bottle Hill, New Jersey, and was succeeded, in 1836, by the Rev. Nicholas Balleis, O. S. B., the present (1890) venerable and much esteemed pastor of the Church of St. Francis of Assisium, Brooklyn, N. Y., to whose kindness the writer of this article is indebted for some of the facts herein recorded. The trustees in 1847, during the pastorate of the Rev. Nicholas Perron, were not so exacting, as he was permitted to preach in French from time to time.

The Rev. P. M. Carbon, a noble and pious priest whose pastorate at the Church of the Holy Trinity extended from

1854 to 1871, the time of his death, introduced into the Diocese the German Community of the School Sisters of Notre Dame, who now have charge of several schools in city and country. In July, 1860, the Church or the Holy Trinity was destroyed by fire, but Father Carbon went to work and rebuilt it, and it rose from its ashes more beautiful than ever. On Nov. 23, 1889, the Centenary of this Church was celebrated with grand and imposing ceremonies. These were participated in by the Most Rev. P. J. Ryan, D. D., Archbishop of Philadelphia; Rt. Rev. W. M. Wigger, D.D., Bishop of Newark, and the late Rt. Rev. Caspar H. Borgess, D. D., titular Bishop of Phacusa. The present pastor 1890) is Rev. Ernest Otto Hiltermann, who built the beautiful Church of the Sacred Heart at Allentown.

Old St. Mary's Church at Lancaster, as has already been stated, was founded by Rev. Father Wappeler, and was attended after his time by Fathers Geisler and Farmer. It was built in 1745, and was simply a log structure. In 1760, it was destroyed by fire, and two years later, it was replaced by a stone building which in those days was regarded as a "very commodious stone structure." It is related that during the building of this Church, the women came daily to mix the mortar, while the men, after gathering stones from the adjacent fields, lent a helping hand to the masons in the erection of the sacred edifice. Among its pastors, after Father Wappeler, the founder of the Mission, we find the indefatigable Molyneux and such sturdy pioneers of the faith as Fathers Farmer (or Steinmeyer), Schneider, Pellentz, Elling, Brosius, Helbon, Rosseter, Stafford, Geissler, Hamm, Montgrand, Fitzimmons, Levermond, Janin, Erntzen, Kohlman; the Franciscan Egan, who afterwards became first Bishop of Philadelphia; the well known DeBarth, whose humility led him to refuse the See of Philadelphia; then the Jesuit Beschter, and Fathers Stoecker and O'Connor, and in 1814, another Jesuit, Byrne, from Conewago. Later on came Fathers Holland and Schenfelder. Father Holland died in 1823 at the age of 37 and his worthy colleague did not survive him.

They were succeeded in the fall of 1823 by the Rev. Bernard Keenan, who for fifty-four years was identified with the history of Lancaster, and who died, Vicar General of the Diocese of Harrisburg, on the 19th of February, 1879, very nearly one hundred years old.

Until 1849, the German and English speaking Catholics had worshipped together, but in 1850, the Germans built St. Joseph's Church. Its first pastor was the Rev. Father Tamchina, whose pastorate extended from Oct. 20, 1850 to April 25, 1851. The Church was enlarged in 1870 by the Rev. F. L. Neufeld, and the basement was fitted up as a school and placed under the care of the Sisters of St. Francis, who had charge of nearly 300 pupils. Father Tamchina was succeeded by the Rev. M. A. Würtzfeld whose pastorate (from June to Sept. 1851) was very short because of failing health

Father John Dudas relieved him, until March, 1852, when Father Würtzfeld returned and served until August 1853, when he was again compelled to give up. The pastors since that time have been Rev. Leopold Habersberger, to May, 1856. Rev. Anthony Schwarz, to June 1866; Rev. Francis L. Neufeld 1871—the present pastor is Rev. Francis X. Schmidt.

In 1870, the corner-stone of a second German Church, was laid by the Rt. Rev. J. F. Shanahan, D. D. This Church (65x125 ft.) was placed under the pastoral charge of the Rev. Anthony F. Kaul, and was dedicated to St. Anthony. It has a parochial school, with 150 pupils under the care of the Sisters of the Holy Cross.

St. Peter's Church, Reading, was founded in 1791. Prior to this the Catholics of Reading worshipped in a little frame structure erected by the early German Jesuits from Goshenhoppen. In this year a brick building was erected near where the Reading Railroad now passes, and in 1844, a more pretentious brick Church was erected. Prior to this, Reading was attended as follows : Rev. George Schoenfelder, 1818–28; Rev. L. DeBarth and Rev. A. T. Pramiwitz, 1820–24; Rev. B. Corwin, S. J., 1824–28; Rev. E. McCarthy, S. J., 1828–34; Rev.

N. Steinbacher, S. J., 1834–39; Rev. F. X. Marshall, 1839–42. From 1842 to 1846, the Mission was attended by the Jesuit Fathers A. Bally, P. F. Dietz, and J. F. Lucas, also by the Rev. Father Donoghue, secular, from Philadelphia. Then Rev. Basil Shorb, 1846–48; Rev. Henry Balfe, 1848–49; Rev· P. H. Lemcke, 1849; Rev. Richard O'Connor, 1850; Rev. P· M. Carbon, 1850–54; Rev. Matthais Cobbin, 1854–55; Rev. James Power, Rev. Rudolph Kunzer, 1860; Rev. Charles J Schrader, 1860; Rev. Francis O'Connor, 1861.

Up to this time the Germans worshipped in St. Peter's with the English speaking Catholics, but in 1861. the Rev. Charles J. Schrader was appointed to build St. Paul's Chuch Father Schrader was a very popular young priest, thorough going and energetic, He hardly saw his work completed when he was called to his eternal reward. He was succeeded by the Rev. George Walmeyer, and he by the Rev. George Bornemann, the present pastor. St. Paul's has a fine parochial school of 600 pupils taught by the Sisters of Christian Charity.

The German Catholics in and around Pottsville, were sufficiently numerous in 1842 to form a congregation by themselves, and Bishop Kenrick sent the Rev. Joseph Burg to build a church for them. A quaint looking stone structure, 70 ft. by 50 ft. was erected and placed under the patronage of St. John the Baptist. Though the congregation increased in numbers, it was not until 1869 that it was found necessary to build a new Church. About this time, Rt. Rev. Bishop Wood purchased a lot at the corner of Tenth and Mahantongo streets for $10,000. A beautiful new Church (160x65 ft.) of dressed Mountain stone, with brown-stone front was erected on this lot by Rev. Bernard A. Baumeister. There was a small school house built in 1849 by that zealous and exemplary priest, Rev. P. M. Carbon, but, as in the course of time, it became too small, and was abandoned. Since the erection of the new Church, the school has been looked after, and now 400 children are taught by the Sisters of Christian Charity.

The succession of pastors at St. John's, up to the erection of the present edifice has been, after Father Burg : Rev. P. M. Carbon, 1849; Rev. Daniel Oberholzer, 1850; Rev. Philip Wegmeyr, 1856; Rev. Francis L. Neufeld, 1859 ; Rev. Franz J. Wachter, 1862; Rev. B. A. Baumeister, 1869.

ACCOUNT OF THE DEATH OF MRS. SETON.—St. Joseph's, Jan. 4th, 1821.
Monsignor :

Two days ago I learned the death of the worthy Superior of the Visitation, which you must have felt very much; and to-day that of our good Mother Seton will be felt likewise by our common Father who derives consolation, in the midst of many troubles, from the piety and labors of such souls. I speak so without hesitation knowing that you were aware of the respect, affection and submission of that excellent soul.

She went last night to her final rest at 2 o'clock. She had a great change these 3 or 4 last days, though she received Communion on Sunday and New Year Monday—it was all her treasure and support. Tuesday, as she was very ill, Mr. Dubois anointed her again, thinking that he was authorized to act thus from her having sufficiently recovered after the first administration of Extreme-Unction. This was for her a very great consolation, placing so much trust in every positive grace, even a simple blessing. He expressed in her name (she being too weak to speak) to her daughters that all her desire was 1st. that they should live united as the Daughters of Charity, and 2d. very faithful to their rules. She asked pardon for any scandal she might have given by the mitigations of the rule granted during her sickness. Mr. Dubois added that it was by his order and that of the physician. Then she herself raised her head a little to thank the Sisters for their kindness and to say to them twice, as one who then fel the happiness of it more than ever : " Be children of the Church—be children of the Church." And as Mr. Dubois commenced administering, she said " Oh, thankful." . . . Last night, I was called up in haste, but when I arrived, she was no more. Her poor Josephine grieving much, has conducted herself as an angel of filial and Christian piety, having scarcely left her one moment for the three or four last months.

Mr. Bruté then asks for prayers in her behalf.

THE CENTENNIAL MONUMENT OF ST. MARY'S
CHURCH, MONROE, MICH.

It was a cold and cheerless day—Thanksgiving. The day set apart for the unvailing of the monument that is to mark the hundredth year of Catholicity in Monroe County, or perhaps more properly speaking, in southern Michigan, Indiana and Ohio. The little pellets of snow and frozen rain hurried along by the cold nor-wester pelted the bare faces of the assembly who gathered to witness the ceremonies with a viciousness that sent the blood tingling through the veins, and no amount of bunting with its warm and lively colors could liven up the scene. From the mast-head of the signal service floated the cold wave flag, from the flag-staff of the Academy building the stars and stripes, as if seeking to qualify the announcement. The contrast was as great as the glow of the rose compared with the ice plant. The weather like that of October 15th, a year ago, was *mal a propos* for the occasion, and the dedication, like the celebration, occurred with nature out of sorts. Snow continued falling nearly the whole day and the thermometer ranged considerably below freezing. Bishop Foley and the visiting clergy, about 20 in number, arrived early in the day and participated in the Pontifical High Mass at St. Mary's. at 10 A. M. At this service, Bishop Foley was celebrant; Very Rev. Monsignor Joos, V. G., assistant; Revs. Schmittdiel and Kelley deacons of honor; Rev. Father Brancheau deacon of the mass; Rev. Lochrain, sub-deacon; Rev. Lochrain, sub-deacon; Rev. Dempsey, secretary of the diocese, first master of ceremonies and Rev. McLaughlin second master of ceremonies. After Mass, the Bishop delivered an eloquent sermon that proved a source of great pleasure to the audience. A select quartett from Detroit furnished the music for the occasion. After service the

Bishop and visiting clergy were entertainned by Fr. Soffers at a genuine old-fashioned Thanksgiving dinner.

At 2:45 P. M., the Cornet band escorted the Knights of St. John from their hall to the Church where everything had been arranged in holiday attire. The little spot in front of the Church was warm with the colors of national bunting and in vivid contrast to the gray clouds that hung like a pall overhead. Across the street, between St. Mary's Academy and St. Mary's Church, hung the national colors and smaller flags mingled in profusion with those of the Irish and Papal colors. Two platforms had been erected in such a manner as to shield the speakers and the band, and they too were made beautiful with bunting. In front of the one upon the left of the church entrance the name of Fr. Frichette, the first missionary was interwoven among the flags, with 1788, the date of his visit. From the front of one upon the left of the church entrance the portrait of Very Rev. Edmund Burke, V. G., the first resident pastor of this city with the date of his arrival, 1794, was placed. This latter platform was occupied by Bishop Foley and the clergy and from here the Bishop delivered his address. It was short, appropriate and fairly teemed with American sentiment. At the close of the address the monument was unveiled amid the cheers of the 2,000 people gathered to witness it, and music by the band. After the blessing there was more music and the clergy, followed by the throng, filed into the church where the " Te Deum " was rendered by the choir, organ and band in unison, making one of the finest musical performances ever heard in old St Mary's. Father Soffers then addressed the audience, thanking them for their attendance, thus closing the dedicatory exercises. In the evening Hon. T. J. McDonnell of Toledo, delivered an interesting oration at the rink, and the Detroit Quartette enlivened the occasion with some· rare selections. During the evening refreshments were served.

The monument as it stands at the corner of Elm Avenue and Anderson Street, facing south, presents to the spectator simply a work of art chiseled from the finest marble; but as he sees and examines it more closely, his thoughts run back a century over the history of the Catholic Church of the country, and not only the history of the Catholic Church of the country but of the State of Michigan, the most of Ohio and of Indiana. It is not only a history of the the Church but an introductory chapter to a century's history of the City of Monroe. From the ground to the top of the star the monument measures 17 feet and 3 inches and weighs 27,000 pounds. The foundation is of Ohio blue sand stone divided into three bases. Upon the south face the second is the word "Centennial" in large raised letters. Upon the second is the following uttered by General Washington :

"May the members of your society in America, animated alone by the pure spirit of Christianity and still conducting themselves as the faithful subjects of our free government, enjoy every temporal and spiritual felicity."

On the east face of the same stone is the date of the founding of the Church, Oct. 15, 1788 ; and upon the west is the date of the Centennial celebration, Oct. 15, 1888. Above this is a sub-die of red sand stone upon which rests a die 22 inches square of Florentine blue marble protected at its four four corners by four Corinthian pilasters of Southampton Falls marble. Upon this die are the representatives of Church, State and Municipality as follows :

Rt. Rev. J. S. Foley, Bishop of Detroit,
Hon. Cyrus G. Luce, Gov. of Mich.
Hon. C. A. Golden, Mayor of Monroe.

Then comes the following:

SOUTH FACE.
This Monument is erected by
Rt. Rev. C. P. Maes, Bp. of Covington.
Rt. Rev. Mgr. Ed. Jos, V. G.
V. Rev. M. J. P. Dempsey, Sec.
Rev. B. G. Soffers, } of St. Mary's.
Rev. F. J. DeBroux, }
Rev. B. Schmittdiel of St. Mich's
Rev. E. D. Kelly of St. John's.

Rev. P. Leavy.
Rev. Chas. Thomas.
Rev. James Ronayne.
Rev. L. J. Brancheau.
Rev. Dan. McLaughlin,

WEST FACE.

Meinrad Fix.
Alex'r T. Navarre.
Wm. Steiner.
C. A. Golden.
J. L. C. Godfroy.
Walter Hackett.
John Davis.
Mrs. Anton Daiber.
Mrs. John Wald.
Ant. Weier, E. Yaeger & Son's.
B. Sturn, G. Martin & Son's.
S. Lauer, H. D. Hoffman.
Ant. Rose, Andr. Baier.
J. & C. Schrauder.
Louis Dubois.
John Bapt. Fix.

EAST FACE.

F. X. Soleau, T Soleau.
Jas. Nadeau, Nap. Nadeau.
M. T. Duval, Meinr. Laprade.
J. O'Reilly, Dennis Kelly.
A. F. Robert & Son's, Geo. Fix.
Mich. Laprade S'r., Jos. Fix.
Hillery Duval & Son's,
E. A. Peltier, P. B. Peltier.
Mrs. M. T. Navarre & Sons.
Bernard Verhoeven.
F. Hugueney, Dave Reaume.
Moses Poupard.
Peter Micheaux.
Joseph Vigneux.
John Lamirande.
Frank Lamirande.

NORTH FACE.

Rev. W. Herwig.
Rev. Thos. Rafter.
Rev. John Van Gennip.
Rev. Geo. Laugel.
Rev. L. J. Wicart.
Rev. John M. Schreiber.
Rev. Bern. J. Wermers.
Miss Helena R. Steiner.
Charles P. Rabaut.
Mrs. M. D. Loranger.
F. X. Tetreau.
Jos. C. Nadeau.
Joseph Kirschner, E. Vanderheyden.
Rev. P. Laughran.
The Knights of St. John.
C. M. & Son, builders.

over this sits a plinth and cap of red Carlisle sand stone, upon which the seal of the county is engraved. A pedestal of buff sand stone surmounts this and is capped by the figure of the Recording Angel. It is cut from Carrara marble, in Carrara, Italy, and is as white as snow. She stands at ease with her book in one hand and quill in the other, and her drapery hanging losely about her. She has six feet of statue and weighs 1250 pounds. The statue was purchased through the firm of John Baird & Son of Philadelphia, who made generous reductions from the original price. To Fr. Soffers' untiring zeal and unfailing good nature should be credited this Centennial mile stone of the history of the spiritual and temporal prosperity of our people.

THE PIONEER FRENCH IN THE VALLEY
OF THE OHIO.

Read before the U. S. Catholic Historical Society, New York,
by Rev. A. A. Lambing, May 24, 1886.

The discovery, exploration and first settlement of the
Western World presents one of the most interesting and
varied pictures to be found anywhere in the pages of history.
The ambition of explorers, the daring of adventures, the
avarice of speculators, the jealousy of powers and the zeal
of millionaires combine to form a panamora without parallel
in the annals of the world. The pen of romance could not
impart a more striking and varied coloring. Spain, Portugal, England, Holland, and France, were there penetrating
into the deepest recesses, mountain, forest and plain, seeking with insatiable thirst whatever could excite cupidity,
from the soul of a savage to the skin of a beaver. But
the methods of exploration and colonization were characterized by the genius of the nation to which individuals
belonged, the influence of the home government, the capacity and aim of the leaders, the climate of the country,
and the strength and disposition of the aboriginal tribes.
This difference is strikingly illustrated in the different
methods of the English and French, with whom we have
exclusively to deal in this paper. The former, left to themselves with nothing but a royal character, ample enough
in its scope, but without any aid towards carrying out its
provisions, thrived and became a hardy race on account of
the very neglect of the home government; a circumstance
which that government learned to its cost when its neglected
children had acquired sufficient wealth to be taxed. For
this reason it is that the English, though far behind the

French in exploration, and the fur trade, were such in advance of them in all that pertained to permanent colonization. Their progress into the interior was slow, but where they once set their foot, they never withdrew it. The frowning range of the Alleghany Mountains, extending along the Atlantic coast at the distance of only one hundred and fifty or two hundred miles, so hemmed them in that they were prevented from crossing that barrier until they had established themselves so permanently on the eastern side as to be able to protect and defend the settlements that might be made beyond in the process of time. Hence we find their progress was steady from the beginning, and if it received an occasional check, it was temporary.

The French, on the contrary, pursued, as a nation, a mistaken policy from the first. It is true, indeed, that some among them, and notably Champlain, wished to follow the proper course; but they were not those on whom the destinies of the colony depended. The high latitude of the settlement and the consequent shortness of the summer season were not favorable to agriculture. But in no place in the New World could a colony have succeeded under the circumstances. The people were adventurers, not colonists; and the company and the minister on whom the success of the colony depended appear to have been bent rather on speculation than the cultivation of the soil. The bane of the New World was felt here as it was by the Spaniards of the South; that of drawing from the country the maximum of wealth for individuals and revenue for the crown with the minimum of outlay. The rivers, concentrating into the interior and connecting with the Great Lakes, and these lying in immediate proximity to the Mississippi, in the highest degree favored exploration; and the well known success of the French in treating with the Indians gave them an additional advantage. For this reason they are found even in the days of Champlain penetrating 700 leagues into the interior. The petty jealousies of rival officers between whom the power was somewhat divided by the Crown with a view of having them watch each other, retarded the execution of any important enterprise, while the brief tenure of office in many cases was a disadvantage equally great.   In short, the French were better explorers than the English, but not so good colonizers.   As a further evidence of this, the population of New France, although it embraced the whole of North America with the exception of a narrow strip along the Átlantic seashore, and comprising more than ten times as much territory as the English, was less than ten thousand. in 1769, more than seventy years after permanent settlement had been begun; while at the time the French power was finally overthrown, it was but one-fourteenth part of that of the English.

But with a rival like the English, urged on not only by the cupidity of the present, and the religious prejudice that served to give it a keener edge, but also by the traditional animosity of centuries of the past, it was not enough to explore a conntry and take nominal possession. This was but a preliminary step; maintaining possession was the touchstone of success.   In no place was this more clearly seen than in the valley of the Ohio River, using, as I do, the term Ohio, as equivalent to that of La Belle Rivière, the Beautiful River, in the sense in which it was employed in the early days by the Indians, French and English, for the water course extending from Western New York to its confluence with the Mississippi.

In the first half of the last century, the English traders, regardless of the claims of the French to all the country lying west of the Allegheny Mountains, had penetrated as far at least as the centre of the present State of Ohio, and had opened up trade with the tribes of that locality. Having to carry their goods but a few hundred miles, in which the severity of winter did not cause them any serious inconvenience or expense, their advantages were so manifestly superior to those of the French, who had to bring theirs all the way from the mouth of the St. Lawrence, and to endure the hardships of a long winter season, that all the tact of the latter was not capable of retaining the natives in their allegiance to the representatives of his Most Christian Majesty. Territorial claims amounted to as little with the Indians as they did with the traders; for according to the ideas of the savages the land was all their own hunting ground, and, though favoring for the present the one from whom they derived the greatest advantages, it was only from interest, or in the hope of one day being able to expel both intruders from the country.

The claim of the French to the Valley of the Ohio by the right of discovery, and that of the English to it as comprised within their several charters, was naturally calculated to engender strife here, and in the end involve the home governments in deadly conflict. The general outline of the history of the war that ensued is too well known to need repetition here, but the details of the French occupation, and later, of their attempt at colonization, may not be so familiar to the student of our history. It is important to determine, if possible, the precise time the French Pioneers first entered the valley of the Beautiful River. Few points of our early history have been argued with greater warmth than that for and against the discovery of this stream by the Chevalier Robert de La Salle, about the year 1670. The most weighty authorities are arrayed against each other; and if less enlightened minds differ, they need not be taxed with either ignorance or credulity. But, though the country owes much to that indefatigable explorer, and though the undertaking would have been in perfect harmony with his inclinations, it is all but certain that the honor of the discovery is not due to him. Subsequently it was to the interest of the French to claim the country on the strength of his supposed discovery, because it was well known to precede any claim that could be advanced by the English; and this they did, as may be learned from various historical documents. That the French discovered the stream, and descended it as far as Attiqué, the present Kittanning, forty-five miles above

Pittsburg, as early as 1730, admits of no doubt. But whether they descended it further or not, it is impossible to determine. Not long after this time the half-breed Peter Chartier, who was married to a Shawanese squaw, went from the west bank of the Susquehanna River nearly opposite Harrisburg, and settled on the Alleghany at the mouth of Bull Creek, about twenty miles above Pittsburg. Devoted at first to the interests of the English, suspicion was soon aroused that he had gone over to the French, and had induced many of the Indians, over whom he exercised great influence, to follow his example. But being untrustworthy neither party coveted his friendship, and he was accordingly banished from his village to the Vermillion country further west, by the authorities of New France, in 1745. He has left his name to two streams to the present day, one twenty-two miles above Pittsburg, the other three miles below. From certain expressions found in Céloron's Journal, it also appears that M. Longueuil paid at least a passing visit to the Indian village of St. Yotoe, or Scioto, about the year 1739; but we have no record of the particulars.

By far the most important event in the history of the transactions of the French up to this time in the Valley of the Ohio was the expedition of Céloron down the Beautiful River in the latter part of the summer of 1749. The English settlements east of the mountains were now in so flourishing a condition as to place them in comparative security, and the spirit of adventure that had hitherto been satisfied with trading with the Indians beyond the Alleghenies, began at length to contemplate the formation of permanent settlements. The proximity to the source of supplies enabled the traders to furnish goods to the Indians on terms more reasonable than those demanded by the French ; a circumstance which naturally gained the good will of the savages. Steps were also taken as as early as 1748 looking to the formation of the Ohio land company to take up and settle lands on the Ohio River. The members succeeded in obtaining from the King of England the grant of five hundred thousand acres of land on the southern bank of that stream between the mouth of the Monongahela and the Kanawha Rivers, with the further privilege of taking up lands on the north side. The Marquis de La Galissonière, then Governor-General of Canada, felt it his duty to consult for the interests of the French Crown by sending an expedition for the four-fold purpose of exploring the country, much of which was still unknown, taking formal possession of it in the name of the French King, expelling the English traders, and conciliating or regaining the Indians to the interests of the French, many of whom wavered or had gone over to the English. The task was beset with difficulties, but delay would only tend to increase them. Accordingly, in the summer of 1749, he appointed Pierre-Joseph Céloron, Sieur de Blainville, Knight of the Royal and Military Order of St. Louis, Captain in the French army, an officer who had already distinguished himself for courage, prudence and energy in the service of Canada, to fit out and command the expedition. In his Journal of the expedition, a copy of which I had made from the original in the archives of the Marine at Paris, he writes: "I set out from La Chine on the 15th of June, with a detachment composed of one captain, eight subaltern officers, six cadets, one chaplain, twenty soldiers, one hundred and eighty Canadians, and thirty Indians."

Although the Recollects were at that time appointed as a rule, to the Chaplaincy of the French forces and expeditions, a Jesuit Father, Rev. Louis Ignatius Bonnecamp, or Bonnquant, was selected on this occasion, most probably on account of his scientific knowledge, for learning no less than religious ministrations, was required in carrying out the objects of the expedition. He was then professor of mathematics and hydrography in the Jesuit College of Quebec, and enjoyed, besides, the reputation of being a distinguished astronomer. The expedition pursued its route by way of the St. Laurence, Lake Ontario, the Niagara

River, Lake Erie, a portage, Chataqua Lake, and Conewango Creek, and entered the Allegheny River at the mouth of the latter stream, July 29th, at a point 188 miles above Pittsburg-

A novel feature of this expedition was the burying of leaden plates at various points, bearing, with the date, an inscription to the effect that the expedition had taken formal possession of the territory in the name of the King of France. A sheet iron plate stamped with the arms of the King was also in each case attached to a tree near by. The first of these plates was deposited with due ceremony at the point at which Céloron entered the Beautiful River.

This manner of taking possession appears to have been peculiar to the French, and to have been employed only on a few occasions. What advantages it possessed it is difficult to imagine, and the more so as some of the plates have not yet been found.

The work of exploring the country and reconciling the Indians now began. Everywhere the Indians were found to have been won over to the English by the superior advantages they offered in trading; and, although Céloron expelled the traders he met, and extorted a promise from them not to return, he knew full well they would not keep it. The protestations of attachment which the Indians made to the French and to their Father Onontio, as they called the Governor-General, he knew were not to be relied on. Indeed, it was only fear that prevented them from breaking out into open hostility, evidence of which appeared on more than one occasion.

Had it not been for these unpleasant features of the expedition, we may imagine with what enthusiastic admiration their keen perception must have feasted on the native charms of that stream which extorted even from the rude, unimaginative savages, the name of the Beautiful River. Having spent all my life along its banks, and having followed its winding course for more than two hundred miles, I can bear witness to its surpassing beauty of its scenery, though the hand of man has robbed it of much of its original charms.   The alternation of wooded hill and bottom land, the outlets of many tributaries, the numerous islands that dotted its bosom, the ripples and eddies of its crystal current must then have presented a panorama upon which the eye could feast with ceaseless delight.

Having descended the Ohio as far as the mouth of the Miami, a distance of about 660 miles, the expedition entered the latter stream and ascended it as far as it was navigable for canoes, made the portage to the head waters of the Maumee, which they descended to Lake Erie, and returned to Montreal, were they arrived November 10th, having journeyed about twelve hundred French leagues.

Father Bonnecamp also kept a journal of the expedition, in which among other things he noted the latitude and longitude of the principal points with considerable accuracy.   These two documents form a very interesting chapter on the early history of the Beautiful River; and the chaplain also drew, a map which furnishes a remarkably correct delineation of the course of this majestic stream, and the location of the numerous Indian villages that dotted its banks, supplies a valuable illustration to the journals.

The result of Céloron's expedition was, that, besides acquiring a more accurate knowledge of this part of their possessions, the French kept a close watch on the movements of the English, and held several councils with the Indians on the Ohio, especially through the influence of the half-breeds, Joncaire brothers, to maintain them in their allegiance to the Governor of New France.

The English, on their part, had not been idle.   The Governor of Pennsylvania continued to negotiate with the Indians, using for that purpose the services of Conrad Weiser and George Croghan, interpreters whose influence with the various tribes was greater than that of any other English colonists of the day.   The former met the various tribes in council at their principal village of Logstown, on the Ohio, about eighteen miles below Pittsburgh, in August and September, 1748. He kept a journal of his travels and negotiations with the Indians. Like the English traders, he came west by way of the Juniata, and crossing the mountains followed the Kiskiminetas to its confluence with the Allegheny. Croghan in company with Andrew Montour was sent on a similar mission to the same Indians in May, 1751, and his journal of the proceedings is also preserved. The Ohio Land Company, too, was on the ground. In 1750, they sent Christopher Gist to the Valley of the Ohio, wish instructions to explore the lands on the southern bank of the river, and report on their quality and fitness for settlement. It is remarkable that, having reached the Allegheny by way of the Kiskiminetas, he went down the west bank, and, passing behind the hill which lies in the present Allegheny city directly opposite the Monongahela River, remained in ignorance of the existence of that stream. He was again sent out on a similar mission in November, 1751, and spent the entire winter in his explorations. The journal of this expedition is still extant.

The way was gradually being paved for a conflict between the French and the English on this side of the water, notwithstanding that the home governments professed to be at peace. The initiatory step was taken by the French. They were anxious to secure their possessions by constructing a line of fortifications extending from the mouth of the St. Laurence to that of the Mississippi. The Beautiful River being the stream which ran nearest to the eastern boundary of their claim, the erection of certain forts upon it was necessary for the execution of their plan. No point was or could have been more important for either nation than the confluence of the Allegheny and Monongahela Rivers, the site of the present city of Pittsburg; and, consequently it is to this point that our attention is to be especially drawn.

In the year 1753, to use the language of the savages of that day, the chain of friendship was broken between the two nations, and the next year the hatchet was dug up. In the execution of their plan the French, in the spring of 1753, built a small fort at Presqu' Isle, on the Southern shore of Lake Erie where the city of the same name now stands; and, cutting a road to the head of canoe navigation on Le Bœuf River, now French Creek, constructed a second fort there immediately after. This determined Robert Dinwiddie, Lieutenant-Governor of Virginia, who claimed south-western Pennsylvania as part of the territory over which he held sway, to inquire into the movements of the French. For that purpose he sent, as the bearer of his dispatches, to the commander of the French at Fort Le Bœuf, at the close of the year 1753, a young man but twenty-two years of age, who was destined to write his name on the proudest page of the world's history—George Washington. Little did the sturdy Scotch governor think, when he introduced this youth into the arena of public life, that he would one day overthrow the power which he represented.

In the execution of his mission, Washington bore letters to the commander of the French forces, took careful notes of all that came under his observation, and returned in the early part of January, 1754. We are indebted to him for the first description of the spot upon which Pittsburg now stands. His report determined the Governor to send a detachment of men to throw up a fortification at the confluence of the Allegheny and Monongahela Rivers. They reached the place in command of Captain William Trent, on the 17th of February, and from that dates the permanent settlement of Pittsburg.

The French were actively engaged in the meantime in carrying out their original plans. During the winter Joncaire had worked with his usual success on the minds of the savages, and had induced them to consent to the erection of a fort at the mouth of the Le Bœuf River, where Franklin now stands. These forts were not meant so much for defence, as for securing the portage from Lake Erie to the Allegheny River; the centre of active operations must be further down that stream. With the completion of the last fort early in the spring of 1754, Contrecœur, who was then in command of the French forces descended the river with an army of French, Canadians and Indians to the number of about a thousand; and on April 16, surprised Ensign Ward who commanded in the temporary absence of Trent. Landing above the unfinished works of the English, he summoned them to an immediate surrender. Having but forty men, there was no alternative; and the French took possession, the English retiring up the Monongahela. Insignificant as this action may appear in itself, in the light of subsequent events it was fraught with the most momentous consequence for both nations. It enkindled the flames of war between the two powers in three quarters of the globe, and despoiled the former after a seven yearss' struggle, of all their possessions; it served to discipline the colonial troops for the approaching contest which resulted in the achievement of American Independence; and it schooled for them a commander who shall ever stand in the foremost rank of the world's heroes.

In order to maintain the claims of their nation, the French built Fort Duquesne on the point of land at the coufluence of the two rivers, and it immediately became, though not wisely, the principal point of attack of the English.

I say not wisely; for had they directed their efforts to the capture of Fort Niagara, they could have reduced Fort Duquesne without striking a blow. Yet, as it was, Fort Duquesne may be said to have been for a time the central point in the world's history. For four and a half years the French held their little fort despite the best efforts of the English to dislodge them. The ill-fated expedition of General Braddock, which resulted in his defeat and death at the Battle of the Monongahela, July 9th, 1755, is too well known to need more than a passing mention. But, notwithstanding this success, fortune frowned on the cause of the French, and they were destined to reap the bitter fruits of their mistaken system of colonization. Little is known of their operations from the defeat of Braddock until shortly before their final withdrawal from the valley of the Beautiful River, except that they made occasional incnrsions into the English settlements, engaged in a few skirmishes and maintained the Indians in their allegiance. But the distance of the fort from the base of supplies, the difficulty, delay and danger of transportation, the time necessary for sending messages to the seat of government, the long march that reinforcements would be required to make to relieve the fort and the continual encroachment of the English settlements rendered their position at all times precarious. The Indians, too, were not to be relied on the moment the fortunes of the French began to waver. Rude though they were, they were yet able to understand the situation, and Christian Frederick Post and other agents of the English were secretly at work striving to alienate them from the French. Petty jealousies, by destroying harmony, also weakened the front the French presented to the enemy; and the successes of the English in the northeast presaged their final overthrow. The trifling successes they gained at Ligonier and near the fort in the early autumn of 1758, were but the last flickering of the taper before it expires. The fact that a large army was advancing under General F orbes, against which they could offer no effectual resistance, cooled the ardor of the savages; and the tardiness with which the English General advanced, by keeping the Indians in suspense, caused them to grow impatient and desert. Nor had the French presents wherewith to retain them. The inability of the French to receive reinforcements in time, or to hold the fort without them, became daily more apparent; and on the 24th of November, 1758, when the English forces were within ten miles of it, they blew it up and retired, some down the Ohio to the Wabash country, others up the Beaver Valley and the rest with their commander, up the Allegheny to Fort Machault at the mouth of Le Bœuf River. The star of the French in the Valley of the

Beautiful River had set never to rise.

Fort Machault was strengthened during the winter, and means of transportation provided with a view of descending the river with the opening of spring and retaking Fort Duquesne before the English, all of whom 'but two hundred, had retired to the east of the mountains, could reinforce it. But the menacing attitude of the English in the northwest made it advisable to await the result of their operations. In the meantime every means was employed to retain the Indians, upon whom so much depended, but they had lost confidence in the French, and cared little to follow them to almost certain defeat. With the siege of Fort Niagara, the forts in northwestern Pennsylvania, were abandoned, and with the fall of that stronghold, August 5th, 1759, all hope was gone. Communication between the east and west was cut off, and the final overthrow of the French power in the New World was at hand. The fall of Quebec, a few weeks later sealed its fate. "The funeral of Montcalm was the funeral of New France."

The French, true as yet to the faith of their fathers, were always accompanied in their expeditions and campaigns by a chaplain, those faithful missionaries and adventurous explorers, whose early letters to their superiors in the mother country must ever be the most valuable documents relating to our early history. The register of their labors in the field now under consideration is still extant, rescued from the dust and mould of archives and published to the world, thanks to the indefatigable labors of one whose name is too well known to need mention here.

During the occupation of Fort Duquesne the French passed up and down the Ohio, but more especially in winter when the severe climate of the north rendered it difficult to carry provisions and munitions of war from the posts on the St. Laurence. But, though they had trading posts on the river, and were scattered here and there among the Indian villages, there is no record of their having formed any permanent settlements. That was not their object even at the fort itself. Possession and occupation were all they aimed at for the present. It was not until more than thirty years later when the country had for the second time changed masters that an attempt was made to plant a French colony on the banks of the Ohio. The history of this colony, besides being painfully interesting, so far as its origin is concerned, is involved in considerable mystery. This I shall endeavor to unravel, with the aid of the best authorities at command. The first reference to an attempt to settle a French colony is found in a letter written by Thomas Jefferson to James Monroe, dated, Paris, November 11th, 1784, in which, among other things, he says : " There is here some person, a Frenchman from Philadelphia, who has drawn up a visionary scheme of a settlement of French emigrants, five hundred in number, on the Ohio. He supposes Congress, flattered by the prospect of such an addition to our numbers, will give them four hundred thousand acres of land, and permit them to continue French subjects. My opinion has been asked, and I have given it : that congress will make bargains with nobody; that they will lay down general rules to which all applicants must conform themselves by applying to the proper officers and not perplexing Congress with their visions . . . and that, therefore, I did not think they would encourage a settlement of so large a body of strangers whose language, manners, and principles were so heterogenous to ours." Nothing more is heard of this scheme; but in May or June, 1788, Joel Barlow was sent to Paris to dispose of lands on the north bank of the Ohio near the mouth of the Scioto. Whether he was commissioned by the Ohio, or by the Scioto land company, was long a matter of dispute; the supposed relation between these two companies was also debated with no little warmth. It may be well for us then to inquire into the relation, if any, that existed between them, and learn further by whose authority so glaring an imposition was practised on so many innocent and unsuspecting people. Says a writer on the subject : " The Scioto Land Company has been the subject

of considerable mystery, and the cause of much misrepresentation. I am not fully informed concerning its origin.
It was probably started during the negotiation of Dr. Cutler
with the old Congress, in 1787, for the Ohio Company purchase. Dr. Cutler arrived in New York July 5th, and carried
on his negotiations for a week; he was then absent another week
on a visit to Philadelphia, where the convention that formed the
federal constitution was sitting. On his return to New York,
the project for the Scioto Company was broached to him
by Col. William Duer, as appears from the following extract
from the Doctor's journal. "Colonel Duer came to me with
proposals from a number of the principal characters in the
city, to extend our contract, and *take in another company*. The
arrangements of Dr. Cutler with the government *made room*
for *another company*. But this other association was entirely
distinct from the Ohio Company. Yet it has been represented
that the Ohio Company was concerned in the alleged wrongs
toward the French emigrants in 1790, who were induced to
come over in expectation of the beneficial acquisition of
land in this quarter, by the agency of Joel Barlow. But
this imputation is entirely groundless. What were the actual
relations and doings of the Scioto Company previous to or
connected with that agency, I have never learned.

  "The arrangements and objects of the Ohio Compaey
are believed to have been very different. The aim of the
Ohio Company was actual settlement by shareholders. ...
The object of the Scioto Company seems to have been, solely and simply land accumulation; to purchase of Congress—
nominally at two-thirds of a dollar per acre—paying mostly
in continental paper money, at that time passing at an enormous discount—so that, in fact, the actual cost per acre
might not be more than eight or ten cents; then to sell at
prices which yield them enormous profits."

  It does not appear that the members of the Scioto Company had any sinister design beyond the securing of great
profit in the purchase and sale of public lands. With this

object in view, they authorized Barlow to offer the lands for
sale in France and invite emigration. but nothing is known
with certainty regarding the specific instructions he received.
The Ohio Company had nothing to do in the matter.   In
1790, Barlow began to distribute proposals in Paris for the
sale of lands on the north bank of the Ohio near the mouth
of the Scioto, at five shillings per acre; the proposals promising "a climate healthy and delightful; scarcely such a
thing as frost in winter; a river called by way of eminence
The Beautiful, abounding in fish of an enormous size; magnificent forests of a tree from which sugar flows, and a shrub
which yields candles; . . . no taxes to pay; no military en-
rollments; no quarters to find for soldiers." The proposals
were readily accepted, and many persons, and even entire
families disposed of their property preparatory to setting out
for this new land of promise. Supplied with title deeds, large
numbers, variously estimated at from five huudred to seven
thousand, embarked at Bordeaux, Nantes, Rochelle and
Havre, two hundred and eighteen leaving the latter port
February 19th, 1791, and arriving at Alexandria, in the District of Columbia, on the 3d of May.

   After spending nearly all they had accumulated from
the sale of their property in France, they reached their
destination by different routes only to find on their arrival
that Scioto Company owned no land, and had scarcely any
existence; and that their title deeds were not worth the paper
on which they were written. How are we to account for this
outrage upon the confiding colonists? Where should the
blame of fraud or mismanagement be laid? The only way
of satisfactorily accounting for it is on the hypothesis that
the Scioto Company expected to buy public securities to pay
for their purchase of Congress, at the excessively low
rates of 1787.   But the adoption of the Federal Constitution,
and the successful establishment of the Federal Government,
raised the credit of those securities and blasted the hopes of
speculation. But as the French were arriving in considerable
numbers, and the purchase was not yet effected, nor likely

to be effected soon, what was to be done? William Duer, Royal Flint and Andrew Cragie, who styled themselves "Trustees of the proprietors of the Scioto lands," applied to General Rufus Putnam and Dr. Manasseh Cutler, two of the directors of the Ohio Company for the purchase of certain interests in that company comprising 196,544 acres. The contract was ratified by the Ohio Company; and the lands of the French settlement of Gallipolis, as the emigrants named the town, were most probably made in consequence of this arrangement. General Putnam, as agent for Duer & Co., provided, at some $2,000 expense, for the accommodation of the French emigrants there, and by the failure of the firm had to lose most or all of it. The Company not only failed in securing the large purchases of Congress contemplated, but did not even succeed in obtaining the interests for which they had stipulated in the lands of the Ohio Company. They did not pay, and the contract with Putnam and Cutler became a nullity. All that was required by the contract, was that the Scioto Company were to pay as much proportionably, as the Ohio Company were to pay Congress, and relinquish to the Ohio Company pre-emption rights, which the Scioto Company was understood to have in reference to lands lying north of the Ohio Company's location. All was failure on the part of the Scioto Company. The French emigrants were planted at Gallipolis, and General Putnam was left to pay some $2,000 expended on behalf of the Scioto Company." Such, according to the best authorities, was the history of the ill-starred speculation.

If we turn from this to the elements of which the French pioneer company was composed, a party more unfitted than they could hardly be imagined, much less be found. It may well be doubted whether the history of the New World, with its endless variety of romantic adventure, furnishes a parallel to the Scioto colony. Transferred from a city life in the French Capital to the depths of a virgin forest, and forced from dire necessity to make the most of things, their situation may be better imagined than described.

Not a few of them were wood-carvers, gilders to his Majesty, coach-makers, friseurs, peruke makers and other artisans and artists whose usefulness in a new settlement few words are needed to declare. They must clear the ground, build their houses, and till their fields. Now, the spot upon which they were located was covered in part with those immense sycamore trees which are so frequently met with along the rivers of the West, and the removal of which is no small undertaking even for the American woodsman. The colonists were wholly at a loss what to do till a happy thought struck them, when they tied ropes to the branches, and while one dozen pulled at them with might and main, another dozen went at the trunk with axes, hatchets and every variety of edge tools, and by dint of perseverance and cheerfulness—for their cheerfulness never forsook them—at length overcame the monsters, though not without many hairbreadth escapes. But here another diffiulty met them. What was to be done with the trunks? A happy thought again led them out. Large trenches were dug in the ground and the huge trunks were rolled in and covered. A situation more painfully ludicrous could hardly be imagined.

Lamentable as their situation was, there were not wanting circumstances to increase their trials. The lands were not their own, and they had no motive for improving them, had they known how ; the location was not healthy; and to these must be added a scarcity of provisions amounting almost to a famine, and occasional incursions of the Indians on the settlement. Yet, notwithstanding the different tempers and pursuits of the colonists in their native land, and the privations and sufferings they had to endure in their new homes, they lived very agreeably together. Their houses were not built in the usual straggling style of a new settlement, but were placed in two rows or blocks of log cabins, each cabin being about sixteen feet square; while at the end was a large room, which was used as a council chamber and ball-room.

They employed American pioneers and hunters to aid

them in clearing the forests and tilling the ground, and the same hunters contributed toward their subsistence from the game which abounded in the forests, and which was very grateful to the palate of the ill-supplied colonists.

But it was evident from the beginning that the settlement must be broken up in time, owing to the people not being able to subsist on the provisions within their reach, or to purchaše lands. Some of them soon found their way to Detroit and Kaskaskia; a few were able to secure lands from the Ohio Company; but the greater part were so poor as to be unable to buy lands and so inexperienced as not to know how to till them even if they had them, or to earn a subsistence in any other way in the backwoods. A few philanthropic persons represented the matter to Congress, in 1795, and that body granted them 24,000 acres of land on the Ohio opposite the mouth of Little Sandy River, to which, in 1798, 1200 acres more were added. This large tract came to be known as the French Grant. The descendants of the original colonists who remained still occupy the spot, but are being gradually absorbed into the general population.

If we turn to the religious history of the colony, for it was composed entirely of Catholics, it will be found to possess an interest not to have been anticipated. Indeed it was all but the successful rival of Baltimore for the honor of the primatial see in the new republic. The history of the proposed see of Gallipolis, so far as it is known, is briefly this : The colony constituted one of the largest Catholic settlements in the United States, and the influence of the French King, to whom the people had formerly owed allegiance, being great, it was used in obtaining from Rome the nomination of a bishop for the settlement; which was not only providing the better for the spiritual necessities of the people, but also securing the appointment of the first prelate for the newly established republic, an honor to which the French were by no means indifferent. The question of the nomination was taken up about the year 1789; and the person selected was the Abbé Boinantier.   Says Rev. C. I. White : " The late Bishop Bruté, in his memoranda, alludes to the fact, stating that the Abbé Boinantier, of St. Roch, Paris, was appointed at Rome in 1789, Bishop of Scioto (Gallipolis).   'I knew Mr. Boinantier well,' said Dr. Bruté; 'he spoke to me of his nomination, and undertook to look for his papers, but not finding them readily, I only learned *ex auditu* this remarkable fact of a see having been established in Ohio as early as that period." The failure of the colony to establish itself permanently put an end to all thought of an episcopal see not only for the present but for ever.

The first visit of a Catholic Missionary to the place was that of Fathers Badin and Barrière during their journey to Kentucky, in 1793, of which Dr. Spalding, says : " The two priests remained for three days at Gallipolis, the inhabitants of which place were French Catholics, who had been long without a pastor.   They heartily welcomed the Missionaries, who, during their stay, sang High Mass in the garrison, and baptized forty children.   The good French colonists were delighted; and shed tears at their departure.   They were but a remnant of a large French colóny of about 7,000 who had emigrated to America four or five years previovsly."

The place is now unimportant, both from a civil and a religious point of view, being without a resident priest, and ministered to by the pastor of an adjoining congregation; and its future prospects are by no means flattering.

MARYLAND CATHOLICS IN PENAL DAYS (1759.)

ADDRESS OF YE ROMAN CATHOLICS TO YE GOVERNOR AGAINST YE £40,000 ACT AS DOUBLE TAXING THEM, WITH COPIES OF FORMER ADDRESSES TO HIS MAJESTY AND YE PROPRIETOR.

1. A fundamental law of the Province confirmed different times allows full liberty of conscience; notwithstanding this, in 1701, the Assembly made a Law for the banishment of all Priests exercising their functions, and soon after passed an Act for the suspension of that law for 18 months in regard of such Priests as exercised their functions in a private family only. Queen Anne in Council by an Order dated at St. James, January 3d, 1705-6, ordered the above Act of Suspension TO BE CONTINUED BY A NEW ACT WITHOUT LIMITATION OF TIME, alledging for reason that THE FORMER LAW TENDED TO DEPOPULATE THAT PROFITABLE COLONY.

2. (This Act of Suspension has never been repealed, notwithstanding since the year 1751 there have been every year Bills brought in for putting in Execution the severest penal Laws, alledging as motives sundry grievances against the Roman Catholics, to all which in general his Excellency Horatio Sharpe, Governor of that Province in his speech of the 24th of April, 1756, to the House of Assembly has the following answer: THE MAGISTRATES ASSURE ME (IN THEIR SEVERAL LETTERS) THAT AFTER A CAREFUL ENQUIRY AND SCRUTINY INTO THE CONDUCT OF THE PEOPLE OF THE ROMAN FAITH WHO RESIDE AMONG US, THEY HAVE NOT FOUND THAT ANY OF THEM HAVE MISBEHAVED OR GIVEN JUST CAUSE OF OFFENCE.

3. Its therefore humbly prayed that no law contrary to Q. Anne's above Act of Suspension be suffered to pass into execution without the previous consent of the crown or proprietor as tending to depopulate the Colony. The yearly

repeated Bills of late for putting Penal Laws in execution have already produced this Effect in some measure, one Gentleman of an affluent Fortune having already sold part of his Lands with intention to quit the country, and many others judging they shall be necessitated to follow his example— unless assured of enjoying their possessions in greater peace and quiet than for these eight years past.

To His Excellency, Hor. Sharpe, Esq. Gov. of Maryland.

The Petn. of sundry Roman Catholics on behalf of themselves and others of the same Communion residing in the Province aforesaid

Humbly Showeth :

That many of your Petrs. preferred a petition to their Honours of the Upper House of Assembly against a Bill then laying before them, Entitled An Act for granting a supply of £40,000 for his Maj^{ties} Service, and for the striking £34,015,6s,0 thereof in Bills of Credit and raising a Fund for Sinking the same by a clause of which the Lands of all the Roman Catholics residing within this Province are doubly taxed, a Copy of which Petn. we herewith offer to your Excell^r.

That notwithstanding the said Pet^r and the reasons suggested therein their Hon^m of the Upper House have thought fit to pass the said Bill.

That therefore our application to your Excell^y becoming necessary, we humbly show to your Excell^y that the Province of Maryland was granted by Charter the 20th day of June, 1632, to Cecilius Calvert, Baron of Baltimore, a Rom. Cath.

That the said Cecilius Calvert Ld. Baltimore's laudable and pious zeal for the Propagation of the Christian Faith was one of the motives for granting him the said Charter.

That in pursuance of the said Charter and his laudable and pious zeal, Cecilius Ld Baltimore caused declarations to be set forth inviting all persons believing in Jesus Christ to transport themselves into Maryland, then a wilderness inhabited by a cruel and savage people, promising an Equality of Freedom and favour and Liberty of conscience to all People so transporting themselves, and to their descendants and further engaged to ratify his said declarations and promises by a perpetual Law.

That in consequence of the said declarations and promises in the 1st Session of Assembly held in this Province, viz: in the year 1640, a perpetual Act passed Entitled an Act concerning Religion which confirmed the said declarations and promises concerning liberty of conscience.

That the same Act was again re-enacted in the year 1650.

That a Rebellion being raised about the year 1652 against Cæcilius Lord Baltimore and his Ld'p making complaint thereof to the then Lord Protector and against Richard Bennett, Esq. and others, his Highness by an order of the 2nd November, 1665, referred the same to the Lords Commissioners Whitlock and Widdrington who made a report which report was referred to his Highnesses Committee for Trade, etc., which committee in pursuance of the said Order took the premises into consideration, and upon proposals made by Richard Bennett and Samuel Matthews for the settlement and peace of the Province which they tendered to the said Committee to which his Lordship at the request of the said Committee gave his answers, which proposals and answers the said Committee for Trade did report unto his Highness together with their opinion and advice concerning the whole state of the case upon which his Lordship on the 23d of October, 1656, sent instructions to his Lieut. and council by a clause whereof his Lordship enjoined that the Act concerning religion whereby all persons who profess to believe in Jesus Christ have liberty of conscience and free exercise of their Religion be duly observed, etc.

That the said Cæcilius Lord Baltimore, on the 30th day of November, 1657, entered into Articles of Agreement with Richard Bennett, Esq., among which is the following article :

"Lastly, the Ld Baltimore doth promise that he will never give his assent to the Repeal of a Law established heretofore in Maryland by his Lordship's consent and mentioned in the said report of the Committee of Trade whereby all persons professing to believe in Jesus Christ have freedom of conscience there and doth faithfully promise upon his honor to observe and perform as much as in him lies the particulars above mentioned, and his Ldp doth hereby authorize and require his Ldps Govern'rs and all other his Ldp's Officers there to give assurance to the people of their due performance thereof," which said Instructions and Articles are in the Council Records Lib. H. H. fo. 1, 2, 3, 4, 5, and fo. 10, 11, 12 to which we humbly beg your Excell' will be pleased to be referred.

That an Act also passed on the 27th of April, 1658 to confirm the Articles between Ld Baltimore &c. and the Commissioners as may appear in Lib. C. & W. H. fo. 134 by which Act, the Act concerning religion is again, tho' not expressly, yet virtually confirmed.

That our ancestors had not the least grounds to suspect that their Roman Catholic descendants would be deprived of the benefit of a law so earnestly contended for by Protestants and so often and so solemnly confirmed at their request and so readily consented to by the Roman Catholics, for it is beyond doubt that Cæcilius Lord Baltimore and most of the Gentlemen then in power were Roman Catholics.

That in consequence of the royal charter and upon the faith of it; upon the declarations and promises of Cæcilius Ld Baltimore and the Act aforesaid, many Roman Catholics, Gentlemen of good and ancient families in the Kingdoms of England and Ireland, and many others of lesser note to avoid the penal laws in force in their native countries, and other vexations to which they were liable at home quitted their countries, their friends and relations and everything dear to them to enjoy these privileges, that Freedom, Liberty and Equality in every thing—here especially—a full liberty of Conscience, and to that end only transported themselves into this province.

That we need not enumerate the many, almost insurmountable difficulties they in their 1st settlement had to struggle with: The country was a vast and one uncultivated forest, the possessors of that forest, a savage and cruel people, with these they were obliged to wage frequent wars : the labour of clearing thickly wooded lands was almost intolerable, the scarcity of Provisions and these are not only of the conveniences but of the necessaries of life, almost insupportable, but above all the distempers and sickness attending a new unhealthy climate were most discouraging.

That the enjoyment of a full liberty of conscience, equal Freedom and equal privileges with their fellow subjects, and the good reasons they had to promise themselves that they should transmit to their latest posterity the same advantages, not only alleviated their hardships and sufferings but comforted them under them.

That they had the strongest reasons to entertain such hopes cannot be denied. A Protestant prince had granted the country to a Roman Catholic nobleman in order to propagate the Christian religion. That nobleman had issued declarations inviting all persons believing in Jesus Christ to repair to it under promise of an equality of Freedom and liberty of conscience : these declarations and promises had been confirmed by the Act concerning religion.

That the Roman Catholics in particular had no reason to suspect any infringement of their religion or Civil Rights, for it appears that in the year 1648 by the Council Proceedings from 1636 to 1657 fo. 183, to which we humbly beg to refer your Excellency, that part of the oath of the Lieut. or Chief Governor of the Province of Maryland was as follows:

"And I do further swear that I will not by myself nor any person directly or indirectly trouble, molest, or discountenance any person whatsoever in the said Province professing to believe in Jesus Christ, and in particular no Roman Catholic for or in respect of his or her religion nor in his or her free exercise thereof within the said Province so as they be not unfaithful to his Ldp or molest or conspire against the Civil Government established here under him, nor will I make

any difference of Persons in conferring of offices, rewards
or favours proceeding from the authority his said Ldp has
conferred upon me as his Lieut. here for or in respect of
their said religion respectively but merely as I shall find
them faithful and well deserving of his said Ldp and to
the best of my understanding endowed with moral virtues
and abilities fitting for such rewards offices or favours
wherein my prime aim and end from time to time shall
sincerely be the advancement of his said Ldps service here
and the Public Utility and good of the Province without
partiality to any or any other sinister end whatsoever and
if any other officer or person whatsoever shall during during the time of my being his said Ldps Lieutenant here
without my consent or privity, molest or disturb any Person within this Province professing to believe in Jesus
Christ merely for or in respect of his or her religion or
the free exercise thereof, upon notice or complaint thereof
made unto me, I will apply my power and authority to
relieve and protect any person so molested or troubled
whereby he may have right done him for any damage which
he shall suffer in that end, and to the utmost of my power
will cause all and every such Person or Persons as shall
molest or trouble any other Person or Persons in that manner
to be punished."

That it also appears from the said proceedings fo. 261,
that in the years 1648 part of the Oath of a Counsellor of
State was as follows :

" I do further swear that I will not by myself nor any
other Person directly or indirectly trouble, molest, or discountenance any Person whatsoever in the said Province
professing to believe in Jesus Christ and in particular no
Roman Catholic for or in respect of his or her religion nor
in his or her free exercise thereof within the said Province so as they be not unfaithful to his Ldp nor molest
or conspire against the Civil Government established
here under him. So help me God and by the contents of
this Book."

That it also appears by Lib, Y. fo. 48 containing a Journal and Acts of Assembly and other proceedings from the year 1641 to 1671 that part of the Oath of fidelity to be taken by the Inhabitants of Maryland is as follows:

"But will at all times as occasion shall require to the utmost of my power defend and maintain in all such his said Ldps and his heirs, just and lawful rights, titles and interests, priviledges, jurisdiction, Prerogative, Propriety and Dominion over and in the said Province and Islands thereunto belonging and over the people who are and shall be therein for the time being as are granted to his said Ldsp and his heirs by the late King of England in his said Ldps Patent of the said Province under the great seal of England not anyways understood to infringe or prejudice Liberty of Conscience in point of religion."

That it also appears the above Oath was enjoined to be taken by an Act of Assembly passed in 1650 by Lib. Y. fo. 46 and 47 which oaths and Acts further evince that the Act concerning religion was deemed an unalterable and Fundamental Law.

That it also appears that all authors who have treated either of the history or settlement of the Province of Maryland, say that all people resorting thither enjoyed liberty of Conscience and an Equality of all Civil Rights.

That the same authors also say that the 1st settlers were chiefly Roman Catholics and that many of them were Gentlemen of Family and Fortune, the truth whereof cannot reasonably be called in question if attention be had to the facts and papers hereinbefore quoted. For the Province being granted to a Roman Catholic, the Act concerning religion having passed, etc., the Roman Catholics looked upon Maryland as an asylum and place of rest for themselves and their posterity.

That notwithstanding several rebellions against the Government here, it continued to be so until the year 1688 or 1689, when a mutinous crew at once ousted the then Lord Baltimore of his Government and made the first breach of the Priviledges granted to all Persons here professing to believe in Jesus Christ.

That the disturbances continuing in Maryland, their Majesties King William and Queen Mary for reasons of State thought fit to take the Government of the Province into their own hands.

That from that period to this time at greater or less intervals many severe laws were made against the Roman Catholics residing within this Province.

That we need not enumerate to your Excellency the several laws by which we are oppressed as your Excellency we presume is well acquainted with them and as they are readily to be found in our Body of Laws, but this we must say, that by these laws we are almost reduced to a level with our Negroes not having even the priviledge of voting for persons to represent us in Assembly; in short, they deprive us of all the advantages promised our ancestors on their coming into this Province and so solemnly and in appearance well confirmed to them and their descendants.

That however grievous and oppressive the laws heretofore enacted against us are they touch not our Property in any other manner than by subjecting us to the payment of 40 £ Poll to the established Clergy.

That the Bill now before your Excellency is the only one by which our load of Taxes is made heavier to us than to our fellow subjects.

That we humbly conceive no just cause or reason can be assigned for laying this unequal Tax.

That we heartily protest and declare that we have never given the Government any just cause of complaint against us and that we have always behaved as peaceable, dutiful and loyal subjects, that not any among us have been called in Question or persecuted for a turbulent or seditious behaviour.

That we have given not only undoubted Proofs in our

Address to the Honble the Upper House of Assembly of our peaceable behaviour to which address your Excellency has been already referred, but of our readiness and inclination to serve the Government and assist our suffering Protestant fellow subjects.

That we are so conscious of our innocence that we defy the most inveterate of our enemies to charge us with even the appearance of a crime.

That if calumny is to fix guilt we own ourselves most guilty, if Slander and palpable notorious lies are admitted in evidence against us, we must be condemned: if it be criminal to be Roman Catholics, we must own ourselves criminals, But we protest no other crimes can be laid to our charge.

That when our Roman Catholic ancestors quitted their native countries that they and their posterity might enjoy Freedom and peace of conscience here they little dreamt that we should be troubled on the score of religion.

That it is evident they did not cross the ocean and encounter all the difficulties they underwent for a temporary enjoyment of liberty of conscience to themselves only.

That they did not fly from Penal Laws foreseeing that their posterity would be subjected to them here.

That we beg your Excellency reflect, that the bulk of the 1st settlers here were Roman Catholics, that they at the expense of their fortunes, and many of them at the price of their blood, without recapitulating the many other hardships they underwent according to the other end of the charter enlarged the King's empire and dominion, and thereby have not only increased the Trade and riches of their mother country but laid the foundation of the present flourishing state of this Province from which his Ldp draws annually noble and splendid fortune and that therefore we humbly conceive his Ldp not only in justice but in gratitude is bound to preserve to us our Rights and Liberties which the double tax strikes at and as his Ldp sensible of your merits has constituted you his Governor and Representative we hope you will not pass the clause we have so just reason to complain of.

That we had not the least reason to suspect that under his Majesties just and mild Government an attempt would be made to invade those our rights which Oliver Cromwell held sacred and did not disturb.

That Oppressions and persecutions have always proved hurtful to States.

That some if not all the Roman Catholics in the Province may be forced into other provinces to the great prejudice of Maryland.

That we are sensible we are charged with disaffection to his Majesties person and Government but we aver it to be a scandalous calumny and a charge unsupported by the least glimpse of a Proof.

That under his Majesties long, mild and happy Reign, his British Roman Catholic subjects have enjoyed an uninterrupted series of Peace and Quiet.

That his Majesties Roman Catholic subjects in his foreign Dominions as far as we are informed equally partake of his favours and affections, and in return pay him a sincere Tribute of love and Duty.

That your Excellency is well acquainted that the Roman Catholics residing in this are in number very inconsiderable compared to the other Inhabitants.

That your Excellency knows this Province is surrounded by populous Protestant Colonies, and that therefore the Roman Catholics must be not only Fools but Mad men to entertain any thoughts of disturbing the peace of the Government.

That we do not charge our enemies with being fools, or madmen, but we submit it to your Excellency to determine what character they deserve who lay such black charges to our doors not only without proof but even without the shadow of probability.

That what we have set forth relating to our duty and Loyalty to his Maj^ᵗⁱᵉ is not mere assertion but contains the sincere sentiments of our hearts, we hope to show by the Copies of the following address, which we here insert. The 1st is an Address to his Majesty on his accession to the throne; The second is an Address to the late Lord; and the third is also an Address to the late Lord on his coming into this Province. To which we add his Ldps kind answer which we humbly hope your Excellency will at this time make good to us.

1st.

To the King's Most Excellent Majesty :

The humble address of the Roman Catholics of the Province of Maryland.

Most Gracious Sovereign,

" We your Majesties most dutiful subjects the Roman
" Catholic Inhabitants of the Province of Maryland under the
" government of Lord Baltimore, Lord and Proprietary there-
" of out of our true and unfeigned sense of Gratitude for the
" great clemency and goodness of your late royal father to-
" ward us, humbly beg leave to express to your Majesty the
" share we bear with the rest of your Majesties subjects in
" the general grief of the British Empire on the death of
" our late most gracious sovereign, and as we have the same
" happiness with them to see your Majesty peaceably succeed
" to the Crown of your great father, we humbly beseech your
" Majesty to give us leave to join with them in our hearty
" congratulations, and in all humility we beg your Majesties
" gracious acceptance of our constant allegiance and duty ac-
" cording to our utmost capacity in this remote part of your
" Majesties Dominions, and we humbly hope by our Loyalty
" and a steady and constant adherence to our duty to deserve
" some share in that tender concern your Majesty has been so

" graciously pleased to express for all your subjects. We
are May it please your Majesty, your Majesties most dutiful
SUBJECTS AND SERVANTS.

2nd.

TO THE RT. HON. CHARLES LD BARON OF BALTIMORE ABSOLUTE
LD AND PROPRIETARY OF THE PROVINCES MARYLAND AND
AVALON,

The humble Address of the Roman Catholics of the
Province of Maryland.

" We your Ldps most dutiful tenants the Roman Catho-
" lics of Maryland humbly beg leave to return your Ldp our
" most sincere and hearty thanks for the honour your Ldp
" has been pleased to do us in sending us your worthy brother
" for our Governor, from whose prudence and wisdom we
" cannot but promise ourselves all the happiness a people can
" wish for.

" We are truly sensible for this and many other instances
" of your Ldp's goodness, how much you have at heart the
" welfare and prosperity of your people of Maryland and beg
" leave, in the humblest manner, to assure your Ldp we shall
" always retain the most grateful remembrance of it; and as
" we had the honour to be witnesses with what tenderness
" and affection your illustrious ancestors cherished this young
" colony so 'tis the utmost pleasure and satisfaction to us to
" see your Ldp tread so closely in their Glorious footsteps.

" We humbly entreat your Ldp would out of your great
. " goodness be pleased to do us the honour to present to his
" most sacred Majesty the tender of our duty and allegiance
" which we humbly offer in an address and we firmly propose
" in conformity to it always to approve ourselves as dutiful
" Subjects to his most sacred Majesty as we have been faith-
" ful tenants to your Ldp and your most noble ancestors.
" We are

May it please your Ldsp,
Your Ldps most faithful Tenants and Humble Servants.

3rd.

To the Rt. Hon. Charles Ld Baron of Baltimore, absolute Ld and Proprietary of the Provinces of Maryland and Avalon, &c.

The humble Address of the Roman Catholic Inhabitants of the Province of Maryland.

May it please your Ldsp:

" We your Ldps tenants the Roman Catholics of this
" Province beg leave to approach your Ldp with sincere con-
" gratulations on your Ldps and Ladys safe arrival into this
" your province which your pious and noble ancestors have
" founded with unwearied application, great zeal, hazard and
" expense to the enlargement of the British Empire and to
" the perpetuating their glorious memory to latest posterity,
" and we have undoubted reason to conclude from your Ldsp's
" prudent conduct in the Administration of affairs that your
" L'dship's character will be no less conspicuous for carrying
" on and encouraging what they so nobly and wisely began.

" Our constant allegiance to his most sacred Majesty—
" our dutiful regard for his royal family and our obedience
" to your Ldps Government will we hope always merit
" your Ldps favourable countenance and protection and we
" assure your Ldp that none of your Ldps tenants exceed us
" in their hearty wishes, for the welfare and prosperity of
" your noble family and of the Province of Maryland.

" It was with great satisfaction we heard your Ldsp was
" called to attend near the person of his Royal Highness
" the Prince of Wales, an honor conferred on few and
" the most deserving. To be so distinguished by your Prince
" sets your merit above the reach of our applause.

" We heartily wish that your Ldsps stay here may be
" as agreeable and pleasing to your Ldp as it is desirable to
" us and that wheresoever you be, after a long and happy
" life, honoured by your Prince, beloved by your tenants,
" you may enjoy the blessings by the Omnipotent prepared

" for the good and just, is the sincere and hearty prayer
' and wish of

My Lord,

Your Ld'ships most Dutiful, most obed't and most

HUMBLE SERVANTS AND TENANTS.

HIS LORDSHIP'S ANSWER.

Gentlemen,

" I thank you for your kind Address, and cannot but
" be in a particular manner pleased with that dutiful regard
" which you express for his Majesty and the Royal family
" the continuance of which will always secure to you my
" favour and protection."

That it cannot with reason be asserted that the fore-going Address were calculated to serve any other purpose or end than that which upon the face of them it appears they were designed to answer.

That from the year 1717 or 1718 to the year 1751 we were undisturbed, and tho' deprived of our rights and Priviledges we enjoyed peace and quiet.

That so many and so great were the hardships already laid on us that we saw no grounds to apprehend more, and that therefore as these Addresses were presented while we enjoyed that peace and quiet, and at such distant periods, and at such times as naturally gave rise to them, as they sprung merely from our inclination, as we might have omitted them without incurring any note of disaffection we doubt not that your Excellency in justice to us will conclude that they were as sincere as they were voluntary.

That we are convinced it would have shocked your Excellency's humanity had there been a clause in the law before you to hang the Roman Catholics.

That we hope it will no less alarm your justice to double tax us without offence for tho' to take away a man's life be a greater sin than to deprive him of his property, the law makes no distinction in punishing the injustice of either transgression.

That we again most solemnly protest we have not committed the least offence against the Government. That we have always behaved as good and peaceable subjects.

That not any among us have been juridically charged with any offence against the government or peace of society.

That therefore the double tax laid on us by the Bill before your Excellency is laid without reason and foundation.

Wherefore and in consideration of the premises and the facts hereinbefore set forth. We humbly pray your Excell'y not to give your assent to the Bill before you whereby our Lands are double Taxed, or to any Bill whereby any particular or partial Tax or other pains, hardships or penalties may be laid on us or any of our communion residing within this province.

And your Petitioners as in duty bound will pray, &c., &c.

PETITION SENT BY THE COMMITTEE OF THE ROMAN CATHOLICS OF NEWCASTLE TO THE CONVENTION CHOSEN TO FORM A CONSTITUTION FOR THE NEW STATE OF MAINE.

To the Hon. Convention to be convened at Portland, on the second Monday in October, A. D. 1819, for the purpose of forming a constitution or frame of government for the State of Maine.

We the Subscribers, inhabitants of Maine and members of the Catholic Church, being a committee appointed specially for this purpose, by a branch of the same Church at Damariscotta, beg leave humbly and respectfully to address your Hon. Body in behalf of the Catholics of Maine.

Nearly three centuries have elapsed, since the Catholic religion has been proscribed by the laws of the country from which our pious Ancestors came. Our Ancestors unfortunately imbibing the spirit which dictated those proscriptive laws, established the same system of exclusion in this happy country. From the first settlement of Massachusetts by Europeans, to our Revolutionary War, the Catholic had been deprived of the Rights of a citizen; and since the adoption of the constitution of this State, no Catholic could hold any office of honor or trust, because he would not betray his conscience or his religion.

The oath of abjuration in that revered instrument, so far as it relates to the spiritual primacy of the Bishop of Rome, no Catholic can take or subscribe. While he is obliged by the law to fight for national rights, while he cheerfully takes up arms in defense of the Honor of his native country, while he pays his just proportion of the public taxes, he lives an alien on the very inheritance of his fathers: and what had he done to be thus disfranchised of the natural and inalienable rights of a citizen? Nothing. But he is a Catholic.

Whatever necessity there might have been in a political point of view, for proscribing Catholics, throughout the British Empire in the sixteenth century; that necessity has certainly ceased in this country. The laws therefore ought to cease also. If to effect a mighty revolution in the religion of a large and respectable portion of the Christian world, penal laws against Catholics were necessary: Now, since that revolution has resulted in the quiet and permanent establishment of the Protestant religion, there no longer exists the least necessity for those laws. In Great Britain and Ireland where those laws were the most severe and of the longest continuance, to wit: from the reign of Henry VIII. down to George III. inclusive, the Catholic is now raised to an equality with his fellow citizens: and shall it be said that the enlightened State of Maine is less wise, less just, less humane than an old and corrupt monarchy? Forbid it Heaven.

Were there any known public and acknowledged dogmata of the Catholic Church hostile to government in general or to republican institutions in particular, the undersigned would be silent: They would be ashamed to approach your Hon. Body and ask for the enjoyment of those immunities, those rights which were given by our Creator to every citizen. But whatever party writers in party times and for party purposes may have said, or whatever religious bigots may have written to establish upon a permanent foundation the Reformation, it is now universally acknowledged by all candid and learned Protestants of all sects that there is nothing in the acknowledged doctrine or discipline of the Catholic Church which is in the remotest degree unfriendly to republican institutions: on the contrary, it is an admitted fact, that the Catholics of the British Empire as well as those of this country always have been strenuous assistants and heroic defenders of the equal rights of man. A reference to Protestant English historians will prove this important fact incontestably.

It is painful to the undersigned, who duly appreciate the blessings of freedom, to be obliged to defend the religion of their ancestry from charges which never had existence except in the brains of designing men who propagated them for the purposes of ambition and self aggrandizement. The God of nature designed that all men should enjoy equal rights and privileges without any regard to their religious dogmata. That religion is a matter between the Creator and creature, and that the creature is answerable for his religious belief to no being but his God, are principles which it cannot be necessary to prove in the enlightened nineteenth century.   If the Catholic demean himself as a peaceable citizen, if he in his religious worship do not disturb the public peace or introduce indecencies or immoralities, tending to the subversion of civil society, if he take up arms and march to the field of battle in defence of the sepulchres of our forefathers and in maintenance of the rights, the honor, the liberties and independence of his country: the undersigned are utterly unable to see why he should not enjoy equal privileges and immunities with his fellow citizens.

The excuse for disfranchising Catholics in Great Britain and Ireland as well as in this country is : that they are obliged by the principles of their religion to bear true faith and allegiance to a foreign power, that is to say, the Bishop of Rome, commonly called the Pope, and it is admitted that were it not for this, the Catholic religion, however enormous and full of superstitions, ought nevertheless to be tolerated in a Protestant State.   The undersigned beg leave respectfully to state in few words to your Hon. Body, the real doctrine of the Catholic Church upon this subject.

She believes and teaches that St. Peter was constituted by Jesus Christ the head, speaker or prolocutor of the Apostles. That as St. Peter made Rome his Diocese, every succeeding Bishop in that Diocese is also by Divine right head, speaker, prolocutor of Christ's Church upon earth. That this primacy is purely spiritual and that no Catholic on earth living out of Italy is any more bound by the principles of his religion to bear true faith and allegiance to the Bishop of Rome, as a temporal Prince, than he is to bear true faith and allegiance to the Emperor of Morocco. We acknowledge the Bishop of Rome to be merely the prolocutor of the Church, simply first among equals. This is all the faith and allegiance Catholics owe him or acknowledge.

This doctrine is proved beyond the power of contradiction in the history of Charles V.. Emperor of Germany, a zealous Catholic : and also by the conduct of tne English and Irish Catholics under the reigns of Henry VIII and succeeding sovereigns. So that were the United States at war with the Pope as in the above and other innumerable circumstances, the undersigned as well as all Catholics except those who live in Italy, the Pope's dominions, would feel it their bounden duty, by the principles of their religion, to take up arms and fight and conquer him by all the means of civilized warfare. Where then is their faith and allegiance to the Pope ? It never had existence except in the illusions of bigotry. As an ecclesiastical personage, all Catholics acknowledge the Pope as the visible head of Christ's Church on earth. In this sense they can never abjure his power. In all other respects the Catholic Church always has and always will readily abjure his authority.

They therefore humbly pray your Honorable Body to place the Catholics of Maine upon an equality with their Protestant fellow-citizens (an equality they enjoy in every other State of the Unon); and that the constitution which you are about to frame as the fundamental law of this State may contain no clause or provision requiring any man to renounce his religion or become proscribed, either to betray his conscience or be debarred of the privileges and immunities of the citizen and as in duty bound will ever pray.

Signed. { JAMES KAVANAGH, MATTHEW COTTRILL, WM. MOONY.

Newcastle, 12th Oct., 1819.

●

NOTES.

"The New York Literary Institution." Letter of F. George Fenwick.

GEORGETOWN COLLEGE, JANUARY 11th, 1856.

Dear Sir:—You must excuse me for not answering your kind favor sooner. I thought it much better to reply by documents than by my own *ipse dixit;* and hence, after examining a number of papers in our Archives, I subjoin more information than you requested, taken from the letters of Father Kohlmann himself and Father Grassi, actual superior of the Missions in and attached to Maryland.

In a letter to Father Grassi, dated New York, 21st of March, 1809, (N. B. F. G. was then at Stonyhurst College, in England,) I find as follows: "Three months ago, Archbishop Carroll, with the agreement of our worthy "Superiors, sent me to NewYork to attend the congregation together with "the diocess, till the arrival of our R. R. Bishop Richard Luke Concan- "non, lately consecrated at Rome. This parish comprises about 16,000 "Catholics so neglected in every respect, that it goes beyond all concep- "tion. My vicar, (Father Benedict Fenwick), is a zealous Father of the "Society, and a man of information. I have brought along with me four "members of the Society, to erect a College in this city, which blessed be "the Lord, is likely to succeed." He then gives a short account of the improvements made in the Church, on which he had already spent 500 dol- lars. Then he continues: " La table Sainte tous les jours remplie qui "étoit deserté auparavant, les confessions generales tout les jours, sans "discontinuer presque (car la plus grande partie de cette paroisse im- "mense sont des Irlandais qui dipuis qu'ils sont venus dans ce pays-ci, "n'ont jamais vu la face d'un pretre.) Trois sermons un Anglais, un "Français, l'autre Allemand, les dimanches, tandis que jusqu'ici on ne "donnoit qu'un en Anglais. Trois catéchismes chaque dimanche, tandis "qu'auparavant il n'y en avoit qu'un." Heretics every day instructed and "received into the Church; sick persons (at least four or five each day), "attended with cheerfulness at the first call; and ordinarily such as stand "in great need of instruction; and general confessions: application made "to all houses to raise a subscription for the relief of the poor, by which "means 3,000 dollars have been collected, to be paid constantly every "year.

In another letter to the same at Stonyhurst, dated 26th of July, 1809 Fr. Kohlmann, says: " We are building a new Church, of which the corner-" stone has been laid with much solemnity six weeks ago, and which we " expect will be finished against the end of next year. It is 124 feet by 81, " of a Gothic style. I wish the Society may have towards that time a Father " at hand to attend this new congregation. . . . . . Mr. Morris, one of our " chief trustees, has purchased five lots of ground, opposite to the front of " the new church, in a healthy and elevated situation, to build a college " upon. . . . . . As to our school, it now consists of about 35 of the most " respectable children of the city, both Catholics and of other persuasions, " among whom four are boarding at our house, and in all probability, we " shall have seven or eight boarders next August. . . . . . Almighty God " is pleased to bless our efforts; it has been observed by several that at the " six o'clock Mass, the church is almost more crowded than it was a year " ago at the last Mass of 11 o'clock; and that there are as many communi-" cants every Sunday, as there were formerly at Easter. It is a fact that " excepting a few individuals, all the rest of the Congregation had entirely " fallen off. If you will look upon as a kind of miracle, the conversion of a " man, who for these six, ten, twenty, forty, sixty years, has lived in a total " forgetfulness of his God and his duty, and begins a new course of life, " worthy of a Christian, then, praised be the Lord, he has done a thousand " such wonders, and is still doing them daily, as almost all our confessions " are of this nature. In short, everyone is glad to see that from the man-' ner in which church and schools are conducted, from the many regular " instructions, from the subscription for the relief of the distressed, and " from the subscription for our new Church, etc., etc., etc., the name of the " Catholic Church has become an object of the highest veneration to the " most respectable characters of this city. . . . . As to our Rt. R. " Bishop Dr. Concannon, I received from our most Reverend Archbishop " Carroll, an extract of a letter written by him to Abp. Troy, (*of Dublin*) " dated Rome, Nov. 19th, 1808. It is as follows: " after remaining four " months in Leghorn and its environs at a hotel, and expending a very con-" siderable sum of money, I (*Bp. Concannon*) was under a necessity of re-" turning to this city. You will do me a singular favour in procuring me " some information from Dr. Carroll. I wish to know what assignment or " provision there is for the support of the new Bishop. You will oblige me " by any information on this head, before my departure from hence, which " will be, God knows when," ' So far Bp. Concannon, Fr. Kohlmann con-tinues : "I doubt very much whether he is ever to come to this country, for " there is no positive provision made; but all depends on the congrega-" tion."

In the same letter, Fr. Kohlmann mentions again that he was charged with all the spirituals, till the arrival of the Bishop. I have not before me

any letters of Fr. Kohlmann during the year 1810, though I think they must
be in the house. The following is information which I received from a lay
brother who is now here with us, and who tells me that in September 1809,
a school was opened in a house in the city situated in Broadway; that the
Rev. Benedict Fenwick, with the four scholastics above mentioned, had the
regulation of it. The names of the scholastics seem to have been Michael
White, James Redmond, Adam Marshall and James Wallace. The three
last afterwards became priests: The first returned to Georgetown and then
left the Society. In 1810, they removed to what was then the country, and
there they remained under the name of the New York Literary Institution,
until its dissolution. Just before it broke up, they had seventy-four boarders attending the the schools. They delivered it into the hands of the Trap-
pists, under their Abbot, Fr. Augustin (I think his name was L'Estrange)
who conducted the school for a short time. While the Jesuits had it, (I
find this in a letter of Fr Kohlmann, dated 4th December, 1811,) the students consisted of the best families, both Protestant and Catholic, and he
was in expectation of building a house capable of holding 100 scholars
at least. He intimates that he intends in the Spring to establish a convent of Ursuline Nuns in the city, and that he wrote to London to Fr.
Betagh, to obtain them for him. He designed also to establish another
Convent of the Nuns of the Presentation, for the purpose of educating
the poorer children; and thirdly, an Orphan Asylum.

I come now to your third interrogatory. *What motives induced the
Society to suppress the Literary Institution ?* I will answer you by quoting
the very words of Fr. John Grassi, who was then our Superior in this
country. His letter to Fr. K. is dated from Georgetown College, Aug.
31st, 1813. " I must implore," says he, 'more than ever upon us the
" peace and charity of our Lord, in the present crisis of the Literary In-
" stitution, in order that the difference of my, from your, opinion on this
" subject, may have no consequences detrimental to that peace, charity and
" fraternal union, which is so proper for those who are joined together
" with the sweet ties of the Society of Jesus. In this spirit, I will now
" proceed to answer your favour of August 21st, being confident that you
" Reverence will read it and reflect upon it with the same disposition.
" You say there is no priest at present at the L. I. I know it; but both
" you and Father Fenwick knew the determination of calling Fr. Marshall
" to Georgetown, and that it was out of my power to send another. This
" very want of subjects has been the greatest reason for abandoning the L.
" I. I received a letter from Fr. Fenwick, in which he communicates to me
" the determination that had been taken; of giving up the L. I. on the 1st
" of November, and he requested the permission, which was granted, to
" keep Mr. Wallace till that epoch. Had he mentioned anything about Fr.
" Marshall's remaining till the same time, I should have no objection to

" it. But as at present the determination is taken of giving it up, it is clear
" that it is useless to be anxious now to send a priest for a month or two.
" However, if, as I am informed, you could succeed to make such
" arrangements as to keep it up, as a thing annexed to the mission, or
" to the Congregation (provided the Society had nothing at all to do with
" it), I would be very glad.

   " The Rev. Mr. Maréchal *(afterwards Archbishop of Baltimore)* a Sul-
" pitian, paid a short visit to this College It is confidently asserted that
" he is to be Bishop of New York, and the great concern he showed for the
" L. I. confirms me in this idea. I exposed to him our situation, the wan-
" of members, and he was sensible that such an Institution is onus insup-
" portabile for us, in the present circumstances, and for several years to
" come. I consulted again quite lately, the Most Rev. Archbishop Car-
" roll on this very subject; and he answered, that as the want of proper
" persons to carry it on is evident, this ought to be represented to those
" who are concerned in it. If there could be found persons who would
" take care of it and continue it on, all the profit would be theirs, etc., etc.;
" that if ever the Society should increase, we would preferably to any new
" establishment, come to its assistance, etc., etc."

   Father Grassi adds: " If ever it should be deemed proper, there could
" be procured an attestation of the Most Rev. Abp. Carroll and Bp. Neale,
" of the real want of subjects, etc., or of our inability to attend the L. I."
Thus far Fr. Grassi. I may remark here that from other letters of Fr. Kohlmann, previous to the date of Fr Grassi's, it appears that he (Fr. K.) was
once favourable to the suppression of that Institution.

   I will add something with regard to the manner in which the College
was conducted, taken from the letters of Fr. Kohlmann. In one, dated 23rd
June, 1812, when Fr. Kohlmann lived in New York, and Fr. Fenwick presided as Rector over the Institution out of N. York, I find the following
words : " Collegium Neo-Eboracense satis bene procedit Præter nostros,
" duo externi magistrorum officio funguntur, boni moratique juvenes. Con-
" victores pietate pariter ac Scientia imbuuntur."

   Besides the four scholastics whom Fr. Kohlmann took with him on his
going to N. York, there were several others who were engaged as teachers
in the College: Such was the Rev. Joseph Gobert, who afterwards was ordained by Archbishop Neale, and for a time was in the College of Georgetown: the Rev. Peter Malou, of whom, perhaps, you will find in N. York,
persons who know more. for he died there than we do. There was also a
Mr. Keegan, a man who had only one arm, who afterwards came among us
at Georgetown, as a hired teacher; and who subsequently went to the West,
and terminated as a Judge, so I am told, in some of the Courts there.

   I have thus, not only, I think, answered to your inquiries, but also
given you other facts which may direct you to a further investigation of the
history of the Literary Institution. There are persons still alive in N. York,
who were actually scholars of that place, and at Philadelphia, there is the
Rev. Fr. Vespré, at St. Joseph's Church. who was for a time a dweller in
the house. I have nothing more to add, except that you excuse me for
being as tardy in my answer. You can appreciate the motives of it which
I mentioned above.

                    Yours respectfully,

                         GEORGE FENWICK.

QUERY.

Mottin de la Balme—A cavalry officer of this name received a commission from the Continental Congress and was killed in an action in the West. Was he the author of " Elemens de Tactique pour la Cavalerie," Paris, 1776; and Essais sur l' Equitation," Amsterdam and Paris. 1773 ?

Mouquet.

BOOK NOTICES.

The Latest Hymn Writers and their Hymns. By the late Samuel Willoughby Duffield. Edited and completed by Prof. R. E. Thompson, D.D. Funk & Wagnalls, 1889, 8vo., 511 pp.

It is with a feeling of self condemnation that we take up this elegantly printed and scholarly volume, impressed with the fact that it is a tribute of Protestant scholars to the gloricus hymns of the Church, and that we have no similar work from a Catholic pen. The day has passed when the liturgy and offices of the Church were scoffed at as relics of heathenism, barbarous and destitute of religious and moral beauty as well as of literary merit. Beginning with the use of hymns and canticles in the earliest period of the Church, we are led through the Syrian and Greek to the Latin hymns, and find historical and critical notes beginning with Fr. Hilary, Pope Damasus, St. Ambrose, Prudentius, Sedulius, St. Gregory the Great, St Bede, the Authors of the " Veni Creator," and " Veni Sancte Spiritus," St Bernard, Thomas of Celano St. Thomas Aquinas, St. Bonaventure, "The Stabat Mater," St. Francis Xavier, to the Hymns of the Roman Breviary.

The volume is supplied with valuable indexes and translations of many hymns are given. It is not often however that the real meaning or spirit of the original has been preserved by modern translators, and the multitude who have failed to render the " Dies Irae " into English shows that its real purport and meaning have escaped the translators who did not meditate before attempting to translate.

While to Catholics there are many statements and judgments in this volume that will excite criticism, the work on the whole is fairly done, and we may be thankful for a manual on the hymns of the Church so comprehensive and so scholarly. In the bibliographical notes we find a reference to a work by Dr. Zardetti, now Bishop of St. Cloud, "Die Kirchliche Sequenz."

ANNOUNCEMENT.

We are happy to learn that Rt. Rev. Bishop O'Farrell has selected and appointed Rev. W. P. Treacy, Historian of the diocese of Trenton. A work of thorough research and of great value may be expected from his pen.

UNITED STATES CATHOLIC
HISTORICAL MAGAZINE.

Vol. III.)   (No. 11.

DONGAN'S CHARTER OF THE CITY OF NEW YORK.

Read before the United States Catholic Historical Society
by John Gilmary Shea.

There is a subject which the Executive Council considered too important not to be commemorated by at best a
brief mention in a meeting of a Society devoted by its very
charter to preserve and make known all that relates to the
history of Catholics in this country.

The act is that by which on April, 1686, New York was
raised to the rank of a city, endowed with property and franchises. It was the act of a Catholic Governor acting in the
name and by authority of a Catholic Lord Proprietor, who
after making New York English and the keystone of a great
colonial system that was to secure to our tongue the pre-
ponderance on this continent, had ascended the throne of
England, the first and only Catholic to rule there during the
last three hundred years.

"The Dongan Charter" is a theme that we hoped to have
treated here by the Irish Catholic Mayor of New York, as
some remarks would come appositely from his lips, filling as
he does the Chief magistracy of a city chartered two centuries
ago by an Irish Catholic Governor.

I regret that the topic does not fall to better hands than
mine, and as I too can plead ill health, I beg your indulgence.

Some years ago, a high city official listening to an important debate in the Chamber or argument in Court heard

constant reference to the Dongan Charter. At last he leaned over to some other official near him and asked in a whisper ; "What *is* the Dongan Charter ?" His friend's blank visage did not require even the movement of his head to show his ignorance. An appeal to another City worthy resulted in no more satisfactory elucidation of the problem, and the high official resigned himself to the prevailing ignorance. But the allusions to "Dongan's Charter" became too much for human nature. He rushed out of the City Hall, secured a carriage on Broadway and ordered the coachman to drive at once to the New York Historical Society. Alighting, he mounted the stairs, and the staircase of that venerable institution was not planned with an eye to the comfort of well fed city offiicials and entering the Library asked of the Custodian of books, his great conundrum ; "What is the Dongan Charter.?" The answer came promptly: it was the charter making New York a city and giving it extensive rights, granted April 22d, 1686 in the name of James II King of Great Britain and Ireland by Colonel Thomas Dongan, an Irish Catholic Gentlemen, then Govenor of the province of New York. But where is this great document. ! " was the next question. "The original in several large sheets of parchment with its seals is preserved in the office of the Comptroller." "What down in the Park ?" "Undoubtedly." "And where can I see a copy ?" "More or less correctly in the City Charter, in many collections of Laws relating to the City and in many of Valentine's Common Council Manuals."

After examining a copy he hurried back, and studying it at leisure set up as a pundit in regard to "Dongan's Charter."

In the remarks about to be presented, I am far from implying in my audience any such ignorance as to the Dongan Charter, or the Governor who granted it, or of the reign and the times in which he lived. Much less do I pretend to give a full or comprehensive account, for it would require a volume to present real facts and sweep away accumulated dust and cobwebs that have long passed for history.

The elevation of New York to the rank of a city was

only one of a series of wisely planned and ably guided acts looking to the future well being and greatness of America. It was important not to the city only and the colony of New York, but to the English empire in America, which the house of Brunswick subsequently received, but lacked statesmanship and honesty enough to retain. The Guelphs lost and lost dearly what the Stuarts consolidated and secured. This to some may be viewing history from a new standpoint, but it is a correct view.

Any one who passes rapidly in mind over the list of English monarchs whose rule extended to this country, will see little interest displayed by any of them in its actual or future prosperity. Elizabeth gave grants, James did the same and wrote a book to injure tobacco, the great staple of Virginia; Charles I made land concessions, but that was all. Cromwell did nothing but involve Maryland and Virginia in strife and confusion. Pleasure loving Charles II of his own impulse would have done as little for America as any of his predecessors; but his brother James was a man of different stamp. Eminently a man of action and administrative ability, James, Duke of York, applied himself during his exile to acquire military experience and saw service under the best general of his time. After the restoration he was made Lord High Admiral of England, and he set to work to increase the efficiency of the British navy. The rules drawn up by him were so wise, so thorough and so practical that they were maintained till our time, and the Nelsons, the Rodneys and the Hoods, the men who made England mistress of the seas, were trained under the system introduced by James, whom venal or careless historians persist in holding up to us as a shallow, bigoted man.

In France he had learned from the numerous books printed on Canada and Acadia, the extent of the French empire in America, and saw how the indifference of the English government was periling not only the future sway of our continent, but the very existence of the two neglected groups of colonies, Virginia and Maryland at the south, and New England at the north, colonies posssessing no common bond or tie, colonies not homogeneous in government, religion or policy.

Reviving an old English claim, James solicited from his brother a grant of the territory colonized by the Dutch and that was wrested by them from the Swedes. As head of the navy he sent over the vessels and force necessary to take possession. New Netherland disappeared from the map, and New York, a new English colony became the connecting link between New England and Maryland, and as his grant included Maine, the British flag floated from the Penobscot to Cape Fear, over a series of colonies in unbroken line. We see his influence too in the grant of the Carolinas to a number of noblemen, completing the occupation of the coast and confronting the French in Acadia at the north, and the Spaniards in Florida at the south.

That the credit is due to James and not to any settled policy of English statesmen is evident, from the fact that this plan had no precedent, and that for nearly half a century after the fall of James not a step was taken to extend the limits of the British coast line his genius had secured.

To develop the province he had himself acquired James transferred the country between the Hudson and Delaware to others who soon peopled New Jersey. His friend William Penn, interested in that colony, soon became Proprietor of Pennsylvania, as all know, by the aid and support of James. In New York he established English laws, introduced English settlers and developed the resources of the province. There he established liberty of conscience. Bancroft says that "no glimpse of it reached James," and that he was "an advocate of toleration without a sense of the natural right to freedom of conscience," but that James was in the full sunshine instead of getting a mere glimpse is proved by his acts. He established religious freedom in New York and lost his throne for endeavoring to establish toleration in England.

Let me quote a more impartial writer, one not biased by hereditary New England hate of James, never forgiven for his endeavor to bring that part of America into harmony with the British constitution.

"Determined to give his American province the franchises its people desired, the Duke of York sought an able colonial governor to take the place of Andros * * * * The man chosen by James was Colonel Thomas Dongan, born in 1634, a younger son of an Irish baronet, Sir John Dongan, and a nephew of Richard Talbot, afterward created Earl and Duke of Tyrconnel in Ireland. Thomas Dongan, of course, gained advancement by his brother's and his uncle's influence at the English court. Dongan was quickly promoted to be a colonel in the royal army, and having been assigned to serve with his Irish regiment under Louis was stationed for some time at Nancy. In 1678 he was ordered home from France, to his pecuniary loss; but was rewarded by Charles with a pension and the appointment of Lieutenant Governor of Tangier, in Africa, under Lord Inchiquin, whence he was recalled in 1680. Dongan was a Roman Catholic, enterprising and active; coveting money, yet "a man of integrity, moderation and genteel manners." His experience in France was an important recommendation, because of the delicate relations between New York and Canada, and the necessity of managing them skilfully on the English side. Dongan was accordingly appointed governor of New York."

Such is the language of John Romeyn Brodhead, historian of our State, a scholar and man of thought, with no bias in favor of an Irishman or a Catholic.

Several new officers came over with Dongan. "The Rev. Doctor John Gordon was also commissioned to be chaplain of the soldiers in New York. An English Jesuit priest, Thomas Harvey, of London, likewise accompanied Dongan, who embarked for America in the old Parliamentarian frigate 'Constant Warwick.' With a considerable retinue Dongan arrived at Nantasket, and set out for New York overland, accompanied some ten miles to Dedham, by a troop of Boston militia, besides several other gents of the town." Brodhead "History of the State of New York, ii pp. 370–375. This was in August, 1683.

About two weeks after his arrival on this island, Dongan summoned the first assembly of the province of New York.

When James became proprietor, such a step with a people ignorant of British laws and government, would have been useless. To give the power to the handful of English who came over, would have been to make a petty minority govern the majority. New York had in twenty years years however developed and James who wished the people to be governed impartially now established a form of goverment in which he aimed to give the legislation to the free-holders, securing on their part a loyal dependence on the British crown, wiser in his generation than the Georges in the next century.

On the 17th. of October, 1684. the seventeen delegates to the first New York Colonial assembly met with the Governor and Council in Fort James, the English fort between the Bowling-green and the bay. The first and grandest of its acts was "The Charter of Liberties and Priviledges," securing the rights of British subjects and establishing entire freedom of concience and religion to all peaceable persons which profess faith in God by Jesus Christ."

Thus is Dongan's name linked with an act and a day memorable in the annals of New York.

But this is not his only claim to a place in history. He at once took a firm stand for New York Colony and its rights. While Thomas Dongan was Governor of New York no infringement on its territoral or other rights, be it from the French in Canada, the over reaching men of New England or the Proprietor of Pennsylvania or the Governors of Maryland and Virginia would be brooked.

He was the bold, skilful, polished but determined upholder of the rights of New York. He was a splendid exponent of state rights.

Towards the French he presented a firm front. The noble missions of the Jesuits among the Five Nations had, as a Catholic, Dongan's warmest sympathy, but France could not make their pious labors the ground of a territorial claim. The territory of the Iroquois was within the limits of New York, and New York would not recognize any claim to a single foot of land in their occupation. He upheld the line of the great lakes as the natural border, and strove to keep the French from any foothold below that line. Seeing the importance of Detroit, he endeavored to occupy it as a key to the West. If the line of the lakes is now the northern boundary of the United States, we owe it to James II and his able lieutenant Thomas Dongan.

Maryland and Virginia had grounds of complaint against the Five Nations. They sought to negotiate with that wonderful confederacy. Dongan put his foot down. They are New York Indians. You can negotiate with them only in my presence and by my sanction. Lord Howard of Effingham came from Virginia to make terms with the Indians under the eye of the Catholic Colonel. His negotiation gave for all-time to the Virginians an Iroquois name. The Dutch interpreter wishing to convey to the Mohawks the meaning of Howard, took the nearest Dutch word he could find, one meaning a hanger or short-sword. This to the Indians was big-knife, and they called the Governor of Virginia Assarigoa, Big-Knife ; and that henceforward became the name for Virginians. Dongan's claim over the Five Nations endures to this day. When the Federal Government was formed, it attempted to pour its legion of Indian agents, contract schemers, and plunderers on the Indians in New York State, especially the Five Nations. Governor Clinton took his stand on Dongan's strong position. "The Six Nations are New York Indians. We tolerate no interference from the general goverment," and this attitude has been maintained.

Towards New England Dongan was equally firm. In the whole line of Colonial Governors there is not one who can be ranked higher than Colonel Thomas Dongan. Brodhead, indeed, accuses him of love of money, but more money was freely voted to him than future governors could wring by flattery or force. And Dongan freely spent the money in the public service. He left office with arrears of salary due him and large amounts advanced from his purse for public needs.

Among the memorable acts of his administartion was that of granting a Charter to the City of New York in the name of the King.

New York had enjoyed a kind of vague existence as a

city. It had the name without the substance. It had no powers that courts would be bouud to recognize.

To place the rights of the city on a firm basis, Dongan in April, 1686, in the name and certainly not without the sanction of King James II, issued a Charter in the name of James as King of England, Scotland, France and Ireland, and also as Supreme Lord and Proprietor of the Colony and Province of New Yord. It recognized New York as an ancient city confirmed all its rights whether by prescription or by any grant, formal or informal, from the States General or himself, or governors acting in their name.

Technically a city requires a bishop, but we were not ready just then to begin our line of bishops. In fact we had to wait sometime.

All lands granted to the city, the public buildings erected, the streets, ferries and all privileges, franchises, rights, royalties, free customs, jurisdictions and immunites exercised by the city were declared to be irrevocably vested in the Mayor, Aldermen and Commonalty of the City of New York. Still more important perhaps was the grant to the City of all waste, vacant, unpatented and unappropriated lands on the island, with all rivers, rivulets, coves, creeks, ponds, waters and water-courses, all land around the city down to low water mark with power to fill in and reclaim

New York was to have a Mayor, six aldermen and as many assistants, a town clerk, a chamberlain, a sheriff, a coroner, a clerk of the market, a high constable and a marshall. Nicholas Bayard was appointed the first Mayor, and of the six Aldermen two bear English and four Dutch names.

The Corporation thus created received power to reguulate trade, markets and fairs, to open new streets and ferries, and to pass ordinances for the government of the city.

The Mayor with the Recorder or some of the Aldermen was to preside in a Court of Common Pleas, and hold a criminal court for the trial of offenders.

Such were the principal topics of this Charter which

declares at its close "that such and no other construction shall be made thereof, than that which may tend most to advantage religion, justice and the public good; and to suppress all acts and contrivances to be invented, or put in use contrary thereunto."

That New York prospered under the Dongan Charter is seen by the tenacity with which the citizens clung to it. When further powers were sought and a new charter issued under Governor Montgomerie in 1730, care was taken to recite the Dongan Charter at full length and confirm it. That was the corner stone.

The able governor Dongan held his office till James in 1688 united the province of New York to New England, and placed all under the administration of Sir Edmund Andros.

Then Governor Dongan retired to his own estate, in the colony. He had acquired lands on Staten Island and Long Island; and had brought over two of his kinsmen, apparently intending to make New York his home and establish the Dongan family here. The fall of James II left New York in confusion. A wild German fanatic, Leisler, seized the reins of government in New York. Left by William III's indifference and neglect to do his will he launched the New York Indians on the French in Canada, and committed a frightful massacre at Lachine, compelling the French on their side to use Indians in war, as they did with fearful effect on New England and New York for many a day.

Dongan had taken no part in favor of the fallen monarch, but Leisler hunted him like a wolf, and the best governor New York had had was glad at last to escape to Rhode Island, and sail to England from the port of Boston where he had been so honorably received.

He reached England to find a foreigner on the throne, his brother the Earl of Limerick in exile, the property of the family confiscated. His own accounts as Governor had never been settled, and New York owed him heavy arrears. He petitioned in vain for the repayment of moneys which he had with public spirit advanced, and for arrears due him. It was not till after long delay that a pittance reached Dongan, a poor reward for long and able services to create a British Empire in America.

When his brother died and the Earldom of Limerick devolved upon him, he sought at least a portion of the immense estates in Ireland which had been confiscated, but the same niggardly policy prevailed.

The great governor of New York, Thomas Dongan, Earl of Limerick, died at last in the obscurity of poverty at London, and was interred in Saint Pancras' Churchyard, the chosen place of repose of Catholics of rank.

The Charter is still preserved intact in the office of the Comptroller of the city, but may easily be marred or destroyed. It is one of the oldest and most interesting documents relating to the city and its rights, and yet one gentleman seeking to consult it, found it used as a foot-rest by a clerk.

In the hope of being able to show the original Charter to the members of the Society, I applied to the Hon. W. Low, to permit it to be brought here this evening in custody of one of the officers of his department, Walter Dongan, a descendent of the great governor, being now one.   He received our application with great courtesy, but expressed his regret that he could not allow it to be removed from his office except under a subpoena from a court of justice.

We are not prepared just yet to involve ourselves in litigation, even with a skilful lawyer for our president ; but I question whether the comptroller has any right to the custody of the Dongan Charter.   He is not one of the ancient officers created by the charter, while the chamberlain is : but there seems no authority for any financial officer to hold the charters and rolls of the city, to be its "Custos Rotulorum."

When it was issued Dongan's Charter was surely committed to the custody of the Mayor, Nicholas Bayard, and the Clerk, John West.   It would seem therefore that the clerk is the proper holder of the same and responsible for its safe keeping.

LIBERTY AND PROPERTY

OR

THE BEAUTY OF MARYLAND

DISPLAYED.

Being a Brief and Candid Search and
Inquiry into her Charter. Fundamental Laws
and Constitution.

By a Lover of his Country.

The following is from a manuscript of the latter part of the seventeenth century, preserved in Georgetown College. The opening is unfortunately missing and there are several lacunæ. It is however, so important that it is here printed in its mutilated condition.

LIBERTY AND PROPERTY

OR

THE BEAUTY OF MARYLAND DISPLAYED.

* * * * * at her birth as I may, say * * * * * * *
* * * * Forces wch prevents all future discords, by a fundamental law giving equally liberty of conscience and an equal share in all rights and privileges are allowed to all christians, but a mutual love, union and concord are secured to them, by strictly forbidding under ye severest penalty's, the least reflection upon another's religion or way of worship. But to advance gradually, and let my arguments search into ye fountain head and begin with Maryland, or when Maryland began to be an English Colony.

It is to be observed that Maryland was first granted by King James I to Sr George Calvert, who was father to ye Ld Cæcilius, he to ye Ld Charles, he to ye Ld Benedict, and he to ye present Ld Charles, Baron of Baltimore, nor must I here omit remarking that ye said Sir George Calvert had for some years served King James ye first, in quality of Secretary of State, a post well known to be of profit, as well as of trust and honor, and consequently such as would be aspired unto by most, and voluntarily laid down by none, without a motive of the highest nature, and such was that of Sir George, who upon a conviction of conscience, thought himself obliged to postpone his temporal to his eternal interest, that is, by embracing the Roman Catholic religion to render himself unqualified for ye abovesaid office of Secretary of State, and the King being apprized and yet probably by Sir George himself, of this his change, was so far from forgetting his past good services, that to reward the same, he constituted him Baron of Baltimore, and passed a Grant

under ye
Governr of the said Provinces   Royal grant
issued after Sir George had declared himself a Roman Catholic and surrendered the Secretary's place.

Now ye said Sir George Calvert not long surviving the
abovesaid grant little could be done during his time towards
the effectual settling of Maryland, wch nevertheless had soon
a happy issue, under the auspicious life and government of
his son Lord Cœcilius, to whom the same grant, as to Maryland, was afterwards confirmed by King Charles I, in an
ample charter granted to the said Ld Cœcilius, who, *pursuing
his father's intentions, and excited with a laudable and pious
zeale, for the Propagation of the Christian Faith, and the
enlargement of ye King's Empire and Dominion, had humbly
besought leave of the King, by his own industry and charge, to
transplant an ample Colony of ye English nation into those
parts of America* now called Maryland, as the Preamble of
ye Charter does word for word appear, and here again I
must observe that ye said Ld Cœcilius was known to be and
professed himself a Roman Catholick, before, at and after
the granting of his Charter, and persevered therein until his
dying day : — so yt Maryland being first granted to Sir
George Calvert, upon the change of his religion, and afterwards confirmed to his son ye Ld Cœcilius a professed Roman
Catholick, it is   to suppose that the Crown designed that they who were to be hereditary Governors of
Maryland should have ye free use of their Religion wth other
privileges they there enjoy.

Cœcilius is no sooner Lord and Proprietor of Maryland
than he spares neither cost nor pains to people and improve
this Province; hence it is, that to encourage others to transport themselves thither, he soon publishes a declaration,
throughout all England and other ye King's dominions, that
whosoever of his Majesty's subjects would go and settle in
Maryland, should not only have a considerable Tract of land
granted unto them gratis, but should there enjoy all Rights
and Priviledges equally and without distinction ; and it was
upon this prevailing encouragement, that many English,

Scotch and Irish, of all religions. Church-men, Dissenters, and Roman Catholics, transported themselves and families : "tho' the chief adventurers," (says the Atlas Geographicus, vol. 5, page 766,) were Popish Gentlemen of good families, who expected full liberty, under a Proprietor of their own religion," especially since by his abovesaid declaration he had promised an equal enjoyment of all Rights and Priviledges unto all.

Now as this appearance of a general liberty in the enjoyment of each one's religion and property, was a great encouragement to ye first adventurers (as Ogilby above cited observes) and furthered much the ready settling of this province: so we find that these adventurers were no sooner settled, but they began to consider how they should insure not only to themselves, but to their late posterity, that for which they had bid adieu to their beloved native soil, I mean the liberty in the enjoyment of each one's Religion. Nor is the Lord Cœcilius

For no sooner were they thus settled and incorporated into a sufficient body to call Assemblys and make laws for themselves (as by their Charter they are allowed) but we behold the whole country voting for and the L^d Cœcifius consenting unto a fundamental law, whereby liberty of conscience is allowed to all that profess to believe in Jesus Christ," as says our above cited author in his new description of Maryland, page 185, and they the L^d Cœcilius "who was at vast expense to improve the Colony," (says another author Atlas Geographicus, vol. 5, page 719) "tho' a Papist procured an Act of Assembly for Liberty of Conscience for all Christians and permitted the dissenters to enjoy the Rights and Priviledges of Englishmen:" by which clause this author clearly shows, that, in his opinion, the Lord Cœcilius had full power to admit and exclude what Religion he pleased or to make his own the chief in Maryland, as W^m· Penn did his in Pennsylvania ; for that the dissenters were allowed "Liberty of Religion and ye enjoyment of ye Rights and Priviledges of Englishmen," was a permission according to this author and consequently an Indulgence of ye L^d Cœcilius and not their

right or due.   Now if any one should hence suspect this
author of being partial to yᵉ Roman Catholics and an enemy
to the dissenters, or ignorant in the History of this Province,
let him but peruse this work and he'll soon find yᵉ reverse,
that is, that he scarce ever treats the first with humanity.
always speaks favourably of yᵉ latter, and if you believe
him in his Preface or Introduction, he was not unprovided
with materials wherewith to compile yᵉ description of
yᵉ whole world and consequently of Maryland.

  That Liberty of Conscience was wᵗ our first Adventurers had most at heart, will clearly appear. to anyone that
considers how strenuously they maintained the same, in the
first Assembly of this province by the abovesᵈ Law of Religion, wᶜʰ by its Preamble, appears to be the first Authentic
Act of this infant Conlony ; whence we have a convincing
demonstration that, as they had transported themselves and
families, upon yᵉ promise and in expectation of this Liberty
so were they firmly resolved to use their utmost endeavours
to fix and perpetuate the same to after ages, and this they did
after the most solemn and sacred manner, by enacting a
fundamental and stable law to confirm and secure this Liberty
unto all christians and that forever as the chiefest of their
Priviledges, and yᵉ most material branch of our Constitution :
and I defy the enemys of Maryland to produce one single
Author, that denys the same, or does not in express terms,
whilst touching upon our Constitution, mention this liberty of
Conscience as a part thereof.   For not only yᵉ above cited
Authors but yᵉ larger Maps of yᵉ English Empire in America,
wᵗʰ a description of each Province in yᵉ margin ; (Robert
Morden in his Geography rectified, 4th. Edition printed at
London 1700 page 596, and Herman Moll in his System of
of Geography printed at London, 1701, in his description of
Maryland, in his North America, page 167 ;) and in a word
all others, do confirm my above assertion that Liberty of
Conscience is allowed in Maryland by a fundamental Law,
that is to continue forever.   To prevent mistake I will
transcribe the words of the two last cited Authors, as highly
worthy our observations; first that this liberty of conscience

was, in prudence, allowed to all by his Lordship, from the beginning, and that it soon after was enacted into a law by the inhabitants wth his Lordship's consent; second, that this Law was not for a time only, but to continue forever, and consequently to be an unchangeable and essential condition of this Plantation; third, that according to these Authors the Law of Liberty of Conscience is so far from being, etc., Robert Morden in ye end of his description of Maryland has these words: "To conclude, the impeopling and trade of this Province, by ye vast expense, care and industry of ye Lord Proprietary hath been improved to that heighth y^t in ye year 1670 there were reckoned near 20,000 English planted there. And that wch keeps them together in the greatest peace, order and concord imaginable, is the Liberty of Conscience wch his Lordship in prudence allows to persons y^t profess Christianity, tho' of different persuasions; so y^t every man lives quietly and securely wth his neighbor, neither molesting nor being molested for difference of judgment in Religion, wch liberty is established there by an Act of Assembly, with his Lordship's consent, to continue forever. "Agreeable to this is what Herman Moll in ye above cited place, gives us in the following words: The Government of Maryland is framed according to ye model of y^t of England and maintained by wholesome laws that tend much to ye advantages of ye Inhabitants; Liberty of Conscience being allowed to all that profess christianity, though of different persuasions so y^t none is molested for difference of judgment in matters of Religion, and this liberty is established there by an Act of Assembly to continue forever; by wch means so many have been induced to settle under this Government, that ye number of ye English in ye year 1670 amounted to near 20,000, and they all live together in the greatest peace, order and concord imaginable." Thus far this Author who agrees so perfectly with Morden and both wth what I have advanced that I cannot but be sensibly rejoiced to find my above assertions thus corroborated by two so credible and impartial authors, whose words are so agreeably corresponding to ye former part of this Treatise that the reader might rationally conclude that I copied after them; and yet I can and do assure him that I had never perused either of these authors till I had writ what goes before ye above citation, and had gathered all before I advanced from our records, other authors and common fame. To observe therefore upon and apply these authorities to my present design I remark, that according to this Author the law of Liberty of Conscience is so far from being inconsistent with our Constitution, altho' our Government is framed, as Moll observes according to ye model of y^t of England, that it is rather the exact fundamental part of our constitution and a wholesome Law, that is, such a law as tends much to the advantage of ye Inhabitants. I remark again that this Law as it was designed, so did it much forward the settlement of this province, in so much that in forty years it numbered nigh 20,000 English Inhabitants, and lastly I remark (w^t should never be forgotten) that the happy fruits of this Fundamental Law of Liberty of Conscience were not only the peopling of this Province in so short a space, but that happy union and agreement of its inhabitants, who altho' differing in their judgements as to matters of Religion, lived nevertheless *together* in the greatest peace, order and concord imaginable.

And now lest some may imagine that this cry of Liberty was only a politick invention to decoy unthinking people and induce them to leave their native soil in quest of that they were never to enjoy, to suspect wch is not only injurious to ye memory of ye Lord Cœcilius, but traduces our worthy ancestors, the first adventurers and compilers of the Law as false and deceitful, and not only enemies to themselves and barbarous to their posterity who might probably be of as different persuasions as were their forefathers, makers of the said law, but (to use ye vulgar expression) no better than a scandalous pack of unconscionable kidnappers, in regard of those that transported themselves, allured thereto by that specious promise of an entire Liberty of Conscience, and an equal enjoyment of all Priviledges: I shall only offer first that such a Law was enacted by ye Lord Proprietor and people, And secondly that ye said Law was religiously ob-

served from ye first settlement of this Province, for above
sixty years without ye least alteration, and even esteemed by
the Inhabitants as their birth-right, the chief of their priviledges, and an essential part of their constitution; and lastly
that the same law was approved of by the Crown appears
for that the same was printed in and diffused thro' all
England, to encourage people to come and reside in this
Province; and thus made so publick that all authors writing
of Maryland mention ye same as I before observed, and yet
it never met with any countermand, check or opposition
from ye crown or government of England, no not even in the
days of Oliver Cromwell, who, altho' he used his utmost
endeavours to extirpate, both ye Church of England and
Popery out of ye whole kingdom, did nevertheless permit
both to enjoy their ancient privileges here in Maryland.

Thus far concerning the Law, its occasion and motives,
its rise and progress, its approbation, continuance and success; now let it speak for itself and make known to all,
that harmonious union, real love and entire agreement w^ch
make up the second distinguishing character of our worthy
ancestors and first adventurers, that settled this Province
upon so noble and so lasting a foundation as I in the beginning did with pleasure observe. Now Rules, as Natu-
ralists well observe and experience makes appear, the first
act and principal effort of each sensitive tho' irrational
being, tends to its own defence and centres in self-preserva-
tion, we cannot doubt but that the first act and chief design
of all rational creatures is, and ought to be directed to this
noble end, first of serving and honouring its maker the
Diety, and then of preserving and if possible, improving its
own existence; and whether our ancestors were not well
apprised hereof, or did not solely aim at this christian as well
as rational end, let their first authentic deed, I mean the
first Law or Act of Assembly they ever made bear evidence,
for here we shall find them first decreeing *Quæ sunt Dei
Deo,* due honour and worship to ye Deity, and then fencing
in and securing their own Rights and Privileges from all
injurys and oppressions to themselves and late posterity,

I omit all further observations, or rather defer them till you have heard the law, wch I will here give you at large, as printed in England, with its title, Preamble and more essential parts.

A LAW OF MARYLAND CONCERNING RELIGION.

"Forasmuch as in a well governed and Christian Commonwealth, matters concerning religion and the honour of God ought in the first place to be taken into serious consideration and endeavoured to be settled. Be it therefore ordained and enacted by the R^t Hon. Cœcilius, Lord Baron of Baltimore, absolute Lord and Proprietary of this Province, with the advice and consent of ye upper and lower House of this General Assembly: That whatsoever person or persons within this Province and the Islands thereunto belonging, shall from henceforth blaspheme God, that is curse him, or shall deny our Saviour Jesus Christ to be the Son of God; or shall deny the Holy Trinity, the Father, Son and Holy Ghost, or the Godhead of any of the said three persons of the Trinity; or the unity of the Godhead; or shall use or utter any reproachful speeches, words or language, concerning the Holy Trinity, or any of ye said three persons thereof, shall be punished with death and confiscation or forfeiture of all his or her lands and goods, to ye Lord Proprietary and his heirs.

"And be it also enacted by the Authority and with ye Advice and Assent aforesaid, ye w^t soever Person or Persons, shall from henceforth use or utter any reproachful words, or speeches concerning the Blessed Virgin Mary, the mother of our Saviour, or ye Holy Apostles, or Evangelists, or any of them, shall in such case for the first offence, forfeit to the said Lord Proprietary and his heirs Lords and Proprietarys of this Province, the sum of five pounds sterling, or the value thereof to be levyed on the goods and chattels of every such person so offending, but in case such offender or offenders shall not them have goods and chattels sufficient for ye satisfying of such forfeiture, or that the same be not speedily satisfied, that then such offender or offenders shall be Publickly whipt, and imprisoned during y[e] Pleasure of y[e] L[d] Proprietary or y[e] Lieut or Chief Gov[r] of this Province for the time being : and that every such offender and offenders for every 2d offence shall forfeit ten pounds sterling, or the value thereof, to be levyed as aforesaid or in case such offender or offenders shall not then have goods and chattels within this Province sufficient for that purpose, then to be publickly and severely whipt and imprisoned, as before is expressed ; and that every person or persons, before mentioned, offending herein a 3d time, shall for such 3d offence forfeit his lands and goods, be forever banished and expelled out of this Province.

"And be it also further enacted, by y[e] same Authority, Advice and Assent that w[t] soever Person or Persons shall from henceforth upon any occasion of Offence or otherwise in reproachful manner or way, declare, call or nominate any Person or Persons w[t] soever, inhabiting, residing, trafficking, or trading or commercing within this Province or within any the Ports, Harbours, Creeks or Havens to the same belonging an Heretick, Schismatic, Idolater, Puritan, Presbyterian, Independant, Popish Priest, Jesuit, Jusuited Papist, Lutheran, Calvinist, Anabaptist, Brownist, Autinomian, Barrowist, Roundhead, Separatist, or other name or term (in a reproachful manner) relating to matter of Religion, shall for every such offence forfeit and loose the sum of ten shillings sterling, or the value thereof, levyed of the goods and chattels of every such offender and offenders, the one-half thereof, to be forfeited and paid unto the Person or Persons, of whom such reproachful words are, or shall be spoken or uttered, and the other half thereof to y[e] L[d] Propietary and his heirs, L[ds] Proprietarys of this Province : But if 'such person or persons, who shall at any time utter or speak any such reproachful words or language, shall not have goods or chattels sufficient and within this Province, to be taken to satisfy the penalty aforesaid, or that y[e] same be not otherwise speedily satisfied, y[t] y[n] the persons or persons so offending shall be publickly whipt, and shall suffer imprisonment without bail or mainprize, until he, she or they respectfully shall satisfy ye party offended or grieved by such reproachful language, by asking him or her respectively forgiveness publickly, for such his offence, before ye magistrate, or chief officers of the town or where such offence shall be given.

"And be it further enacted by ye authority and consent aforesaid, that every person or persons within this Province, that shall at anytime hereafter profane the Sabbath or Lords Day, called Sunday, by frequent swearing, drunkenness, or by any uncivil or disorderly recreation, or by working on that day (when absolute necessity doth not require) shall for every offence forfeit two shillings six pence sterling, or the value thereof and for ye 2d offence five shillings sterling or the value thereof and for the 3d offence and for every time he shall offend (in like manner) afterwards, ten shillings sterling, or the value thereof : and in case such offender or offenders shall not have sufficient goods or chattels within this Province to satisfy any of ye aforesaid penalties respectively hereby imposed for profaning ye Sabbath, or Lord's Day, called Sunday, as aforesaid, then in every such case, ye party so offending shall for the first and second offence, in y^t kind, be imprisoned till he or she shall publickly in open Court (before the chief Commander, Judge or Magistrate of that County Town or Precinct, wherein such offence shall be committed) acknowledge ye scandal and offence he hath in y^t respect given against God, and ye good and civil Government of y^t Province, and for ye third offence and for every time after, shall also be publickly whipt.

"And whereas the inforcing of Conscience in matters of Religion, hath frequently fallen out to be of dangerous consequence, in those commonwealths where it hath been practiced, and for the more quiet and peaceable Government of this Province, and the better to preserve mutual love and unity amongst ye inhabitants here ; Be it therefore also by ye Ld Proprietors, with ye Advice and Assent of ye Assembly ordained and enacted (except as in this present act is before declared and set forth) that no person or persons whatsoever, within ye Province or ye Islands, Ports, Harbours, Creeks or

Havens thereunto belonging, professing to believe in Jesus
Christ, shall from henceforth be any ways troubled, molested
and discountenanced, for or in respect of his or her Religion,
nor in the exercise thereof within this province or the islands
thereunto belonging, nor any way compelled to ye belief or
exercise of any other Religion, against his or her consent, so
as they be not unfaithful to ye Ld Proprietary, or molest or
conspire against ye civil Government established, or to be
established in this Province under him and his heirs. And
that all and every person and persons, y^t shall presume contrary to ye Act, and the true intent and meaning thereof.
directly or indirectly either in person or estate, wilfully to
wrong, disturb or trouble, or molest any person or persons
whatsoever within ye Province professing to believe in Jesus
Christ. for or in respect of his or her Religion, or ye free
exercise thereof within ye Province otherwise than is provided for in ye Act, that such person or persons so offending
shall be compelled to pay treble damage to the party so
wronged or molested for every such offence ; shall also forfeit twenty shillings sterling in money, or the value thereof;
half thereof for the use of the Ld Proprietary and his heirs,
L^ds and Proprietaries of this Province, and the other half
thereof for the use of the party so wronged or molested as
aforesaid ; or if the party so offending as aforesaid, shall
refuse or be unable to recompense the party so wronged, or
to satisfy such fine or forfeiture, then such offender shall be
severely punished by publick whipping and imprisonment
during ye pleasure of the Ld Proprietor or his Lieutenant or
Chief Governor of this Province, for the time being, without
Bail or Mainprize.

"And be it further also enacted by ye authority and
consent aforesaid, that ye sheriff or other officer or officers
from time to time to be appointed and authorized for that
purpose of ye county, town or precinct, where every particular offense in this present Act contained shall happen at
any time to be committed, and whereupon there is hereby a
forfeiture, fine or penalty imposed, shall from time to time
distrain and seize ye goods and effects of every such person

so offending so aforesaid, against this present Act, or any part thereof, and sell the same, or any part thereof for the full satisfaction of such forfeiture, fine or penalty as aforesaid, restoring to ye party so offending the remainder or overplus of ye said goods or estate, after such satisfaction so made as aforesaid."

Behold ye first and fundamental Act of this Province, a law to stand forever and worthy of our noble ancestors. A law that gives ease to tender consciences, induced thousands to transport themselves hither, and united all in ye strictest bonds of peace and good neighbourhood, and as ye promised enjoyment of this law was ye chief inducement to many of our forefathers to settle here, so it is to be hoped that all lovers of their country will not only value the same as they did, but do their utmost to secure unto themselves and transmit to late posterity this so essential a part of our happy constitution; for as ye intended scheme of ye Liberty of Conscience gave the conception and this law brought it forth; so ye observance of this law has nourished, brought up and perfected this our province; nor can we question but a body politick, as well as natural, is left preserved by ye continued influence of those means to which it owes its existence and production and consequently since this Law of Religion was our first, our chief, our fundamental Law, and ye dearest branch of our Constitution, by which we live, grow up and flourish, to strike hereat, would be to unhinge ye Government, destroy our foundation, and reduce this flourishing Colony to ruin and confusion; besides the great injustice would be done to those whose forefathers were prevailed upon to become residents in this Province by this fun-Law, which like ye conditions of Plantations, was to be inviolable and unalterable.

But to return to ye law itself and make some reflections thereupon, I observe—first; That as ye service of God and union, peace and concord among one another, were w^t our Ancestors did so highly value and endeavour to settle, so are they w^t we their descendants should have most at heart, if we would copy after so noble a pattern, or share in a like happiness. Secondly ; This was their first Act and design to be their last, as I may say ; y^t it is was to be perpetual, as ye authors above cited do allege. Thirdly ; To this Act it is to be attributed, y^t our Province became so well peopled and flourishing so soon, as ye same authors observe. Fourthly : It would be not only a hardship, but an injustice to deprive those of the benefit of this law, to enjoy which was ye only motive that induced their forefathers to leave their native soil and settle here. Fifthly ; This Law, as it it was made to be perpetual, is an inherent birthright of each Marylandian. Lastly; as this Law and the enjoyment thereof has peopled our Province, and made it ye most happy and most flourishing of all ye British Colonys, so ye cessation or annulling thereof would be, not only injurious to our late Posterity, but would render us a divided and unhappy people, and *tend much to depopulate this his Majesty's so profitable colony,*" as the Lords Commissioners do observe in their Remonstrance to ye late Queen of blessed memory, of which more hereafter ; but to pursue our history.

. Under ye protection of this fundamental law, christians of all persuasions lived, intermixed, in y^s Province, in Peace and good neighbourhood ; nor was there any difference to be seen, save only in their different places, and manner of worship, in Divine service ; at other times, and in other places, they all agreed as neighbours, friends and brothers, whilst some of all persuasions (that is to say, those that were thought most fit and capable) employed promiscuously places of Honor, Trust and Interest, and this for sixty years and upward ; during which time all christians enjoyed not only ye free use of their religion, but an equal share, in all their Rights, Places and Privileges : So y^t whenever a Counsellor, or Burgess, a Judge or Justice, was to be chosen. or appointed. his Religion was neither a help nor a hindrance, and nothing came under consideration, but his integrity, Parts and Capacity, were he Churchman or Presbyterian, Quaker or Roman Catholic ; and hence it is to be presumed that this country was never better served, nor would it be, than in those halcyon days, when neither his Lordship nor ye People were debarred, he from appointing, or they from chosing, the most knowing and proper persons, be their persuasions what it would. Nor was ye equal enjoyment of Privileges confined to Religion and Offices only ; no, there was also an entire liberty and full enjoyment of all other rights, privileges and immunities for all subjects of Great Britain, as to buy and sell, to take profits and enjoy, to transmit to their heirs, or to convey or bequeath unto any other w^t goods or chattles, lands or hereditaments, and in a word, all their estates, or any part thereof, whatever, real or personal : So y^t Clergy and Laity of all persuasions have taken up land of his Lordship, bought of and sold to each other and succeeded to Estates by bequest or Inheritance, without doubt or scruple, and the Lord Prop^{ty} has not only allowed thereof but acted therein, in and from ye infant years, as I may say of their Province, as it appears upon our Records (A. B. and H. Fol. 27.) where land is granted to Thomas Copley, or according to his assignment ye said Copley having Rights, as ye above cited record observe, to twenty-eight thousand Acres of Land for servants imported into y^s Province, though ye said Thomas Copley was known to be both a Priest and a Jesuit, and such did publickly profess himself.

Nor can this be wondered at, since both Clergy and Laity of all persuasions, and consequently of ye Roman Catholicks among ye rest, were ever deemed to be qualified to purchase, buy, sell or possess any lands or estates in Maryland. For First, they had a law that empowered them so to do, a fundamental and Perpetual Law, the law of Religion, where as above appears among other things it is enacted "that no one shall be any ways troubled, molested, or discountenanced for or in respect of his or her religion," and can there be a more severe discountenancing, or a more disagreeable molestation, or a more sensible troubling, than to deprive a man of his birthright, to rob him of his subsistence, and render him incapable to buy, sell, or enjoy any estate whether real or personal, and this upon account or in respect of his Religion. Secondly ; The usages and customs of Maryland have ever approved thereof ; the courts have acknowledged it, and that ye Crown has consented thereto, we may conclude, since ye law y^t was its foundation, was printed in and published through all England and made publick, y^t all Authors treating of this Province, mention ye same, and yet it was never contradicted or reversed by ye Crown, as I before observed. Thirdly ; There neither is, nor ever was a law of Maryland to render them unqualified, to purchase and enjoy, to inherit or succeed unto any estate, either real or personal : and y^t ye Penal Laws of England extend not hither was for seventy years and more the opinion of all in Maryland in courts and out of courts. Tho' some of late to secure w^t may be justly deemed an Englishman's birthright, ye enjoyment of all beneficial laws, or laws of Privilege, wch were made in England before our first settlement, have unwarily advanced too much, in claiming all ye Laws of Great Britain : for should we examine into necessary consequence thereof so extensive a claim might be found to be not benefical, but highly prejudicial to, if not destructive of our constituion. But to leave the more exact and convincing solution of this difficulty to ye gentlemen of ye gown, I shall only observe we can rationally desire no more than to bring with us the Laws of Privilege ; ye others being rather a burden on, and hinderance to a new Colony, than any benefit or advantage : and to have a power of making Laws, for ourselves and consequently of re-enacting here such laws as either have been (since our first beginning to make laws) or shall be made from time to time in England, wch we shall judge agreeable to our constitution, and for our advantage ; whilst others that may be repugnant to or inconsistent therewith, are void and of no force. Nor can we wonder, if many such laws should pass in England, since ye Parliament is neither knowing of, nor interested in our affairs; and whether it be better for us who are so highly concerned in improving this Colony, and so feelingly sensible of our own interest, to make our own laws or to leave them to be made by such who are strangers to our constitution, and not only ignorant of but perchance unconcerned for our advantage, is so easy for an unprejudiced person to determine, that I believe most will join with me, in advising such as will still insist for all the laws, to supercede this claim, till they have obtained two things of the Crown ; the first is, that our province may be freed from the unnecessary trouble and expence, of having Assemblys, for if all the laws of England should extend hither and we are not allowed to contradict yᵉ same, or to make laws contrary to them, as by our charter we are forbid to do, to have Assemblys, would be an unnecessary charge and a superfluous trouble. The second is to obtain leave yᵗ our freeholders may chose a sufficient number of delegates from among themselves that may be Representatives, and both sit and vote in yᵉ British Parliament, for wᵗ can be more reasonable, than that we ourselves should have a vote in those laws yᵗ are to bind us : and yet whether either of these would be granted by yᵉ Crown, or if granted, would be beneficial to this Province, I leave the disinterested and impartial to be judges.

But to return to our first and fundamental law; if what has been advanced be true, viz: that this law was to be perpetual, a branch of our constitution, and yᵉ birthright of a Marylandian, it may be asked, whence comes it ? then yᵗ at present, there is not yᵗ equal share of all privileges enjoyed either by yᵉ Quakers or yᵉ Roman Catholics; to wᶜʰ question I give our Saviour's answer: "Ab initio non erat sic," "from yᵉ beginning it was not so." It's true both yᵉ Quakers and yᵉ Roman Catholics, be they otherwise never so well qualified, nay and superior to many by their probity, judgment and erudition, as it may possibly sometimes fall out, are nevertheless excluded from all offices; "but from yᵉ beginning it was not so," and what is still harder, neither Quakers nor Roman Catholics are allowed to have a vote in yᵉ making of any law, tho' they and their late posterity must be bound by yᵉ same, "but from yᵉ beginning it was not so." And what is yet more severe, yᵉ poor Papist, (I may call him so without offence, tho' it was penal by our first Law, "sic tempora mutantur!") yᵉ Papists, I say, can neither vote in nor out of yᵉ house, neither be nor send a representative, but "from yᵉ beginning it was not so." That

Maryland should make these dissentions, and suppress those who most contributed to her first settlement, for (as Atlas Geographicus observes) "The chief adventurers were Popish Gentlemen of good families" is much to be wondered at. But that Maryland should deem a Papist unworthy to be a petty juryman or constable, whilst the Crown thought a Papist sufficiently deserving to be both her Proprietary and hereditary Governor, is most surprising. That Maryland should be worse than her promise, and deny ye enjoyment of her fundamental law to any of her people, whose fathers were allured by the same to become her inhabitants, is more wonderful as well as more deplorable. I forbear enlarging on so melancholy and ungrateful a subject, lest our enemys should glory in our mother's weakness, or my love to Maryland should be questioned by the unwary. To silence those I would have them reflect, y^t Maryland, whilst herself, was never guilty either of partiality to some or of severity to others of her children; and to prevent the mistake of these I solemnly aver that my only motive of and design in w^t I have here touched upon, was to stop ye mouths of ye malicious, to heal our wounds and wash away all spots or blemishes that may be pretended to be discovered in our once so well united, so beautiful and so amiable Maryland, y^t it has ever been most justly esteemed the happyest Colony of ye British Empire.

I say Maryland whilst herself, and I meant whilst governed by that noble and worthy family of ye Calverts, to whom it was first given, by whom it was first settled, and under whom, it grew up and flourished to ye envy as well as admiration of her neighbouring Colonies. During this time, which was for sixty years, our Proprietary was our Governor who was truly *Pater Patriæ,* a father of his people and had their interest and prosperity at heart, because his own if not ye same, was nevertheless so interwoven therewith, that an injury to his people must necessarily be a loss to him ; so hence what he had promised, and our assembly enacted into a stable law, Liberty of Religion and an equal enjoyment of all privileges was allowed to all without distinction, and that not as an indulgence or a favour, but as their undoubted right, and an unalterable condition of their or their fathers' first settling here.   Thus we enjoyed both peace and plenty during the civil wars in England and amidst all its unhappy changes we alone were unchangeable and still the same until the revolution, when our unhappy country could not escape the common deluge, and w^t was done here in opposition to our lawful Government could not fail of an approbation at Home, tho' in that unhappy conjecture the first fomenters of our disturbances were called to England and tryed for their lives; nor would they have escaped, it's thought, or their proceedings been unpunished, had not their judges thought that Maryland only copyed after England, and (as one of ye Lords was heard to say) to condemn them would be to censure themselves.

From this epoch we may date our changes, not only in Government, but in manners, love and union, to and with each other; then it was prejudice and party set up their unhappy standards, and Religion which till then lay quiet and undisturbed, was discountenanced, brought to ye Bar and confined to much narrower limits than she enjoyed before; and yet I do not find, either in history or upon record, that she was ever accused, much less legally convicted, of any trespass or offence against crown or state.   But such was the will, such ye pleasure of our new Governors sent in by the Crown, Governors that were strangers to our constitution, and unconcerned for our prosperity; Governors that came to fleece and not to feed; to raise their own fortunes not to advance ours; Governors who instead of healing our wounds, widened our breaches, fomented our divisions, and when no other crimes could be detected, made the Religion of some high treason, or at least a mark of disgrace, and a hindrance not only to promotion, but to ye usual common and undoubted Rights and Privileges of a Marylandian. Hence they impose and require such oaths and conditions to qualify for office, that the Quakers and Roman Catholics are excluded from places; though for sixty years fidelity to his Lordship was ye only requisite; this was the first and open breach of our Constitution, and directly contrary to our above cited fundamental Law: tho' as to all other rights and privileges, both yᵉ Quaker and Roman Catholic held their usual and equal share for fourteen years longer, that is till 1704, when Governor Seymore out of a pique against some private persons of yᵉ Roman Catholics (who when the Governor had modestly demanded a purse well lined, had yᵉ indiscretion or impudence, as it was then deemed to refuse the same) resolved, Haman-like for one Mordekæus, to ruin all; hence he puts his engines to work and at length brings forth an Act, entitled : "An Act against the growth of Popery," wᶜʰ might have been more justly styled *An Act to extirpate Popery, Root and Branch,* because thereby their Clergy was forbid all exercise of their functions, and consequently the whole body was debarred of yᵉ use of their Religion. But that it was not yᵉ design of the Burgesses to carry things to that extremity, and how little a hand our country had therein, appears by the unwelcome reception this law met with, for when yᵉ Roman Catholics complained of this hardship, the Assembly men unanimously declared that it was neither their design nor desire to forbid the free exercise of their Religion, and upon this the Governor is addressed so yᵗ yᵉ same Assembly might be called again wᶜʰ accordingly was done three months after yᵉ former, and there and then yᵉ very same Assembly declared by and in a new Act for yᵉ purpose made, and to suspend yᵉ former Act, that their real intent was not to deprive yᵉ Roman Catholics of yᵉ use of their Religion as by yᵉ preamble of yᵉ said suspending Act more clearly appears : this suspending Act was to continue for eighteen months, or till yᵉ Queens' pleasure should be notified therein, and this Act was further continued for twelve months longer, by a third Act to yᵗ purpose made April, 1706. From wᶜʰ Acts I infer first that neither Governor Seymore nor our Assembly were of opinion that yᵉ penal laws of England extended hither, for to what end should they trouble themselves, or risk such a severe check, as they had from yᵉ Crown by making a law for yᵗ for which the Laws of England had more severely provided, had they dreamed they had Laws ready made, in force and more severe. Secondly, that the general voice of the whole country is, that none should be debarred of ye use, or be oppressed for or in respect of their religion. Well but how does this Law of Seymore relish at home? Not at all; for as the council records of England make appear, the Lords Commissioners of Trade and Plantations were highly offended thereat and weighing the injustice as well as ill consequences thereof, first advised with the Bishop of London, and, then, with him, addressed the Crown in an humble remonstrance; wherein they set forth and complain among other things, that this Law would deprive the Roman Catholics even of the private use of their religion, tho' in the most inoffensive manner, wch their Lordships *humbly* conceived was not her Majesty's gracious intention, and that ye rigorous execution of ye said Act would in a great measure tend to depopulate that her Majesty's profitable Colony; for these and other reasons they humbly pray that her Majesty would be graciously pleased, by her royal letter to direct the Governor of Maryland to represent to ye Assembly of that province, That the Second Act (y^t is ye Act suspending y^t against ye Papists) be continued by a new Act or clause of an Act without limitation of time. This report or remonstrance was signed thus by—

Whitehall, ye   H. LONDON.   WM. BLAITHWAYTE.
third of Jan'y   DARTMOUTH.   JOHN POLLEXFEN.
    1705-6.   PH. MEADOWS. MATHEW PRIOR.

And here, before I proceed to the order sent hereupon to our Govr by ye Queen and Council, I must observe that it was the joint opinion of the Lords Commissioners of Trade and Plantations, and ye Bishop of London, first that ye exercise of ye Popish Religion tho' treason in England is inoffensive and therefore Lawful in Maryland. Secondly that to deprive the Roman Catholicks in Maryland of ye use of their Religion was neither the gracious intention of her late Majesty Q. A. of blessed memory, nor is it of his present Majesty. Since ye same motives still remain, indulgence to his peaceable subjects, and the advantage of so beneficial a

Plantation : for Thirdly to deprive yᵉ Roman Catholicks of
yᵉ use of their Religion *would in a great measure tend to depopulate this Profitable Colony.*   Because many, as their Ancestors had quitted their native Country, and preferred
Maryland thereto, upon this consideration because there they
might enjoy their Liberty and Religion, would be tempted
to imitate their example, were they deprived, of this benefit,
and transport their families and effects to some other country,
where they might peaceably enjoy the same.   Fourthly That
yᵉ will of yᵉ Crown is a Law to Maryland, as well as to yᵉ rest
of the Plantations, wᶜʰ are therefore governed by yᵉ Prerogative, and not by the English Parliament and that we have
power to make laws for ourselves, is a grant of yᵉ Crown and
no inherent right, or such, as is independent of yᵉ Royal Pleasure: this is but a necessary consequence from their Lordships
asking and her Majesty sending her positive order that such
a Law should be enacted, whether our representatives
approved thereof or no ; for there is no exception allowed of,
nor conditions specified, such as, in case they should be
willing and consent thereto.   Lastly their Lordships thought
it both just and reasonable that yᵉ Roman Catholicks should
forever enjoy the free use of their religion, and that power
of depriving them thereof ought only to be lodged in the
Crown ; and therefore they petition yᵗ yᵉ Act by wᶜʰ the use
of their Religion was allowed them, should be continued by
a new Act or clause of an Act without limitation of Time,
and wᵗ is to exist without limitation of time I think is to be
perpetual, or, wᶜʰ is the same, is to last forever.

    Well, and wᵗ then, some perchance may say, these Lords
are neither our law-makers nor infallible, and perhaps they
asked for more yⁿ the Crown either could or thought fit to
grant, and might be answered, as yᵉ Apostles were, with a
"Nescitis quid petatis, you know not wᵗ you ask." For her
Majesty could not but be sensible, how dear the suspending
power had cost her Royal Fathers, and therefore she would
never hazard her Crown by ordering such an Act to be made,
wᶜʰ would be a suspending of yᵉ Penal Laws of England with
a witness, for it is petitioned to be without Limitation of

time, that is, for ever; if ye said Penal Laws of England
should be found to extend hither. This I must acknowledge
is a weighty and startling difficulty and such as might justly
have deterred, both ye Lords Com^{rs} from asking and her
Majesty from granting any such thing, had there been but
ye least conjecture possible of the Penal Laws of England extending hither. Besides their petition would have been vain,
for to w^t end should they solicit ye Queen to obtain an order
y^t ye Roman Catholicks should not be prosecuted by
Govr Seymours law, if they, that is the Roman Catholicks
were liable to be prosecuted by the much severer Penal
Laws of England, as they would, no doubt, were these in
force in Maryland : would this secure to ye Roman Catholicks
the inoffensive use of their Religion or prevent the depopulation of this profitable Colony, to free ye Roman Catholicks
from ye lesser Penaltys of Seymours law, if they might be
prosecuted upon and punished by ye Penal Statutes of
England. If suffer they must, it mattered not by w^t law or
statute, whether of Maryland or of England: for as a criminal
is not pardoned or freed from his punishment if die he must,
tho' you change his gallows into a scaffold, and hanging into
beheading ; so it is but a trifling advantage, for a person
that is arraigned, to take away ye milder whilst you indict
him upon a severer statute ; and such would have been the
case of ye Roman Catholicks, such ye Petition of ye L^{ds} Com^{rs}
of trade and Plantations, and such ye Royal favour, should
ye penal laws of England include y^s Province.

Well but the L^{ds} Com^{rs} petition and her Majt^{ys} Royal
grant are not y^t ye penal laws of England should be suspended, but y^t a law of Maryland should be repealed or
suspended by another law : why yes, I allow all this, but
must beg leave to believe and observe, y^t this is a convincing demonstration, y^t the L^{ds} Com^{rs} petitioning and
ye Queen and Council granting, both thought and knew that
the penal laws of England did not extend hither; and y^t no
law besides y^t of Seymours could debar the Roman Catholicks of ye use of their Religion, the reason is clear for had
their Lordships or her Majesty imagined the severer Penal

Laws of England were here in force, or any others made in Maryland to yᵉ same purpose, they never would have trifled away their time, nor have troubled themselves about Seymours Law, wᶜʰ was almost word for word yᵉ same with one made for England in yᵉ 11 and 12 of W (III) and was yᵉ milder of yᵉ two ; nor have given so superficial a relief to the distressed ; nor have so weakly provided against so great an evil, as yᵉ depopulation of so profitable a Colony. And had our Govʳ and Assembly thought as much, viz : yᵗ yᵉ Penal Laws, reached to and included Maryland they might have spared themselves yᵉ trouble, escaped yᵉ odium and not exposed themselves to yᵉ danger of a reprimand from yᵉ Crown, by executing yᵉ laws already made, rather than by making a new one of their own ; and from hence I infer that neither England nor Maryland, neither Govʳ Seymour and our Assembly, nor yᵉ Lᵈ Comʳˢ of Trade and Plantations, nor yᵉ Queen and Council were of opinion yᵗ yᵉ Penal Laws of England extended hither.

But least any should mistrust that this order of yᵉ Crown was fraudulently procured, or surrepticiously obtained, or that no lawyers were advised with, or few or none of yᵉ Councellors present when this business was transacted, I'll give my readers the satisfaction of a true copy of a transcript thereof, signed by yᵉ Clerk of the Council, and corroborated with yᵉ seal of his office. It begins as follows—

At yᵉ Court at St. James, yᵉ 3d of January, 1705,

Present

The Queen's most Excellent Majesty

His Royal Hˢˢ Prince } George of Denmark }	Lᵈ Gt.Chamberlain	Earl of Radnor
	Lᵈ Chamberlain	Earl of Bradford
Lord Keeper	Lᵈ Poulett	Lᵈ Ch. Jus. Holt
Lord President	Mr. Bertie	Lᵈ Ch. Jus.Trevor
Duke of Somersett	Mr. Boyle	Mr. Vernon
Duke of Ormond	Mr. Secre'y Hedges	Mr. How
Duke of Bolton	Mr. Secre'y Harley	

Upon reading this day at yᵉ Board a Report from yᵉ Lords Commissioners of Trade and Plantations, in yᵉ following words : "May it please yʳ Majtʸˢ etc." (then follows yᵉ said Report, yᵉ substance of wᶜʰ having been given above I shall here for brevity sake omit yᵉ same, and continue yᵉ copy from yᵉ end thereof, that is, only give yᵉ order yᵗ follows this report, and was given there.)

"Her Majesty in Council was pleased to approve thereof, and to order as it is hereby ordered, that Col. John Seymour, Her Majesty's Govʳ of Maryland do forthwith represent to yᵉ Assembly there, that yᵉ Act above mentioned (that is in the report) for suspending the prosecution of any Priests of the communion of yᵉ Church of Rome incurring yᵉ penaltys of an Act of Assembly, entitled; An Act for preventing the growth of Popery, by executing his function in a private family of the Roman Communion, but in no otherwise whatsoever: be continued by a new Act or Clause of An Act without limitation of Time, according to yᵉ said report and yᵉ said Commissioners for Trade are to cause this signification of her Majesty's pleasure to be transmitted to yᵉ said Govʳ of Maryland by yᵉ first conveniance that shall offer."

JOHN POVEY.

And now the candid reader and impartial judge, by comparing yᵉ Report and order thereupon, and weighing well both yᵉ request of the Lords and yᵉ order of yᵉ Queen in Councill, their design and method of proceeding, their words and expression, may safely conclude how groundless and unjust a surmise it would be to imagine, either that yᵉ report was fraudulently procured, or that yᵉ order was surreptitiously obtained; or yᵗ no lawyers were advised with or yᵗ few of yᵉ Councill were privy and approving of yᵉ grant For first, the Lords Commissioners before they applyed to yᵉ Crown, had (as they say in their report) "considered of both wᶜʰ Acts" (yᵗ is yᵉ Act against yᵉ growth of Popery, and yᵉ Act suspending yᵉ same) "and advised thereupon with yᵉ Rt. Rev. father in God, yᵉ Lᵈ Bishop of London, to whom the care of Ecclesiastical matters in yᵉ Plantations do belong." Secondly, this consideration was mature and made at leisure, and their resolution not taken in a hurry there being above twelve months between yᵉ passing of yᵉ last Act and their report, that being Dec. 9, 1704; this Jan. 3, 1705/6. Thirdly, they neither add to nor conceal part of yᵉ truth, but confine themselves to yᵉ two mentioned Acts and their natural and obvious consequences. Fourthly, they apply to most proper persons, first advising wᵗʰ yᵉ Bishop of London, and then addressing to yᵉ Queen and not to yᵉ Queen alone, but to yᵉ Queen in Councill, where, as by their names appears, were not only yᵉ chief of yᵉ nobility present, but many of yᵉ most eminent lawyers of England, tho' one, Holt alone, might have been sufficient. I would here conclude this subject, and with it my whole discourse, did not yᵉ above order of yᵉ Queen in Councill call upon me to draw some inferences from thence and add some observations thereupon: to be brief therefore, I infer first; That yᵉ Penal Laws of England do not extend to Maryland, and that there neither is a law of Maryland, nor can be made, (without an order from yᵉ Crown) to debar any of yᵉ use of their religion, I say any, because in yᵉ vulgar notion yᵉ Rom. Catholicks may be thought the most obnoxious (how just I know not): for what safety would yᵉ Roman Catholicks have received by having this Act suspended, had any other law in force whether of England or Maryland, forbid yᵉ use of their Religion, and that no such law ought to be made, may be gathered from her Majᵗʸˢ ordering that Act of Seymour to be suspended for ever, or, as yᵉ words are, "without limitation of time," wᶜʰ is much yᵉ same, as I above observed. For to order that they should never be prosecuted by yᵗ Act of Seymour, is tacitly to acknowledge and declare that there was no other law by wᶜʰ they could be prosecuted, and a virtual injunction of never making any other such law, before or till yᵉ Royal pleasure be therein notified, as the words of yᵉ Act made in compliance to the abovesaid order do impart.

I infer secondly that yᵉ Queen and Councill, as well as yᵉ Lᵈˢ Comʳˢ and Bishop of London, thought there was a wide difference between England and Maryland so that w^t might be treason there, might be both innocent and lawful here; otherwise they would not have condemned a law in Maryland, wch only copyed after one in England and allowed ye Roman Clergy to do y^t here, wch might cost them their lives there.

I infer thirdly that they all esteemed Seymour's proceedings not only as an undeserved hardship but as an injustice done to ye Roman Catholicks, and therefore the order is absolute that ye indulgence or Liberty of Religion shall be without limitation of time, and y^t *forthwith* such a law be made : and for this end the L^ds Com^rs are *required* to send the order *by ye first convenience y^t shall offer*, to ye Govr of Maryland, and why such order or such haste, unless they had thought it agreeable to both our charter and constitution y^t such liberty should be allowed to all inhabitants of this Province.

And here I must observe that we cannot doubt but ye L^ds Com^rs having obtained their request did punctually comply with ye injunction, ye Queen was pleased to put upon them and send the abovesaid instructions to ye Govr of Maryland, and since ships are continually setting out for y^t Province all January and February (the order being given on ye 3rd of January) we must likewise conclude y^t ye Govr had notice thereof before ye next Assembly met wch was on and from ye 2nd to ye 19th of April following, tho' he took no care to comply therewith, nor even intimated ye same, as we can find, but continued ye suspending Act by a third Act for twelve months more : and in ye ensuing sessions, wch was in the year following, he made ye Act agreeable to ye Queen's order, tho' even there he minced ye matter and instead of making it as it was petitioned for by ye L^ds Com^rs and ordered by ye Queen in Councill, to impart y^t ye suspension should be "without limitation of time,"words it thus in the title : "During ye Queen's pleasure," and in ye Preamble of ye Act,he says that her Majesty,Q A.order was y^t ye suspending Act should be continued by another Act or Clause of an Act "without any other limitation of time, than until her Majesty's further pleasure be declared and signified * * * thereof," whereas yᵉ words of yᵉ order are very plain, yᵗ yˢ suspending Act be made *without any limitation of time:* it's true yᵉ Lᵈˢ Comʳˢ in their report, after they had prayed yᵗ such an Act might be made *"without any limitation of time,* subjoined those words, wᶜʰ *subjects yᵉ continuance or repeal thereof at all times to yʳ Majesty's Royal Pleasure* which words were no part of the order, and therefore wᵗ yᵉ Govʳ had to do with them I know not; and can only bear this sense that altho' such a law will be perpetual and unchangeable by any power in Maryland, yet yᵉ same, as all other laws of Maryland are, will be subject to yᵉ Royal Pleasure, as to their continuance or repeal. That he meant yᵉ same yᵗ yᵉ Queen had ordered, we must suppose, and by her Majesty's words yᵉ law must be interpreted: but why he did not comply with the order till fifteen months after, whereas he held an Assembly twelve months before yᵗ and three months after yᵉ order was given. Perchance time may declare to those who are more skilled in politicks, than I either am or desire to be, and to bid farewell to my impartial reader, hoping he'll excuse my language, style and other deficiencys, and assuring him that it was a real love for both my country and truth and not an overfondness to appear in print, that prevailed upon me first to write and then to publish wᵗ little I knew of our charter and constitution. I conclude, that as Liberty of Religion and an equal share in all Priviledges laid yᵉ foundation of yˢ Province and brought it to perfection, so I hope that all well wishers to this Province will contribute all they can to continue and preserve the same, since all things are best preserved by the same means by which they were first produced.

FINIS.

THE GENESIS OF THE EARLY HISTORY OF
DETROIT. BY RICHARD R. ELLIOTT.

Until within a few years, the "Cadillac Papers," were generally recognized by local writers as the documentary history of the founding, and of the first decade of the existence of the French colony of Detroit. The originals of these documents are on file in the archives of the Marine and Colonies, of the Government of France.

While Minister of the United States to the Court of Louis Philppe, 1836-1842, General Louis Cass, at his own expense, employed Pierre Margry, a young gentleman of ability, to examine these archives, which, it should be remarked, were voluminous, and in a very chaotic condition, and to make transcripts of such documents as related to the history of Michigan and especially of Detroit, during the French colonial era. These transcripts, when completed, were submitted to the General, who in some instances required, and received from M. Margry, explanations and marginal notes. Upon the return of General Cass to Detroit he placed these transcripts at the disposition of such of his fellow-citizens as were interested in local historical research; among them were several letters, memoirs, and statements, though not all, of M. de la Mothe Cadillac, the founder of Detroit. These were called the "Cadillac Papers."

The documents copied by M. Margry, are in some respects unimportant, but those relating to Detroit shed a great deal of light upon the first years of the young colony, and he who shed this light, was the founder himself.

In 1853, while engaged in editorial work in Detroit, Mrs. E. M. Sheldon obtained these transcripts from General Cass, and becoming deeply interested in their contents, conceived the idea of having them published. She procured their translation and adding other historical matter, issued in 1856, "The Early History of Michigan, from the first settlement to 1815," N. Y., A. S. Barnes & Co.; Detroit, Kerr, Morley & Co., pp. 409. This book contained the genesis of the history of Detroit, during the earlier years of its existence; and for thirty years has been quoted without hesitation, by distinguished writers on local historical snbjects.

It is not my purpose to refer to the first four chapters, nor to that part of the work which treats of a later period than 1710; but it would be as well to state, that in 1842, the State of New York sent John Romeyn Brodhead to Paris, with instructions to transcribe all documents on file in the archives there, relating to the colonial history of New York; these transcripts were subsequently very ably edited by Dr. E. B. O'Callaghan. Those in which we in Detroit are mostly interested, will be found in New York Colonial Documents Vol. IX, 4⁰, 1112 pages. This work contains collateral information of importance, supplemented with valuable notes by the editor, and covers a period extending from 1631 to 1744.

In the fifth chapter of Mrs. Sheldon's work, at page 99, may be read, "The directors of the Company of the Colony were Jesuits, and it was at their solicitation, aided by the united petition of the Jesuit Missionaries already established in different portions of the Northwest, that they succeeded in obtaining from the Governor General the appointment of Father Vaillant to accompany M. de la Motte Cadillac, and establish himself as missionary at Detroit.

M. Cadillac was a zealous Catholic, as his correspondence abundantly testifies, but he was a Franciscan and a cordial hater of the Jesuits; this fact was undoubtedly well known, as he did not hesitate to speak his sentiments in his official letters, and in his private correspondence; and a disposition to thwart his plans and purposes was soon manifested by that powerful and completely organized body. Many of the difficulties which subsequently arose in the colony, are clearly traceable to these personal dislikes.

Most readers would probably infer from the text that the trading company mentioned was owned and managed by Catholic priests, by Jesuits; and that the founder of Detroit was a member of the Order of St. Francis, or in other words, a priest of the Franciscan Order. The Canada Company, the corporate name of the trading company mentioned, owned in France and managed by seven Canadian directors, at that time, had the monopoly of the commerce of New France. When Cadillac founded the post of Detroit, the directors arranged a treaty with the Governor General, which gave this company control of the trade of Detroit.

The worst foes the missionaries encountered in their work of evangelization among the Indians, were the factors and traders of the Canada Company; who freely exchanged brandy with the Indians for their furs, and the unstinted supply thus obtained, worked ruin to soul and body. On this account particularly, this monopoly was energetically opposed, both in the Colony and in France, by the missionaries of the Society of Jesus. The cause of much of Cadillac's trouble with the Canada Company, arose from the fact, that two of their factors at Detroit were detected in private transactions and reported to Quebec.

The two parties implicated were related to some of the wealthiest directors of the company at Quebec, who persecuted Cadillac on this account, and sought the destruction of the post and colony.

Consequently when the founder of Detroit was in Montreal in 1704, he was arrested at the suit of the directors mentioned. Father Vaillant accompanied Cadillac ostensibly to perform the missionary work around the post, while Father Delhalle, a Recollect, was commissioned as chaplain. Both were exemplary priests, both having special duties. Father Vaillant was one of the most esteemed missionaries in Canada, as the annals of Canadian history will testify.

The sudden departure of Father Vaillant from the post of Detroit has been a puzzle to local writers. But the cause was very simple. Soon after the arrival of Cadillac he sent messengers to the lake tribes of Indians,

inviting them to come down and make their homes at Detroit. Now these tribes were under control of a missionary
system, which had its centre in Michilimacinac. To remove
and come to Detroit would break up these Indian missions,
and this, the Jesuits, who conducted them, did not deem
salutary for the spiritual or temporal interests of their
neophytes. Hence their opposition, not so much to the establishment of the post and colony, but to the designs of
Cadillac against their missions. The latter found Father
Vaillant unwilling to co-operate with his plans and the
missionary chose to leave, but not in the manner stated by
Cadillac, but by canoe by way of the Lake Erie shore.

In the trial which resulted from the charges made by
the Canadian directors of the Canada Company, Cadillac was
acquitted, and in this connection occurs the writing of his
vindication and the acceptance by Mrs. Sheldon as facts, of
what was simply fiction, and in the acceptance of this fiction,
the utterance of what, being founded on a falsity, was still
more fictitious.

Impatient at his being prevented from returning to his
post after his acquittal—"M. la Motte appealed to the Colonial Minister; by the next vessel he received orders," says
Mrs. Sheldon, page 140, "to appear before Count Pontchartrain at Quebec. He obeyed these orders and remained
at Quebec." Now comes the masterpiece of historical fiction
as will be seen below:

"Highly indignant," begins Mrs. Sheldon, in chapter
vii, page 142, "at the supposed failure of all his plans in
regard to the establishment of Detroit, Count Pontchartrain
met Cadillac with bitter reproaches.

"He was, however, permitted to make his defence, and
the conversation which ensued between them was soon
after committed to writing by M. la Motte, accepted by the
minister as correct, and is still preserved among the colonial archives in Paris. The reader will find the following
translation more satisfactory than any modern statement
of facts."

This memorable meeting of the Secretary of State and

of the Marine and Colonies, under Louis XIV. and M. de la Motte Cadillac, is described as having taken place at the Chateau of St. Louis in Quebec the year heretofore stated.

Mrs. Sheldon's translation begins at page 142 and ends at page 204. It opens as follows: "Whence comes it," exclaimed the Count when Cadillac was brought into his presence, "Whence comes it, that you have failed to establish Detroit?"

Without continuing the further quotation of this paper, I shall refer to pages 144 and 146 in which the founder of the post speaks in a scurrilous manner, perhaps badly translated, of Father Vaillant. It was in connection with the disparagement of the standing of Father Vaillant, that the fictitious nature of the account of this interview was discovered.

In 1883 I began to write a history of Detroit from a Catholic standpoint, relying much for the earlier years upon the "Cadillac papers."

When the first ten years had been gone over, I submitted the manuscripts for the correction of such errors as it might contain, to Dr. John Gilmary Shea, in conformity with my custom of deferring to his judgment in all historical questions. Judge of my astonishment when I received the following letter from Dr. Shea:

ELIZABETH, N. J. April 22d, 1883.

My Dear Sir:—I have read your manuscript with interest; the "Cadillac papers" given in Sheldon, require close study and comparison with other documents. The conversation with Pontchartrain is evidently fictitious.

His correspondence with the Governor and Intendant, shows that he never came to Canada. This style of imaginary conversations is not uncommon; and as this document cannot be used as history, we may suspect some others of the same coinage.

There must be exaggeration in regard to Father Vaillant, whose stay at Detroit was very brief, as he appears a few months after in New York State.

I have always felt that these "Cadillac papers" must always be confronted with contemporary documents before accepting their statement.

There is so much Detroit matter, moreover, that the founder need not occupy too much space and rash statements can be avoided.

Had the Secretary of State come from France to Canada, so important a fact could not escape Charlevoix, De la Potherie, and the Canada historians in our day; there would be in the annals of the convents, Ursulines, Hotel Dieu de Quebec, etc., some mention of the fact, but there is no trace of such a thing.

Yours most sincerely,

JOHN GILMARY SHEA.

R. R. Elliott, Esq.

Here was the strong fabric of our historical gospel history levelled to the ground by a few words from Dr. John Gilmary Shea,. The response to my appeals to local writers was not flattering to Dr. Shea, who was unmercifully accused of partisanship on the side of the Jesuits. The Cadillac papers were endorsed as the only reliable records of the times.

Convinced that Dr. Shea was right, I determined to investigate the subject in the interests of history. I then wrote to my friend Bela Hubbard, who was at the time in Europe.

DETROIT, November 26, 1883.

BELA HUBBARD, Esq., Paris.

My Dear Sir:—You are aware that General Cass, while Minister of the United States to France, employed M. Pierre, Margry, to take copies of the "Cadillac papers," on file in the archives of the Marine and Colonies, in Paris; which documents he very generously placed at the disposition of his friends interested in historical studies.

These papers have been translated and published in Mrs. Sheldon's work, from which quotations have been made from time to time, and quite recently by Judge Campbell.

Much of what we all believed to be the exact details of the first settlement of Detroit, has been drawn from these papers and published without fear of contradiction.

Having occasion to submit a memoir, which I had prepared on the "Colony of Detroit," for revision to Dr. John
Gilmary Shea, I was surprised to learn from him that the
authenticity of Cadillac's statements was doubtful.

Dr. Shea says, he does not believe that Count Pontchartrain, Secretary of State and for the Marine and Colonies
came to America at the time stated by Cadillac, in his account of the interview he had with the Minister at Quebec,
on the occasion of his trial there, upon the charges preferred by the directors of the Canada Company.

Dr. Shea says, he finds no records of such a visit in the
archives of the convents and religious houses of Quebec and
Montreal, and advises, that the statements af Cadillac, should
not be accepted, without corroborative testimony.

I am sure Judge Campbell will be pleased, and I shall
feel greatly obliged, if, while in Paris, you can ascertain the
truth regarding the alleged visit of the Count de Pontchartrain to America, at the period mentioned.

Respectfully,
Your obedient servant,
RICHARD R. ELLIOT.

In the following January I received the following response:

My Dear Mr. Elliott:—Your favor of November 26 last,
found me in Spain, and as it was not my intention to return
to Paris, where alone were to be found means for investigation, before spring, I wrote to M. Pierre Margry on the
subject propounded in your letter.

M. Margry is unquestionably the greatest living authority on early Canadian history—and he has access to the
archives.

He did me the honor to reply on the 28th of December
last. As his letter relates in part to matters foreign to your
inquiry I retain the original, but translate for you such portions as have interest in that connection. My Sir Oracle, as
you will see, is as hard to interpret, as other celebrated
oracles of old; I therefore took the liberty of again appeal-

ing to him, asking him to be more explicit ; making use of Judge Campbell's name, and urging the importance to history of clearing up a matter which so directly concerned the veracity of Cadillac, and stating that it could not be difficult to determine from the documents in the archives in Paris, whether Count Pontchartrain visited Canada or not in 1704. To this appeal M. Margry promptly responded, and I send you his letter herewith.

I have also attempted a translation, to the best of my ability, (which is small) and which I presume is not entirely accurate.

M. Margry's chirography is somewhat cramped, and there are sundry erasures which cloud his meaning; perhaps Judge Campbell, who must be familiar with his writing, and is au fait in French, will assist you in in a better rendering of of its meaning.

I trust M. Margry's theory will prove satisfactory; as the Italians say *"si non vero e ben trovato."*

Yours truly,

B. HUBBARD.

The following is the translation of M. Pierre Margry's letter to Mr. Bela Hubbard:

PARIS, 39 Chaussé d' Antin.

January 9, 1884.

SIR:—The Count Pontchartrain never came to Quebec; evidently those who accept this idea are deceived, the statements of Mrs. Sheldon and of Judge Campbell to the contrary, notwithstanding.

But they would be equally deceived, were they, on this account, to discredit the statements made by de la Mothe Cadillac, in connection with his pretended interview with Count Pontchartrain.

These throw themselves upon the memoir of Nov. 14, 1704; to say that Count Pontchartrain was in Canada, since Cadillac held discussion with him ; while others deny that he was there, but admit that he wished to make it appear that he was there.

In truth I am astonished that these two ideas should have entered their minds.

In effect, Cadillac did not intend by his memoir of Nov. 14, 1704, to repeat a conversation which had not taken place, but in placing fictitiously *en scene*, the Minister and himself, giving their mutual replies, he sought to render more apparent the correctness of his own conduct. .

He put into the mouth of the Minister, the observations, the objections, to which he, Cadillac, should triumphantly respond, thus aiding the Minister to think as he, Cadillac desired.

Cadillac prided himself upon his ability as a writer, having for Judge of the law a young Minister who admired people of spirit and Cadillac, the *savan* knowing it, sought to interest him by this dialogue, in which he anticipated his thoughts. Fontenelle had published Dialogues of the Dead, Cadillac imagined for himself a dialogue of people very much alive, but living far away from each other. It was original in management and piquant. There, sir, is my answer.

I regret that the rigors of history do not permit me to be more gallant with Mrs. Sheldon. As to Judge Campbell, whose work upon Michigan is otherwise very acceptable, he will pardon me if he remembers the *mot* of a French magistrate; "the Court renders judgments and not services." I can meanwhile assure him in all sincerity, that it will give me pleasure to be agreeable to him at all times.

Receive the expression of my most distinguished consideration.

PIERRE MARGRY.

Mr. Bela Hubbard,

Hotel de Londres, San Remo, Italy.

This correspondence triumphantly vindicated the reputation for thorough historical accuracy, of Dr. John Gilmary Shea; it shatters our idols here, and leaves us the necessity of confronting every line we may use, from the "Cadillac papers," with some corroborative testimony that will establish its authenticity.

In closing I beg to add the following in regard to Father Vaillant.

Rev. Francis Vaillant de Gueslis, ordained at Quebec, 1675, (Liste Chronologique), Missionary at Fort Hunter, 1679; with the Mohawks, 1683. With Denonville's expedition against the Senecas in 1687. Envoy to Governor Dongan in 1688; at Detroit in 1701; with the Senecas in 1703–7; N. Y. Col. Doc. ix, 672.

This in a few brief sentences, is the index to the career of a distinguished Missionary.

RICHARD R. ELLIOTT.

DESTRUCTION OF AN EARLY LIBRARY. "Governor Moore, with about five hundred more of this Colony, lately made an irruption into Florida, with hopes of taking the Castle of St. Augustine from the Spaniards, but were unfortunate, being forced to raise the siege and come home overland. This expedition. I am afraid, will cost the country £8,000. Our men did much mischief to the Spaniards by burning the town of St. Augustine and their Convent, and by other ravages through the country. They brought us hither a few prisoners (amongst which are three Franciscan friars) and about £200 worth of Church plate, which Governor Moore promised to our Carolina Churches and meeting houses."

"And to show what friends some of them are to learning and books, when they were at St. Augustine they burnt a library of books worth about £600, wherein were a collection of the Greek and Latin Fathers, and the Holy Bible itself did not escape, because it was in Latin. This outrage was done as soon as they arrived, by the order of Col. Daniel, who is one of our Lord's deputies and of the Council here" Rev. Edward Marston to Rev. Dr. Bray, Charleston, Feb. 2, 1702. Doc. Hist. P. E. Church, S. C. 1 pp. 11–12.

LETTERS RELATING TO THE DESTRUCTION
OF THE URSULINE CONVENT,
CHARLESTOWN, MASS.

We are indebted to Rev. Thomas A. Reid, S. J., for the following letters, found among the papers of Mr. Benjamin Hawkes, now in the possession of his daughter, Mrs. Luther F. Brooks.

NAVY YARD, CHARLESTOWN, AUG. 12th, 1834, NOON.
MY DEAR H—

I arrived here safe although not so early as usual and am well. We had last night one of the most daring and successful mobs in this town that has perhaps ever been witnessed in this country if in any other.

I believe I told you something about a young nun that caused some excitement in this community last week, and of which a satisfactory account could not be obtained. The citizens, if they can be properly called such, of this town and Boston determined upon removing what they thought a nuisance, assembled in small squads about in this town at an early hour last evening, and about eleven o'clock set fire to a tar-barrel on one of the hills, half a mile from the Convent. This was a signal for joining all the squads in one and for action; they then proceeded to the Convent and demanded admission, they were told from the Chamber by the Lady Abbes, that they could not be admitted, but if they would come in the morning they might have free access to every part of the premises. This did not satisfy them, they kicked at the doors, broke the windows, but could not enter; they then procured axes and stove the front door in and a part of them entered; they were met by the Abbess, who expostulated with them and even (it is said) threatened them, but it was all of no use. They told her she must quit the house and every other person who was in it, and at the same time forced her from it. The nuns then escaped by a side door, the persons inside then with torches explored every part of the Convent, threw out of the windows the furniture of every description and unhung the doors, kindled a fire with them in the middle of the parlours and commenced destroying Pictures (very valuable) Pianos, Harps and everything they could find, the fire at the same time raging.

The bells which began to ring on the burning of the tar-barrel and afterwards stopped, now began again to ring, and the engines again came from Boston. The noise was so great I could not sleep and after trotting from room to room looking at the fire I resolved to go to it and know what it was, it was a mile and a quarter from my lodgings and when I arrived and saw what was doing I was completely thunder-struck to see a building of brick, as large as the Franklin building in front, with two wings in rear, of half of the size of the front, an elegant Chapel or School, another large building covered completely with a running vine, large out-buildings and about forty cords of wood all on fire at once, and a dancing and infuriated assembly of men throwing the furniture into the flames. I confess it reminded me of the worst days of revolutionary France; after I arrived they fired several small buildings which I presume were wash-house, storehouse, woodhouse and etc., and at half past two I left them in their work of destruction and traveled to my lodgings. About five o'clock this morning they set fire to a large old dwelling house and barn full of hay belonging to the Convent and inhabited by the males who worked in the gardens and lands round the house; they then retired. When I was there, there was twelve or fifteen engines standing round and the enginemen looking on and although the canal runs within a few hundred yards of the Convent, not one drop of water was thrown on the buildings. The whole es-tablishment was said to cost $100.000. The land alone is left of all of it. How differently it must have looked this morning from what it did yesterday morning, the gardens and walks were the most elegant that I ever saw. E. H. Derby's es-tablishment although it cost $80.000 is not to be named the same day with it for beauty and height of cultivation ; it is gone and with it the reputation of Boston and vicinity for an orderly city and the land of steady habits. All Europe and nearly all the world consider, as you very well know, such institutions as this sacred and holy ; there is no knowing what the end of this will be ; I fear there will be both blood and treasure expended before the Catholics will be appeased; to think otherwise, would be to presume that they were much more virtuous and forgiving than other Christians, you will have more of it soon. Part of the Commissioners of the Navy have arrived but have not visited the yard yet, but probably will on Thursday, I had a pleasant talk with the Commissioner yesterday he said E—s would be off in a day or two.

What I was talking with you about (George) can be obtained ; perhaps it will be well for him to come up here during the vacation and show the folks here his cleanly face and hands and pleasant manners. You had better not say anything to him about it, as he may blab it to all the world. My love to all the little ones, the baby in particular, and for yourself accept the assurance of my everlasting esteem and respect.

Yours B. H. Jr.

Four o'clock P. M. We have had a shower, some thunder and lightning but not much ; there appears to be more with you. The companies of Militita were ordered to be in readiness at a moment's warning to repel any riot that may occur in this vicinity. It is feared that the Irish may resent the injury done last night. The nun is well: had been seen by her friends last Saturday and could have left the Convent at any moment had she chosen ; there was therefore no cause their doing what was done last night.

Good bye, ever yours,

B. Hawkes.

NAVY YARD, Charlestown, Thursday aft., Aug. 14, 1834.
MY DEAR HELENA.

I yesterday afternoon received a few lines and a newspaper from you, and sent you a letter written the day before. I have no news to communicate; the excitement raised about the Convent has not yet subsided and I fear it will not until blood is let or property destroyed.

Last night almost every person in the town stood guard; the Police officers were multiplied, the draws on the Bridges were raised, and all persons not armed were desired to keep indoors, which I assure you was no restraint on me. I think at present no further attempt will be made by any one to violate the laws.

The Navy Commissioners and the Secretary visited the Yard this forenoon and were received with great attention; the Commissioners may stay a day or two but the Secretary will start soon for Washington.

You will not receive this until after George's exhibition, therefore nothing is necessary to be said about the distribution of the tickets. You and the girls must go if you please, I fancy you will have no very great treat.

Afternoon Friday.—My love to the little ones, I will be with you to-morrow; in meantime I am respectfully,

Yours,

B. HAWKES.

A CATHOLIC MEDAL IN MASSACHUSETTS. — Mr. S. L. Joyce, of Scituate, Mass., reports that recently in his town some workmen dug up a Portuguese coin and a brass medal, with the Blessed Virgin and the Holy Child on one side, with the legend Dilecto Carmelo, and on the other St. Anthony of Padua, holding the Infant Jesus, with the legend San Antonio, D. P. No Catholics are known to have lived in the place till about thirty years ago.

ILLINOIS AND MIAMI VOCABULARY
AND LORD'S PRAYER.

We are indebted for this relic of the old Catholic Missions to Wilberforce Eames, Esq., of the Lenox Library. The manuscript was at some one of the old missions early in this century, as words from it and the Lord's Prayer are given in the "Notice sur l' Etat Actuel de la Mission de la Louisiane," Paris, 1820, p. 49; Turin, 1822, p. 51.

It is a manuscript of 4 ll. containing 7 unnumbered pp. in double columns, 4to, and is in the Lenox Library. It was apparently written in the latter part of the seventeenth or early part of the eighteenth century. On the verso of the last (blank) page is the endorsement "Commencement d' un Dictionnaire de Langue Sauvage."

There is also a copy of this manuscript in the library of the American Philosophical Society, Philadelphia. It was made by Mr. Duponceau and forms No. LII of a collection recorded by him in a folio account book, of which it occupies pp. 159–162.

Like the original, it is without indication of date or name of author.

Elémens pour servir à la formation d' une grammaire des langues sauvages des Nations des PIAN, des ILLINOIS, des MI, lesquelles nations s' entendent parfaitement les unes les autres quoiqu' il y ait quelque différence dans leurs langues.

Elements to serve for a formation of a Grammar of the Indian languages of the Pian(keshaw), Illinois and Mi-(ami) Indians, tribes which understand each other perfectly, although there are some differences in their dialects.

Il n'y a point d' articles.   There are no articles.

Pronoms personnels.—Personal pronouns.

Moi,	*I,*	Nirλ
'Tu, toi,	*thou, thee,*	Kira
Lui,	*he,*	Ouirλ
Nous,	*we,*	Nironan
Vous,	*you,*	Kironac
Ceux-là,	*they,*	Ouironac

Pronoms réels—Real pronouns.

Une chose, *a thing,* onann. Il faut nommer la chose pour déterminer le pronom. The pronoun cannot be determined till the thing is expressed.

Pronoms possessifs.—Possessive pronouns.

Mon, mien.	*mine,*	Ni	{ uni avec la chose { united with the thing
Ton, tien,	*thine,*	Ki	" "
Son, sien,	*his,*	Oui	" "
Nos, notre,	*our,*	Nironan	" "
Vos, votre,	*your,*	Kironac	" "
Leurs, leur	*their,*	Ouironac	" "

Exemples,—Examples.

Mon chapeau,	*my hat,*	Niouioukoen
Ton chapeau,	*thy hat,*	Kiouioukoen
Son chapeau,	*his hat,*	Ouiouioukoen
Nos chapeaux,	*our hats,*	Nironacouioukoen
Vos chapeaux,'	*your hats,*	Kironacouioukoen
Leurs chapeaux,	*their hats,*	Ouironacouioukoen

Moi-même, myself, n' ajoute rien au pronom simple. Adds nothing to the simple pronoun Nirλ.

Noms principaux.—Chief nouns.

| Dieu, | *God,* | Kissernanetou | (maître de la vie) master of life |

Eglise, *Church*, ANAMEANAMECUŃQUE
(endroit ou l' on prie—place where they pray.)

Prêtre, *priest*, MECATEOCOROIATT (robe-noire.—black gown.)

Tout le monde,	*everybody,*	CIAKAMETOSEGUIAK
Français,	*French,*	OUAMATICOSIAH
Anglais,	*English,*	ANKIRASSI
Américains,	*Americans,*	MASSIPHA
Ciel,	*Heaven,*	KISIK
Beautems,	*fine weather,*	OUANEKISIK
Soleil,	*sun,*	KISIPOL
Lune,	*moon,*	KISIS
Etoiles,	*stars,*	RANKHOÁ
Terre,	*earth,*	ASCKIKHE
Fusil,	*gun,*	PAPIGOINÉ
Mer,	*sea,*	KECICAMENGUE
Rivière,	*river,*	SIPÜNG
Arbre, bois,	*tree, wood,*	TAOUANE
Beaucoup,	*much,*	MISSIRITOM
Peu,	*little,*	TAKAKOM
Homme,	*man,*	ININ
Hommes,	*men,*	ININIOK
Femme,	*woman,*	ICKOÉ
Femmes,	*women,*	ICKOEOK
Air, vent,	*air, wind,*	WOOUTIN
Vie,	*life,*	PEMATIS
Bon,	*good,*	OUAOUANECHEG
Mauvais,	*bad,*	MIANSEHKEG
Hache,	*axe,*	TACAHACAN
Corne,	*horn,*	OUIOUIRÀN
Capotte,	*coat,*	PISICλ
Souliers,	*shoes,*	MAHKISSINA
Bas,	*stockings,*	TAPA
nourriture,	*food,*	MICIPEN
pain,	*head,*	PAHCOISICAN
eau,	*water,*	NIPI

farine,	*flour,*	NOQUIMIN
Maïs,	*Indian corn,*	MICIPI
Chasse longue,	*a long hunt,*	MAMALAOUR
Chasse d'un jour,	*a day's hunt,*	NINAUTONAMAOUR
jour,	*day,*	KISIK
nuit,	*night,*	PECKONTEIG
matin,	*morning,*	CHAJEHPAH
soir,	*evening,*	CRACOIK
année,	*year;*	KICKATOUR
automne,	*autumn,*	TEGNAGHEGH
hiver,	*winter,*	PIPOUNGH
Printems,	*spring,*	MIROUCKAMENGH
Eté	*summer,*	NISSINONGH
chaleur,	*heat,*	LIRITEGH
froid,	*cold,*	RIPAHNOM
langue,	*tongue,*	WILEI
Mort,	*dead,*	WEEPEH
fête,	*festival,*	WIIDIP
bras,	*arm,*	NINIHKECK
jambe,	*leg,*	NICKAHTA
pied,	*foot,*	WISSIT
oreilles,	*ears,*	NITTAGAI
Visage.	*face,*	. . . .
yeux,	*eyes,*	ISCKENGJCONGH
bien,	*well,*	KENTERANN
mal,	*ill,*	MIANLECKECK
Oui,	*yes,*	HAHA
non,	*no,*	MANENTOUI
bonjour,	*good day,*	KICKOA SITORCHEMON
reponse,	*response,*	OHOH
Priere,	*prayer,*	ANAMEHOA
Diable,	*devil,*	MATCIMANETOU
Esprit,	*spirit*	NAMISITCHÉ
Ecriture,	*writing,*	{ MASSANACICAN NIPIEIKEO

Vérité,	truth	ERAMOUCHÒ
Mensonge.	falsehood,	KIRACKICKEI
amour,	love,	TEPAIÉHO
haine,	hatred,	SENCHIRCOECOK
guerre,	war,	NANTOPANIH
paix,	peace,	NACKOMANDITIOK
Pere,	father,	NOSSACK
mere,	mother,	MECKIλ
Mari,	husband,	NAMPEHEMAN
femme,	wife,	OUIONÒ
frère junior,	younger brother,	SIHMAN
frère ainé,	elder brother,	SILENSA
soeur,	sister,	MISSEN
fils,	son,	KOISSO
fille,	daughter,	TAHANÀ
chevelure,	scalp,	TIPAGAN
mains,	hand,	NICH
sang,	blood,	MISKOM
cheveux,	hair,	NISSISSAH
chefs,	chiefs,	CHIMAOK
pipe,	pipe,	POAGAN
Tabac,	tobacco,	ASSEMANOHAN
sac à fumer,	tobacco bag,	TOPAC ANIMOTÉ
Couteau,	knife,	MARISSA
armée,	army,	TANCAPECIK NATOPANECIK
feu,	fire,	SCOTTÉ
pluie,	rain,	CHIMIALEH
maison,	house,	OUITIAME
un,	one,	NICOTE
2		NIHSSON
3		NIHSSONI
4		NIHONI
5		NIAHARANGH
6		KACKATSOUI
7		SOATATSOUI
8		PARAHARÉ
9		NICOTEMANECKI
10		MITATSONI

11		MITATSONI-NICOTE ATSÍ
&c. ajoutant,	*adding,*	ATSÍ
20		MISOUMATENÁ
30		NISSOIMETENλ
40		NIHONI METENA &c
100		NICOTOAGEH
200		NISSON AGEH
1000		MITTAHSOAK
10,000		KICIOUAK
Argent,	*silver,*	SOONRIH
vol,	*theft,*	KIMOHOTENGH
aujourd' hui,	*to-day,*	NOUGON-INOKI
demain,	*to-morrow,*	OUABANK
matin,	*morning,*	CIAJESSλ
hier,	*yesterday,*	ARACAHÉ
cheval,	*horse,*	NICOTE-CASHIÓ
chien,	*dog,*	OREMὸ
ours,	*bear,*	MOKKUOH
boeuf,	*ox,*	RENONSOAH
chevreuil,	*deer,*	MONSOAH
chat,	*cat,*	ASSEOPAN
mouche,	*fly,*	MOUSSIAC
castor,	*beaver,*	AMEKOÁ
poisson,	*fish,*	CHICONESSλ
oiseau,	*bird,*	PINEUSEU
outarde,	*wild goose,*	NICAK
cygne,	*swan,*	OUABANKIA
cocq d' Inde,	*turkey,*	PIREOUAH
pigeon, tourterelle,	*wild pigeon,*	MIMÍ
vieillard,	*old man,*	KIOUSHIAH
jeune,	*young,*	COJONSÁ
jeune fille,	*young girl,*	COESSENSAK
tonnerre,	*thunder,*	NTATCAOUONE
avant,	*before,*	NITAM
chanter,	*to sing,*	NACAMOHOK
parler,	*to speak,*	KAROSSI
parle donc,	*speak then,*	KAROSSIRὸ
aller,	*to go,*	NIAROH

venir,	to come,	PIOUOH
Je suis retourné,	I have returned,	NTTAPOHEHÁ
J'aime cela,	I like that,	NTTAPATÀ
Je ne l'aime pas,	I do not like that,	NISSENCORAHECO
dépêche-toi,	hurry,	OUIOUIPICAOUÉ
allez doucement,	go softly,	OUIKKI
Je suis,	I am,	NIRONAI
J' en ai,	I have,	NNTATTOU
Je n' en ai point,	I have none,	NNTATTOUSSONS
tu en as,	thou hast some,	KITTATTOU
celui-là en a,	he has,	OUIRATTOUCH
nous en avons,	we have,	NITTATTOUMENÁ
vous en avez,	you have,	KIROACHITTATOU
ceux là en ont,	they have,	OUIOUACATTOUOK
Je suis malade,	I am sick,	NIMENTA
Je me porte bien,	I am well,	KIRAKIMENTA
Je ne mourrai jamais,	I shall never die,	ANSI CAOUCNIME PESOUKA
acheter, } vendre, }	to buy, to sell,	NTATAVOAH (traiter)
donner,	to give	KIMIRI
prendre,	to take,	NIMAHAMÉ
laisser,	to leave,	NAKATAMOKANE
faire,	to do,	NIVOASITTOU
commencer,	to begin,	KINNTA
finir,	to end,	SAYÉ
demander,	to ask,	MIRIROÚ
répondre,	to answer,	CAROSSIRÓ
craindre,	to fear,	NICOEHSSÁ
souffrir,	to suffer,	PEH KENTAROARE
gouter,	to taste,	GOUTANTÒ
tuer,	to kill,	NDANKIA
fuir,	to flee,	MANCIAOUÍ
manger,	to eat,	MIRNIICI
boire,	to drink,	NINICENÉ
dormir,	to sleep,	NÉESSÁ

Notre pere faites nous la charité, *Our father do us the charity,*
KISSEMENETOU KITTIMINAOUERÒ

Qu' as tu a vendre? *What have you to sell,* KECKONEIA ETA-VOEIAN

Une paire de souliers, *a pair of shoes,* MAKISINON KITATAMIRÉ

Il ne m'a rien donné, *he has given me nothing,* NIMIRI COSSI OUIKIKOU

Je m' en vais dormir, *I am going to sleep,*   NEESSA—CATA

Allons ensemble à la chasse, *let us go hunting together,* MAMA-OUÉNATON AMAOUIKA

Dinons ensemble, *let us dine together,*   MAMAOUÉ MICITAOUI

Pourrais-je rester chez vous cette nuit ? *May I stay with you to-night?* OUAHI NINÉ PACATA INOKI

Combien voulez vous de cela ? *How much of this do you wish?* TAMI TASSU CATAMEHMANA

C'est trop cher,   *It is too dear,*   OUISSA KINANTOTAH

Tu es avare,   *you are stingy,*   ISSOUKIRÉ

Je vous remercie,   *I thank you,*   OUAOUAHINOU CKITACAM

Va-t-en,   *get out,*   MAN-CIAROU

Tous les hommes mourront, *All men will die,* CEHEKI KINÉ ESSEMINA

Connais-tu le bon Dieu ? *Dost thou know God?* ENKOH KISSE-MANETOU RETAMA

Je ne le connais pas, *I do not not know him,* ENKIKKEN RE-TANSON

Je le connais,   *I know him,*   H ! H ! ENKIKKEN RETAN

Etes-vous de la priere ? *Do you belong to the prayer?* ENCOUH KIRÀ NARNEAK

Pourquoi ne pries-tu pas Dieu, *Why dost thou not pray to God?* KEKOANÉ ONCIANAMEA SEON

Etes-vous baptisé ? *Are you baptised?* ENKOU SA SEPAREKOK

Mais c'est inutile, parcequ' il ne prie pas Dieu, *But it is useless because he does not pray to God,* H ! H ! SA SEPAREKOK

Ne pensez-vous pas à la mort ? *Do you not think of death?* NEPÉ AN KI REPOASSÈ

Il ne faut point s'enivrer, *You must not get drunk,* KATAKI ONSKE BI KEKÒ

Je suis blanc, rouge, jaune, *I am white, red, yellow*, NIVOA BISSÉ, MISKOI, NASSAROAK.

Je suis noir, bleu, vert, *I am black, blue, green*, MACATE OSSI, OSKIPAKIA.

Le vent du sud,   *South-wind*,   SAVANINOTIN

ORAISON DOMINICALE.—LORD'S PRAYER.

Nossak Pemenke Kitaope, ceckimitousegnia tepará kissolimi, kirah debeheretamocané, cecki nironan, kirah cehecki deberetan ouahé aposi pemenki. Inoki micipeneh miricane. Oueni perà kirò cehecki mereo akek kisitojangh rapini-irà ni oueni piraki cehecki mereo akek nivoesit tacou. Catanossa deboe tavieh cané mereo akek kekoa sitojangh. Cecki mací mereo akek pakitamocané peroi nironan. Ouajak deboata ouiakann.

A.   M.   D.   G.

THE DIOCESE OF BROOKLYN.

By Marc F. Vallette.

Fuit homo missus a Deo cui nomen erat Joannes.

The Diocese of Brooklyn was established by His Holiness Pope Pius IX, in 1853. It comprises Long Island, in the State of New York. The Indians are said to have called this island Sewanhacky, Wamponomon and Paumanake. The early Dutch settlers called it Matouwacs or Long Island, while to the early Catholic explorers (Spanish) it was known as the Isle of the Holy Apostles. Surely, no name could have been more appropriate than this latter, for it seemed to have been a forcast of that apostle "sent of God, whose name was John," and who, more than two hundred years later was to be its first resident representative of Peter, the Prince of the Apostles.

Fifty golden years have passed away since three young men, class-mates at Mt. St. Mary's, Emmittsburg, Md., knelt in old St. Patrick's Cathedral, New York, before the valiant Bishop Hughes, and received, at his hands the grand commission that sent them forth to preach Christ and Him crucified. They were Edward O'Neil, Francis Coyle and John Loughlin. On October 18th. 1840, these young men, full of zeal and energy chose "the better part" and devoted the rest of their lives·to the service of their fellow men, at the altar. From that day forth they had no father save God ; no mother save Mary; no wife save the Church; no children save their flocks· They might "suffer but they knew in whom they believed"* They "were set for the rise and fall of many." Father Coyle

---

*Vim patior, sed scio cui credidi.

was assigned to the missions of Sandy Hill, Lansingburg and Waterford. Father O'Neil became Treasurer and Professor of Natural Philosophy and Chemistry at St. John's College, Rose Hill (now Fordham); while Father Loughlin was assigned to St. Patrick's Cathedral (Mulberry Street, New York,) of which he became Rector in 1848. While attached to the Cathedral he went for a time to Utica to assist the Rev. Father Quarter.

Fathers O'Neil and Coyle "have fought the good fight" and are now, we trust, enjoying the reward of their labors. Father Loughlin was reserved that he might plant a tree the wide spread branches of which were to offer refuge and consolation to the wounded hearts of thousands of the children of God.

In 1849, the Rev. John Loughlin was appointed Vicar General of New York, and in the same year we find him at the Seventh Council of Baltimore acting as Theologian to Bishop Hughes. He served in the same capacity at the First Plenary Conncil of Baltimore, in 1852. The Fathers assembled at this Council proposed to the Holy See the creation of several new Dioceses, among them the Diocese of Brooklyn. Pope Pius IX, of holy memory, approved of their designs and by an Apostolic letter of July 29th, 1853, erected the new Sees of Brooklyn, Newark and Burlington, Vt., in the province of New York. When it became necessary to make a choice of a ruler for the new See of Brooklyn, the eyes of the assembled Fathers fell upon the Vicar General of New York.

On the 30th day of October, 1853, old St. Patrick's Cathedral was thronged to witness a ceremony very unusual, in those days. Three worthy laborers in the vineyard of the Lord were to be elevated to the dignity of the episcopate— they were Very Rev. John Loughlin, V. G., or New York, for the new See of Brooklyn ; Very Rev. Louis de Goesbriand, V. G. or the Diocese of Cleveland, for the new Diocese of Burlington, Vt., and Rev. James Roosevelt Bayley, Secretary to Archbishop Hughes, for the new See of Newark, N. Y. Bishop Bayley was promoted to the Archiepiscopal See of Baltimore in 1872 and died in 1877. Bishop de Goesbriand had been a missionary and co-laborer of the late Bishop Rappe, in Ohio, and on the elevation of the latter to the See of Cleveland became his Vicar General and was laboring in that capacity when the Bulls came making him Bishop of Burlington. In June 1890, he celebrated the fiftieth anniversary of his ordination. He still lives to carry on the work of his Divine Master. The consecrator of these three new Bishops was the Most Rev. (afterwards Cardinal) Cajetan Bedini, Papal Nuncio to the Brazils and then on a special visit to the United States. The consecration sermon was preached by the Most Rev. Archbishop Hughes.

Bishop Loughlin lost no time in entering upon his new field of duty. The Catholics of Brooklyn received him as Catholics should, and on Nov. 9th. his installation took place in old St. James Church now became the Cathedral of the new Diocese. It would be difficult to describe the joy that filled the hearts of the little flock that went forth to welcome its future shepherd. Many Catholic Societies from New York joined those of Brooklyn in a grand procession, and over one hundred priests, (a large number for those days) from New York, Jersey City and Brooklyn, took part in the solemn ceremonial. It was, indeed, a happy omen ; it was the beginning of a glorious work; the bow of promise was set in the heaven; another John had come "to give testimony of the light that all men might believe through him," and, "to those that received him, he gave them power to become the sons of God."

Prior to the year 1822 there was not a Catholic Church on Long Island, but in that year (on January 1st.) the Catholic inhabitants of the Village of Brooklyn resolved that "whatever they did in word or work" should be done all in the name of the Lord Jesus Christ: giving thanks to God the Father, through Him. They wanted " their children instructed in the principles of our Holy Religion" and "more convenience in hearing the word of God themselves."

A society was formed, with the approbation of the Rt. Rev. Bishop Connolly, of New York, for the purpose of securing the ends in view and on January 7th. (1822) the first meeting was held at the house of Peter Turner, (father of the late Vicar General Turner) at the S. E. corner of Washington and Front Streets. Associated with Peter Turner were James M. Laughlin and William Purcell. It was found after a careful examination, that only seventy men were able to give any assistance in the good work undertaken, and some of these, not being able to contribute money, generously offered the labor of their hands. On the 2d. of March eight lots of ground were bought at the corner of Jay and Chapel Streets for $800; of this amount $500 was paid in cash and a mortgage was given for the balance. It must be borne in mind that these good men, while acting with the approval of the Bishop of New York, under whose jurisdiction Brooklyn was at that time, were also working under great disadvantages. They were without the aid of a priest and although they made many earnest and repeated requests for one there was none to give them. They were entirely dependent upon the kindness of Very Rev. Dr Power, of St. Peter's Church, Barclay Street, New York, who whenever opportunity offered crossed East river in a row boat and said Mass in a private house. Sometimes his place would be taken by Fathers Philip Lariscy, Richard Bulger, A. McCauley, Michael O'Gorman, Patrick McKenna and others, and these good Fathers would offer up the Holy Sacrifice of the Mass in Mr. Dempsey's " Long Room," in Fulton Street. The first Mass celebrated in Brooklyn was by Rev. Philip Lariscy at the residence of William Purcell at the N. E. corner of York and Gold Streets.

Perseverance such as these good Catholics displayed in the face of so many difficulties, could not go unrewarded; they had purchased ground for the erection of a church and also for a burial ground; they had had this ground blessed on the Feast of St. Mark, (April 25th,) by the Rt. Rev. Dr. Connolly, and they had taken courage from the kind words of Rev. Father Bulger, who preached on that occasion. Slowly but surely the first Catholic Church in Brooklyn advanced towards completion. On Dec. 31st, 1822, the following Trustees were incorporated under the general Act: George S. Wise, Peter Turner, William Purcell, D. Dawson,

P. Scanlan, W. McLaughlin and J. Rose. The work went on but still it was impossible to give them a resident Pastor.* On the 28th of August, 1823, Bishop Connolly dedicated the new church to the honor and glory of God, under the invocation of St. James. The interior of the church was yet unfinished, and upon an altar constructed of a few boards roughly put together, the Rev. John Shanahan said the first Mass. The sermon was preached by the Very Rev. Dr. Power. On the 12th of the following month J. Mehaney was appointed school-master and sexton, with the care of the burial ground which had just been leveled and fenced in. The amount of money expended up to this time was $7,118.16 The most strenuous efforts were still made to secure a resident Pastor. The Rev. Father McKenna, who had ministered to these persevering and energetic Catholics, with some degree of regularity, died on the 4th of October, 1824, and was buried in St. James' churchyard. This was a severe blow to the new and struggling congregation; they were not discouraged, however. In January, 1825, they sent through the Very Rev. Dr. Power, some $220 to Ireland, to the Rev. Father Duffy, in the hope of obtaining his services as their pastor; but as he declined to come, at that time, the money was returned. It was not until the April following that Dr. Power, acting as administrator of the Diocese of New York, (the Bishop being in Europe at the time) was able to send a pastor to St. James.' This was the Rev. John Farnan, who became "the first resident clergyman and who received $600 a year and house rent free." The Rev. John Farnan labored at St. James' until 1832. In 1828 he introduced the Sisters of Charity, who took charge of a school opened in the basement of the church. In 1832, Father Farnan was succeeded by the Rev. John Walsh. Father Walsh made his studies at Montreal, and was ordained in 1827 by Bishop Dubois. He is regarded by many of the old Catholics of Brooklyn as the real founder of the Mission. His pastorate extended over a period of ten years and was marked by zeal for the welfare of his people. Besides St.

*Bishop Connolly had only eight Priests in his entire Diocese at this time.

James' Father Walsh visited the Catholic families at Sag Harbor, Flushing and Staten Island. In 1834 an Act was passed "incorporating the Roman Catholic Orphan Asylum Society in the City of Brooklyn, in the County of Kings." From this we see that the building of the church was soon followed by a move towards the education of Catholic children and a tender care for the orphan.

During his pastorate at St. James' Father Walsh was assisted successively by the Rev. James Dougherty, who died on March 29th, 1841; the Rev. Philip Gillick, Rev. Patrick Donaher, and the Rev. J. McDonough. In 1842 Father Walsh was transferred to Harlem, where he died in 1852. His successor at St. James' was the Rev. Charles Smith.

In the mean time the Catholics of Brooklyn had been increasing in numbers. They began to scatter over the city and soon St. James' was too far away to suit the convenience of those who lived the other side of Fulton Street. The truly Catholic perseverance which had marked the early struggles of the people of St. James' had strengthened their faith and awakened a spirit of self-sacrifice. Cornelius Heeny, a man of means, and of heart too, was ready to do his part towards the erection of another church. In 1835 he gave a piece of land, valued at $8,000, situated at the corner of Court and Congress Streets, and in the following year a new church, under the invocation of St. Paul was erected here. It was built of brick, 72 feet by 125 feet, at a cost of somewhere about $20,000. The debts incurred in its erection were shared by the generous people of St. James,' a truly Christian but somewhat unusual proceeding nowadays. St. Paul's Church was dedicated by Bishop Dubois and his Coadjutor, the Right Rev. John Hughes, D. D. The first regular Pastor was the Rev. Richard Waters, who remained only two years, (1838—1840) but in that time he opened a parochial school which he placed under the care of the Sisters of Charity, and he inaugurated other good works. He was succeeded by the Rev. Nicholas O'Donnell, O. S. A., who, with his brother, the Rev. James O'Donnell, also a Hermit of St. Augustine, came from Philadelphia and labored, not only at St. Paul's, but at many places on Long Island. Father Nicholas O'Donnell was evidently a man of learning and of literary tastes. It was under his editorial management that the first issue of the *Catholic Herald*, the first Catholic paper published in Philadelphia, appeared on January 3rd, 1833. In 1844 he appeared, in connection with his brother, the Rev. James O'Donnell, and the Very Rev. John Hughes, (afterwards Archbishop of New York) in a suit against the County of Philadelphia, to recover damages for the wanton destruction of St. Augustine's Church, (Philadelphia) during the Native American Riots of that year. In 1846 he was recalled to Rome, much to the regret of his parishioners at St. Paul's.

Father O'Donnell was succeeded by the Rev. Joseph A. Schneller, whose long pastorate is still remembered by the older Brooklynites. He was ordained by Bishop Dubois in 1827, and was identified with the Jesuits in the early part of his career. He was a man of literary tastes and was for a time connected with the *New York Weekly Register* and *Catholic Diary*. Before taking charge of St. Paul's he had been pastor of Christ Church, New York, and of St. Mary's Church, at Albany. While in the latter place he engaged in controversy with the Rev. Dr. J. N. Campbell, pastor of the First Presbyterian Church in that city and replied to his pamphlet entitled "Papal Rome." He also published a reply to the Rev. Dr. Sprague's pamphlet entitlet "Protestant Christianity contrasted with Romanism." Father Schneller died Sept, 18th 1862, and was succeeded by the Rev. Robert Maguire.

. In the meantime, Father James O'Donnell had been extending the field of his labors to Williamsburg. In 1841 he built St. Mary's Church. Three years before (1838) Father Dougherty went over from St. Mary's Church (Grand Street) New York, and said Mass in Williamsburg, in a stable on Grand Street. This was not, as some suppose, the first Mass said in Williamsburg, because records show that Father

John Walsh, of St. James' and his assistant, Father Bradley, visited Flushing, Staten Island and Williamsburg in 1837, and they may have gone there as early as 1836. In 1839 Flushing was visited once a month by the Rev. Michael Curran, who also attended Harlem and Throgg's Neck. Father O'Donnell was connected with St. Mary's Church until 1844. From here he ministered to the Catholics at various points on Long Island. We find traces of his work at Jamaica, Sag Harbor, Flatbush, and elsewhere. He died in Boston, April 7th 1861.

The successor to Father O'Donnell at St. Mary's Williamsburg, was the Rev. Sylvester Malone, the present (1891) greatly beloved and justly respected Pastor of the Church of SS. Peter and Paul. He was born at Trim, Ireland, on May 8th 1821. He came to this country in 1838 and at once entered the Seminary at La Fargeville, Jefferson County, N. Y. and a year later he was transfered to St. John's Seminary, Fordham, when he completed his ecclesiastical studies. On August 15th, 1844, he was ordained priest by the Rt. Rev. John McCloskey, D. D., coadjutor to the Bishop of New York. With him were ordained Rev. John Sheridan, Rev. Thomas McEvoy, Rev. William O'Reilly, Rev. Matthew Higgins, Rev. George McCloskey, Rev. Patrick Kenny. Of these seven priests then ordained, Father Malone is the only survivor. We shall have occasion to refer to him in connection with the church of which he is now pastor.

The year 1841 was a church-founding year for the Catholics of Williamsburg. It was in this year that the Rev. John Raffeiner, the "apostle of the Germans" in this section of the country, gathered his scattered countrymen around him, and out of his own purse bought ground and erected a church, which his pious soul led him to dedicate to the Most Holy Trinity.

Old St. James parish had been growing all these years, and another division of the parish was made in 1842. This time the new church was dedicated to the Blessed Virgin, under the title of the Assumption. This church had been commenced some years before by Father Farnan, while under ecclesiastical censure. It was his intention to establish an Independent Catholic Church, but as his congregation did not respond to his needs, the church remained in an unfinished condition for some years. In 1841 it was bought by Bishop Hughes, who placed it under the pastoral charge of the Rev. David W. Bacon. He completed the building and had it dedicated under the above invocation, on June 10th, 1842. Father Bacon was a hard worker and hesitated at nothing. He would dress the altar himself and he has been known to cut out the cassocks worn by his altar boys. His congregation grew rapidly and demonstrated the necessity for further church extension. He was largely instrumental in the erection of the Church of St. Mary, Star of the Sea, but before its completion he was called to a higher dignity and a broader field. He was consecrated Bishop of Portland, Maine, in 1855. His successor was the Rev. William Keegan, who had been his assistant for some time.

Father Keegan was born in Kings County, Ireland, in 1824, and came to this country in 1842. He graduated from St. John's College, Fordham, in 1849, and continued his theological studies and acted as Professor, until October 16th, 1853, when he was ordained by the Most Rev. Cajetan Bedini, Archbishop of Thebes and Papal Nuncio to the United States. He was almost immediately appointed Assistant at the Church of the Assumption, and, on the promotion of Father Bacon to the See of Portland, he became its Pastor. It was not long before he enlarged and beautified the church. Some time later he erected, what was then, one of the finest parochial school houses in the country. In 1880 he was appointed Vicar General of the Diocese, and he held that honored position up to the time of his death, May 10th, 1890.

We have seen that old St. Mary's Church (North Eighth and First Streets,) Williamsburg, was commenced in 1841 by Father James O'Donnell. It was an unpretentious wooden structure, but it was a start; and the Catholics of that day, for a long distance around, were wont to bury their dead in its immediate vicinity. The little church has long since disappeared, but the old tomb-stones stood for fifty years and told the Catholics of to-day who had been the founders of their parish. Last year (1890) they disappeared, the dead were removed to Holy Cross Cemetery and the ground will probably be sold for business purposes. The history of the old church, though brief, is not devoid of interest because of the mighty tree that grew from this little mustard seed. It was dedicated in 1843 by Bishop Dubois and the sermon was preached by Father O'Donnell. On the same day a Temperance Society, the first in Brooklyn, was established by the Very Rev. Dr. Felix Varela, V. G., of New York. In 1844, just after his ordination, Rev. Sylvester Malone became its pastor. He found a debt of $2,300, no small amount in those days, staring him in the face. His people, too, were scattered over a large extent of territory, for his, parish extended to Hallett's Cove on the North, Myrtle Avenue on the south, Middle Village on the east, and the East River on the west. Before the end of three years, by energy and trust in God, he secured not only the payment of this debt but in the purchase of a site for a new church in a more eligible locality "convenient for the Catholics of the fourteenth as well as those of the thirteenth ward, which were the only settled sections of Williamsburg," at that time. On May 11th, 1847, Bishop Hughes laid the corner-stone of the present church of St. Peter and Paul, (Second Street near South Second) and work proceeded so rapidly that it was dedicated to the service of God on Sunday, May 8th, 1848. The years that followed were years of labor and suffering to the good pastor and of anxiety to his people. In 1849 Father Malone fell a victim to that dreadful scourge, the small-pox, contracted while attending to his duties. Scarcely had he recovered when the cholera broke out in his parish. It is needless to say that the good priest was at his post and that he again shared the maladies of his people as well as their troubles. Misfortunes never come alone, and hardly had he recovered from this second attack when the scourge of ship-fever fastened its grip upon him. St. Peter and St. Paul prayed for him and Father Malone, happily, lives to this day to bless a flock by whom he is revered.

> "He wears the marks of years well spent,
> Of virtue, truth well tried, and wide experience.
> Age sits with decent grace upon his visage
> And worthily becomes his silver locks."
> ——— ———the poor, the pris'ner,
> The fatherless, the friendless, and the widow,
> Who daily own the bounty of his hand,
> All cry to Heaven, and pull a blessing on him."

A nature like Father Malone's shrinks from that publicity which personal interest too often courts and his wishes should be respected. It may be permitted to say of him, however, that he holds a place in the hearts of non-Catholics as well as in those of his own people. In 1854 he went to Rome to be present at the definition of the Dogma of the Immaculate Conception. During his absence the anti-Catholic prejudice that had manifested itself in the burning of churches in Philadelphia and elsewhere, and in the destrution of Orphan Asylums in Boston, reached Williamsburg, and threatened Father Malone's church. As the Know-Nothing rioters advanced they were met at the church door by Mayor Wall (a non-Catholic) who declared that he would protect his absent friend's church, if it cost him his life. The church was saved and stands to-day as a noble monument to charity and good will among men.

As far back as 1846, the Catholics of Gowanus and vicinity were looked after by the clergy of the other churches, as the opportunity offered. Father Peter McLaughlin gathered them together in a small wooden structure and organized a parish. The old church was replaced by a much more suitable edifice in 1850. St. Patrick's Church at Fort Hamilton, was built in 1849.

It was a long distance from old St. James' and the Church of the Assumption to Father Malone's Church in Williamsburg, and yet they were "adjoining parishes." The number of Catholics was growing in this long stretch of territory and they began to feel that there ought to be a church situated somewhere in the Wallabout region. The Catholic laymen of old St. James' had gathered together, subject to the Bishop, of course, and built a church and then waited until the Bishop could give them a priest. Why could not this be done again? There was a public house on the old Newtown Road (now Flushing Avenue) kept by a Mr. Mackey, an Irish Catholic. Here, some time in the early forties, a number of Catholics were wont to meet and talk' over the need of a church. They were earnest men and meant business. They agreed that each man should contribute a certain amount and finding that they had every prospect of success, they began to look around for a suitable lot. Their patron saint befriended them. A small frame Methodist meeting house on Kent Avenue near Willoughby Avenue, was purchased with two lots of ground, from the minister, who found fishing more profitable than preaching, for something like $3,000. These happy sons of Ireland immediately set to work to make such alterations as would transform their new property into a Catholic Church. This done they petitioned Bishop Hughes to send them a priest, but he had none to give them; yet, with the example before them of the old St. James' people twenty years before they had "learned to labor and wait," until, finally, in 1843 the Rev. Hugh Maguire, who had been laboring among the French Canadians of St. Lawrence County was given them as Pastor. Before six months had passed away he found it necessary to enlarge the old church. Later on a basement was added, in which he opened a school for the children of his constantly growing congregation. Ten years had passed away since the first meeting at Mackey's "house of call," and the little mustard seed had been growing steadily. Brooklyn no longer had to depend on New York for its priests. It had now a Bishop of its own and his far-seeing eye was not long in telling him that a new and much larger church must be built at once. The corner stone of the present beautiful edifice was laid on November 5th. 1854 and the new St. Patrick's Church was dedicated to the service of God in August 1856. The old church was turned into a school house and was used as such for many years. Among its teachers may be mentioned Manly Tello, Esq., editor of the Cleveland *Catholic Universe*, and Mr. John Gallagher, now principal of the Brooklyn Training School for Teachers. The old building in time, gave way to the splendid Academy for boys, which was placed under the care of the Franciscan Brothers. The girls were provided for in the large asylum back of the school and conducted by the Sisters of Mercy. After a pastorate of nineteen years Father Maguire was succeeded by Rev. P. C. Fagan, (1862 to 1865); Rev. E. G. Fitzpatrick (1855 to 1872) and by the present, (1891) pastor the Rev. Thomas Taaffe.

" Father Thomas " as many of his people love to call him, was born at Dromard, County Longford, Ireland, in 1837. He made his ecclesiastical studies at the well-known missionary college of All Hallows where he was ordained, in 1863. He came to this country immediately after his ordination and labored, successfully at the churches of St. Mary, Star of the Sea, and at our Lady of Mercy, in Brooklyn. It was while at the latter place that he evinced that executive ability which pointed him out to Bishop Loughlin, as the man who alone was able to lift St. Patrick's Church out of the financial difficulties in which it was involved. Hardly had Father Taaffe put the church of Our Lady of Mercy on its feet and was justly entitled to a season of rest, when he was sent to face a debt of over $70,000 at St. Patrick's.

He had taken the vow of obedience to the will of his superious and without a murmur, he removed to his new field of labor. But before he could begin to cut down that debt he was obliged to put $20,000 more to it. The parochial house was unfit for habitation; his congregation was growing and would soon require more priests to meet their wants. A suitable house must be provided and that immediately. The work was undertaken ; the house was built and two additional lots were purchased for school purposes ; and what is better still, the church is now out of debt.

We have spoken of the church of the Holy Trinity which Father Raffeiner had built on lots purchased with his own money, in 1841. The German Catholics of Williamsburg

Had been growing to such an extent that their old church became too small to accommodate them, and on June 29th 1853 the Most Rev. Archbishop Hughes laid the corner-stone of a second and larger church of the Holy Trinity. Father Raffeiner labored here until 1861 when he went to his reward. Few priests have done more for their people than good Father Raffeiner. He was born at Mals, in the Tyrol, on December 26th. 1785 and received in baptism the name of John Stephen. From his tenderest childhood he displayed those qualities of piety, firmness and perservance which distinguished him in after life. His early manhood was not devoid of struggles. The agitated condition of his country and the imprisonment of Pope Pius VII, made him almost despair of reaching ordination. For a time he devoted himself to medicine, with no little success, but his yearning for a life in which he might spend himself for the benefit of his fellow men grew stronger with his knowledge of the inner life of men. He resolved to resume his theological studies at his old home in Tyrol. On May 1. 1825, at the age of forty he had the happiness of seeing the realization of his life long desires ; by receiving the commission that enabled him to cure souls as well as bodies. In 1832, he came to America to minister to to the needs of his country-men in these regions. He arrived in New York on January 1. 1833, and was warmly received by Bishop Du Bois who prevailed upon him to remain in New York. From that time until the day of his death he devoted himself to the service of God and of his people. He extended the fruits of his labors to Boston, Buffalo, Syracuse, Patterson, etc., and at the time of his death he could point to thirty churches in New York State that owed their origin and prosperity in one way or another to his zeal and devotion. Of his labors in Williamsburg we have already spoken. He died in July 16th 1861, and was succeeded as pastor of the church of the Holy Trinity by the Rev. Michael May, the present honored Vicar General of the Diocese of Brooklyn.

Very Rev. Michael May, V. G., was born at Waldkirch, Bavaria, June 2d 1826, and was ordained on July, 19th 1851. After eight years of service in his native land, he determined to come to America and arrived in New York on March 2d, 1859. Bishop Loughlin accepted his services and, at once, assigned him to duty at the church of the Most Holy Trinity, Father Raffeiner found him *ein priester nach dem herzen Gottes.* and felt that he would have, in Father May a successor who would carry on the work of the parish as he had planned it. The care of the young, the orphan and the sick commended themselves to him, and his wisdom and prudence may be seen in the magnificent church he has reared to the service of God; in the flourishing schools with their 1500 children ; in the Orphan Asylum with its 400 inmates, in the hospital which has during the last year opened its doors to 1,647 males and 622 females besides the 400 who received dispensary treament.

Bishop Loughlin has not failed to manifest his well deserved appreciation of Father May's work by making him Vicar General.

(To be continued.)

NEW YORK IN 1831.

From an introductory letter from Lady Wellesley I was privileged to call on the Catholic Bishop of New York. He is a pleasant and intelligent man, and has a cast of countenance very similar to what we often find in pictures of cardinals and popes With this gentleman I had a long conversation, during which he flattered me by saying that I should obtain much encouragement in America. He informed me that there were upwards of 30,000 Roman Catholics in and about New York. A large flock he observed and many of them very ignorant; but I find a great deal of good feeling among them and a tractableness which is very gratifying.

"The Catholic Bishop made a somewhat curious remark, which I did not soon forget ; that the Protestants and Roman Catholics are approximating rapidly toward each other and that we shall be Catholics in the end."

Rev. Isaac Fidler's Travels in 1831. Published in 1833.

WAS THERE A JESUIT COLLEGE AT KASKASKIA

IN THE DAYS OF THE FRENCH?

After the English conquest of Canada and the occupation of the territory North-west of the Ohio by British authority, references are found in correspondence and in time in print, to a Jesuit college at Kaskaskia, Illinois. As the Jesuits had all been carried off at the cession of the country to England in pursuance of orders from the Superior Council at New Orleans, there were no Jesuits in Illinois when the British troops after great endeavor reached Fort Chartres to take possession of the Western Country, although one Father, Sebastian Meurin in time was allowed to return to the Spanish side of the Mississippi and eventually took up his abode in Illinois. English writers, therefore, in speaking of a Jesuit College could not speak of any actually existing in Illinois, but of something that they had been led to believe existed under the French rule.

The earliest reference is in a letter written June 27. 1779 (Michigan Pioneer Collections, Vol 9. p 338) "The Kaskaskia is no ways fortified, the fort being still a sorry pinchetted enclosure around the Jesuit College."

In the Prefatory Advertisement to The American Practical Brewer and Tanner, By Joseph Coppinger, New York 1815 we read : "The more so, when it is known that in the reign of Louis XIV., the merchants of Bordeaux presented a memorial to that monarch praying him to put a stop to the importation of the wines of Kaskaskias into France, as likely, if permitted, to be injurious to the trade of Bordeaux. There was at that time a College of Jesuits established in that country, the superiors of which caused the wine to be cultivated with great success, and quantities of it were at that time sent to France."

Any account of such a College must be sought in French writers between 1700 and 1763. Charlevoix, the Historian, visited Kaskaskia and wrote from there October 20th. 1721. " I arrived at the Kaskaskias the next morning at nine o'clock. The Jesuits had a flourishing mission there, which has just been divided into two, as it was deemed expedient to form two villages of Indians instead of one. The most populous is on the bank of the Mississippi. Two Jesuits, Father le Boullanger and Father de Kereben have spiritual charge; half a league lower down is Fort Chartres, a gunshot from the river. Mr. Dugué de Boisbrilland, a Canadian gentleman, is Commandant there for the Company to which this post belongs; and all the space between begins to be settled by French people. Four leagues further down, a league from from the river, is a large settlement of French, almost all Canadians who have a Jesuit, Father de Beaubois, as parish priest. The second village of Illinois is two leagues off, and further inland. A fourth Jesuit, Father Guymonneau has charge of it. The French are very comfortable here. A Fleming, employed by the Jesuits, has taught them to plant wheat which succeeds well. They have horned cattle and poultry." " The French village is bounded on the north by a river, the banks of which are so steep, that although the water sometimes rises twenty-five feet, it rarely leaves its bed."

It is evident that he found no educational establishment there, all his fellow religious being employed on the mission.

There are several letters from Jesuit Fathers in the Illinois country in the Lettres Edifiantes et Curieuses, all of which are given in English by Bishop Kip in his " Jesuit Missions," but there is not a word in any of them that can give the slightest foundation for any theory that the Jesuits had a College at Kaskaskia. The "Bannissement des Jesuites de la Louisiane " (Paris 1865) is equally silent. It is a contemporary document, and mentions only six chapels and houses occupied by the Fathers (pp 35-36) but has not a word about a College. The account of the seizure of their property at Kaskaskia (pp 35-6) mentions only their residence.

Jefferys in "The Natural and Civil History of the French

Dominions in North and South America" London 1760, describes the Illinois country (pp 137-8) but the story of a College at Kaskaskia finds no support in his pages. None of the French documents collected by J. R. Brodhead or B. P. Poore allude to such a College, or to any one as teacher or pupil there, or any allowance made for its maintenance.

It would seem therefore that English writters after the loss of the territory by the French, originated the story, using the word College, simply as equivalent to Residence.

CONDITION OF ST. PETER'S CHURCH NEW YORK IN 1800.

Jan, 10. 1800. The trustees of St. Peter's. N. Y. write in most respectful terms to Dr. Carroll, and represent that the Rev. Mr. McMahon would no doubt be very useful to the large, (and they wished they could say, flourshing) Congregation ; but the great difficulty was to provide for his support. They request Dr. Carroll to suggest by what means he contemplates the revenue of the church to be increased, while they suggest that this result would probably be obtained by having "suitable prayers and sermons in the afternoon on Sundays," two charity sermons in the year," and your admonition to the clergy to interest the numerous offspring of Catholics in this city in the Christian doctrine, which they are totally ignorant of." This the people had been long expecting. The following was the income at that time.

		Expenses.	
Rent of Pews, - - -	$1120		
Collections about -	360	Rev. O'Brien's salary	$600
	$1480	House rent - -	345
		Interest on Loan -	315
		Contingencies -	125
			$1385

Debt of the Church

Loan from Trustees individually · - -	$2000
" " U. S. Bank - - - - -	2000
" " Dom. Lynch, and Thos. Stoughton -	2500
	$6,500

GONZALO DE MENDOZA'S "HISTORIA DE LAS CO-SAS MAS NOTABLES, RITOS Y COSTUMBRES DEL GRAN REYNO DE LA CHINA," AND ITS PLACE IN AMERICANA AND NEW MEXICANA.

As a matter of Bibliography it may seem strange to some that a work on China can have any place at all in collections of books on American history in general or New Mexico in particular. The work of Mendoza contains, however, as an Appendix, an "Itinerary of the New World". describing the travels of a party of Franciscan Fathers around the world, crossing Mexico from sea to sea. Their description of New Spain gives it a place among Americana. This work ran through more than twenty editions between 1585 and 1655, in Spanish, Italian, French, English and Latin, a fact which proves its great popularity. All these editions come properly under Americana. But there are two types of Mendoza's Historia and some of the editions follow one and some the other. The editions of one type contain very interesting matter relating to New Mexico, while in editions of the other type this part is entirely wanting. Hence some editions are valuable from the fact that they contain early printed accounts of New Mexico, and come into collections of books on that ancient province, while the editions of the other type have no place at all among New–Mexicana. Without some guide it is impossible to tell whether a copy described in a catalogue contains an account of the early missionary visit of the Franciscan Friar Agustin Rodriguez to the Pueblos of New Mexico or not. The following notes are given to prepare the way for a complete bibliography of Mendoza's China.

A. The first edition appeared in Spanish at Rome in 1585, with the title "Historia de las Cosas mas Notables, Ritos y Costvmbres, del gran Reyno dela China, sabidas assi por los libros delos mesmos Chinas, como por relacion de Religiosos y otras personas que an estado en el dicho Reyno. Hecha y ordenada por el muy R. P. Maestro Fr. Ioan Gonzalez de Mendoça de la Orden de S. Agustin, y penitenciario Appostolico a quien la Magestad Catholica embio con su real carta y otras cosas para el Rey de aquel Reyno el año. 1580. Al Illustrissimo S. Fernando de Vega y Fonseca del consejo de su Magestad y su presidente en el Real delas Indias. Con vn Itinerario del nuevo Mundo. Con Privilegio y Licencia de su Sanctidad. En Roma, a costa de Bartholome Grassi, 1585, en la Stampa de Vincentio Accolti.

It is a small octavo of 440 pages, with 29 preliminary and three blank pages. On page 341 is

Ytinerario del Padre Cvstodio Fray Martin Ignacio, de la Orden del bienauenturado Sant Francisco, que paso ala China en compañia de .otros religiosos de la misma Orden, y de la Provincia de S. Ioseph, por orden del Rey. D. Philippe nestro Señor, y de la bvelta que dio por la India Oriental y otros Reynos, rodeando el Mundo, donde se trataran las cosas mas notables que entendio y vio en la jornada, y los ritos, ceremonias y costumbres, de la gente que toparon, la riqueza, fertilidad, y fortaleza de muchos Reynos por donde paso, con la descripcion que conforme a la noticia que tuuo de ellos pudo hazer."

This Ytinerario extends to page 440 and contains no New Mexico matter.

B. The next year another edition appeared at Madrid, with nearly the same title, adding however after the date 1580, " Y nueuamente añadida por el mesmo Autor"—"And newly added to by the same Author." It was printed at Madrid by Querino Gerardo Flamenco for Blas de Robles.

It is an octavo volume of 368 leaves, 24 preliminary and 16 supplementary pages. On leaf 268 is

Itinerario y Epitome de todas las cosas notables que ay desde España, hasta el Reyno de la China, y de la China

a España, boluiendo por la India Oriental despues de hauer
dado buelta a casi todo el mundo. En el qual se trata de
los ritos, cerimonias, y costumbres de la gente que en todo
el ay, y de la riqueza, fertilidad, y fortaleza de muchos
Reynos, y la descripcion de todos ellos. Hecha por el pro-
prio antor deste libro, assi por lo que el ha visto, como
por relaciv verdaderissima que tuuo de religiosos Descalços
de la Orden de Sant Francisco que lo anduuieron todo el
ano de 1584.

The Itinerary in this second edition enlarged by the
Author is not that of Father Martin Ignacio, but a new one
prepared by Fray Juan Gonzalez de Mendoza himself. It
begins on leaf 268 and ends on leaf 208 (misprint for 308)
Chapter VII, folio 286 is "On New Mexico, and its discovery
and what is known there of." Chapter VIII, folio 289 "Continues the Discovery of New Mexico." Chapter IX, folio 294
"Continues about New Mexico and the things seen therein."
Chapter X, folio 297 "Continues about New Mexico," thus
giving 30 pages to this early account of New Mexico.

The Roman edition A is followed by that of Valencia,
1585 ; Madrigal, Madrid, 1586 ; the Italian translations,
Rome, 1586 ; Muschio, Venice, 1586 ; Venice, 1587-8 ; the
Spanish, Bellero, Antwerp, 1596.

The second edition B with the Itinerary by Mendoza,
and including the New Mexico chapters is followed by the
Spanish edition of Medina del Campo, 1595 ; the French
translation of Luc de la Porte, Paris, 1588-9 ; the Latin,
Frankfort, 1589 ; the French by Perier, 1589 ; the French,
Jean Arnaud, 1606 ; the French, Lyons, 1609 ; the French,
Rouen, 1614.

As to the Italian editions by Avanzo, Venice,1586-88-90 ;
Genoa, 1586 ; the German translation, 1589 ; Bologna, 1589 ;
Paris, 1600; Geneva, 1606; Lyon, 1606; the writer cannot say.

The London Edition 1588 followed A, but introduced
the New Mexico part from the French of Luc de la Porte, so
that it belongs to both categories. It has been reprinted by
the Hakluyt Society, London, 1853-4.

The Latin edition Frankfort (1589) and the Dutch, Amsterdam, 1595, give only three books and have no Ytinerario.

After the works of Cabeza de Vaca, 1542 describing Narvaez's expedition and its results, the work of the Gentleman of Elvas, 1557, describing De Soto's, and the accounts of Father Mark of Nice, and Coronado in Ramusio, 1565, this is the next account of explorations within the limits of the United States. Though three centuries have elapsed there are still names and places to trace the course of Espejo's journey to rescue the missionaries. New Mexico, the Rio del Norte and Conchos rivers, Zia, Acoma, Zuñi, the Queres and Taos tribes still remain memorials of the past.

Espejo's narrative was printed at Madrid in Spanish in 1586 ; and reprinted the same year in Paris by Richard Hakluyt. An edition of 1636 is also referred to.*

The Missionary Journey of Friar Augustine Rodriguez, O. S. F. to New Mexico and the Expedition of Don Antonio Espejo to discover his fate.

From the "Historia de las Cosas mas Notables, Ritos y Costumbres del gran Reyno de la China," of Father John Gonzalez de Mendoza, of the order of St. Augustine.

I. Of New Mexico, and its Discovery and what is KNOWN THEREOF.

I proceed to treat of New Mexico, which as being so new a thing it will I believe be a matter of much interest.

I have already said in the said (fifth) chapter that in the year 1583, fifteen provinces had been discovered which the explorers called New Mexico in the mainland of New Spain, and I promised to give an account of the discovery, as I shall do with the greatest possible brevity, because if all they saw and knew was to be set forth diffusely, it would be necessary

*I am indebted for much kind assistance in this notice to Wilberforce Eames, Esq., of the Lenox Library.

to make a special history of them. The substance of it is, that in the year 1581, a religious of the order of Saint Francis, named Friar Augustine Ruyz, (1) who resided in the valley of St. Bartholomew, (2) learning by the report of certain Concho Indians, who treated with other Indians known to them, called Passaguates, that to the northward, travelling always by land, there were certain great towns, never known to our Spaniards or discovered, he with the zeal of charity and of the salvation of souls, asked leave of the Count of Coruña, Viceroy of the said New Spain, and his superiors to visit them, to endeavor to learn their language, and that known baptize them and preach the holy gospel to them. Having obtained permission of the aforesaid, taking two other companions of his same order, (3) he set out with eight soldiers, (4) who voluntarily wished to accompany him, to carry out his Christian and zealous intention. After some days march they reached a province called of the Tiguas, distant 250 leagues north of the mines of Santa Barbara, where they began their journey. In this province on a certain occasion the natives killed one of the two companions of the said Father. (5) He and the soldiers who accompanied him, seeing and deploring this event, and fearing that some greater harm might result from this, agreed with common consent to return to the mines from which they had set out, considering that the party with them was very feeble to resist the events which might arise so far from the settlements of

(1) Rodriguez, a native of Niebla near Seville in Spain, and a lay brother. Torquemada, Monarquia Indiana, iii p. 626; Vetancurt, Cronica de la Provincia del Santo Evangelio, iii, 298

(2) Now Allende in Chihuahua. The Conchos who occupied the valley which still bears their name, belonged to the Mexican family of languages. Pimentel, Cuadro Descriptivo i p 65; Orosco y Berra, Geografia de las Lenguas, p. 55.

(3) They were priests, Fathers Francis Lopez, and John of St. Mary, a Catalonian.

(4) Commanded by Francis Sanchez Chamuscado. The names of all are given by Villagra in his poem Historia de la Nueva Mexico. See U. S. Cath. Hist. Mag. i p. 172.

(5) Father John of St. Mary set out alone for Mexico to obtain other Fathers and was killed the third day; Torquemada iii, p. 627; Vetancurt, Menologio Franciscano, iv p. 412. The soldiers set out before Father John.

the Spaniards, and so far from necessary aid. The two surviving religious not only did not share this opinion, but rather seeing an opportunity to execute their good desire, and so great a harvest ready for the table of God ; seeing that they could not persuade the soldiers to push their discovery further, remained in the said province with three Indian boys and a half-breed whom they had brought with them, it seeming to them that though they remained alone, they were safe there, from the affability and affection with which the natives treated them. When the eight soldiers arrived at their desired point, they at once sent a report of what had happened to the Viceroy, in the City of Mexico, which is 160 leagues distant from the said mines of Santa Barbara. The religious of Saint Francis greatly regretted that their brethren had remained, and fearing that the Indians would kill them when they saw them alone, began to excite the courage of some soldiers to return to the said province with another religious of the same order called Friar Bernardine Beltran, in order to rescue the two said religious from danger, and continue the enterprise undertaken.

At this juncture there was at the mines for some purpose a gentleman from the City of Mexico, named Antonio de Espejo, a native of Cordova, a wealthy man of much courage and skill, zealous for the service of his Royal Majesty, our Lord Philip II. When he heard the desire of the said religious and the importance of the matter, he volunteered to undertake the expedition, spend part of his substance and risk his life in it, if permission could be obtained from some person representing his Majesty. This the said religious obtained, and it was given by Captain John de Ontiveros, Superior Alcalde for his Majesty in the towns called the Four Cienegas, which are in the government of New Biscay, 70 leagues from the said mines of Santa Barbara, not only permitting him to go, but also to raise people and soldiers to accompany him and aid in carrying out his Christian purpose. (1)

The said Anthony de Espejo took up the matter so ear-

_____

(1) Torquemeda, ili p. 359.

nestly that in a few days he gathered the necessary soldiers and supplies for the expedition, expending on it a good part of his estate, and he set out with them all from the valley of Saint Bartholomew on the 10th day of November, 1582, taking for what might occur 115 horses and mules, and a supply of arms, munitions, and provisions and some servitors.

He directed his march northward, and two days after met a number of the Indians called Conchos in rancherias or villages of straw houses, who, as soon as they recognized the Spaniards, having long had intercourse with them, came forth to receive them with signs of joy. The food of these Indians and of the others in this province, which is a large one, live on the flesh of rabbits, hares and deer, which they kill, and of all which there is a very great quantity. They have much maize which is the corn of the Indies, pumpkins and good melons, and plenty of them : and there are many rivers which contain a great quantity of very good fish of various kinds : they almost all go naked, and the arms they use are the bow and arrow ; and they live under the rule and lordship of Caciques like the Mexicans. No idols were found, nor could they learn that they worshipped anybody, so that they readily consented that the Christians should set up crosses, and they seemed well pleased with them, after they had been informed by our people of their meaning which was done through the interpreters they took along ; by their means they learned of other towns to which the said Conchos guided them, escorting them more than twenty-four leagues, which were all settled by people of their nation, who came out peacefully to receive them, in consequence of the notice which the Caciques sent from town to town.

After making these twenty-four leagues they reached another Indian nation called the Passaguates, who lived in the same manner as the said Conchos, their neighbors, and who treated them in the same way, guiding them four days march further, by the action of the Caciques in the manner already explained. On this march our people found many silver mines, of much and very rich ore according to the opinion of those who understood. A day's march from these they reached another nation called the Tobosos, (1) who on seeing the guise of our people, took to the mountains, leaving their houses and towns deserted. It was afterwards known that some years before some soldiers who were in search of mines passed there, and carried off some of the natives captive. This made the rest of them afraid and suspicious. The Captain ordered them to be called, and assured that no harm should be done them, and he assumed so friendly a manner, that many came to whom he gave food and presents, welcoming them and declaring through the interpreter that they had not come to injure anyone. By this means they were all quieted, and consented to the erection of crosses, and the mystery of them was explained. They showed signs of great satisfaction on receiving them, and in token thereof accompanied the Spaniards as their neighbors had done, till they placed them in a land inhabited by a different nation, distant some twelve leagues from theirs. They use the bow and arrow and go naked.

II. The Discovery of New Mexico Continued.

The nation to which the said Tobosos guided them was called Iumanos, whom the Spaniards also call Patarabueyes (2.) They have a large province with many towns and a large population. The houses are built of mason work, with flat roofs. The towns are laid out with order. All the men and women have their faces, arms and legs striped. They are a corpulent race, and more civilized than those hitherto seen ; and they had abundant provisions, and many game animals and birds, and a great quantity of fish, by reason of having great rivers which come from the north, and one as large as the Guadalquivir, which empties into

(1)   The Tobozos were spread over Coahuila, Durango, Nueva Leon and Chihuahua ; but their language is lost.   Orozco y Berra, pp. 61, 66.   Benavides includes them among the fierce and savage tribes, p. 7.

(2)   This tribe was in the valley of the Pecos and in Chihuahua   It was to this tribe that V. Mary de Agreda was believed to have appeared and instructed them in Christianity.

the North Sea. (1.)   It contains many lakes of salt water, which evaporates at a certain time of the year, and makes very good salt.   They are a warlike people and showed it at once, because they attacked us with arrows the first night we encamped and killed five horses, wounding as many more badly, and they would have left none alive had not the sentinels defended them.   Having done us this bad turn they deserted the place and ascended a neighboring sierra, to which the Captain proceeded next morning with five well armed soldiers, and an interpreter named Peter, an Indian of this very nation, and by good reasons he calmed and pacified them, making them return to their town and houses, and inducing them to notify their neighbors that they were not men who injured anyone, nor intended to take their property. This he easily effected by his prudence and by giving the caciques some strings of glass beads which he took for the purpose, hats and other trifles : in consequence of this and of the good treatment given them, many of them accompanied our people for several days, always marching along the bank of the great river above mentioned.   All the way there were many towns of Indians of this nation, which continued for the space of twelve days, during all which, notified by the caciques from town to town, they came out to receive our people without bows or arrows, and brought them abundant provisions, and other presents and gifts, especially hides and chamois-skins very well dressed and not exceeded by those of Flanders.   This people were all dressed, and it was found that they had some light of our holy faith, because they made signs of God, looking up to heaven, and they called him in their language Apalito, and they recognized him as Lord from whose bounty and mercy they confessed that they had received life and natural existence, and temporal good.   Many of them with their wives and children came to the religious, who, as we have said, accompanied the said Captain and Soldiers, to be blessed by him and have the sign of the cross made on them.   When he asked them from whom they had

(1)   Here they evidently reached the Rio Grande.   In old times the Pacific was the South Sea, and the Atlantic the North Sea.

acquired this knowledge which they possessed of God, they replied, from three Christians and a negro who had passed there and remained some days in their land.   According to the signs which they gave, it was Alvar Nuñez Cabeça de Vaca, Dorantes and Castillo Maldonado, and a negro, who had all escaped from the expedition with which' Páfilo de Narbaez entered Florida, and after being a long time in slavery, they came upon these towns, God-working by their means many miracles, and healing with the mere touch of their hands many sick persons, in consequence of which they left a great name in all that land.   All this province remained peaceful and very quiet, in token whereof they accompained and served our people several days along the banks of the river mentioned above.

In a few days they reached a great town of Indians, who sallied out to receive them in consequence of the report which they received from their neighbors, and brought them many very curious things of different colored feathers, and many cotton blankets with blue and white stripes, like those brought from China, to sell and exchange them for other things. They all, men, women and children were dressed in very good and well dressed chamois skins, and our people never could learn what nation they were, for want of an interpreter who understood their language, although they conversed with them by signs.   When some stones with rich metal were shown them, and they were asked whether there were any such in their land, they replied also by signs that five days march thence westward, there was a great quantity of it, and that they would guide us there and show it to our people, as they subsequently did, accompanying them for the space of twenty-two leagues all inhabited by people of that same nation, who were immediately followed up the same river by another nation much more populous than the last, by whom they were well received and entertained with many presents, especially with fish, which was infinite, by reason of some great lakes existing near there, which produce them in said abundance.   They remained among them three days, during which they performed for them by day and night many dances in their fashion with pecular expression of joy. How this nation was called could not be ascertained for want of interpreters, although it was understood that it was great and wide spread.   Among them they found an Indian of the Concho nation who told them and indicated that fifteen days hence westward there was a very wide lake, and near it very great towns, and houses of three and four stories, and well dressed people, and the land of much provisions.   He offered to conduct them there.   Our people rejoiced at this, and omitted to carry it in to effect only to execute the project with which they began the journey, which was to go northward to relieve the religious mentioned above.

What they particularly noted in this province was that the climate was very good, the lands very fertile, and game, both beast and bird, abundant, and much rich ore, and other other especial and profitable things.

From this province they followed their route for the space of fifteen days without encountering during that time any people amid the great forests of pine trees like those of Castile ; at the end of this time, having marched in their opinion eighty leagues they came to a small rancheria or town of a few people, and in their poor straw houses they found a great quantity of deerskins, as well dressed as those of Flanders, and much very good white salt.   They were very hospitably entertained during the two days they remained, after which they were accompained by them some twelve leagues to some large towns, always marching along the Rio del Norte already mentioned, till they reached the land which they call New Mexico.   The whole bank of the said river was lined with immense forests of white poplars, and in some parts they were four leagues wide, and also with many walnut trees and wild vines like those of Castile.   Having marched two days through these poplar and walnut forests, they came to ten towns, situated on both banks of the said river, without counting others which were seen further inland.   In these there seemed to be a large populotion, what they saw exceeding ten thousand souls.   In this province they were treated with many entertainment, and they were con-

conducted to their towns where they gave them much food and poultry of the country, and other things and all with great good will.   Here they found well built four-story houses with fine rooms, and in most.of them there were estufas for the winter time.   They were dressed in cotton and deerskin, and the dress both of men and women, is like that of the Indians of the Kingdom of Mexico, and what caused most surprise was to see that all of both sexes, went shod with shoes and boots of good leather with soles of cow-hide, a thing which up to this time they had never seen.   The women have their hair well combed and arranged, and wear nothing on the head.   In all these towns there were caciques who governed them as among the Mexican Indians, with officers, to execute their commands, who go through the town, crying aloud the will of the caciques, and execute it.   In this province our people found many Idols which were adored and especially that they had in every house a shrine for the devil, to which they were accustomed to carry food and other things. In the way that among Christians we have crosses by the wayside, so they have a kind of high chapels where they say the devil rests and recruits when he goes from town to town: these are highly adorned and painted.   In all their cultivated and planted fields which are very extensive, they have at one side of them a portal with four columns, where the laborers eat and take their noon-rest, because they are a very industrious race, and are ordinarily at work.   It is a land of many mountains and pine-woods.   The arms which they use are very strong bows and arrows tipped with flint, with which they can pierce a coat of mail, and macanas, which are clubs half a yard long, and set full of sharp flints, which can cut a man in two, and also bucklers of raw cow-hide.

III.   CONTINUATION IN REGARD TO NEW MEXICO, AND

THE THINGS SEEN THERE.

After being in this province four days, and at a short distance from it they came to another called the Province of the Tiguas, which contained sixteen towns, in one of which called by name Poala (1) they found that the Indians had put to death the said two Fathers, Friar Francis Lopez and Friar Augustine, whom they had set out to seek, and also three boys and a half-breed. When the town folk and their near neighbors saw our people, touched by the remorse of their own conscience and dreading lest they should be punished, and vengeance taken for the death of the said Fathers, they durst not stay; but leaving their houses deserted, they fled to the neighboring mountains, from which they could not be induced to come down, although efforts were made to allure them by all devices. They found in the towns and houses much provisions, and an infinite quantity of native poultry, and many kinds of ore, some of which seemed very good; it could not be ascertained clearly how great the population of this province was, as the people had fled to the mountains as already stated.

Having found that those they sought were dead, a council was held to decide whether they should return to New Biscay, from which they had set out, or proceed further. In this opinions differed. But as they heard there that east of that province and far from it, there were great rich towns, finding himself so near, the said Captain Anthony de Espejo agreed with the opinion of the religious already named, Father Bernardine Beltran, and the majority of his soldiers and companions, to continue the discovery till they saw where it ended, so as to be able to make a clear and certain report to his Majesty as eye witnesses, and so conforming to this they determined that leaving the camp there, the Captain with two companions should carry out his desire, as they did in fact. After two days march they reached a province in which they saw eleven towns, and in them many people, exceeding in their judgment 40,000 souls (2). It was a very fer-

---

(1) Called also subsequently Puaray. It was near Sandia and Isleta. It was apparently like them a town of Tioas Indians. Benavides, 21, and thus allied to the Taos and Picuries. Oñate found on the wall of a house the death of the missionaries painted by the Indians.

(2) Apparently the Queres. Benavides, p. 22.

tile and productive land, the boundaries of which touched
directly those of Cibola, where there are many cattle, in the
skins of which they are clothed, and in cotton.   They follow in matter of government the system held by their neighbors.   There are indications of many rich mines. and accordingly they found ores of them in the houses of the Indians,
who have and worship idols.   They received them in peace
and gave them food.   Seeing this and the nature of the land
they returned to the camp from which they had set out, to
inform their comrades of all the above.

On reaching the camp, as just stated, they heard of another province called that of the Quires, which.was six leagues
off up the Rio del Norte, and when they set out for it and
came within a league of it, a great number of Indians came
out to receive them in peace, and ask them to visit their
towns. and when they did so they were well received and entertained.   They saw only five towns in this province, in
which there was a very great number of people.   What they
saw exceeded 15,000 souls, and they adore idols like their
neighbors.   They found in one of these towns a magpie in a
cage, such as used in Castile, and umbrellas like those
brought from China with the sun and moon and many stars
painted on them.   On taking the altitude here, they found
that they were at $37\frac{1}{2}°$ N.

They left this province and marched in the same direction and fourteen leagues thence they found another province
called the Cunames, where they saw five other towns, the
chief and largest of them being called Cia, (1) which was so
great that it contained eight plazas ; the houses were plastered and painted with colors, and better than those that
had been seen in the other provinces.   The population which
they saw seemed to exceed 20,000 souls.   They presented to
our people many curious blankets and eatables very well
prepared, and they regarded these people as more curious,
and more civilized than any that they had yet seen: they
showed them rich ores and some ranges near by whence they

(1)   Now Zia or James River.   The Amejes may be the James.

obtained them. Here they learned of another province, which was to the northwest and they resolved to visit it.

When they had marched about six leagues they reached the said province, which is called that of the Améjes, which contained seven great towns, and in them by their estimate 30,000 souls. One of these seven towns they said was very great and beautiful, but they omitted to visit it, both because it was beyond a mountain range, and for fear of some disastrous result, if they divided their force. The people resemble those of the neighboring province, as well provisioned and governed.

Fifteen leagues from this province, always marching westward, they found a large town called Acoma; (1) it contained 6,000 souls and is situated on a high rock, fifty men's stature high, inaccessible except by a stairway made in the very rock, at which our people were greatly astonished; all the water there was in the town was cistern water.

The leading men came peaceably to see the Spaniards and brought many blankets, and well dressed chamois-skins, and a great quantity of provisions. They have their cultivated fields two leagues off, and draw the water to irrigate them from a small river which is near, on the bank of which they saw very large rose bushes like those of Castile. There are many ranges of mountains with signs of mines, although they did not visit them, the Indians being numerous and very warlike. Our people remained three days in this place, on one of which the natives made them a very solemn dance, repairing to it in very fine dresses, and with very ingenious games in which they take extreme pleasure.

Twenty-four leagues thence westward, they came to a province called in the language of the natives Zuny, (2) and the Spaniards call it Cibola; it contains a great number of Indians. Francis Vazquez Coronado was in it and left many crosses set up and other marks of Christianity, which have always remained standing. They found also three Christian Indians who had remained of that expedition, whose names

---

(1)   See Benavides, p. 33.
(2)   Benavides, p. 35.

were Andrew of Cuyoacan, (1) Gaspar of Mexico, and Anthony
of Guadalajara, who had almost forgotten their own language
and knew that of the natives very well, although after conversing with them for a time they understood easily. From
them they ascertained that sixty days march thence there
was a very great lagoon or lake, on the shores of which there
were many great and goodly towns, and that the natives had
much gold, as an indication of which they wore gold bracelets
and earrings : and that as the aforesaid Francis Vazquez
Coronado had very positive information thereof, he had departed from this province of Cibola to go there, but after
marching twelve days he could find no water, and resolved
to return, as he did, with the resolution to come again expressly but afterwards he could not carry out his plan, because
death arrested his steps and thoughts.

IV.   New Mexico Continued.

At the report of said wealth, the said Captain Anthony
de Espejo wished to hasten there, and although some of his
companions shared his counsel, the majority and the religious
were of a contrary opinion, saying that it was time to return
to New Biscay from which they had started in order to make
a report of what they had seen. This the greater part put
in execution after a few days, leaving the Captain with nine
companions, who agreed to follow him. After having assured himself very thoroughly of the aforesaid riches, and of
the abundance of very rich ore there, he departed with his
said companions from this province, and marching due West,
after having made twenty-eight leagues they came to another
very large province, (2) in which there seemed to them to be
more than 50,000 souls, whose inhabitants when they knew
their coming sent them a message, saying that if they did
not wish to be killed, they must come no nearer their towns.
To which the said Captain answered that they did not come

---

(1)   Culiacan.
(2)   Apparently the Moquis.

to harm them, as they would see, and that therefore he asked them not to carry out their hostile designs, and he gave the messenger some of the things he had : he succeeded so well in calming our people and appeasing the excited minds of the Indians, that they freely allowed them to enter, as they did with one hundred and fifty friendly Indians from the province of Cibola already noted, and the three Mexican Indians of whom mention has been made.

A league before they reached the first town, more than two thousand Indians came out to receive them loaded with provisions, to whom the Captain gave some things of little value which seemed to them of great, and they esteemed them more than if they had been gold. Coming nearer the town which is called Zaguato, a great multitude of Indians came out to welcome them, and among them the caciques, making such demonstrations of pleasure and joy, that they scattered quantities of Indian meal on the ground for the horses to tread on. With this pomp they entered the town and were very well lodged and feasted, which the Captain paid in part by giving all the leading men hats, glass beads, and many other things which he had for such presents.

The said Caciques then sent messengers to all in that province notifying them of the coming of their guests, that they were very courteous men and did not injure them: this was enough to make them all come loaded with presents for our people, and to importune them to go and enjoy themselves in their towns, which they did, although always with watchfulness as to what might happen. The said Captain accordingly used caution, and told the caciques, that as the horses were very fierce and had been told that they wished to kill them, it would be necessary to make a fort of masonry to keep them and prevent the injury they wished to do the Indians. The caciques believed it so completely, that in a few hours they collected so many people that they built the said fort desired by our people with incredible speed. Moreover when the Captain announced that he wished to depart they brought him a present of 40,000 cotton blankets, painted and white, and a great quantity of handkerchiefs with tassels at the corners and many other things and among others rich specimens of ore which indicated much silver. They found among these Indians a very clear knowledge of the great lagoon above mentioned, and they corroborated what the others had told of the wealth and of the great abundance of gold.

The Captain relying on this people and their good disposition, after some days agreed to leave there five of his men with the other friendly Indians, that they might return to the province of Zuny with the baggage, and to go with the four who remained, lightly equipped to follow up certain indications he had of some very rich mines ; carrying this out he departed with the guides he had and when he had marched due west forty-five leagues he reached the said mines, and obtained with his own hands very rich specimens containing much silver, and the mines which consisted of a very wide vein were in a range easily ascended, as there was a road open to it. Near them were some towns of mountain Indians, who showed friendship, and came to receive them with crosses on their heads and other signs of peace. Near this place they found two considerable rivers, on whose banks there were many vines bearing very good grapes, and great walnut trees and much flax like that of Castile, and they told by signs that beyond those mountains there was one more than eight leagues broad, but they could not understand how it could be so near, although they made signs that it ran towards the North Sea, and that on either bank there were many towns so large, that compared to them, those in which they were, were but suburbs.

After having obtained all this relation, the said Captain departed for the province of Zuny, where he had ordered his said companions to go : and when he arrived there in health, having followed a very good road, he found his five companions in it and the said Father Bernardine with the soldiers who had resolved to return as we have already said, but who had not yet set out for certain reasons. The Indians had given these very good treatment, and everything necessary in great plenty, doing the same afterwards with the Captain and those who came with him, whom they came out to welcome with marks of joy ; they gave them abundant provisions for the march which they were to make, asking them to return soon, and bring many Castillas (so they call Spaniards) that they would give all food, and that to do so more easily they had sowed that year more grain and seeds than in all past years.

At this time the said religious and the above mentioned soldiers adhered to their first determination, and agreed to return to the province from which they had started, with the design already expressed ; this was upheld by Gregory Hernandez, who had been ensign on the expedition. When they had departed, the said Captain remaining with only eight soldiers resolved to proceed as he had begun, and ascend the Rio del Norte, as he did. And having marched about sixty leagues towards the province of the Quires already mentioned, twelve leagues thence to the eastward, they found a province which is called the Hubates, where the Indians received them in peace, and gave them much provisions and information that near there there were very rich mines which they found and took from them good bright ore, with which they returned to the town from which they had set out. They estimated the population of this province as high as 25,000 souls, all well clothed in painted cotton blankets and chamois-skins well prepared. They have many pine and cedar forests, and the houses in the towns are of four and five stories. They here obtained information of another province, one day's journey distant, called that of the Tamos, (1) in which there were more than 40,000 souls. When they reached there, the inhabitants would not give them food or admit them into their towns ; on account of this and the danger in which they were, and some of the soldiers being sick, and being so few as we have said, they determined to march for the land of the Christians, and they did so in the beginning of July in the year 83, being guided by an Indian

___

(1) This seems to be the Taos, rather than the Tanos tribe. From this point Espejo apparently marched down the valley of the Pecos.

who went with them and took them by a route different from they followed in coming, down a river which they called de Las Vacas(1)by reason of the great multitude of them along its banks, down which they marched 120 leagues, meeting herds constantly. From this they passed to the Rio de los Conchas by which they had entered and the valley of Saint Bartholomew from which they set out at the beginning of the exploration. When they arrived they found that the said Friar Bernardine Beltran and his companions had arrived safely at the said town many days before, and had proceeded thence to the city of Guadiana. In this town the said Captain Anthony Espejo made a very accurate report of all the aforesaid, which he forwarded at once to the Count of Coruña, Viceroy of that kingdom, and he to his Majesty and the Lords of the Royal Council of the Indies,that they might make such orders as seemed well, which has already been done with great care. May our Lord aid this affair in a manner that so many souls redeemed with his blood may not be condemned, from whose good understanding (in which they surpass those of Mexico and Peru, as we understand from those who have treated with them) it may be presumed that they will easily embrace the Gospel law, abandoning the idolatry, which now holds most of them. May God do this as he can, for His honor and glory, and the increase of the holy Roman Catholic faith.

I have dwelt on this Relation more than was required for the Itinerary, and I have done so intentionally. as it was something new and little known, and it appeared to me would not displease the reader.

---

(1) Bison River.

POINTS FROM THE ECCLESIASTICAL HISTORY

OF CATTARAUGUS COUNTY, N. Y.

It may be pleasing to the members of the Society to receive a detailed, yet concise historical account of Catholic Church matters from this County.

The first successful attempt at an embodiment of Catholicity in Cattaraugus County, N. Y. may be dated back to the year 1847, when the late amiable and saintly bishop, Rt. Rev. John Timon, C. M., ascended the episcopal throne of the diocese of Buffalo. On taking possession of his see, he found but very few Catholics, and only a few scattered missions. Owing to his apostolic zeal and the aid of Divine Providence he soon had the happiness to witness a rapid, almost instantaneous, increase of Catholic life and piety in this once barren soil.

The first missionary stations opened were Ellicottville and Cuba ; and later on, Allegany and Olean. The last two, in particular, owe their present flourishing condition to the pioneering of the Franciscan Fathers of whom we shall presently speak.

There was an influx of Catholics into this locality in 1851, when work was commenced on the Erie Railroad ; and Bishop Timon knew it would be impossible for the two priests, Fathers McKenna and Walsh stationed respectively at Ellicottville and Cuba, to attend their spiritual wants.   There was a scarcity of priests in this quarter of the diocese ; the only others who visited it were Rev. T. McEvoy, who was afterwards stationed at Rochester, and was buried at Allegany; Father Doran, who endeavored to establish a mission at Chipmunk ; and Rev. John Loughlin, the present Bishop of Brooklyn, who celebrated Mass at Allegany, in the house of

Mr John Shaw. The bishop realized the necessity of establishing missions for the new arrivals but had no priests to spare. He was relieved from the difficulty in the following manner, which resulted so happily to the interests of Catholicity in this section of the country.

Mr. Nicholas Devereux, a noble-hearted Catholic gentleman, had settled some time previously in Western New York. Owing to favorable circumstances, he very soon acquired vasts tracts of land in Cattaraugus Conuty. This he parcelled out, at moderate prices, to the new settlers ; and as he was always actuated by the princlples of Charity, he permitted them to pay for their portions by installments, according to their abilities. He even gave some lands away gratuitusly. A true son of Holy Mother Church, he not only provided for the temporal interests of his fellow-men, but he also had an ardent desire to promote their spiritual welfare. Having received his early education and true Christian training under the Franciscan Fathers in Ireland, his native country, he always pseserved a special love for that order, and cherished the hope of seeing them one day establish a House in this vicinity. In order to have this ardent desire realized, he made it known to Rt. Rev. John Timon, with whom he stood on terms of intimate friendship. This design corresponded exactly with the bishop's wishes in the matter, and steps were immediately taken to put it into execution. This was in the year 1854, a year of absorbing interest to the universal Church of Christ, when the Dogma of the Immaculate Conception of the Blessed Virgin Mary, the constant and universal belief of the faithful from the time of the Apostles, was about to be defined. The glorious Pontiff, Pius IX., desired the presence of the Prelates of the Catholic world, in order to give all possible lustre and solemnity to the Definition. Bishop Timon was among the number called to the shrine of the Apostles, the once superb city of the Caesars, the new brilliant focus of Catholic doctrine, the seat of the vicar of Jesus Christ on earth. He told Mr. Devereux the news of the invitation to Rome. The latter rejoiced exceedingly on receving this intelligence. Now the happy moment was approaching to open negotiations with the proper authorities, about obtaining Missionary Fathers for the new settlement! He promised to do all in his power to further the project, and even offered himself as travelling companion to the Bishop, as he was himself anxious to see Rome and its illustrious Pontiff, Pius IX.

Passing over the usual incidents and inconveniences of a journey by land and sea in those days, we find them in Rome, the same year, 1854. Their first thought was to thank God for their safe arrival ; then they hastened to tender their respects to the Holy Father. They unfolded their plans to His Holiness who, after listening attentively, imparted the Papal Benediction, and spoke encourging words, for their success. In the next place they repaired to the then Head-Superior of the Franciscan Order, Most Rev. Father Venantius. The reasonableness of their petition commanded itself to him, and they received his consent and approbation.

Four members of the great Order of St. Francis of Assisi, three priests and one lay brother, voluuteered and exchanged a life of contemplation and activity under the azure sky of Lavinium for the inclement climate and woodlands of Western New York. These pioneers, whose names deserve to be handed down to posterity, were : Very Rev. Father Pamphilo, O. S. F., Very Rev. Father Samuel, O. S. F., Rev. Father Sixtus, O. S. F., and the Venerable Brother Salvador, O. S. F. The first of these, Very Rev. Father Pamphilo, was appointed Warden, or Superior, of this brave little band of Franciscans.

Full of zeal for the glory of God and the salvation of souls, the missionaries set out from Rome on the 9th day of May, 1855, and after an unusually short voyage, reached the American shores on the 19th of June, the same year. The first mission assigned them was Ellicottville, New York, from which was attended Allegany, and, later on, other adjacent stations. Soon after, Mr Devereux gave them a suitable tract of land in the township of Allegany, Cattaraugus County, and it was determined that some of the Fathers should here form a second abode. On their arrival, they resided for a time in the private dwelling of Mr. John McMahon. Not long after, however, with the assistance of their liberal patron and the generosity of good neighbors, they were enabled to erect their first building which then formed St. Bonaventure's College and Seminary. The Church of St. Nicholas, called after the patron Saint of Mr. Nicholas Devereux, was also erected about this time. The Fathers took up their abode in their new home on the eve of the Feast of their glorious Founder, St. Francis of Assissi, October, 3rd 1858. God blessed their undertaking. The mission increased rapidly : shortly afterwards other members of the Order arrived from Europe, and postulants from the surrounding towns who desired to become children of St. Francis were added to this number. In the following year, 1859, they opened their public Institution, with chairs of the various departments of science. Very soon they were enabled to meet the Rt. Rev Bishop's desire of attending, from Allegany, the adjacent Catholics of Olean, Cuba, Belmont, Humphrey, Little Valley, Great Valley, Cattaraugus, Franklinville, and other places, where they either erected churches or enlarged such as they already found. The bishop at that time needed his small number of secular priests in other localities of his vast diocese.

Thus began the Mother House of the Franciscans of the Eastern Province. Notwithstanding the many difficulties placed in their way, they always succeeded ; nothing could cool the burning zeal of the devoted sons of St. Francis.

In the course of time, the monastery and spacious church were erected. The Institution increased in the number of professors and students. In 1888 a large Alumni-Hall was built, to which was added a fine library containing over 6,000 vols. on all branches of Literature and Science. A novitiate has also been established from which a goodly number of young men are regularly received into the First Order of Friars Minor. A vast number of priests who daily ascend the altar of God in almost every diocese throughout the the country, were trained under the Coat of Arms of the humble Seraph of Assisi and still hold the Franciscans and St. Bonaventure's College and Seminary in grateful remembrance. This is well attested by the large number of clergy and laity who come from great distances to attend the Annual Commencements, of which the thirteth anniversary has already been celebrated.

Another institution, coeval with the College and Seminary, that has done a great deal of good for Catholicity is St. Elizabeth's Convent–Academy, conducted by the daughters of the Third Order of St. Francis. Uniting a contemplative life to the Christian training of young ladies, they have endeavored for many years to guide their pupils in the path of rectitude ; to give them a solid education, ornamented with all the modern accomplishments, and to fit them to preside as true Christian mothers in their future homes.

This is not the only Franciscan Mission to which the American Catholics are indebted. We find it recorded, that there was one to the Canadian Territories over two centuries and a half ago. Also, it is an historical fact that it was a Franciscan Friar who first offered the Holy Sacrifice of the Mass in the city of Monterey, California ; and Christopher Columbus, the discoverer of America, was a Franciscan of the Third Order. In the South-east and South-west of the United States, we also find the Order laboring for God's Holy Church.

It will be gratifying to the friends of piety to know that the Third Order, founded by St. Francis in A. D. 1221, is in a most flourishing condition, under the vigilant care of the Fathers. Branches have been established in various parishes conducted by the secular clergy, who have had ample opportunity to witness the beneficial influence among their flocks. Their testimony has been so unmistakable that constant requests are received to organize new congregations of Secular Tertiaries. We should not omit mentioning, in connection with the Order, the Arch-Confraternity of the Cord, which renders its wearers participants of innumerable spiritual favors.

NOTES.

EARLY CATHOLIC AFFAIRS IN NEW YORK.

From the reminiscences of the late Mrs. Eliza Quinn Howard we extract the following : " The first remarkable incident that produced a lasting impression upon the mind of the writer, was being led by the hand to view the remains laid out in state, of the Rt. Rev. Bishop Connolly, in old St. Peter's Church in Barclay Street. It is said they were viewed by over three thousand people, and were a novel sight to both Catholics and Protestants. The history of our two first Churches, and the experiences of the Catholics of that time, were conspicuous for incidents, that will never be recorded in history; yet were filled with acts of self-sacrifice, poetry and even romance, that would far exceed in interest the pages of the modern novel, but are only registered in the books of the Recording Angel.

It is with a mixture of exultation and sadness that the writer remembers the Christmas mornings of her early days, when she plodded through the untrodden snow, a walk of two miles, to be present at the five o'clock mass at St. Peter's Church, in Barclay Street, no sound disturbing the harmony of both Earth and Sky, save the salutation of "Merry Christmas" from all passing wayfarers.

In those days Goodyear and galoshes were unknown and as for surface cars and elevated roads, they did not exist in the wildest dreams of the imagination, though now they hasten many on their path to Paradise.

Thus did catholic parents foster the faith of children, who have subsequently filled our pulpits, one of whom has worn as "Newman" says, "the royal robe both of empire and of martyrdom," men who have administered the laws of justice, and women who in the sacred garb of charity have devoted their lives to the relief of the helpless and the aged.

Before the introduction of the Sisters of Charity at St. Peter's—the ladies of the congregation taught the Sunday School classes, among whom the families of Binsse, Burtsell, Manahan and Glover were conspicuous.

The missionary spirit still exists among their descendants. From a Burtsell the writer learned the definition of " Trinity:" It may not be irrelevant here to relate an incident connected with St. Peter's Church. The sexton, Sheils by name, was a distinguished feature of a class that is now obsolete, the English Beadle. One of the pictures of the past was seeing him in peruke, and short clothes, mount the pulpit stairs to place the Gospels upon the velvet cushion. He would take a survey of the assembled congregation through his spectacles ; puffing out his cheeks and giving a dissatisfied shake of his head, at the tardy occupants filling the pews. His frown was fearful. Among the children in the catechism class with the writer, was a little girl of perhaps six or seven years. The question came to her, "Who is the visible head of the Church on earth?" She replied "Grandfather Sheils."

In 1830 the Sisters of Charity opened a day school at St. Peter's; Sister Jerome, lately deceased, was placed in charge of it and upon her arrival, it fell upon the writer's lot to carry her her first meal. Always upon meeting the good Sister, in after years, she would refer to this incident, as the first hospitality extended to her in this city. The school was opened in an old wooden building forming the eastern boundary of the yard adjoining the church. The present School and Sister's house were built years after under the direction of Rev. John Power. His portrait, which adorned the mantel of the Sister's parlor, has been presented to the Historical Society by Sister Mary Francis."

CORRESPONDNCE OF ARCHBISHOP CARROLL AND BISHOP CHEVERUS.

Bishop Cheverus to Archbishop Carroll.

BOSTON, October 10th, 1811.

MOST REV. FATHER.

We have still here the two monks of La Trappe, and the sister of the *tiers-ordre*. They are in the greatest anxiety concerning Father Vincent. Not a word from him have they received these six weeks. Nothing can be more edifying and pleasing than their conduct. The Sister is a very sensible woman and would, I think, make an excellent instructress of youth. Should her expected companions not arrive, I think she would be a valuable acquisition to the Sisterhood at Emmitsburg. . . . All those who have had the happiness to know you, here and in Damariscotta, never fail to enquire about you with tender anxiety. All unite in the wish that you may long be preserved, to edify and preside over the Church of J. C. in the United States. Permit me to subscribe myself, with filial respect and affection.

Most Reverend Father,
Your obedient, humble servant and son in J. C.,

✠ John Bishop of Boston.

BOSTON, December 31st, 1811.

MOST REV. FATHER.

I am happy to have an opportunity to renew to you at this season the assurance of my heartfelt respect, gratitude and filial love. Most beloved and venerable Father, may God in mercy to his Church preserve your inappreciable life *ad multos annos!* It is the prayer of every Catholic throughout the United States; I indulge the fond hope that it will be heard. I understand that you enjoy a good state of health, and no intelligence can be more pleasing to me.

Most Reverend Father,

Your obedient, humble servant and son in J. C.,

✚ John Bishop of Boston.

BOSTON, August 31st, 1812.

MOST REV. FATHER.

I was favored the day before yesterday with your esteemed letter of the 25th. I thought the idea of our assembling next November was given up. The Right Rev. Bishop Egan wrote to me last June, that the Right Rev. Bishop Flaget could not come.

When two years ago we fixed the time of our next meeting, I supposed, I understood, it was in the hope, that we should be able to hear from the Holy Father, that the vacant sees of New York and New Orleans would be occupied, etc. But as unhappily everything remains in the same situation, where we left it two years ago, you must excuse me when I say, that I do not see either the necessity, or even the great utility, of a Provincial Council being held at the present moment. In this opinion my venerable and most dear friend Dr. Matignon fully concurs.

I will say nothing of my being obliged to come back here at the most severe season, and the most unfit for travelling.

I am just returned from an excursion of two months and a half in the District of Maine. Had I thought I must go to Baltimore I would not have remained so long. I am more of a Parish Priest than of a Bishop, and it is believed that a new absence will be hurtful to the congregation here, besides burdening Dr. Matignon with duties, too heavy for his weak state of health, although his zeal seems never to think them too painful. Our good and amiable Dr. O'Brien is indeed willing to lend a helping hand, particularly as to the pulpit; but yet the above remark stands good.

Besides the above, an objection almost insuperable, is the expense. Were I to complain of my poverty I would be wrong and ungrateful; but many of our poor people have no employment, and all feel the distress of the times, without excepting my good friends, Messrs. Kavanagh and Cottrill, who have met with heavy and repeated losses. I really do not know at present one of my Diocesans to whom I could apply with a good grace, even for $10.00 The dear Dr. Matignon and myself have but one purse, but it is now an empty one. However we live from day to day, and a kind Providence supplies our daily wants.

If you think the Council must be held, could not a vicar general elected *ad hoc* be my attorney and answer every purpose? In this case, I would propose my learned, pious and venerable friend Dr. Dubourg. If however, Most Reverend Father, you point out any one you would prefer, I would immediately write to him or to Dr. Dubourg, if it meets your approbation. Permit me also to add that the present distracted state of this country, the shocking scenes which . . . induced Dr. Matignon and myself to doubt of the propriety of holding our assembly just at this time, and particularly of holding it in your city. I need not add, I hope, that I do not even dream of any personal danger. To conclude: I have not forgotten this part of my consecration oath, *Vocatus ad Synodum ibo*. If therefore, Most Reverend Father, you order me to come, I must and will obey, but if the above reasons appear to you sufficient to justify you in dispensing with my attendance, I most humbly and earnestly beg that you will grant me such dispensation. I have the honor to be with the most profound veneration,

Most Reverend Father,

Your obedient, humble servant and son in J. C.,

✠ John Bishop of Boston.

Dr. Matignon and Dr. O'Brien[*] Mr. and Mrs. Stoughton, your little god-daughter, etc., etc., present their best respects. My respectful compliments to Rev. Mr. Fenwick, Mr. Mertz, Mr. Moranvilliers, and all the Reverend gentlemen at the Seminary.

BOSTON, December 30th, 1812.

MOST REV. FATHER

All your children in J. C. unite in fervent prayers for the preservation of your invaluable life. God in mercy to his Church will hear us, and grant health and strength to our guide and pattern, dear and venerable Father, *ad multos annos*. My respectable and dear friend Dr. Matignon, and also Dr. O'Brien and Mr. Brosins, cordially unite with me in this wish, and in assuring you of their profound respect. Since I was honored with your esteemed favor, in answer to my letter concerning the intended Council, I have heard that our dear and R R. brother of Bardstown, has come to Baltimore. I regret his disappointment, (though I think that at all events, his visit to his holy brethren is not an unpleasant one ;) but he and they are wrong, in attributing to me the postponement of the Council. I merely expressed to you my reasons for not holding it at present, and you were pleased to write to me that they appeared *decisive*. Had you judged them of no weight I was ready to go, without calculating any personal inconvenience. But I must say that I am still of opinion that the

---

[*]Rev. Dr. O'Brien had gone to Boston in May.

Council may be postponed, and I know of nothing that makes the holding of it in the present circumstances, either necessary or even particularly useful.   Rev. Mr. Badin writes to Dr. Matignon, that there are some intricate questions concerning marriage which are to be examined, but it appears to me that the gentlemen of the Seminary may examine these questions and then submit them to you. Your decision would become our rule in our respective Dioceses.   The R. R. Bishop of Philadelphia has written to me ; he wishes we would meet, but says only that some important matters might be settled.   What these matters are he does not even intimate.   It is certainly extremely inconvenient for me to go, but yet any order from you, my venerable Father, will be obeyed wihout delay or reluctance.   The Consul has been unwell and also your little god-daughter ; they are getting well and unite with Mrs. Stoughton in respects and the wishes of the season.

I beg my affectionate and respectful compliments to our R. R. Brother of Bordstown, Rev. Mr. Fenwick, and all the Reverend gentlemen in Baltimore.   With sentiments of the highest veneration, I have the honor to be,

Most Reverend Father,

Your most obedient, humble servant and son in J. C.,

✠ John Bishop of Boston.

The good and amiable Mr. Brosins has got a few young men to whom he gives lessons in Mathematics. I begin to hope he may be enabled to remain with us. What a pity that his health is so precarious? The dear Dr. O'Brien is in good health.

QUERIES.

GANILH'S POEMS.—Rev. A. Ganilh, a priest who was on the mission in the West and Southwest, published a volume of English poems   Can any reader give us the title?

V.

SICUT LILIUM INTER SPINAS. There is preserved in the Cathedral of New Orleans, a large silver gilt plate with a coat of arms on it. These arms are a lily on the centre of the shield. Above it on either side and below it, a branch with thorns. The motto is: "Sicut lilium inter spinas." Can any of our readers inform us whose bearings these are?

F. J.

COUNCILS AND SYNODS.—The editors will be glad to learn of any printed acts of Provincial Councils and Diocesan Synods on Statutes not included in the list given in this Magazine.

BOOK NOTICES.

HISTORY OF THE UNITED STATES OF AMERICA, DURING THE FIRST ADMINISTRATION OF THOMAS JEFFERSON. By Henry Adams, 2 volumes, 12mo, New York: Charles Scribner's Sons, 1889.

The history of the United States, from the close of the Revolutionary war to the second war with Great Britain, is practically unknown to the generality of American readers. No classic work covered the period, and few but students would delve through a series of works to gather facts and form a judgment for themselves. Mr. Adams in this work, which gives him a high rank as a careful and judicious historian, does much to bring the period in part at least before the ordinary readers. The key to our whole political history lies in the study of the events and opinions which led up to the Constitutional Convention of 1787, in the adoption of the Constitution, in Washington's work in putting it into operation, in the rise of two antagonistic policies, the Federalist and the Republican, in the defeat of the Federalists and the accession of Jefferson to the control of the destinies of the nation. To present well the eight years administration which has left so deep an impress on American politics, which began so hopefully, and ended in such bitter disappointment alike to the President, his party and the country was a task worthy of a historian, and certainly Mr. Adams gives a work that will long retain its place as a book of value, and one to attract readers usefully. Jefferson was a theorist, compelled to assume the active work of administration, and his whole administration was an effort to cling to theories which events rendered impracticable, and in yielding he sacrificed the fundamental principles of his policy. The great event of his first administration was the purchase of Louisiana from France. Theoretically opposed to the acquisition of new territory, holding it to be contrary to the Constitution of the United States, Jefferson was driven to the point where he must either sacrifice what he constitutionally sought, or secure still greater advantages by straining unduly the powers conferred by the Constitution of 1787. Economy and reduced taxation had been the cry of his party, yet the first step of his administration plunged it into difficulties which forced Congress to reimpose taxes. Jefferson had opposed the Navy, but in three months found it necessary to employ frigates to defend the national honor. Leaning towards France, events forced him to conciliate England and to seek to stand well with her, only to receive the unkindest treatment in return. The result of his first administration, while it disappointed his party and the people, did not prevent his re-election by 162 votes against 14.

History of the United States of America during the second administration of Thomas Jefferson. By Henry Adams. 2 volumes, 12mo, New York : Charles Scribner's Sons, 1890.

In the second administration of Jefferson the salient points are the Florida negotiations, Monroe's treaty, Burr's Conspiracy, England's contemptuous treatment of America evinced in the attack by the Leopard on the Chesapeake and the great mistake in policy of laying an Embargo, the resultant schism in the ranks of the Jeffersonian Republicans, the rise of a disloyal British party among the New England Federalists, the humiliation of Jefferson at the hands of former friends, the repudiation of his system, and his inglorious retirement to private life.

The only consolation was that he had driven New England federalists to show their lack of patriotism and love of country in their scheme to place New England under English protection, a secession not to independence, but to a hostile power.

The whole story of Burr's conspiracy and Wilkinson treachery has never hitherto been so carefully studied or so graphically presented. The Leopard's outrage on the National Flag, which after nearly a century still rankles in American hearts is well and graphically told. We read with interest the poitraiture of John Randolph, as given in the history of his schism ; those of Talleyrand and Napoleon in the story of the negotiations with France. But throughout all we feel that it is the narrative of a period of national humiliation, of wrongs borne rather than have recourse to arms, yet which gradually made war necessary, when no due preparation had been made for it. The work is an attractive one and lures the reader on, though his indignation rises at every page at the part which the government and people were forced to play. "With a sigh of relief which seemed as sincere and deep as his own, the Northern people saw Jefferson turn his back on the White House, and disappear from the arena in which he had for sixteen years challenged every comer."

ANNOUNCEMENTS.

The Abbé H. Gosselin, parish priest of St. Ferreol, has issued the most thorough and extended life of the Ven. Francis de Laval, first bishop of Quebec and now visits France for material to produce a second edition.

NOTE.

"Liberty and Property" was written after Queen Anne allowed the Maryland Catholics a modified toleration. It is important from its broad ground that acts of parliament did not bind the colonies, because they were not represented ; while the very fact that the colonial legislatures were not created by parliament but by royal prerogative, showed that parliament's power did not extend to the colonies.

UNITED STATES CATHOLIC
HISTORICAL MAGAZINE.

Vol. III.)   (No. 12.

REMINISCENCES OF NORTH CAROLINA,

By His Eminence James Cardinal Gibbons.

CARDINAL's HOUSE, Baltimore, Md., February, 1891.

Gentlemen and Friends of the United States Catholic Historical Society of New York :

Having been invited through your Secretary, Mr. Marc F. Vallette, to furnish some matter of interest to your admirable Society, and taking up the subject of North Carolina, as suggested by Dr. John Gilmary Shea, it is a source of pleasure to me to give the following hasty sketch, embodying some Reminiscences of Catholicity in that state.

In calling up memories of my labors in that Vicariate, as its first Vicar Apostolic, I am carried back to the early years of my Episcopacy, nearly a quarter of a century ago. My mind reverts to scenes there as dear to my heart as a first-love, to scenes in fields of labor rich with spiritual harvests.

It was in the Second Council of Baltimore, held A. D. 1866, and presided over by the zealous Mt. Rev. Dr. Martin J. Spalding, D. D., Archbishop of Baltimore, as Apostolic Delegate, that North Carolina was proposed to the Holy See for a Vicariate. The National Council, naturally enough, took into warm consideration the religious state of the South; for its people had just emerged from the horrors of a civil war, and were in a condition of mind and heart to welcome the consolations of religion.

After a period of more than twenty years I am more than ever convinced, that the erection of the Vicariate of North Carolina was a special direction of the Holy Ghost—that the

time had come when the God of all consolation was to pour
out his graces on the souls of men, enlightening their minds
with the light of the true faith. The Southern people had
been in a measure prepared. For in the late war almost the
entire male population of the South had been marshalled
into armies (North Carolina furnished 50,000 men,) which, in
camp and field and hospital, were enabled to behold the
Catholic Church in her most beautiful form of divine Charity. Many of these soldiers who had been taught to hate
the Church, were won by the exhibition of her charity.
They returned to their homes with sentiments of respect and
reverence, and prepared somewhat to receive instruction at
the hands of the priests.

Having been consecrated Vicar Apostolic of North Carolina, I at once painfully experienced the poverty and isolation
of the charge. Humanly speaking, I felt myself sent out
alone to a strange country among strangers, to a state where
few Catholics were to be found, where there was little or no
immigration, and none to be expected. My clergy numbered but two priests, the Rev. Mark S. Gross and the Rev.
Lawrence P. O'Connell. I could only say to myself and
to them ; *"Deus providebit."* In the Vicariate everything
had to be created. Missionary priests had to be procured
(and they were not to be had for the asking for North Carolina;) schools to be established; missions organized, and the
people at large instructed in the principles of the Catholic
Faith. In the midst of these difficulties I realized the worth
of the admirable "Society for the Propagation of the Faith,"
which annually remitted me pecuniary aid for the work of
the Vicariate. I can scarcely see how the work could have
gone on without such aid. The certainty of the annuity was
a relief to my mind, whilst it gave a stimulus to fresh undertakings as well for the conversion of the people, as for
the preservation of the faith among the few.

I was warmly encouraged in my trying vocation by His
Grace, my dear friend, Archbishop Spalding, who promised
to aid me in my difficulties, and I was also indebted to the
late Rt. Rev. Bishop Patrick N. Lynch for the services of the

Rev. H. P. Northrop (now the Bishop of Charleston,) who lived in Newberne, and who attended, for the most part at his own expense, many missions.

At the time of my taking charge it was estimated that there were not more than eight hundred Catholic souls in the state, scattered amidst a population of fourteen hundred thousand Protestants. North Carolina has about the same extent of territory as England. This was the wide field which myself and three priests were to travel over, ministering to the spiritual wants of the widely separated Catholics, preaching in season and out of season, in Church, house, Meeting House, Masonic Lodge, Lecture Halls, and in open air, to large congregations, curious to hear a Roman Catholic divine.

I was not, however, the first bishop in the field. A great man had gone before me, the learned and eloquent Bishop England, whose diocese embraced the states of Georgia and the two Carolinas. The most remote Catholic settlements received his episcopal visitation. He was preeminently the pioneer bishop of the Southern states. His example, in sustaining every labor of mind and body, edified and supported me in my charge. In a region eminently Protestant he championed the Faith with tact and power. None could stand before him. The most learned felt honored, even in defeat by Bishop England. His talents and attainments were truly great ; but more admirable far was his apostolic zeal for the conversion of souls. It inspired him to disregard all labor, to endure every trial.

I set out for my Vicariate in company with Archbishop Spalding. His Grace was full of hope for the conversion of the Southern people a hope not quite disappointed in his day, and to whose more complete fulfilment influences are now leading. Our party arrived in Wilmington N. C. on Friday evening October 30th, 1868. We were met at the depot by the Rev. M. S. Gross in company with a Catholic delegation. His Grace, the Archbishop, and myself, and the Rev. B. J. McManus, of Baltimore, were escorted to the home of Col. F. W. Kerchner, the most prominent Catholic of the city, who entertained us for the night. My little flock welcomed us with sentiments of the greatest joy; and I reciprocated the warm attachment then displayed, and ever afterwards entertained, by the Catholics of Wilmington. Mgr. James A. Corcoran had been their devoted pastor for years, but had just then left for Europe, to take part, with other eminent theologians, in preparing for the Vatican Council. The company present at my installation was His Grace, Archbishop Spalding, the Rev. Dr. T. Birmingham V. G., and the Rev. Dr. J. J. O'Connell (both of the Charleston Diocese,) Rev. H. T. Northrop, Rev J P. O'Connell, and the Rev. M. S. Gross. I remember that the audience, composed of the most intellectual people of the town, was large and most respectful. The Catholic congregation numbered about four hundred souls. His Grace did honor to his pulpit reputation by a discourse of an hour's duration on the unity of the Church. I preached at Vespers on the Communion of the Saints, the Feast of the day.

I remember, on the Saturday after my arrival, witnessing, from the porch of Col. Kerchner's residence, a political torch-light procession of colored people. I learned that this element was the leading political factor in the state, as it was, at the time, in the South generally. While right thinking men are ready to accord to the colored citizen all to which he is fairly entitled, yet to give him control over a highly intellectual and intricate civilization, in creating which he had borne no essential part, and for conducting which his antecedents had manifestly unfitted him, would be hurtful to the country as well as to himself.

After the departure of the Archbishop and Father McManus I was left to feel the loneliness of my situation, more trying than its material poverty. My sole clerical companion in Wilmington was the Rev. M. S. Gross. Our accommodations here (we had no house) consisted of two small bed-rooms and two other small rooms, one for an office and the other for a library, attached to the rear of the little church. But my work ahead left no leisure to breed home-sickness. Everything had to be started ; missions inaugurated, schools established, priests to be had, conversions to be made. The last item was the first great work, one which called for extensive travelling, and much elementary preaching. I started out, with Father Northrop, to visit Newberne, and his district of a hundred miles and more in extent. At Newberne we found a congregation of seventy-five souls. Prominent among them was the Hon. Judge Mathias Manly, son-in-law to Judge Gaston. It is asserted sometimes, by the enemies of the Church, that a good Catholic cannot be a good American citizen. Gaston disproves so wanton and gratuitous an assertion. He was the best citizen and the most learned judge North Carolina ever had. Permit me here a moment's digression, to say a word in reference to this renowned Carolinian. There is no man whose memory is more tenderly enshrined in the hearts of the people of North Carolina than that of Judge Gaston. His name is a household word in every town and hamlet throughout the old North State. His parents were married in Newberne about 120 years ago. His mother was a pious English Catholic lady. His father warmly espoused the cause of American Independence, and on that account he was an object of special hatred to the British and the Tories. When the English, aided by Tories, made an attack on Newberne in 1781, the first object of their assault was the elder Gaston, who, with his wife and two little children, fled to the river in hopes of escaping from his pursuers. He jumped into a boat, leaving his wife and children on the shore. His trembling wife fell on her knees and begged the soldiers to spare the life of her husband, and not make her a widow and her children orphans. But, heedless of her entreaties, they fired over her head, and slew him before her eyes and those of his children. Hence it was afterwards beautifully said of young Gaston that "he was baptized to liberty in his father's blood."

From that moment Mrs. Gaston spaired no pains in the religious and moral training of her children. She was then perhaps the only Catholic lady in Newberne. Her son lived to fill one of the highest positions in the state, that of Judge of the Supreme Court of North Carolina, to which he was elected in 1834.

Up to the year 1835, a clause remained in the constitution of North Carolina, forbidding a Catholic to hold certain important offices of trust.   Judge Gaston was a member of the Convention which that year framed a new state Constitution.   He delivered a speech in favor of Catholic emancipation, which, for theological learning, soundness of argument, consummate tact, and sublime eloquence,has seldom been equalled in the halls of legislation.   By that speech, unaided and alone, he struck the fetters off the feet of his Catholic brethren, and established religious liberty in North Carolina.

Judge Gaston was always fond of referring to his mother, and he attributed to her not only the heritage of his faith, but also those high moral qualities which endeared him to his fellow citizens.

From Newberne, accompanied by Father Northrop, we visited the distant out-missions, preaching and administering confirmation at various posts.   Our visits seemed to cheer the faith of every household.   At Newberne I learned, with grateful feelings of the daring and timely intereference of a Capt. McNamara, of the Federal Army, whereby a Catholic Church was saved from desecration.   Riding past the edifice and observing a body of persons about its door and apparently in charge of it, he asked their business.

"We have occupied this church for school purposes," said one of them, advancing and speaking for the rest.

"Where is your authority?" demanded the Captain. ,

"Our authority," the school-mistress replied, "is that of the United States Government and of Jesus Christ."

"Well," rejoined the Captain, "that is pretty good authority; but, as a Federal Officer, I am wont to obey *written* instructions.   Can you show papers from the sources you have mentioned?

The teacher stood silent and crest-fallen, when the Captain added :

"As you can't produce the papers my order is that you

vacate this Church at once; and enter it no more for such purposes."

From Newberne we visited Edenton, where we found a large brick church, built altogether through the untiring efforts of a resident Catholic lady, who solicited aid for the purpose. Here we met the distinguished family of Judge Moore, at the time late converts to the faith. We had travelled hundreds of miles and the Catholics were few and distant. Yet I could not but remark the number of very distinguished persons whom God had raised up as so many lights in the land to honor, to declare, and to spread the Catholic Faith. These distinguished Catholics drew the attention of the people to the Church and inclined them to study its doctrines.

A few months later I made my visitation to Western North Carolina, reaching first the City of Charlotte, whose Rector was the Rev. Lawrence P. O'Connell.* He was a veteran in the service, a well-tried, faithful self-sacrificing priest, whom I appointed my Vicar General. He had served as a Chaplain in the army of Virginia. Not merely content to minister to the spiritual wants of Charlotte, Father O'Connell, though infirm from rheumatism, visited outmissions, and labored zealously for the conversion of the country people. He had, near the town of Concord, a whole congregation composed exclusively of converts. It was a Lutheran settlement, and a people whose ancestors were German. It happened that the Lutheran minister delivered a violent tirade in his Church against the doctrine of the Real Presence. A member present was roused to investigate the subject. His reading led him finally, by the grace of God, to abjure Lutheranism, and to embrace the Catholic Faith. The spirit of truth seemed to pour itself out on the hearts of the people. Religious investigation became wide-spread, and family after family were received into the fold of the Church. These people, like many others in North Carolina simple, sincere, and religious were those other sheep spoken of by our Lord whom He would

---

*Very Rev. Father O'Connell died since this paper was written.

bring into His fold.   Rev. Father O'Connell was kept busy instructing and baptizing the people of that district, who shortly afterwards erected a church.

Visiting Salisbury, I became the guest of the Fisher family, and confirmed the two daughters of Colonel Charles Fisher, a gallant Southern Soldier, killed in the battle of Bull Run.   The family had become converts.   I found myself, a Catholic Bishop, occupying the very same room in Col. Fisher's residence, formerly given to Bishop Ives, when he was the Protestant Episcopal Bishop of North Carolina. The Fisher family is one of the oldest and most intellectual in the State.   The eldest daughter, Frances, is the southern writer known as *Christian Reid*.   The family had been Episcopalian.   Salisbury has now a Catholic congregation, school-house and church.   In my visitations I could not but remark, how many Catholic families, single or in groups of two or three, were settled over the state.   Whilst I saw in this isolation a danger to themselves (that is, to their faith,) yet I saw also how they were a means for the enlightenment of others.   Their homes became little centres of Catholicity all over the state.   The few zealous priests regularly visited them, sustaining and encouraging the Catholics, and helping on the work of conversion.   Books of religious instruction were in great demand.   They supplemented the work of preaching.   The great Bishop England, on his first visit to a mission, little or great, began to form a library for the diffusion of Catholic truth among the people.   This medium of conversion I fully recognized.   A good book is a powerful ally.   The sermons, preached in the missions to audiences almost exclusively non-Catholic, were particularly prepared for them, and aimed entirely at their conversion.   Hence, they were partly moral and partly doctrinal appeals to the heart and mind in the interest of truth that can save the soul.   At the urgent instance of Father Gross I wrote then *"The Faith of our Fathers."*   Catholicity made such advancement, by way of conversions, that places which had but one or two families, and some that had none, are now

Catholic mission centres, with their congregations, church and schools.

It was while I was absent in Europe at the Vatican Council, in 1870, that a letter came through the post, addressed "To any Catholic Priest of Wilmington, N. C." The Rev. Father Gross received the letter, which was one of inquiry about the doctrines of the Catholic Church, and from Dr. J. C. Monk. A correspondence was opened between us after my return from Rome. I recommended certain Catholic books. Dr. Monk procured these, and, having more fully instructed himself and family in the faith, he with his household were all received into the Church. He came to Wilmington, after a journey of nearly a hundred miles, by private conveyance and railway, to make a profession of faith. I baptized the family, and learned with the deepest interest of the circumstances that had led to his conversion, and of his hopes in regard to the community in which he had lived all his life as a prominent physician.

"None of the Protestant denominations," said he, "could satisfy me. Tneir modern origin, their contradiction of one another, their diverse constructions of the Bible, made me lose faith in Protestantism. I was casting about for the one true Church, when by chance (as we say) I came upon a sermon on "The True Church," delivered by Archbishop McCloskey, and printed in the New York Herald. The truth came to me on the wings of the Press. The sermon was a light from Heaven. It led me to find the Church of Christ in the Catholic Church. Furthermore, the books of instruction plainly showed me that it is the Catholic Church only which delivers all the truths of the Bible to be believed. I found the whole truth in Her."

This was a very remarkable conversion. The finger of God was here. Nor was this conversion to be barren of results. Dr. Monk returned home, after receiving my promise of a visit to his family. In due time the Rev. Father Gross visited Newton Grove, and to a great throng in the open air preached on the true faith. From that time an earnest inquiry into the tenets of the Catholic Church sprang up

among the people.   Dr. Monk was a providential man for
the diffusion of the faith.   He was highiy respected, and, as
a physician, had access to every family in all that region.
His zeal to enlighten the people was surpassed only by his
solid piety and good example.   Possessed of means, he lib-
erally aided in every way for the spread of the faith.   A
few months later I redeemed my promise by a visit to Newton Grove.   The trip came near imperilling my life.   I
remember it was the month of March.   The day of my de-
,parture opened with difficulties.   The railway train left very
early in the morning.   Rising at four o'clock, I found the
weather cold and rainy.   The carriage failing to call for me,
I was compelled, with the help of a boy, to carry my large
heavy valise, packed with mission articles, then the distance
of a mile to the depot.   As I travelled northward, the rain
became a furious storm of sleet and snow.   Reaching the
station, I found the brother of Dr. Monk, who had come to
meet me, and on horseback, too, with axe in hand, to cut our
way through the forests.   For the sleet and snow had covered
the country, and bowed to the earth, and in many places,
across our course, the pine saplings that grew in dense bodies
up to the margin of the road.   A neighbor was with him to
take me in his buggy.   We started.   It was a journey to be
remembered—a journey of twenty-one miles in the teeth of
wind, rain, sleet and snow.   After a short exposure I was all
but frozen by the violence of the storm and the intense cold.
We had ridden a number of miles when, to my delight, my
friend drew rein at his own house.   I entered the hospitable
door, and the change was most grateful—-from cold and
misery to warmth and comfort.

In a few moments the good housewife had brought in a
hot bath for my frozen feet, and the husband a supplement
in the way of a hot drink.   The generous hospitality restored,
in a very short time, my almost perished frame.   They were
both strangers, yet the closest friends could not have treated
me more kindly.   I remained for dinner, and, as the weather
became clear, we proceeded on our journey.   Next morning
being Sunday, I celebrated Holy Mass in Dr. Monk's house,

and preached there, later in the day, to an earnest audience. The religious interest was profound. It promised to become, as it truly did, a religious movement of the whole district towards the Catholic Church.

Regular appointments were made for a visit by the priest ; and, in a short time, the brother of Dr. Monk, with his family, embraced the Catholic faith. The congregations that met on the occasion of the priest's visits to Newton Grove were so large that it became necessary to erect a temporary structure of rough boards for their accommodation.

This Tabernacle answered admirably for the services, which were arranged to suit the primitive state of affairs in that section. The priest appeared in the rostrum in his secular dress, and, after prayer and reading of the Scriptures, delivered a long instruction on the Catholic Church or some one of its doctrines. The preaching, directed at the conversion of the people, was necessarily simple in its character, historical and didactic. Catechisms and books of instruction were freely distributed after the sermons. An attractive feature of these services was the singing, by select voices, of beautiful hymns. In the beginning, the Holy Mass, even on Sunday, was celebrated privately. Strange that in the 19th century the exclusive discipline of the Holy mysteries, insisted on by the primitive Church, should be found necessary. Yet so it was. It was absolutely necessary first to instruct the people in the doctrines of the faith, before the "mysteries of the Church," with their holy ceremony and strange ritual, could be fitly and profitably celebrated in their presence. The priest, at regular intervals, visited the people, and made use of books and the zeal of the converts in spreading the truth.

Opposition, however, was encountered. A crusade of petty persecution was inaugurated by the Protestant preachers. Joint meetings were held, *revivals* and *conferences*, wherein such coarse misrepresentation and abuse were poured forth, as to displease the honest country folk attending, and to hurt seriously the influence of the preachers. In vain were the people advised against and forbidden to attend the Catholic services. They came in greater numbers and more eager still, to compare the statements of the Protestant preachers with the instructions to be found in the sermons of the priest and in the Catholic books and catechisms.

The Catholic movement daily gathered strength by the accession of the most respectable families in the vicinity. Within a short time the number of conversions warranted the erection of a church and school-house. On their completion this apostolic mission became firmly established, and continues to prosper. Up to date some two hundred souls have been baptized.

This is but one of the several missions that have sprung up in the Vicariate. Another somewhat similar was started by three brothers, Irish peddlers, who settled in the interior. The priest was engaged to go a distance of eighty miles, to baptize their children. Strange! These Catholic men could not read, yet they became the founders of a mission. Their families, after proper instruction, were baptized and received into the Fold. The country people of the neighborhood were assembled and instructed; and, finally, the Church of the Good Shepherd was built. A Catholic school here rooted the faith in the hearts of the children.

One of the missionaries from this mission went still further into the interior and visited the "classic" precinct of Chinquepin, a village in the dark pineries of North Carolina, where live a most primitive people, blissfully ignorant of the outside world. Here he met an old Irish woman that had not seen a priest for forty-five years. Her faith, she said, was still as fresh as the sod of her native home, and her prayers, embalmed in the old Irish tongue, were never forgotten or omitted. It seems that the faith had been brought to Chinquepin by a convert lady, who advised the Rev. Father of the presence of this good old Irish soul in the back-woods. Chinquepin grew into a mission of converts, with chapel and school.

After my translation to the See of Richmond, there was inaugurated in Wilmington a mission-house. Three priests, the Rev. Fathers Gross, Moore and Wright, made the force.

Each one in his turn travelled a distance of nearly three hundred miles, giving a month to the out-missions. Another, at the same time, visited the families of the less distant places; whilst the third served the flock at home. The change of life and scene and labor was most agreeable. The missionaries, too, by living together, gave support and comfort to each other.

I remember another instance of a remarkable conversion. I was called on in Wilmington to marry a convert lady to a farmer, who proved to be a Baptist deacon. This lady, on going to her new home, succeeded, by God's grace, in enlightening her Protestant husband. He embraced the Catholic faith, and became its zealous promoter, being the founder of St. Peter's mission and school.

I recall, with grateful memory, the faithful and efficient service, on the eastern missions, of the Rev. J. J. Reilly, and that of the Rev. James B. White at Wilmington, and also at Raleigh, where he secured a most valuable church property at a cost of nearly thirty thousand dollars, all of which money he obtained himself, at home and abroad, by long and persistent effort.

I could not but recognize that what artillery is in warfare, schools and colleges, under the direction of religious men and women, would be in the Vicariate. It was a day of rejoicing, therefore, when I brought to Wilmington in 1869, a colony of Sisters of Mercy from the Mother-house at Charleston, South Carolina. This congregation of Sisters had been established by Bishop England, who gave them the rule of St. Vincent, and the religious dress of Mother Seton. They knew the South from an experience of fifty years in teaching its children. I considered that these Sisters would understand the people and bear up under our peculiar difficulties. The move was successful. The colony increased in numbers and usefulness, and founded convent schools at Wilmington, Hickory and Charlotte.

A good general, in order to make a strong stand in the country he designs to hold, sets about establishing a well garrisoned fort. Spiritually, I regarded in this light, the foundation in North Carolina of a Benedictine Abbey. I gave the matter serious reflection and awaited the opportunity. Kind Providence granted my wishes. It was in 1873, that the Rev. Dr. J. J. O'Connell, who had retired after the war to his extensive farm near Charlotte, whence he attended the country missions, favorably discussed with me the foundation of a Benedictine College. I at once besought the Ven. Rt. Rev. Arch Abbot Wimmer, of St. Vincent's Abbey, Pa., for a colony for the Vicariate. Just at that time a similar petition had been sent in, seeking a colony for a far more favored diocese. It was the true spirit of God in this venerable servant, that moved him to choose the poorer Vicariate of North Carolina. The colony was sent to me.

It was Abbot Wimmer's child from the beginning. To make this colony in North Carolina a success, nothing was spared, neither money, nor talent, nor subjects. The Rev. Dr. O'Connell having entered into an agreement for the transfer of his estate of five hundred acres for the establishment of a Priory and College, the Benedictine Fathers and Brothers duly arrived and took possession. The pioneer Prior was the Ven. Fr. Herman Wolf O. S. B., formerly a Lutheran minister. He served three years. His able successor was the Rev. Placidus Pilz O. S B., who erected, under many difficulties, a commodious brick building, an important addition to the humble frame structure of Father Wolf. For years the North Carolina Benedictine foundation struggled on under every difficulty. Its patronage had been so small, expenses so great, and the conviction of complete failure entertained by so many, that the question of its further support became a topic of discussion in the Chapter of the Abbey in Pennsylvania. But Abbot Wimmer did not despair. To him the cross was the sign of ultimate and permanent triumph.

At this juncture a number of Benedictines (of St. Vincent's Abbey,) young and full of zeal, volunteered to go to North Carolina, if allowed to take with them an abbot of their own choice. Abbot Wimmer considered that should the North Carolina priory be erected into an abbey, it might rise out of its difficulties and prove a success. The Chapter, therefore, accepted the offer, and elected and sent forth the Rev. Father Leo Haid O. S. B., with his volunteers. Rome having confirmed the action, Father Haid in the Pro-Cathedral in Charleston, South Carolina, Nov. 26th 1885 was consecrated, by Bishop Northrop, Abbot of Mary–Help Abbey, North Carolina. At the time I was absent in Rome.

Under the zealous administration of its new head St. Mary's College received another life. In a short time the number of students had so grown that it became necessary to erect two extensive additional buildings. God's blessing rested signally on the College and the new Abbey. Those who had loudly condemned the movement as a foregone failure, were now vigorous in its praise. Abbot Haid gave a wise and successful administration, and made himself worthy of higher honors. In the council of the Rt. Rev. Bishops of the Province he was chosen Vicar Apostolic of North Carolina. The Holy See having confirmed the choice, in 1887, in the Cathedral at Baltimore, he was consecrated to his high office.

A visit which I made the same year to Mary–Help Abbey, is one of my most pleasing North Carolina reminiscences. What a change had taken place! On the site of the frame tavern, a hundred years old and of revolutionary fame, that had served as the first shelter for the Benedictine Fathers, now stood several commodious brick buildings. In the midst of a wilderness had sprung up an Abbey and College, a House of Prayer and Learning, and centre of missionary zeal. The broad acres around were tilled by the brotherhood, those religious men, whose forefathers in the faith had taught the best art of husbandry to the nations of Europe. I regarded this Abbey with unbounded satisfaction. In its seminary I beheld the nursing mother of a native Southern clergy. In the College attached, Southern youth were offered a seat of learning where they could receive thorough christian education. My intimate knowledge of the poverty of the past made me keenly relish the richness of this spiritual foundation. In my judgment, it is most intimately related to the best interests of Catholicity in the south land.

With me, as first Vicar Apostolic of North Carolina, the primary difficulty was *to get* a missionary priest, the second to support him, the third to provide for his spiritual comfort. For he must needs go forth alone to his distant work ; and few of them had a home of their own ; none, a community to which to return. But now I recognized that the Benedictine Abbey would remedy these difficulties.

I saw, too, in it the hand of God for the conversion of the people. His Providence, in the line of great works, is ever the same. In the past the main instrument for the conversion of nations (England, Germany, and Italy, especially) was the Benedictine order. The advent of the Benedictines will aid in the conversion of the South. During my visit I learned that a number of candidates, both for the priesthood and for the order, had presented themselves.

The work on the Southern missions is humble and laborious, entailing many sacrifices. Bnt the faithful missionary is discharging the first duty of his calling (the endeavor to win souls,) and giving to his Divine Master the sincerest proof of his love.

In closing this hasty sketch let me emphasize my indebtness to the Very Rev. Mark S. Gross. He was ordained in 1868 for the dicoese of Baltimore ; but, immediately after ordination, volunteered his services for mission work in North Carolina. He was my *fidus Achates*, ready for every good work, and loved and honored wherever known.

J. CARD. GIBBONS,
ARCHBISHOP OF BALTIMORE.

Baltimore, Feb. 18th, 1891.

THE SURRATT CASE.

A True Statement of Facts concerning this Notable Case.

By Rev. J. A. Walter.   Read before the United States
Catholic Historical Society, May 25th, 1891.

Among the open letters of last April number of the
"Century," I find one referring to the priest who attended
Mrs. Mary E. Surratt.   As I am the priest alluded to in this
article, I must positively deny that I prohibited Mrs. Surratt
from asserting her innocence.   I thought of answering this
letter at once, but as I had an article prepared years ago on
the Surratt case, in which I had determined to make public
my statement of this notable case, I deemed it best to defer
the answer till the present time.

The object of this article is to make manifest the truth
in this case and thus vindicate the innocence of Mary E.
Surratt.

It may be asked, why this delay of twenty-five years?
The answer is a simple one.   It takes time for people to lay
aside prejudices, so that they may form a just judgment on
a question of this character.   The whole country was con-
vulsed with horror at the assassination of its Chief Ruler,
and the people had run mad with excitement.   Time alone
could quiet the deep feeling embittered against every one
who might have been suspected of having anything to do
with the crime.   Amidst all this excitement, I had determined in my own mind to wait twenty-five years before I
would give to the public a clear and full statement.

The public mind has had time to quiet down and men
can now calmly listen to reason.   Very few persons at this
date believe that Mary E. Surratt knew anything about the
plot to assassinate the President.

Now as to the facts of the case—President Lincoln was assassinated at Ford's Theatre, Tenth near F Street, Northwest, on the 14th of April (Good Friday) about 10 o'clock P. M. John Wilkes Booth was his murderer. It was, in my opinion, the act of an insane man and no friend to the South. This I said on the next day to several friends, stating that it was my firm belief that it was the work of a madman, and was concocted within the past twenty-four hours. I felt convinced that if the parties had reflected on what they proposed doing, the act would never have been consummated.

Mary E. Surratt, whose name has been associated with this awful tragedy, was a quiet amiable lady. She had removed from the country a few months previous to the murder of the President, resided on H near Sixth Street, Northwest, and was in St. Patrick's parish. I was not acquainted with her and never spoke to her until the eve of her execution. I received a letter from her dated Sunday, April 23rd, 1865, asking me to come and see her. She was then in Carroll Prison. I went on Tuesday morning, April 25th, but she had been removed to the Penitentiary, and I was told by those in authority at Carroll Prison that no one would be allowed to see her. On Wednesday, July 5th, 1865, I learned that the trial was over. On Thursday at 10 o'clock A. M., I went to the War Department and asked Col. Hardie for a pass to visit Mrs. Surratt, who had requested me to visit her when in Carroll Prison some three months previous. Col. Hardie told me that Secretary Stanton was not in and asked me if I was in a hurry about it; I told him I was not. He then replied that he would let me have a pass in a few hours. When I returned home, and whilst at dinner, an orderly came with a pass signed by Col. Hardie. I gave the usual receipt for the same, and going to the door with the orderly I remarked to him that I had read all the evidence of this trial, and, as regards Mrs. Surratt, there was not evidence enough to hang a cat; besides, you cannot make me believe that a Catholic woman would go to Communion on Holy Thursday and be guilty of murder on Good Friday. Shortly after the orderly had left, Mr. John F. Callan and Mr.

Hollohan, a boarder at Mrs. Surratt's house, called and informed me that the execution of Mrs. Surratt was to take place next day. To act so hastily in a matter of this kind was certainly strange on the part of the Government. Whilst talking to these two gentlemen, Col. Hardie came in and seemed much excited; I requested him to walk into the parlor, leaving the two gentlemen standing in the hall. He then said to me "Father Walter, the remarks you made to that young man," meaning the orderly who brought me the pass, "have made a deep impression on him; I was afraid that the pass I sent you would not answer, so I have brought you one from Sec. Stanton, but I want you to promise me that you will not say anything about the innocence of Mrs. Surratt." I replied coolly and deliberately "You wish me to promise that I shall say nothing in regard to the innocence of Mrs. Surratt. Do you know the relation existing between a pastor and his flock? I will defend the character of the poorest woman in my parish at the risk of my life. Thank God I do not know what fear is, I fear neither man nor devil, but God alone. You wish to seal my lips; I wish you to understand that I was born a freeman and will die one. I know where all this comes from, it comes from your Secretary of War, whom a Congressman in my breakfast room two weeks ago, called a brute. Of course I cannot let Mrs. Surratt die without the sacraments, so if I must say yes, I say yes." He then gave me the pass signed by Secretary Stanton. This was about 2,30 P. M., Thursday, July, 1865. That afternoon I went to see Mrs. Surratt to make arrangements to give her Communion next morning. I also called to see the President, having Annie, Mrs. Surratt's daughter, with me. On entering the gate at the President's house I met Hon. Thomas Florence, ex-member of Congress from Pennsylvania. He remarked, "Father Walter, you and I are on the same errand of mercy. The President must not allow this woman to be hanged." We went into the Executive Mansion and up stairs to a room next to the one occupied by the President, Andrew Johnson. There I met Col. Mussey, Secretary of the President, Preston King and one other person. I requested Col. Mussey to go in and ask the President if he would see me. He returned and said the President would not see me. Again, at my request, Col. Mussey went in telling the President that I would not detain him five minutes. This was denied me. I made another attempt, and told Col. Mussey to say to the President that I did not ask for pardon or commutation of sentence, but asked ten days reprieve to prepare Mrs. Surratt for eternity. This reasonable request was also refused. Annie, Mrs. Surratt's daughter, was in like manner refused an interview with President Johnson. The President sent me word to go to Judge Holt. I went with Annie to see this man, but it was perfectly useless. He had no more feeling for the poor daughter than a piece of stone; he referred her to the President. The poor child, with eyes streaming with tears, was left without any sympathy from this cold, heartless man. I said to her "Come Annie, it is battledoor and shuttlecock, the President sends you to Holt and Holt sends you to the President." This was Thursday afternoon, the day before the execution. On the following morning I went at seven o'clock, carrying with me the Holy Communion which I gave to Mrs. Surratt in her cell. I remained with her until the time of her execution, which was about 2.30 P. M. I can never forget the scene witnessed on that sad occasion. Poor Mrs. Surratt had been sick for several weeks and was quite feeble, she was lying on a mattrass laid on the bare brick floor of her cell. Certainly this was not the way in which to treat the vilest convict just before execution. While I was trying to comfort this poor good soul, her daughter had just returned from another unsuccessful attempt to see the President; she addressed her mother in these words: " Mother are you resigned? Her mother replied, "Yes, my child." Again she spoke "Father speak to mother and ask her if she is resigned." Her mother replied, "Annie, my child, this is no place for you, go to your room." Without a word this dear child, with broken sobs, left the cell and retired to one of the rooms in the Penitentiary. Shortly before the hour of her execution, Mrs. Surratt was brought out of her cell and was sitting on a chair at the doorway. It was at this time that she made clearly and distinctly the solemn declaration of her innocence. She said to me in the presence of several officers "Father I wish to say something." "Well what is it my child?" "That I am innocent" were her exact words. My reply was, "You may say so if you wish, but it will do no good." These words were uttered whilst she stood on the verge of eternity, and were the last confession of an innocent woman.

When the time arrived for the execution, she was carried to the scaffold by two soldiers, because she was too weak even to stand on her feet. On the scaffold she asked them not to let her fall. All the religious services had been performed in her cell, so as to save her from being too much exposed to the public gaze. At the signal the trap fell; I looked over the platform and saw that she had died without a struggle. I went immediately to see Annie and try to give her some consolation. When I told her that it was all over she gave way to her intense feelings, but one word was sufficient to calm her.

I had left my carriage within the walls of the Penitentiary when I first came before the execution, but when I went to look for it, it was not to be found. I asked General Hartranft, ex-Governor of Pennsylvania, who had charge of the execution, to let me have a conveyance in order to take Annie, Mrs. Surratt's daughter, home. He immediately ordered an ambulance, and with Annie and a friend, I left the enclosure. I found my carriage outside and transferred Annie with her friend to it and then drove to Mrs. Surratt's house on H Street near Sixth Northwest. I would here state that General Hancock was simply commander of tne Military Division comprising the District of Columbia, and General Hartranft was the officer in charge and superintended everything. Shortly after the execution of Mrs. Surratt, an article appeared in the New York Tribune accusing Secretary Stanton of refusing me a pass to visit Mrs. Surratt, unless I would promise to say nothing regarding her innocence. It seems that at this time Horace Greeley and Secretary Stanton were not on good terms. Mr. Forney, Editor of the Philadelphia Press and Washington Chronicle, denied the charge that Secretary Stanton had refused me a pass on terms as stated above. Two reporters of the Tribune called on me to ascertain the truth of the matter; I told them what had occurred between Col. Hardie and myself in relation to the pass. Of course they drew their own conclusions from what I told them. I said to them that I wished to have nothing to do with the quarrel. The next day they published verbatim what had passed between Col. Hardie and myself. Col. Hardie thought proper to write an article in the "National Intelligencer," calling me some harsh names and saying I was not a proper person to have attended Mrs. Surratt. I paid no attention to this article, but attended to my duties just as if nothing had happened. Some friends met me on Pennsylvania Avenue on the morning of the publication and asked me what I was going to do about the article. I simply told them that I would do nothing; if Horace Greeley and Col. Forney chose to quarrel in their newspaper, they might just fight it out among themselves. Evidently someone at the War Department must have been alarmed, for Major General Hancock was telegraphed to go and see Archbishop Spalding, so as to prevent me from asserting the innocence of Mrs. Surratt. I received a telegram from the Archbishop's Secretary, asking me to keep quiet and saying that the Archbishop would write me a letter by the evening mail. The letter came. It was no order, but simply a request that I should keep quiet in regard to the innocence of Mrs. Surratt. My answer was, that what he requested was hard to comply with, but I would try to do so. Archbishop Spalding told General Hancock that he also believed Mrs. Surratt was an innocent woman. At the present time I think there are few persons in this country who are not of the same opinion. Let any one quietly and calmly sift the evidence given in this trial and the same conclusion will be reached. Let us examine this evidence.

Mrs. Surratt's guilt could only be in consequence of her

son John H. Surratt's guilt. She was concerned in the conspiracy to murder President Lincoln only in as much as he was one of the conspirators. Now, John H. Surratt had nothing whatever to do with the conspiracy to murder President Lincoln; in fact, he knew nothing about it. He came to Washington on the 4th of April, took supper at home, changed his clothes and left for Elmira the next morning. The testimony of Susan Jackson, Mrs. Surratt's servant, was correct as to facts, but she mistook the date, saying it was April 14th. It was ten days previous to the 14th of April. It is strange that the hotel register in Elmira could not be found: someone had made away with it. Whoever it was, he did not know that John H. Surratt had telegraphed to New York to know where Booth was. I saw the Telegraph register in Mr. Bradley's office on which his name, John Harrison, the name he assumed, appears on the date April 14th. If he were one of the conspirators, he certainly ought to know where the chief conspirator, Booth, was, and it was his business to have been on hand in Washington and not in Elmira, New York, some 400 miles distant. When he read the account of the assassination of President Lincoln on the morning of April 15th, he was utterly astounded when he saw his name in connection with the plot and supposed it must have been done by some parties of whom he had no knowledge. He immediately left for Canada and remained concealed there several months. He has been accused of deserting his poor mother. This is not true. He sent a person to Washington, furnished him the means, and was ready to give himself up in her defence. This friend saw the counsel of his mother. They advised the friend to return and tell John H. Surratt to remain in Canada, for there was no danger that his mother would be convicted. Everyone knows that had he come to Washington, he would have been placed in the dock with the other prisoners and condemned with them. Prudence and common sense demanded the course he followed. Now John H. Surratt being in Elmira, how was he to be transported these 400 miles so as to be in Washington in time for the assassination of the President? Mr. DuBarry, Master of Transportation of the Northern Central Railroad, proved that there were no trains running on that day by which he could possibly have reached Washington.

Again; a handkerchief of John H. Surratt's was found in a car going North after the 14th of April, and this fact was adduced as evidence that he was escaping from Washington on his way to Canada. This handkerchief was lost by Mr. Hollohan, who boarded at Mrs. Surratt's, and it had by mistake, been placed in his bureau drawer. He was on his way to Canada with Detective McDevitt to try to find Surratt and lost it out of his pocket.

Again; two soldiers going down H Street and passing Mrs. Surratt's house, swore that Mrs. Surratt put her head out of the window and asked what was the matter. But during the trial of John H. Surratt it was in evidence that Mrs. Frederica Lambert, and not Mrs. Surratt, was the lady who talked to these soldiers. Mrs. Surratt's house was on H Street, between Sixth and Seventh, Mrs. Lambert's residence was on the same street but a square below. Both houses had high porches, hence the mistake.

At the trial of Mrs. Surratt, Mrs. Lambert was not aware of this evidence being given in the trial, but read it in the papers when John H. Surratt's trial was going on. She mentioned this fact to her son, who is a very worthy lawyer of Washington. He advised her not to say anything about it, but she insisted that it was her duty to make known the facts to the lawyers, Bradley and Merrick, who were defending John H. Surratt. This she did, and her evidence will be found in his trial.

Again; John T. Ford testified that no one knew that the President was to be at the theatre before twelve o'clock, yet Mrs. Surratt had ordered a carriage at ten o'clock (two hours previous) to take her to Surrattsville. She went down toere to attend some business in connection with her husband's estate. She was coming out of the house about two o'clock in the afternoon when she met Booth, who requested her to take two packages wrapped in newspaper, one containing a bottle of whiskey and the other a spy-glass, and give them to Mr. Lloyd at Surrattsville. She went down to this place, did not see Lloyd, but gave the packages to his sister-in-law. What this poor lady did anyone would have done, without suspecting that any harm was intended : she thought she was simply doing an act of kindness and nothing more. The fact of her ordering her carriage at ten o'clock shows that it had no connection whatever with the assassination of the President.

Every trivial circumstance was brought forward as positive evidence of guilt, when there was not the slightest ground for such a conclusion. I am convinced that if President Johnson had given me a hearing on the day preceding the execution, he would not only have saved the life of an innocent woman, but would have prevented a blot that will forever remain as a stigma on the Government of these United States.

This would have given ample time to examine the evidence on which she was convicted and this examination would have provec her innocence.

J. A. WALTER.

DON JUAN DE OÑATE, FOUNDER OF
NEW MEXICO.

Don Juan de Oñate was the son of Don Cristobal de Oñate one of the Conquistadors of Mexico. He married Doña Isabel Cortes Moctezuma, daughter of Hernan Cortes and of a daughter of the unfortunate emperor of Mexico. In his Nobiliario Genealogico (Madrid 1622 p 414) Lopez de Haro says : "Don Juan de Oñate, Adelantado of New Mexico, true to his valor and miltary instinct, after serving the crown of his royal sovereigns in his early years, till the present year 1620, with honor to his illustrious name, and the fame of his most distinuished house, with arms, horses and means, in the bloody battles which he fought with the Chichimecos, and unconquered tribes of savage traits, discovered the mines of Zichu, los Cnarcas and San Luis, teeming with immense wealth and settled Spaniards there. He was the discoverer and conqueror of another New Mexico, new provinces and kingdoms, subjecting to the King's arms countless tribes, which in New Mexico have submitted to the precepts and laws of the holy Gospel and the Roman Church, to the glory of his name, making him immortal in the histories of both hemispheres. The companions of his conquests and hardships were Don Cristobal de Oñate, his oldest son, lieutentant governor and Captain General, who at a tender age displayed the courage of his illustrious forefathers ; Don Juan de Zaldivar, his Maestre de Campo, whom the Acoma Indians treacherously slew, death in his youthful days baffling the hopes which the New World had conceived of his unconquerable courage. Don Vicente de Zaldivar his brother, also Maestre de Campo on this expedition, proceeded to avenge his death and giving battle to the Acomese, conquered them and destroyed the impregnable fortress of Acoma. They were notable persons in the service of God and of arms in that world, displaying the valor of the illustrious house of Zaldivar, well-known in Biscay for the nobility of its ancient landed house." (1)

After the expedition of Don Antonio de Espejo to New Mexico in 1582 to ascertain the fate of Friar Augustine Rodriguez and his fellow missionaries, Don Juan de Oñate solicited the royal license to reduce that province to the Spanish crown. This he obtained January 26th, 1588. But in the long formalities other orders were issued, July 19th, 1589, January 17th, 1593 and June 21st, 1595, so that it was not till August 24th, 1595 that Don Luis de Velasco, the Viceroy of New Spain issued his edict giving Oñate the official authority to undertake the proposed expedition. Ten thousand dollars were given to Oñate, six thousand being a loan from the royal treasury, and all the official transactions were concluded by the 30th of September.

Meanwhile the Count de Monterey arrived as Viceroy, and was informed by his predecessor of all the steps taken. Oñate accordingly with the approval of the new Viceroy, raised his standard on the plaza of Mexico. and discharging twelve cannon in front of the Cathedral invited men to join him as soldiers or settlers. Having gained some adherents he proceeded to Nombre de Dios where he gathered a force of 1500 men, including soldiers and settlers. For the spiritual care of the new settlements and the conversion of the natives Father Peter de Pila, then Commissary General of the Franciscans in Mexico selected as Superior Father Roderic Duran, who with Fathers Diego Marquez, Balthazar, and Christopher de Salazar and some others, joined the expedition. Wagons loaded with provisions and implements, seeds for planting grain and vegetable, horses, cattle, sheep and other domestic animals formed part of the outfit. Just as Oñate was about to proceed, an officer of the Viceroy appeared and handed him a letter from the King dated May 8th, 1596, enclosed in a longer and more detailed one from the Count

---

(1) Duro, " Don Diego de Peñalosa" Madrid, 1882 pp. 180-1. Villagra, " Historia de la Nueva Mexico," Alcala, 1610.

de Monterey forbidding him to continue the expedition and to return, if he had already set out, under penalty of being regarded as a traitor to his Majesty.

Oñate was thus left on the frontier with a large number of people to disband or maintain, and cattle to pasture and care for. He had expended 15,000 ducats in his preparation, and could only set to work to obtain at Mexico and Spain the revocation of the orders. It was not till a final order of the King, April 2, 1597, removed all the obstacles, that the expedition was enabled to move. He broke up his camp at Nombre de Dios in March, 1598, and with eighty heavy wagons and his herds, began the march. Only one missionary, Father Diego Marquez, remained with the force, but a new superior of the mission, Father Alonso Martinez, with other Franciscan Fathers soon joined Oñate. (2)

They reached and forded the Rio Grande del Norte, the Alcahuaga of the Indians (3) and on Ascension day, April 30, 1598, Don Juan de Oñate by an official act took possession of New Mexico in the name of the King of Spain. (4)

(1) These orders are given in Duro, p. 152.

(2) Torquemada, "Monarquia Indiana" 1 pp. 671-2.

(3) Barcia, Ensaio Cronologico, p. 170.

(4) Documentos Ineditos, xvi pp. 88; 306, 316. Villagra, p. 120.

LETTERS OF MR. WILLIAM PEASELEY AND HIS WIFE ON MARYLAND AFFAIRS, 1642.

I.

After the departure of my man with the letter, I received this enclosed from my Lord Baltimore, by which it will appear that his mind is changed. I went to him nevertheless this morning and debated the business with him as earnestly as I could, but I cannot prevayle with him. Hee is stiff in his resolution, saying that hee will prepare his demaunds within these two dayes which may be sent over by the next Post, and the answere transmitted hither before the going away of the shipp, which will be a month hence. And hee conceives there will bee no such necessity of sending those two gentlemen thither by this first shipp, in case the answere cannot come to his lordship, by the departure of this first shipp, for hee sayes there will goe other shipps after her thither. However hee is resolute that none shall bee sent, until hee have satisfaction; this is the substance of all our discourse; I am sorry I have fayled in doing that good and service I desired, so I take my leave and rest

Your humble and affectionate servant,

Lincolnes Inne Fields, 1 October 1642.　　　W. P.

II.

Deare Sir,

I have bin with my Brother but have bestowed my paines to no purpose, for in this business he is inexorable, untill all conditions be agreed upon betweene; the particulars are not worth relating, for both of us talked too much, since the effects of our discourse prooved no more to my content. I am onely satisfied in this; that what can hath been done in this business, and for the event I leave it to him who I hope will turne all things to the best; I cannot possibly waite upon you my selfe, our time is so short and our business so much, but I am as ever,

Your most affectionate friend and servant,

October 5th, 1642, ANN PEASELEY.

Mrs. Cotton presents her service to you and so doth Mr. Webb.

———

III.

I have prevailed for the present employment for two of yours, as is desired; upon confidence and promise that hee shall have satisfaction in his just and reasonable demaunds. and if it possibly may bee, before their departure, which was much pressed and importuned, for hee sayth the best shipp that goes now directly thither under the command of Ingle, the master, will bee ready to sett sayle from Gravesend about a fortnight or three weeks at the furthest, so as by that time an answer may come from Mr. Knott to his demaunds; but that shall not hinder their departure. Hee desires to see and speake with the gentlemen that hee may judge of their disposition and fitness for such a work. I pray therefore let them be sent to him as soon as may bee. So I rest.

Your humble and affectionate servant,

Vlt-7-bris. ——— W. P.

STATISTICS OF ST. ANNE'S CHURCH, DETROIT, IN THE LAST CENTURY.

	Baptisms	Marriages	Burials
1703 to 1710	94	3	13
1720	44	7	15
1730	106	16	44
1740	156	27	73
1750	235	24	114
1760	363	70	216
1770	351	80	217
1780	476	60	182
1790	551	80	219
1800	914	167	367
	3289	534	1460

MARIN DE LA MARGUE.

A Foot Note.

By Edmond Mallet.

"The excessive rains and vast quantity of snow, which had fallen, prevented our reaching Mr. Frazier's, an Indian trader, at the mouth of Turtle Creek, on Monongahela River, until Thursday the 22d. We were informed here, that expresses had been sent a few days before to the traders down the river, to acquaint them with the French general's death, and the return of the major part of the French army into winter quarters. "Washington's Journal of a Tour over the Allegany Mountains, 1753."

The French never had officers of the rank of general in the Ohio valley. Reference is here made to Captain Pierre Paul de la Margue, Sieur de Marin, a distinguished Canadian officer of troops of the marine, who was commandant of the army of the Ohio from April, 1753, to the time of his death, which occurred at the fort of Rivière aux Bœufs, on October 29th, 1753

Marin was born in 1692, at Montreal, and was married to Marie Joseph Guyon-Desprets in that city in 1718. One of his sons, the Marin *fils* of the Canadian chronicles, was not less distinguished than was his father.

As early as 1727, Marin was a partner in the Sioux Company, which established Fort Beauharnois on Lake Pepin in Minnesota. In 1739 he was ensign in the troops and was characterized in official dispatches as "a perfect commandant." In that year he negotiated peace between the Foxes and the Sacs. The Sioux having requested him to found a new post in their country he was sent, in 1750, at his own solicitation, to re-establish friendly relations between them and the French and their Indian allies, and to explore the head waters of the Mississippi to ascertain whether the source of the great river of the West, leading to the Pacific ocean, could be found at the height of lands. In 1752 he was relieved by his son, also a captain of colonial troops, and was sent to take armed possession of the Ohio valley, which was about to be occupied by an English land company.

Captain Marin arrived at Niagara from Montreal, with five hundred men, in April, 1753, and found the advance guard of his army, under Captain Baby of the militia, preparing to march into the interior by the Lake Chautauqua route. Marin changed the plan of campaign, and advanced to the point of land extending into Lake Erie called the Peninsula, in French *Presqu'île*, where he erected the first of three forts which he was to build that season. Leaving Captain Le Gardeur de Repentigny in charge of the fort, he pushed forward and erected a second fort at the mouth of a stream called Rivière aux Bœufs. It was his intention to erect a third fort that season, at the confluence of Rivière aux Bœufs and the Allegany river, where de Joncaire had an outpost, but he failed to accomplish his design, ill health, dissentions in his party and the necessity of sending the militia and habitants back to Montreal before the close of navigation on Lake Ontario, having made it impossible.

He was made a Knight of the Order of St. Louis just before his death, which was caused by dysentery contracted whilst superintending the erection of his forts. He was buried in the cemetery of the fort at Rivière aux Bœufs by Father Baron, the chaplain of the expedition, assisted by all the principal officers of the army, among whom was Captain Le Gardeur de Repentigny, who assumed command of the army pending the arrival of his relative, Captain Le Gardeur de St. Pierre who had been dispatched from Montreal to relieve Marin at the first intimation that he was dangerously ill.

CORRESPONDENCE BETWEEN HENRY CLARK
BOWEN GREEN, M D. AND VERY REV.
WILLIAM TAYLOR, 1824-25.

Dr. Green was born at South Berwick, Maine, April 3rd, 1800 of old New England stock, his original ancesters having come over with Roger Williams, and the ground first settled by the family on Rhode Island havihg remained in its possession to recent times. Henry C. B. Green was educated at South Berwick Academy and at Harvard College where he was graduated in 1819. Four years afterwards he married Elizabeth Hartley of Saco.

He entered on the practice of medicine at Saco and soon acquired reputation as a learned and skilful physician. From his boyhood the subject of religion occupied much of his thoughts, but he saw nothing around him except the various sects of Protestantism. These he examined one after another and became dissatisfied with all, being a man of great intellectual power and sound judgment. This reason obliged him to reject all as having no right to teach or guide him. At this time he had no opportunity of knowing the Catholic Church or of seeing any of our books. He was therefore considered an infidel, although in his heart he was deeply religious and felt great anxiety. Whilst in this state of mind at the age of 27 he had a severe fit of sickness and his life was despaired of. He recovered, however, and the question of religion interested him more deeply than ever. He had recourse to fervent prayer and knowing nothing better, he began again to study the Bible, which some years before he had laid aside as a sealed book, that he could not penetrate though he respected it. With no other instructor than divine grace he discovered the Church, and her perpetual existence and authority to teach as established by our Lord. About this time some Catholic book fell into his hands by apparent chance, and he saw at once and believed the Catholic Church. His conviction became immediately his rule of action. He seized the earliest opportunity to come from Maine, where he was then practising medicine to Boston where he learned that priests resided. There he was received into the Church. In the year 1836 he removed to Boston with his family for the sake of their religious instruction. No man was more universally respected.

NOTE OF REV. J. M. FINOTTI.

I did not know HENRY BOYNTON C. GREEN personally, as he had been summoned away from this world three years before my coming to Boston. The first time I heard of his honored name was under very sad circumstances. On the of , 1852, I was called in great haste to the bedside of a young lady, a carriage waiting for me at the Bishop's house, (corner of Federal and Franklin Streets) and a lady in great distress urging me not to delay one moment. I was a stranger in Boston and I cannot to-day remember the street to which I was led. I found a young lady suddenly taken with hemorrhage of the lungs, attended with a mother's care by the venerable Sister servant of St. Vincent's Orphan Asylum, Sister Ann Alexis, to whom, I have since learned, Dr. Green had been tenderly attached as a brother to her and a father to her poor orphans. All withdrew from the sick room, and in my private interview with the death smitten girl, I found her perfectly conscious of her state, resigned, nay most willing to die. I had been informed that an accepted lover was in the house; even that engagement suggested not the least hindrance to the total disengagement from this earth. The friends were called in and in their presence I administered all the Sacraments of the Church, and continued reading the prayers of the Church, until, if I remember well, she breathed her last peacefully, and holding to her lips the emblem of salvation. On my return home I informed Bishop Fitzpatrick of the *call* I had, whereupon he started up to visit the patient, from which I dissuaded him for the reason that Elizabeth Green was dead. He immediately wrote to one of her sisters in Maine, to have the distressing news conveyed to Mrs. Green. I remember to have myself mailed the letter. As I returned home, I met the Bishop walking up and down that "old piazza," in connection with which so many recollections are stamped in the heart of the old clergy and laity of this Diocese. It was then that I learned to revere the name of Dr. Green, one of the *best* of men, and *great* in the avocation of his life. Since then I have had no intercourse with the family; I know none of them, with the exception of one of the Doctor's dear children, whom I have met in 1854.

Whilst lately searching general data in Dr. Green's life for some other purpose, such a flood of light and such a volume of information came upon me, that I thought it my duty to arrange all the information I had in a memoir, digested the best way I could, urged on by the interest of religious fellowship and the veneration, aye more, gratitude, I felt in my heart toward Dr. Green, who, were he living to-day, would be the leading star of his profession, and the unequalled of representatives of the Catholic Church in Massachusetts. But God reckons in mysterious ways. Let us bend our head in genuine sorrow.

May the example of Dr. Green teach us and prove an admirable pattern for the Catholic how to be true and fearless, to the professional man how to be *conscientious* and charitable, to the citizen how to be unswerving from the principles of eternal justice, and unselfish in the service of his country.

———

LETTER I.   DR. GREEN TO REV. W. TAYLOR.

Saco, May 9th ,1824.

It will no doubt be a matter of surprise to you, sir, to find yourself addressed by an utter stranger and it may seem impertinent, but my apology must be (as I can offer no other,) that I can not of course have an introduction to you and I earnestly desire information which I can apparently seek from no one so properly as you.

The object of my letter is this ; the importance of having some well settled principles of religion has suggested itself to me for sometime past and of late more particularly ; and I feel the necessity of some well grounded hope that my faith and devotion rest upon the proper and true foundation ; but in these days of doubt and scepticism, when one says: "Lo! here is Christ," and another " Lo! there" the mind cannot easily determine which is the true path and by halting between opinions is left in a doubtful and dangerous state.

Such is, if I mistake not, my own situation and feel the necessity of religion; I revere my Maker and respect his word as given in the Scriptures, but am left in doubt to which of the denominations of those calling themselves Christians I could conscientiously attach myself, were I worthy.

But I feel a desire, which is unconquerable, to make some inquiries with regard to the Catholic faith. Educated a Protestant I can have no prejudices in its favor from education, but (as part of my education was acquired in Boston,) I have listened with admiration to the eloquence of Bishop Cheverus, I have loved and admired the benevolence of of his character, and have concluded that the religion can not be corrupt in its principles whose professors are so exemplary,

In fine I have a prepossession in favor of the Ancient Church, which weighs much upon my mind, so much that I wish to become more acquainted with its principles, and to have removed from my mind the scruples I entertain with regard to it, or be convinced of its errors altogether.

With these feelings then, Sir, I have presumed to address you, and ask you, if you would condescend to give me occasionally some instruction with regard to, and point out some way in which I may become acquainted with the principles of the Catholic faith. Should you thus condescend, the scruples alluded to, shall be expressed in some future communication, with the hopes that you will pardon the intrusion I have thus made upon you, through my assurance of the sincerity of my intentions I subscribe mysely,

Yours,

HENRY B. C. GREEN.

LETTER II. REV. W. TAYLOR, TO DR. B. C. GREEN.

BOSTON, Mass. 17th May, 1824.

DEAR SIR.

I have been prevented, by professional engagements, from sending a more seasonable reply to your letter of the 9th, Current. I am fully persuaded you possess a laudable anxiety to discover the truth and it will afford me much pleasure to assist you in your inquiries and to facilitate, as much as possible, the attainment of your object.

We are not to adhere to religion from the accident of birth or the prejudice of education ; we should adhere to it from evidence, and we have received our mental faculties to search and to investigate, not to remain in a state of torpid inertion and languid indifference. We should have a strong conviction that the religion which we profess is conformable to the eternal mind, and the detection of that fact is the most noble and the most important investigation which can engage and occupy the attention of men.

If I read your letter correctly, you admit the divinity of the Christian Religion; but amidst the subdivisions of it into so many jarring sects, you seem confused and bewildered. I think it possible to furnish you with a clue which will unerringly conduct you through the windings of the labyrinth and introduce you to the cheering light of truth.

I wish you would direct your attention to the first establishment of the Christian Church by the Great Teacher himself, to the conversion of the Gentiles, to the precise words in which our divine Redeemer conveyed his splendid promises, promises which He must, as the con-substantial

Son of God have fulfilled, and promises which have secured and protected the Christian edifice from the violence of the storm and the buffeting of the tempest. Ask how it has happened that the Christian Church has been thus divided? Was it so from the beginning? Discuss the claim of every sect to scriptural and primitive Christianity and see whether in the number you will not find one which has prescription and biblical evidence in its favor; one church having over her portals the words Unity, Sanctity, Catholicity, Apostolicity. A church which received the promises from the lips of Jesus Christ and which, by an unbroken hierarchy, a visible ladder, enables you to trace your connection with his sacred person. A church which has been consistent and invariable from the commencement and which (whatever may be the external forms which she adopts to enlist the body in worship) places the kernel of Religion in the heart which adores the Father through the beloved Son "in spirit and in truth." Ask and ascertain, after prayer and meditation, whether the Reformers did not, under the specious pretence of removing and rescinding excrescences, touch the trunk of the tree? and whether they did not lay, by their principles, the foundation of that motley group of sects which are daily springing up with the rapidity of mushroom and vegetation? We do not take our Religion from the vices or virtues of Believers or Teachers, but from the pure Word of God and from the belief of the Christian Church throughout the world "Quod ubique, quod semper, quod ab omnibus." Tell the captain of some coaster to call on me and I will send you some books which will assist you in your pious efforts.

I am, dear sir,

Your faithful servant,

WILLIAM TAYLOR.

_____

LETTER III. DR. GREEN TO REV. W. TAYLOR.

SACO, May 25, 1824.

The receipt of your excellent letter of the 7th instant gave me much gratification, the more so perhaps, as previous to my addressing you I had entertained fears that you would not be inclined to notice a communication from one of whom you knew nothing, and who if you did, would probably have no particular claim to your attention.

Your construction of my letter was correct with regard to my admission of the Divinity of the Christian Religion, and my desire is to obtain access to the fountain whence flow its sacred truths, unmixed with error and untainted by innovation.

I have no hesitation in believing (unless my heart deceives me) that the great Head of the Christian community possesses the full power and will, as the "Consubstantial Son of God," to reward and fulfill to the utmost his promises to them. But there are many sects who call themselves *Christians*, who agree in acknowledging the Divinity of the Scriptures and in many other important points, and yet who differ in many respects, seemingly essential to their being united in one bond and one body, and who mutually deny the orthodoxy of each other's faith.

The inevitable consequence of this is confusion, at least it is so as respects the effect produced in my own mind, and I look round with no little solicitude to discover which is the true Church of Jesus Christ.

The considerations which you mentioned have previously struck me with much force, and I have reflected how many centuries have rolled away and yet the Catholic Church stands through all the changes of time and the dilapidations of ages; itself (apparently) unchanged and (for aught I know) invariable in its doctrines and consistent in its principles. These facts have suggested themselves to me in much force, and for some time past I have resisted the prejudiced sarcasms so frequently (among Protestants) uttered with regard to the Catholic faith.

But sir, while I confess to you the prepossessions existing in my mind in favor of the Ancient Church, I must as freely acknowledge my scruples with regards to some points of its character and its reputed Creed. To trace the steps of the

"Visible Ladder" by which in reflection we can ascend to a connection with the person of our Blessed Redeemer, must be delightful and calculated to excite the noblest feelings of our nature. But is the evidence decisive that this is the Church which possesses the distinguished privilege of having received its promises from the lips of Jesus Christ? Is it certain that its hierarchy has been unbroken, and that no link has been severed in the chain by which its claim of connection with primitive Apostolicity is entertained?

These questions no doubt will savor to you strongly of ignorance, and this I freely confess, and as my object is to become better informed, I shall with gratitude improve the opportunity you offer of sending me some books.

Accept, sir, my thanks for your kindness in noticing my letter, and my best wishes for your prosperity.

With much respect I remain,

Your faithful servant,

H. B. GREEN.

_____

ETTER IV. REV. W. TAYLOR TO DR. GREEN.

BOSTON, Mass. 4th June, 1824.

MY DEAR SIR.

I have regularly received your last letter and send you by Capt. Flatley a few books calculated to assist you in your inquiries relative to the important subject which engaged your attention.

I particularly recommend to your perusal "The End of Religious Controversy" by Dr Milner, and I have such a high opinion of the book that I would say it is the best and the most able defence of the Catholic Religion (the Chapter or Letters on Miracles, excepted) which I have read.

I will be always happy to see you or to hear from you.

And believe me, my dear sir,

Yours sincerely,

WILLIAM TAYLOR.

LETTER V. DR. GREEN TO REV. W, TAYLOR.

Saco, June 19, 1824.

Dear Sir.

Being absent from home when Capt Hartley arrived, and since my return having been occupied by professional duties and domestic concerns, I have been unable before this time to acknowledge the receipt of your last letter with the books accompanying.

Capt. Hartley informs me to receive the books as my own. The loan of them would have been considered as a great kindness, but as you generously choose to present them, I should ill requite your goodness, were I to do otherwise than to receive them and tender you my grateful thanks for them ; at the same time I assure you they shall be attentively considered.

I understand you contemplate visiting the State of Maine this summer. Should you do so, it will give me much pleasure to see you and I hope you will not pass by without calling on me, as you must pass through this town on your . way to the more eastern part of the state. Hoping still to hear more from you I remain with the highest respect.

Your obedient servant,

HENRY B. C. GREEN.

LETTER VI. REV. W. TAYLOR TO DR. GREEN.

Boston, Mass. 22nd 1824.

My Dear Sir.

I have received your letter of the 19th, and am pleased to know that you received the books. I regret much that the binding was not more superb but I am persuaded, from your letters, that you are more attentive to solids than to surfaces and that a book will be recommended to your judgment by its contents.

To you, my dear sir, sincerely disposed to discuss the truth, I would recommend a serious perusal of historical works on the state of Europe at the period of the Reformation. In your closet, without prejudice, reflectingly examine the works of Catholics and Protestants and rancorous feeling long since subsided, you can dispassionately compare the evidences of both sides of the question, and and draw correct and logical inferences. The Roman Catholib Church, as you well know has been much misrepresented and I may add caricatured by the Reformers, and those who possess and are influenced by their spirit. The Christian Religion by the bigots of Europe has been occasionally made use of as a political instrument; in some countries it was and is at present connected with the state but it suffered much by such an unnatural union. The Ancient Church is represented in the United States as partial and inclining to Monarchy and despotism in her policy and constitution, but the assertion is made and believed by those who are strangers to the history of past ages. Permit me, my dear sir, to direct your attention to the numerous Republics which started into existence, and were fostered by the Catholic Church, Republics rivalling in splendor the Commonwealths of Greece, and far exceeding them in stability and duration; I mean the Italian Republics and those on the coast of Dalmatia. Look at the Cantons of Switzerland free and happy before religious fanaticism sowed the seeds of dissention amongst them and behold the four Protestant Cantons yielding to a foreign faction and surrending their liberty without discharging a cannon or striking a blow. I mentioned in my former communication that a law does not cease to be less pure because its maxims are disregarded and its principles despised. I allude particularly to the independent spirit of the Ancient Church and beg leave to add that her enlightened members and distinguished scholars have always opposed themselves to unscriptured pretentions and papal unsurpations.

If I go to Maine I will see you and Lady and if you come to Boston you will see and dine with your friend.

WILLIAM TAYLOR.

LETTER VII.   DR. GREEN TO REV. W. TAYLOR.

SACO, July 26, 1824.

DEAR SIR.

After a serious and attentive perusal of the books you sent me, and from all other evidence and information I can gather with regard to the subject, I find my mind much more inclined to the Catholic faith than when I first addressed you. But as religion is something so sacred and important and something which cannot be changed as the fashion of a garment, I should wish to be certain that I was "well persuaded in my own mind" that the religion I should profess wore every mark of certainty as to its truth and possessed my full and unwavering faith, lest having embraced a system without these essential conditions, its principles before they were firmly rooted be choked by the thorns and wordly vexations or blighted by the temptations of perverse doctrine. I have little doubt remaining (I may say none) that the Catholic Church is the only Church which has existed as one Church since the days of the Apostles and that the Protestants are gone off from, instead of reforming it; its practical principles and moral inculcations, as far as I understand them, are pure and unexceptionable but some points of its doctrine seem "difficult and hard to be understood." That which causes the greatest degree of doubt and uneasiness in my mind is the doctrine of the *Eucharist.* Although I am far from saying this cannot be so, I perceive something in my heart very like a feeling which would actuate me to say with the disciples of old. "This is a hard saying: who can hear it." I do not intend by any means to reject everything I cannot understand; I well know that many things are a mystery not to be compassed by human reason, the doctrine of the Trinity I firmly believe, although I can no better understand it, than I can understand that of the real presence in the Eucharist, but I do not find that full faith in my heart, with respect to this latter, which is present with regard to the former. My anxiety to become settled in my religious principles is undiminished or rather increased; and the consideration of the subject through the means you furnished me, has removed many or most of the scruples I entertained with regard to the Ancient Church and has given me a higher estimation of it in many particulars than I before possessed. The principal cause of hesitation is that alluded to, the doctrine of the Eucharist. Can you, my dear sir, who already have bestowed so much attention to my inquiries that, I fear I shall weary you with my importunities, direct me to an examination of this very important point in any manner which will be more likely to cause me to receive it?

It would give me great satisfaction to see and converse with you, and I hope I shall have the pleasure before long of seeing you in Maine.

I can make no calculation when I shall visit Boston, having no business calling me there save that of visiting a valued friend. Should I find it practicable to go there the coming fall, I shall make it a conspicuous part of my errand to visit you.

With sentiments of respect and esteem,

I remain, sir, yours &c.

HENRY B. C. GREEN.

LETTER VIII.   DR. GREEN TO W. TAYLOR.

SACO, September 4, 1824.

DEAR SIR.

Persuming from your silence that you do not intend continuing a correspondence which (although short in its duration) has been productive of much pleasure and instruction to me, I can not on my part suffer it to cease without expressing to you the gratitude I feel for the kindness you have shown me since its commencement.

I was (as I probably now am) utterly unknown to you and produced no warrants that my intentions were good or my enquiries sincere, but you treated me as a friend. It is not my habit, sir, nor I have the faculty of making high wrought compliments or ardent professions and therefore shall attempt none here : but while I tender you the meagre

offering of my thanks permit me to assure you that the remembrance of your kindness will not be easily eradicated,
and that I should be very happy in the reflection could I
expect ever to reciprocate it.

The clouds of doubt (relative to the subject mentioned
in my letter to you of the 26th July) still hang over my mind
and prevent my desiring to be received as an unworthy Son
of the Catholic Church; but as I hope I shall not be suffered
to fall into error, so I hope that my search after truth will
ultimately be crowned with success. Professional duties and
engagements have so far prevented me from visiting Boston,
.but I still intend it, when I can consistently with the circumstances of my situation.

Suffer me to remind you of your promise to visit me
should you come into Maine, and indulge in the hope that
the period of your visit here may not be very distant.

May prosperity attend you, my dear Sir, and when in
your prayers no worthier object engages your attention,
breathe one aspiration for

                                        HENRY B. C. GREEN.
                    _____

LETTER IX.   REV. WM. TAYLOR TO DR. GREEN.

                              BOSTON, Mass., 26 October, 1824.
MY DEAR SIR,

I have received your two last letters and be assured I
would have long since replied, had I not been prevented by
professional drudgery. My society here is numerous, about
three thousand, and these two months I have had no clergyman but myself to attend to their spiritual necessities. If
you knew moreover the elements which compose this Society
you would readily excuse me from answering regularly your
polite and friendly communications.

If I recollect (for I can't lay my hand on your letters) you
stated that you found some difficulty in submitting your
understanding to the belief of "the Real Presence" of Christ
in the Sacrament of the Eucharist, and you stated that
though you considered the Trinity a greater mystery that

You believed it because the evidences which commanded your assent struck you as more distinctly stated in the Sacred Scriptures. I beg leave to refer you to Bossuet and also to Milner's End of Controversy, for a statement of the evidence of our faith on the subject of the Real Presence and its consectary Transubstantiation. When we, Catholics, assert the Real Presence of the body of Christ, we mean certainly his glorified body. It is the same body which was immolated on the cross, and which atoned for our transgressions, which purchased for us " the inheritance ; " but it is that glorified body to the properties of which we are strangers and with which we are totally unacquainted. The body which appeared in the midst of the disciples " when the doors were closed for fear of the Jews, " the body which Mary Madgalene took for that of a gardener, and the body which the disciples at Emmaus recognized "in the breaking of bread."

The facts of Scripture which the Catholic Divines cite in defence of this doctrine are : First, the words of institution (recorded in the Gospels) " This is my body," etc., etc., Second, the words of promise in the sixth chapter of John. The inhabitants of Capharnaum understood our Lord in a literal sense, and He, so far from undeceiving them, confirmed the sense in which they understood him, and many of them walked no longer with him. Third, the Doctrine of the Apostle St. Paul, in his epistle to the Corinthians.

Both Protestants and Catholics acknowledge that the present belief of the Catholic Church on this mystery was general and universal at the period of the Reformation. If, as our Protestant brothers contend, a figurative not a real, Presence were the belief of the primitive Church, the change could not take place or the one faith be substituted for the other, except suddenly or gradually; now it strikes me as absurd in morals and involving a repugnance to suppose a change in either way.

Suddenly would be to suppose that the Christian world would go to bed Protestants and get up in the morning professing the Catholic faith, and the change occurring gradually is equal y absurd. For instance to suppose that a change could take place in one church and then in another and so on, on so vital a point and so apparently contrary to the testimony of our senses and conceptions of our minds, insensibly creep into all churches and become universal, is supposing what could never occur. In the darkest ages some manly and *unslumbering* Master spirit would rise up to assert its native dignity and prevent the forging of such fetters for the human mind. Faith is a gift of God without which we cannot please him and in the awful mysteries of our religion as well as in Metaphysics when we carry our enquiries too far and attempt to know the length and breadth of things which in their essence transcend the limits of our conception, we often suffer the shipwreck of faith and are engulfed in a vortex of perplexity and doubt " non plas sapere quam oportet sapere sed sapere ad sobrietatem."

I am your sincere and faithful friend,

WILLIAM TAYLOR.

LETTER X. DR. GREEN TO REV W. TAYLOR.

SACO, 8th December, 1824.

MY DEAR SIR.

After a fatiguing journey I arrived home in safety and found my family and friends in good health, but found my professional and domestic concerns requiring so much of my attention, as to prevent, until now, the performance of the agreable task of addressing you. The kindness and attention with which I was received and treated by you and your friends while in Boston has left very agreable impressions upon my feelings and the only alloy to this pleasure is the circumstance of the obligation lying wholly upon me and that I was not able to make any return by way of reciprocation. I do not despair however of an opportunity which shall permit me to evince to you that your friendly and very disinterested attentions are duly appreciated.

I have the happiness to find, that although the important

step which I have taken and which has now become necessarily public, has excited the surprise of many and perhaps the vexation of some, yet that most of my nearest friends look upon it without any feelings of horror, and those whose orinions I value most, without scarcely those of disapprobation. I esteem this as a source of happiness because although it is our duty to overrule our natural affections when they controvert us in matters of conscience, yet the solicitude of near and dear friends, when opposed to our sense of duty, is a strong temptation to swerve from it and one which we are fortunate perhaps in being delivered from.

I shall not neglect to continue my investigations with regard to the subject of religion, as I feel that I have but just entered its confines, and I am quite sensible too, that what I possess of it is merely a *bud* which will require every attention to prevent its being blighted and destroyed by the chilling atmosphere of doubt and conflicting passions, with which the human heart, unillumined by the light of religion and faith is ever surrounded. I have reason to be grateful that a ray of divine truth has at length penetrated (as I fondly hope) this gloom, and I must continue to petition that by unremitted exertion I may be enabled to remove the rubbish which now obstructs it, until it shines forth in the full splendor of its perfection.

I am happy in the privilege you have given me in permitting me to continue my correspondence with you, and shall consider it as an important means of supporting me forward in the way I have taken.

Please to present my respects to Mr. Byrne, to the Superior of the Convent, to Mr. and Mrs. Walley (when you see them) and others of your friends whom I had the pleasure of meeting, and be assured, my dear sir, that the warmest esteem and respect is cherished toward you by

HENRY B. C. GREEN.

LETTER XI. DR. GREEN TO REV. W. TAYLOR.

SACO, January 10th, 1825.

MY DEAR SIR.

This letter will be handed to you by Mr. Jonathan Tucker, Jr., a merchant of this town, who is a very much esteemed friend of mine. His character is one of firm and strict integrity, and his standing as a moral man very high with all who know him.

I take much pleasure in introducing this gentleman to you as after a mature and candid investigation of the subject, he finds his feelings strongly biased in favor of the Catholic faith, as his conversation with you will more fully unfold.

I have already written you one letter since my return from Boston, but have not experienced the pleasure of receiving one from you, but I still expect it when your weighty duties will permit you to spend a few moments upon so insignificant a correspondent as I am. I hope this opportunity will soon occur and that you will consider that I am here far removed from you like "a sheep having no shepherd," and in most of my feelings and opinions in matters of religion alone. There is one subject in particular upon which I wish to consult you; it is that although I consider myself as one of your flock, I am still one of the *Parish* in my own town and am thus giving my mite in support of a Calvinistic minister. Can I conscientiously do this, and is it my duty to do so, when according to the laws of this State, by merely giving notice of the act to the clerk I am from that time discharged? I have some scruples upon the consistency at least of this course, and wish for your opinion of it.

My imagination not unfrequently carries me into your society and joins me with you in your exercises, which always inspires me with the wish that it was in my power to be present in reality; but although the body be confined to one small spot of earth, the immortal mind is unsusceptible of such trammels and flies over many miles of seeming distance to the communion of kindred spirits.

I hope soon to hear from you and to learn when you will probably visit Maine, as I wish much to see you and am anxious that my infant child should receive the rite of Baptism from your hands, in which desire my wife also joins me.

Please to present me with sentiments of respect to those of your friends I had the pleasure of meeting, and be assured of the regard and esteem with (which) I remain,

Yours, etc.,

HENRY B. C. GREEN.

LETTER XII. REV. W. TAYLOR TO DR. GREEN.

BOSTON, MASS., 18 January, 1825.

MY DEAR SIR.

I thank you sincerely for the kind letter and accompanying book and friendship which I received from Mr. Tucker. I have been much pleased with this gentleman's acquaintance and I look at him as virtually a member of our church. My dear Sir, you will dispel prejudice and materially serve the cause of truth. I am pleased that your friends do not rashly condemn the important step you have taken, and you must be prepared to see and hear the weapons of ridicule substituted where no argument can be advanced. You have judgment and information to shield you from such attacks, and you have on record in the inspired writings, a precedent calculated to console you. "The Apostles went forth from the Council rejoicing that they had been found worthy to suffer contumely for the name of Jesus Christ."

When the weather becomes better, if God spare me health, I will pay you a visit. I send you a few books. "Pastorini" I borrowed, and request you will return it after the attentive perusal to which it is so justly entitled.

With affectionate regards to Mrs. Green, believe me,

Your devoted friend,

WILLIAM TAYLOR.

Politeness of Mr. Tucker.

LETTER XIII. DR. GREEN TO REV. W. TAYLOR.

* SACO, March 3, 1825.

MY DEAR SIR,

The acknowledgment of the receipt of your letter and the accompanying books (by Mr. Tucker) has been deferred until this late period, from some other causes than my inclination, or a slight regard of the obligation I owe you in respect to them. The sickness of this season, added to my usual routine of business, has since then kept me much employed and sometimes fatigued me too much to leave me capable of answering your friendly communications with the interest they certainly merit. I am happy in learning you found my friend Mr. Tucker worthy of your regard, and I consider his character such as would do honor to any society in which he is found. I have read " Pastorini " and feel very grateful to you for the trouble you have taken about it on my behalf ; it shall be returned by the first opportunity. I am much pleased with it ; it has rendered intelligible in some measure a book, which before I read this, seemed enveloped in an impenetrable cloud. As you mention, and as I before anticipated the shafts of ridicule and satire are not unfrequently levelled at me, but I have no fear on that account. The walls of the fortress under whose protection I have attempted to throw myself I well believe are too far impregnable to suffer by the attacks from such feeble weapons, and I have much more dread of the weakness and sinfulness of my own heart than of all the artillery of such assailants.

Religion at the present day seems quite too much a theme of speculation and we have much reason to tremble lest we *speculate* and theorize until we are lost. My constant wish and prayer is that in proving " all things " I may " endure to the end " in holding " fast that which is good. "

The anticipation of your expected visit affords me much pleasure and I hope that no accident will prevent you from its accomplishment. In the mean time let me assure you, my dear sir, that the reception of a letter from you affords me so much gratification that I am certain you will not refuse to grant it, when you have a leisure moment you can without inconvenience bestow upon me.

I recollect, with much gratitude, the attentions I received from you and your friends in Boston and should be very happy to have it in my power to reciprocate them. Please to present me to them with sentiments of much esteem, and believe me your very much obliged friend,

HENRY B. C. GREEN.

_____

LETTER XIV. REV. W. TAYLOR TO DR. GREEN.

BOSTON, 20th April, 1825.

MY DEAR SIR.

I have only time to thank you for your last kind letter. If I do not answer you, in course, you will not, I am persuaded, ascribe my silence to neglect or inattention. If I continue to reside permanently in Boston (a matter very probable), I intend soon to associate with me one or two pious and well informed clergymen who, sharing and participating in my labors, will afford me a few moments to correspond with my dear and valued friends. I hope I can execute my intention and pay you a visit next month. Every morning at the Altar I recollect you and pray for your presesent prosperity and future happiness. I hope the dear Mr. Tucker enjoys his health. Before I depart from Boston I will write to you that unless serious professional engagements may call you to a distance, there may be no disappoinment in our projected interview.

I did not notice "your case of conscience" relative to the support given by you to the Calvinist Minister. I leave you to your own good prudence and sense and should you continue your generosity to him I can't see how it could be deemed a relinquishment of principles on your part when you neither accept of his ministry nor attend at his church. I wish to send the dear Mrs. Green and yourself a copy of the Doway (English) translation of our Bible with notes and I will thank you to tell any friend of yours coming to Boston to call on me for the book. With best respects to Mrs. Green and to Mr. Tucker.

I am, my dear sir, your devoted friend,

WILLIAM TAYLOR.

LETTER XV. REV. W. TAYLOR DR. GREEN.

BOSTON, 26th April, 1825.

MY DEAR SIR.

This will be handed to you by my dear brother Clergyman, the Rev. Dennis Ryan of Whitfield in your state. As my visit to Saco can't take place before the latter part of May I have requested Mr. Ryan to call and see yourself and dear lady and Mr. Tucker. Any attention you pay to my associate, the Rev. Mr. Ryan. will be deemed as immediately directed to the person of, my dear sir,

Your sincere friend,

WILLIAM TAYLOR.

Politeness of Rev. Dennis Ryan.

LETTER XVI. DR. GREEN TO REV. W. TAYLOR.

SACO, 27th April 1825.

MY DEAR SIR.

It was with great pleasure I received your letter of the 20th, inst. and the assurance it conveyed that I might expect to be gratified by a visit from you soon. I hope you will write me as you proposed and give me a little notice of the time I may expect to see you, as I sometimes make excursions which keep me absent a day or two, and I should be extremely sorry to have this happen when you visit me.

I am pleased to learn that you consider your permanent residence in Boston as a "matter very probable" and if such should be your wish I hope you will be gratified.

I return you "Pastorini," with many thanks for the use

of it, and for the trouble you have given yourself about it, on my account; the perusal of it has afforded me much interest and instruction.

Mr. Tucker is in the enjoyment of his usual good health and he desired me to present you his respectful esteem.

I hope your health has not suffered during the prevalence of the late very uncomfortable epidemic from which very few have escaped. It has caused me to be exposed to a considerable degree of fatigue, but otherwise it has not affected me much.

I thank you for your intention of forwarding to me the Bible you mentioned and Capt. Hartley (who will hand this to you) will take it, if you please.

With many wishes, for your prosperity and happiness together with usual. esteem, I remain, sir,

Your much obliged friend,

HENRY B. C. GREEN.

Politeness of Capt. Hartley.

LETTER XVII. REV. W. TAYLOR TO DR. GREEN.

BOSTON, 29th November, 1825.

I thank you much for your late affectionate letter and for the handsome token of esteem with which you thought proper to aceompany it. I will certainly retain it during life in my possession.

I expect the recently consecrated bishop here on next Sabbath, and as soon as I surrender to him my spiritual and temporal authority, I will embark for France and the Atlantic now lies in black prospective before me. I regret much that I can't see yourself and dear wife, and friends before my departure but I never will forget you in my sacrifices and prayers and I will recollect you with tender feeling of love and friendship. I will send you a few books by Rev. Mr. Ryan and on my arrival in France will be your coustant and regular correspondent. Perhaps you would yet send me one of your children for the purpose of receiving his education in France, which may be advantageous and would not extinguish his partiality for the institutions of his own dear free and prosperous country.

Embrace your dear wife and children for me and cherish the hope that we may meet where painful separations are unknown.·

Believe me, my dearest sir,

Your sincere friend,

WILLIAM TAYLOR.

TRUSTEE DEFIANCE OF CATHOLIC DISCIPLINE. The following advertisement in the Norfolk (Va) Herald, of Sept. 27, 1819, will show to what lengths the trustees went in the old times, and how completely they had lost all Catholic spirit. A priest was appointed to Norfolk by Archbishop Marechal, yet these men assumed to "discard him from the Church" and notified the Congregation that this duly appointed priest "should never be permitted to officiate there or in any burying ground belonging to it." They really prevented the priest from fulfilling his priestly duties at the grave of a young lady. These men drove many out of the Church, themselves leading the way. It is a wonder that they did not order all their unfortunate dupes to become Protestants.

ADVERTISEMENT—TO THE PUBLIC.

An unpleasant occurrence took place yesterday, at the gate of St. Patrick's Church in this Borough, in consequence of the persevering malignity of a Clergyman discarded from that Church. Although public notice was given to the congregation, so far back as three weeks or a month, that "he should never be permitted to officiate there, or in any burying ground belonging to it,"—yet supported by persons who have been misled by his false principles and intrigues, he had the audacity, in defiance not only of the public notification, but also of a written notice warning him on the morning of yesterday, that he would not be permitted to enter into said Church or any of the premises thereunto belonging, to attempt to go and officiate there over the corpse of a young lady of eminent virtue and respectable family. We cannot but regret that so disagreeable an affair has occurred, particularly when the remains of so amiable a young lady and the feelings of so respectable and respected a family were involved; and that duty to ourselves, and respect for our Church and congregation, forced us, by excluding an intruder to do an act, which, though particularly levelled against him—malice, perhaps, will not fail to construe, as intended to insult the dead and to hurt the feelings of the living.

THE TRUSTEES of St. Patrick's Church, Norfolk.

PAPERS RELATING TO THE FRENCH SETTLE-
MENT AT GALLIPOLIS.

Copied by Col. Bernard U. Campbell, from originals in
possession of General Walbach.

Done at Paris, the 3d of Feb 1790.   Enregistré Nicolau.

Mr. Peter Spurche will have the right on his arrival in
America to put himself in possession of 50 english arpens,
(called acres) adjoining the land of the company of the
Scioto, situated between the Ohio and the Scioto rivers, in
1st or 2nd township of the 18th range, of which 50 acres the
survey will be made.

Fifty acres for himself and his heirs forever to enjoy
in full property, provided that the annual rent of one bushel
of wheat to the acre, good and receivable American measure,
be paid into the hands of the company's agent, after the
second year, and also from year to year. The large building
timber which Mr. Peter Spurche will find upon the fifty
acres granted to him will belong to him in property, and he
will have the right of transporting the produce of his lands
upon the vessels of the company, upon paying only his part
of the freight, in faith of which the present have been
signed by two of the Directors of the Company and by Mr.
Peter Spurche.

SPURCHE.   WILLIAM PLAYFAIR.   T. A. CHAIS DE SOISSONS.

———

At Paris, this 10th day of February, 1790.

Knowing the distinguished intelligence and the desire
of obliging of Messrs. DeBarth and Thiebout, members of
the society of 24, first setting out for America, counting
moreover with confidence on their friendship, I beg these
gentlemen to choose for me and take possession in my name

of five hundred acres, or arpens english, which I have bought upon the banks of the Ohio. I wish also to place my possession near that of Messrs. De Marnezia and the locality and the apparent fertility of the land, do not put any obstacle to it. I desire my land to be watered by some water course susceptible of the establishment of a mill ; I dare not add as a motive for my request, my sincere remembrance of the care which they will take of my interest.

GAVAULT BON DE MAUBRANCHE.

At Paris, the 11th of February, 1790.

We, the undersigned, purchasers of 2,000 acres, which are not embraced in the society of Messrs. DeBarth and Thiebaut, and the title of property of which is mentioned, declare that we have given, and do give by the present letter of attorney, full power to Mr. DeBarth, in our name, to cause two squares of 1,000 acres each to be marked out joining each other, and in the place which will appear to him the most advantageous for fertility and position, and at the same time as near as possible to the Ohio river, and to the common lands of the aforesaid Society; to use all necessary diligence for us and to cause himself to be placed in possession in our name and to enable us to enjoy and use it in all property, and to obtain every confirmative act of property,&c.

DUPORTAIL.   ROCHEFONTAINE.

I certify that the above are the signatures of General Duportail and Major Rochefontaine mentioned in my certificate on the other side. Paris, 11th, 1790.

[SEAL.]   J. BARLOW.

I certify that General Duportail and Major Rochefontaine have each purchased 2,000 acres of land of the Scioto company, one half of which is to be taken in the society of the 24, of which Mr. DeBarth and Mr. Thiebaut are agents, and the other half as near as may be to the said society's lands, agreeably to the rules given by me for laying out the lands of the said Scioto company and their certificate to be considered as valid as a deed of sale for 2,000 acres. Paris, 11th of February.

I approve the above title of 2,000 acres.   J. BARLOW.

———

Paris, 7th of February, 1790.

I certify that General Duportail, General de la Valette and Major Rochefontaine, have each of them bought one thousand acres of land, in company with the gentlemen for whom Messrs. DeBarth and Thiebaut are the attorneys. The above 3,000 acres are to be delivered as making part of the 24,000 acres for which the said DeBarth and Thiebaut are the agents and attorneys.

J. BARLOW.

———

Paris, 11th February, 1790.

The above erasures of the name of Smith are made by me. The above thousand acres each for General Duportail and Major Rochefontaine are the same as mentioned in the certificate here adjoined, to be taken in the society of 24 persons.

J. BARLOW.

———

Notice upon the purchases of different parts of lands. lying between the Ohio and the Scioto, bought at Paris by the agents of the company of the Scioto, of which the undersigned, members of the Society of 24, are charged to take possession as well for themselves and their associates, as for other persons of their friends not members of said Society; but who have made purchases and desire to place themselves in proximity with the establishment of the 24.

SOCIETY OF THE 24.

Names of the Purchasers of the Society.	Dates of the Contracts.	Quantity of Acres purchased;
1 Claude Francois Adrien, Marquis de Lezay Marnesia.	January 14th, 1790	1,000
2 Jean Paul Guerrin,	" 14th, "	1,000
3 La Com^{se} de Beauharnois par Mr. de Marnésia her father.	" 15th, "	1,000
4 De Bondy,	Idem "	1,000
5 Claude Abel, Marquis de Vichy.	Idem "	1,000
6 Claude Leopold Perrotin de Barmont.	January 18th, "	1,000
7 William Playfair,	Idem "	1,000
8 Jean Antoine Chais de Soissons,	Idem "	1,000
9 Jean Joseph DeBarth, father.	January 20th, "	1,000
10 François Meinrad Joseph DeBarth Bourogue.	" 21st, "	1,000
11 Charles Antoine, Louis Thiebault.	Idem "	1,000
12 Jean Joseph DeBarth for Mr. de Saulegue.	January 23rd, "	1,000
13 Jean Joseph DeBarth for Mr. de Blondeau.	Idem "	1,000
14 Francois Auguste de Gréville,	January 25th, "	1,000
15 Jacques Duval d'Epremenil,	Idem "	1,000
16 Jean Daniel Smith,	February 2nd, "	1,000
17 Dominique Benoit, Vicomte de Bellon.	" 8th, "	1,000
18 Etienne Jean Gayault, Bon de Maubranche.	Idem	1,000
19 Etienne François Schwend aujourdhui Mr. le Cte de Tresigny	February 10th, "	1,000
20 General Duportail, Cert. of Mr. Barlow, Feb. 11, 1790,		1,000
21 General de la Valette,	Idem	1,000
22 Major de Rochefontaine,	Idem	1,000
23 Mr. Barlow, General letter of Att'y of Feb. 8, 1790,		1,000
24 Mr. le Mrs. de Gaville, Cert. of Mr. Barlow, Feb. 11, and resolve of the same month.		1,000

OTHER PURCHASES OUT OF BUT IN PROXIMITY WITH THE

TOWNSHIP OF THE TWENTY-FOUR ASSOCIATES.

M. Mrs.

Names of the Purchasers.	Date of the Contracts.	Quantity Acres.
Marquis de Marnezia	January 11th, 1890	20,000
The same,	" " "	100
The Count de Gourcy,	" 16th, "	300
The same,	" 23rd, "	200
Mr. De Barth (father)	" 24th, "	1,000
The same,	" 25th, "	1,000
Mde La Ctsse de la Ville Bague,	" 29th, "	1,050
De Quinzon,	" 29th, "	2,100
Spuitter,	" 29th, "	1,050
De Préville,	February 2nd, "	400
D'Epresmenil,	" 11th, "	10,000
Bon de Maubranche.	" 11th, "	5,000
General Duportail,		1,000
Major de Rochefontaine,		1,000
		44,200
	Society of the 24,	24,000
	Total,	68.200
More, Mr. DeBarth for his workmen,		1,300
		69,500

At New York, on the 20th May, 1790, DeBarth.

———

June, 1790. To Mr. DeBarth at Alexandria; from Col. William Duer of the city of New York, to my father, before his leaving Alexandria with the company of settlers for the lands in Ohio.

My Dear and Very Respectable Friend.

I have received your letter of the 29th of May. The conduct of the purchasers and of the B————————e has caused me much uneasiness, and the more because I know

well you are troubled with all that can interrupt the prosperity of our establishment. Yet, my dear friend, it is
necessary to exercise firmness, all that is in reason will be
done, all that is not ought not. By his sacrifices dictated by
caprice or injustice I will do nothing but encourage the spirit
of science which already rules too much. Our determination
will be sent to-morrow and I doubt not that it will have your
approbation. I write to Thiebeau on the subject of the em-
barrassment that Boulogne has caused to those engaged : he
will show you my letter ; by the post which departs to-morrow
yov will have from me a long letter : adieu and believe me
always your faithful friend,

WILLIAM DUER.

The Marquis Maurnesia. Messieurs Barth and Thiebaud.

Marietta Nov. 9th, 1790.

GENTLEMEN.

I have learned from Col. Thompson since my arrival
here that you are anxious to be on your lands as soon as possible, with many other circumstances relative to the emigrants
in general, I am sorry that any accident has prevented you
so long from taking possession of your purchase, and I feel
myself very unhappy that I did not arrive sooner but my de-
tention was unavoidable, I am not yet ready to determine on
every matter which I find connected with the business, but I
beg you to rest assured that no time will be lost or any exertions wanting on my part either in forming the necessary
arrangements or in the execution of the business. The first
object of attention I conceive to be your determination with
respect to the place where you will locate the 24,000 acres to
which your associates are entitled and the spot where you
wish the houses should be built for your accommodation, for
till this is done it will be improper to send on the people etc.
for the purpose of building the houses. That you may be able
to make the best choice, I should advise that at least some
of your associates with a number of your people, should go

down and reconnoitre the several tracts mentioned in your contract with Mr. Barlow, and to facilitate this part of the business, I will send two surveyors with some assistants and a party of about twenty Rangers, etc., for protection. With respect to the house lots and four acre lots at Chickamaga Creek, I shall provide for their immediate survey and allotment to individuals; but it is my duty to inform you that the ground proper for house lots at that point will not admit of half the number proposed by Colonel Duer, that should the number be extended to one thousand the greater part will not be worth having, I therefore advise that you relinquish your claim to house lots and four acre lots at Chickamaga, on condition of receiving a donation of the like at the place where you shall fix for building your town. This I conceive will be much for your interest as well as convenience, both of which I am sure Colonel Duer intends to promote; but his want of information with respect to the situation at Chickamaga, has led him into an error in this respect. I shall be happy at all times to be honored with your communications and ready to suggest every idea which I may judge promotive of your interest or that of any of the french emigrants. I have the honor to be with great respect and esteem, Gentlemen,

Your most obedient and very humble servant,

RUFUS PUTNAM.

Marquis Maurnesia, Mr. Barth, Mr. Thiebaud and other gentlemen of the 24 Associates.

———

MARIETTA, November 13th, 1790.

To the Gentlemen composing the 24 Associates.

Gentlemen:

I have ben honoured with your letter of the 10th, in answer to mine of the 9th instant, to which with the utmost defference I answer. The agents for the Scioto Company

did very early concert measures for the lodging and defence
of the French Settlers on their arrival; at the same time
they had the attention to prepair other buildings in a better
stile for the accommodation of the gentlemen of the twenty-
foure, who should first arrive in full expectation that they
would occupie them with their workmen, untill others could
be constructed or you yourselves should be enabled to build
your own houses on the ground you should fix on for your
new city.   But at this period, gentlemen, it seems for per-
ticuler reesons best known to yourselves, you do not choose
to occupy the buildings errected and you demand that Car-
pinters and other workmen sufficient to erect buildings
capable to lodge you and your people be instantly furnished
to you.   As this circumstance could not be foreseen it must
not appear extreordinery to you that it is impossible for me
satisfie your demand so soon as you could wish, but gentlemen
by reasonable delay I trust every obstical may be removed,
at present I have not the means to encounter this new and
unexpected expense ; nor will it be prudent to attemp another
establishment untill the event of the expidition against the
Indians is known and perhaps not till the detachment of
troops expected for your protection shall arrive ; in the the
mean time, gentlemen, should you please to adopt the plan
that I proposed in my letter of the 9th, instant, viz : appoint
a committe of your company with power to reconnoitre and
fix on the spot with surveyors etc. to accompany them, which
business may be accomplished in twenty-days ; you will be
able to determine the form and qualety of the buildings for
your first lodgment that will be requisit for your conveneance
and accommodation, and I shall be much better able to judge
of the workmen necessary for the execotion of the business
by that time ; also we shall doubtless know the event of the
expidition against the Indians, (which could never have been
foreseen neither by yourselves nor the Sioto company) and
be better able to judge of many other matters that must
meterially affect our future opperations.   I have the honor

to be with great respect and esteem, gentlemen, your very obedient and very humble servant,

RUFUS PUTNAM.

To the Gentlemen composing the 24 Associates.

————

MARIETTA, November 26th, 1790.

Memorandum of a bargain between Mr. DeBarth and Rufus Putnam, viz : the latter agrees to sell to the former a lot of land lying on the Ohio River, at the first Creek below Fort Harmer, containing one hundred and eight acres, and is number 22 in the one hundred and sixty acre Division of the Ohio Company. The consideration to be four hundred dollars, to be paid the first day of January, 1792, with interest at 6 per cent. from the first day of January, 1791, for the security of which payment Mr. DeBarth will draw bills on Mr. William Duer, of New York. Mr. DeBarth is to enter and occupie the lands whenever he pleases, and the necessary writing to be executed within twenty days, or as soon after as shall be required by either party.

RUFUS PUTNAM.

————

CATHOLICITY IN CONNECTICUT. In December, 1854, John Kennedy, a Catholic at South Manchester, Connecticut, was evicted by his landlord, because he had permitted a priest, Rev. Mr. Brady, to say mass in the house. When the new church was dedicated, November 13th, 1876, a majority of the inhabitants were Catholics.

PHILIPPE THOMAS DE JONCAIRE.

A Foot Note.

By Edmond Mallet.

"Monacatoocha informed me, that an Indian from Venango brought news, a few days ago, that the French had called all the Mingoes, Delawares, &c., together at that place, and told them that they intended to have been down the river this fall, but the waters were growing cold, and the winter advancing, which obliged them to go into quarters, but that they might assuredly expect them in the spring, ... they and the English would join to cut them all off, and divide the land between them ; that though they had lost their general, and some few of their soldiers, yet there were men enough to reinforce them, and make them masters of the Ohio.

"This speech, he said, was delivered to them by one Captain Joncaire, their interpreter in chief, living at Venango, and a man of note in the army" "Washington's Journal of a Tour over the Allegany Mountains, 1753."

Phillipe Thomas de Joncaire, captain of colonial troops of New France, was the eldest son of Louis Thomas de Joncaire, Sieur de Chabert, a native of Providence, France, and of Marie Madeleine Le Guay, a native of Canada, of Norman origin, who were married in Montreal in 1700. De Joncaire, the elder, who was king's interpreter, and lieutenant of colonial troops, was taken captive by the Senecas previous to 1700 and was saved from burning at the stake by an act of courage which so impressed the Indians that they adopted him as a member of their tribe. After his exchange the Indians still considered him as their adopted son, and at their solicitation he was sent by the Governor of Canada as "resident" or Indian agent, in the Seneca country. His influence among the western Iroquois was as great as was that of Sir William Johnson with those of the eastern cantons. When, in 1740, he died at Niagara, the Senecas went to Quebec to weep for him and to request the privilege of adopting his two sons Philippe and Daniel.

Philippe Thomas de Joncaire was born in Montreal in 1707, and married Madeleine Renaud in his native city, in 1731. Much of his early life was spent in western New York with his father, and he, too, wielded great influence among the Indians in behalf of the French. His brother Daniel de Joncaire, Sieur de Chabert and de Clausonne, was born in Montreal in 1716, and in 1740, he marched against the Chicasaws, in Alabama, with Lemoyne de Longueueil's expedition organized in Canada, to co-operate with Bienville's troops from Louisiana, and D'Artaguiette's from the Illinois country. He married Marguerite Rocbert de la Morandière in his native city in 1751.

The de Joncaire brothers, both of whom were officers in in the colonial troops, were in the celebrated expedition conducted by Céleron de Blainville to renew the taking of possession of the Ohio valley in 1749. In the following year Philippe Thomas de Joncaire erected fort La Presentation on the Oswegatchie, (near the present city of Ogdensburgh.)

He was with Marin's army in the Ohio country in 1753 and he was sent by this commander to winter with the Indians in the interior with the view of winning them over to French interests. Washington found him at the Indian village at Venango in November of that year, and he referred to him as an active, energetic officer wielding great influence over Indians. He built fort Machault at that place in the following spring, and remained in the country with his brother, until the fall of fort Niagara in 1759. In the articles of capitulation of that fort he signed as Captain of the Marine, and his brother Chabert signed as Captain attached to the Guienne regiment of regulars.

De Joncaire emigrated to France after Canada was ceded to England, whilst Chabert remained in America and settled in Detroit, where he died in 1771. One of his grandsons, François Joncaire Chabert, was a member of the first legislature of the Territory of Indiana, organized in 1801.

INDIAN MYTHOLOGY,

Paper read before the Houghton County Historical Society
and Mining Institute, by V. Rev. E. Jacker.

The most prominent and interesting figure in Otchipwe
mythology is undoubtedly, Menabosho, the hero of Longfellow's poem, Hiawatha. From the fact that the history of
a similar character, figuring in analogous primeval events,
opens the legendary circle of a number of Indian nations,
even in South America, almost conclusive evidence is derived,
that our Menabosho is not a mere fiction of the red man's
poetical imagination, but a real historical person, and one
whose period of life reaches back beyond the time when the
red race lost its national unity in consequence of its dis-
persion over this vast continent; nay, probably beyond the
date when the ancestors of that race set out on their wanderings from the original seat of mankind in the eastern
hemisphere. This latter supposition would greatly gain in
probabilty, if we should discover, in the traditions of the
eastern nations, anything closely resembling the Indian myth
of Menabosho, Hiawatha, Tarenyawagon, or their antitypes
in South America.

But let us hear the tale itself, or rather some of the principal traits of the myth, in one of its manifold versions. For
it must be borne in mind, that in American mythology the
same process of poetical transformation has taken place, by
which the simple traditions of ancient Greece, have under the
hand of Homer and later poets, become such a rich and ever
varied compound of mythological tales. The gifted Indian,
who delights in repeating to a raptured audience his Menabosho tales, embellishing them with curious additions of his
own invention, is therefore very appropriately called "a dyer,"
or "one who colors things;" which seems to be the meaning

of the Otchipwe term, "edisoked" or "adisokewinini." And
no wonder, if the character and feats of that assumed historical personage, Menabosho, appear through the medium
of the intervening ages in the shape of a fanciful mirage,
rather than of a correct representation of reality. Enough,
however, is left of the original form, to allow a probable in-
ference as to the real character of the person, of which that
hero is a curiously distorted reflection.

Menabosho appears first as survivor of a general in-
undetion, and second, as the teacher of civilization. The tale
of the deluge is as follows :

The cnemies of Menabosho, the Manitos, (beings endowed with superhuman power, personifications of the great
natural agencies,) having in vain tried to destroy him by
divers other means, finally engage the Great Lake itself in
war against their common foe, and caused it rapidly to rise
above its banks. Finding the destructive element encroaching
on him, the hero calls upon his friend, the badger, to dig
channels, through the neighboring mountain ridges in order
to drain the inundated portion of the earth's surface. The
faithful friend performed the task, and the vestiges of the
stupendous wotk are still visible in the manifold ravines,
deep dales and defiles, which intersect the mountainous regions of the earth. But it is to no avail. The water continues
rising. Menabosho in vain takes refuge on the highest point
of land. The steadilv rising flood forces him to climb a fir-
tree. But soon the fugitive's head is all that appears above
the immense sheet of water. "Stretch thyself, stretch
thyself," he ehtreatingly addresses the tree that supports
him, and the tree obeys : it grows rapidly ; but the water
follows as quick. "Stretch thyself, fir-tree, grow, grow."
Menabosho begs again and again, and for some time meets
with the same ready obedience on the part of the friendly
tree. But, alas ! its strength proves inferior to that of the
powerful element in the inimical Manito's service. "Menabosho, I can no more," the fir-tree sighs at last, as it finds all
further efforts, to grow higher, utterly fruitless. In his
pressing danger the hero now surveys the surrounding sea

and discovers divers water-fowls and amphibious animals swimming about. They gather around him, for they are all his brethren ; they love him, and will forsooth cheerfully assist him. The duck is the first, Menabosho calls upon. "Brother duck, brother duck!" he cries. What is thy demand, Menabosho?" "I wish, brother duck, thou wouldst dive to the ground, to bring up some earth for me." "Very well, Menabosho! I will, I will." The friendly fowl dives ; but its strength fails, before it reaches the bottom, and it returns no more. No time is to be lost " Brother diver, brother diver!" cries Menabosho. "Brother diver, wilt thou be able to fetch some earth for me?" "I shall try, Menabosho!" The diver disappears in the fathomless depth—and is seen no more. "Brother otter, brother otter!" is now the cry. "What is thy wish, Menabosho?" "O, wouldst thou not quickly fetch some earth for me!" "I shall do my best," the other replies ; dives, and meets with the duck's and the diver's fate. At last the muskrat comes in sight. "Brother dive, dive, I want some earth." Yes, Menabosho!" says the muskrat ; dives, reaches the bottom at an immense depth, and returns with a very small portion of earth in its tiny paw, reaches the same to Menabosho and at the same moment dies from exhaustion. But Menabosho is saved. For the pinch of earth, rubbed over the palm of his hand and from thence blown out in all directions over the surface of the water, soon forms an immense piece of solid ground. This is the great island of America, the home of the Indian race.

So much of Menabosho, as the survivor of a general inundation. In regard to his achievements as teacher of the arts of peace, such as agriculture, fishing, medicine, picture-writing, and of a well regulated worship—such as the Indian uneerstands it—it will be enough for our present purpose to state, that almost everything that characterizes man as a social being, and as conqueror in the contest with nature, is ascribed to Menabosho ; he is the source of all that is human in man. If to this the circumstance is added that our hero is believed to have, at his final departure from the Otchipwe land, retired to the glacial regions of the north, where he is still living, and from whence he is expected to come again, enough points of comparison have been obtained to sustain the assertions that our Otchipwe Menabosho is identical, not only with the Iroquois Tarenyawagon, or the Hiawatha of the Dacotahs (which nobody doubts) but even with the Manko Capak of the Peruvians, the Amalivaka of the Tamanacs, with Bochica of Bogota and Votan of Yucatan, not to mention other similar heroes whose names are connected with the tradition of a great inundation and with the institution of civil government or regular religious worship, with the introduction of agriculture, or of whatever the respective nations deem their highest boon of happiness or superiority.

Thus, according to Peruvian traditions, Manko Capak started from an island in Lake Titicaca, upon which the sun, rising for the first time after the great flood, shed his first rays ; he arrives in Cazco, clears the rivers and forests, instructs the people, and becomes with . his wife and sister, Mama Oilke, the ancestor of the royal family.

Amalivaka, having crossed the sea, arrives in Guiana, where he becomes the father of the Tamanac tribe ; under his rule the people enjoy a golden age of peace and plenty, until he finally returns again to the opposite shore. On the high-lands of Bogota, Bochica drains the Lake of Funzha, which by rising had inundated the earth, establishes civil institutions and returns to the north.

Votan, the national hero of the Chiapanese, in Yucatan, has come from the north, immediately after a great and general flood has subsided, and finally retraces his steps in the same direction. He is said to have been the first man and sent by the deity to distribute the Indians' lands.

Are such striking coincidences confined to the western continent ! By no means ; we find them sometimes, even with the minutes details, when we cross the Pacific and review the half historical, half mythological traditions of the Chinese, the Hindoos and the Egyptians.

At the threshold of Chinese historiography, we meet the patriarch and first emperor Yao, under whose reign the water rose "as high as heaven," but he, with the assistance of his

.

minister, Shin, drained the earth by creating the great rivers and canals of China.

In India, according to the epic poem Mahabharat, all men were destroyed by a flood under Manu, who became the ancestor of a new race. The annals of Cashmere, which are considered as the oldest document of India, commence the history of the present period of the world with the patriarch Cacyapa, who drained the everflowing waters of Lake Satisaras, and with the assistance of the gods, peopled the country anew.

The Egyptians call their first human ruler Menes. He too saved Egypt from a general inundation by digging the bed of the Nile.

In like manner, the history of other ancient nations commences with a flood, and however the tale may have been localized or poetized, some facts remain always discernible, which almost compel us to identify those traditions with the biblical relation of the deluge, contained in the first book of Moses, the oldest of all historians. Thus we have discovered our Otchipwe hero, Menabosho, (or Longfellow's " Hiawatha,") to be an old acquaintance of ours, a Noah in Indian disguise. If the Noah of the bible, if the Chinese Yao, the Egyptian Menes, and the Manu of India are identical persons, a fact, which scarcely allows a doubt, the Otchipwe Menabosho must be added to the list. Even the first half of Menabosho's name bears a close resemblance to those of Manu and Menes. The second half of the word might be derived from the verb " bos " which means " to embark ; " and Menabosho would be, " Manu, who embarks." But this coincidence is probably quite fortuitous. The almost tender friendship, which exists between Menabosho and all kinds of animals, could also have been mentioned as a point of resemblance between him and Noah, to whose saving ark all creatures gathered. Even the calling to assistance of four aquatic fowls and animals, and their going in search of earth, could be placed in juxtaposition with Noah's letting loose four birds, once a raven and three times a dove, for the sake of exploring the state of the earth. Still, on these particulars much less stress is to be laid than on the coincidence of the principal facts, that of Noah and Menabosho having been saved in the flood, and that of their having been the teachers of civilization after the great event.

Another circumstance might deserve more attention. Menabosho, and almost all of his American antitypes, are represented as having returned to the place from whence they originally came; they are considered as being still alive there, and expected to reappear at some unknown future period. The Asiatic traditions, on the contrary, are silent on this point. How will this discrepancy be accounted for? Perhaps simply thus:

Noah, the ancestor of the whole human family, is for the Indian at the same time the representant of the white race, or of that portion of mankind which remained in or near the original seats of the human race. Accordingly, almost all the above mentioned South American heroes (as also the ancestor of the Toltecs, Quetzalcoatl,) are represented as white and bearded men, altogether superior to the race that owes to them whatever it possesses of the elements of civilization. And in stating that those heroes are still living in their old homes, the simple truth is implied that the white race, from which the Indians themselves originally departed, still occupied the countries beyond the sea, and that the time will come when the separated brethen are to meet again. In the lapse of centuries this was forgotten, or rather no more properly understood by the Indians, many of whom became inclined to consider themselves aborigines, (created on the soil they inhabited.) They retained their old traditions, but knew no other way of explaining them, than by assuming that those white and bearded patriarchs first came to them from beyond the sea and again returned thither.

Menabosho, although superhuman in many of his feats, is generally represented as having human shape, acting like a man, and even sometimes showing the weakness and the follies of man. At all events he is the first man that appears in Otchipwe traditions. May we then conceive him as bearing the double character of Noah and Adam? He is the grandchild of Misakamigokwe, or Earth personified; for "Misakamig" signifies everywhere on earth, and the ending "okwe" gives the term the female gender. His father is the wind, (westward or northward, according to our different renderings of the tale.) Hence, Adam made of earth and enlivened by the divine breath, and Menabosho, descendant of the Earth, and son of the Wind, how closely do they resemble?

But are the Indians the offspring of Menabosho or the creation of his hands? Our Otchipwe story-tellers are at a loss to answer this question. According to them Menabosho is at first the only man on the newly created or restored continent, and all at once he is surrounded by a crowd of untutored Indians, whom he teaches, calling them his cousins, or his uncles and aunts. Where do they come from? For a solution of this difficulty it might be answered, that their wild hunter-tribes, having so far departed from the type of a superior humanity, as represented by Menabosho, would no more believe themselves to be his descendants. They remembered him as a great benefactor, but lost sight of him as their own progenitor. Not so, indeed, the more cultivated nations of Mexico, Yucatan and Peru. They considered the above mentioned heroes, if not as the ancestors of the whole nation, at least as those of their royal and priestly clans.

If the ancient works can be proved to have been abandoned more than four hundred years ago, the cause of the miners' departure or disappearance cannot be sought for in the occupation of the country by the warlike Ojibwa tribe, and it is in vain to look for well founded traditions among the latter, relating to the former occupants or rather visitors of the copper region. But the hypothesis of their having been expelled from, or utterly destroyed in their homes in the Ohio and Mississippi valleys gains much in probability.

Before concluding I would request your attention to a few remarks on another subject. The account given by our Ojibwa neighbors of their first meeting with the white men, is worth hearing. My authority is the old man, mentioned before, the "Smoker of Pure Tobacco." He related as follows:

"Once upon a time a rumor was spread among the Indians on Lake Superior that men of strange appearance coming from beyond the "Great Salt Lake" had arrived in the great river of the East. Excited to the highest pitch of curiosity, they would see with their own eyes what seemed incredible to them. So a number of stout-hearted Indians started in three large canoes on the perilous journey, risking their lives in the investigation of truth. They slowly descended through lakes and rivers, accomplished a number of tedious portages, and often found themeselves in the utmost destitution by means of a scarcity of food. But at last they arrived in the neighborhood of the village built on a steep rock (Stadacone, Quebec.) The first signs they perceived of the presence of strangers, were trees sawed clear through near the root. This is the work of none but "Manitos" (beings endowed with superhuman power,) they said, and accordingly proceeded with the utmost caution. Finally they beheld trees sticking in the water and logs thrown over them (a wharf) and persons standing on the top. After holding a council they resolved to make their hearts strong and to proceed at any risk. When they approached the place they were ignorant of what would happen them. But the Frenchmen received them with the greatest cordiality, saluted and entertained them as brothers and would not allow them to turn the stems of their canoes, till aftei having passed a winter in the settlement and been fitted out with firearms, utensils, wearables and other stores. The party arrived on Lake Superior after an absence of three years and was received as men risen from the dead. From that time every year a large party of Indians descended to the settlements on the great river of Canada to exchange their furs against the goods of the white men, until the French themselves came into the Ojibwa country and established their trading posts."

This is the relation of the old man. How far it agrees with historical truth is hard to say ; but I am inclined to credit at least the substance of the narrative. That the account of the strangers' arrival at the lower St. Lawrence should have been borne from tribe to tribe until it reached the forests of the Lake Superior country, long in advance of the first adventurous traders is quite natural. And to a tribe so fond of rambling as the Ojibwas have always been, the character and direction of the way could not be unknown, leading as it was to a country inhabited by their own ancestors at not very remote a period. Nor is it unlikely that curiosity alone should have prompted those children of the woods to start on a journey replete with dangers, both real and imaginary. Even as late as the beginning of the present century members of the same tribe (some of them perhaps still living) left their peacable wigwams on the shores of Lake Superior, passed by the rapids of St. Marie and through the Straits of Mackinaw, and coasting along the western shore of Lake Michigan went as far as the present site of Milwaukee and Chicago, to see a great object of curiosity, a real, living Manito, whom rumor had said to exist in those regions. Like many other traits, erroneously ascribed to the Indian character by superficial observers, that of a stupid indifference toward strange and curious objects, may be found in some individuals and perhaps in some of the most savage tribes ; as for our Ojibwa neighbors, I have seen their curiosity (when not restrained by considerations of politeness or by timidity in the presence of strangers) wrought to as high a pitch, as it would be in any white man.

But I fear I am too much encroaching on your patience, and conclude with the request that you will excuse my deficiencies with the want of leisure to digest the matter, together with the difficulty of experience in treating subjects of this kind in the English language.

THE DIOCESE OF BROOKLYN.

By Marc F. Vallette.

II.

If the Catholics of the Eastern District of Brooklyn had been increasing in numbers and building churches in which they might practice the religion of their choice, their brethren in the Western District were not behind them. They, too, needed more church room. St. Paul's had become too far away from St. James' and the good Catholics in the intervening space must needs have a church of their own. Rt. Rev. Bishop Hughes had foreseen this and he soon organized a new parish, which he placed under the charge of the Rev. Charles Constantine Pise, D.D. Near the corner of Sydney Place and Livingston Street, stood the Church of the Emanuel which the Episcopalians had built ten years before and which they were now anxious to sell. Dr. Pise bought it and on December 30th, 1849, after having been remodeled, it was dedicated to the service of God under the invocation of St. Charles Borromeo.

There is an incident connected with the early history of this church which will be of interest to Catholics. It was here that the Rt. Rev. Levi Silliman Ives, Episcopal Bishop of North Carolina, ordained the Rev. Donald McLeod. Some years later bishop and minister met again in this same church, but the church had since become a Catholic church, the Bishop had become a Catholic layman and the minister had become a Catholic priest.

Dr. Charles Constantine Pise was born at Annapolis, Md. on November 22nd, 1801. His father was a native of Italy and his mother a Philadelphian. After completing his studies and graduating at Georgetown, he began his novitiate as a Jesuit and was sent to the Roman College to pursue his theological studies. The death of his father compelled his re-

turn to his native country and his withdrawal from the
Society of Jesus. He soon after became professor of
Rhetoric at Mt. St. Mary's College, Emmittsburg, a position
he held until 1825, when he was ordained by Most. Rev.
Ambrose Maréchal, Archbishop of Baltimore. After serving
for some time as assistant at the Cathedral in Baltimore, he
was assigned to St. Matthew's Church, Washington. While
here his brilliant talents and his courteous manners attracted
the attention of Henry Clay, at whose instance he was unanimously elected Chaplain to the United States Senate. In
1832 Dr. Pise visited the Eternal City and while there passed
a splendid public examination at the College of the Sapienza,
earned his degree of Doctor of Divinity and received the
ring and other insignia of his office at the hands of His
Holiness Pope Gregory XVI. His writings merited for him
the Cross and Spur and the title of Knight of the Holy
Roman Empire. In 1838 he again visited Europe and he described his wanderings through Ireland in his *Horæ Vagabundæ*.
Bishop Du Bois invited him to New York and soon made
him rector of the Church of St. Joseph. He was afterwards transferred to old St. Peter's and from there to the
Church of St. Charles Borromeo, Brooklyn, where he labored
until his death, May, 1866.

Few men, if any, have done as much for Catholic literature in our country as Dr. Pise. In 1830, while in Baltimore,
he was editor of the *Metropolitan* the first Catholic Magazine
published in this country. In 1842 he was associated with
the learned Very Rev. Felix Varela, D.D., in the publication
of the *Catholic Expositor* of New York, a magazine of great
merit. Besides his magazine work, Dr. Pise wrote a *History
of the Church*; *Father Rowland*, a novel; *Aletheia*; *St. Ignatius and his Companions*; *Christianity and the Church*;
Indian Cottage; *Letters to Ada*; *Pleasures of Religion*;
Zenosius, or The Pilgrim Convert; *The Acts of the Apostles*,
in verse. Among his masterly translations may be mentioned
De Maistre's *Soirees in St. Petersburg*, and *Hymns from the
Roman Breviary*. His poetical writings are numerous and
full of genius.

In manners Dr. Pise was always courteous and refined, and in his many controversies he never forgot that he was a gentleman ; hence he never made enemies of his opponents. He was passionately fond of music and painting, and his choir and the decorations of his church evidenced his fine taste.

In 1858 Dr. Pise established a parochial school with over two hundred pupils. This school opened prosperously, but difficulties arising it became necessary to suspend it for a time. There is now a flourishing school of over 500 pupils. The girls are under the care of the Sisters of Charity and the boys under the Franciscan Brothers.

We have not room, in an article of this kind, to dwell upon the many resplendent qualities which endeared Dr. Pise not only to his own people, but to Catholics in general; and even to those of other creeds. The educated and refined gentleman never fails to make his influence felt by those around him. His death was a severe blow to his parish and to the church at large, but his mantle fell upon worthy shoulders.

Dr. Pise was succeeded by the Rev. Francis J. Freel, D.D. one of the assistants at St. James' Cathedral. Dr. Freel was born in Ireland, in 1840, and made his ecclesiastical studies at the famous Urban College of the Propaganda, in Rome. Like his predecessor, he was a gentleman of culture and fine taste. He immediately applied himself with energy and good will to continue the work of Dr. Pise. In December, 1866, he purchased seven lots on Livingston Street, for which he paid $22,000. It was his intention to erect a larger and more imposing church edifice than the one his congregation then occupied. This determination was hastened by an untoward event. In the night of March 7th, 1868, the church took fire from a defective flue, and notwithstanding the most strenuous efforts of the firemen, the entire building with its valuable stock of church music, beautiful paintings and costly furniture, was soon reduced to ashes. Dr. Freel, at the risk of his life, rescued the Ciborium and its sacred contents, some other sacred vessels and some of the most valuable of the vestments. This fire was a sad blow to the people of

St. Charles'; but in less than three weeks after the disaster
ground was broken for a splendid new church of Philadelphia
pressed brick, with a frontage of seventy feet on Sydney
Place, and a depth of one hundred and thirty feet on Livingston Street. The corner-stone was laid in August, 1868.
For eighteen years Dr. Freel continued the work entrusted
to him. His new church, with its beautiful interior decorations continued to attract the *elite* of our city, but the poor
were not neglected. Dr. Freel looked after the education of
the children of his parish, and as we have seen, he placed
the parochial school on a firm and flourishing basis. He
died in March, 1884, and was succeeded by the Rev. Thomas
F. Ward, the present (1891) incumbent.

St. Benedict's (German) Church was founded in 1852,
on Herkimer Street. In 1874 a beautiful new structure
one hundred and thirty-seven feet, by sixty-five feet was
erected on Fulton Avenue near Ralph Avenue, at a cost of
some $60,000. The old building in which Rev. M. Ramsauer
used to say Mass was transformed into a school house and
placed under the care of the Sisters of Christian Charity,
whose mother house is at Mallinckrodt, near Wilkesbarre,
Pennsylvania.

St. Joseph's Church, on Pacific Street near Vanderbilt
Avenue was founded in 1853 by the Rev. P. O'Neill. The
church was afterwards enlarged by the Rev. Edward Corcoran, the present pastor, and the parish is now one of the
most flourishing in the city. There is a fine church, a handsome pastoral residence, an Academy under the Sisters of St.
Joseph, a parochial school with five-hundred boys taught by
the Franciscan Brothers, and five-hundred girls taught by
Sisters of St. Joseph. Father Corcoran is a man of prompt-
ness and everything in the parish moves with clock like
regularity.

The year 1853 was an eventful year in the history of
Catholicity in Brooklyn. Churches were springing up in
various parts of the city, old St. James' became a Cathedral
and Brooklyn had now its own Bishop, in the person of the
Rt. Rev. John Loughlin, DD. (whom, may God long preserve

to us). He was preconised on July 19th, 1853, and his first official act, as Bishop-elect, may be said to have been the laying of the corner-stone of the Church of the Immaculate Conception, (corner of Maujer and Leonard Streets,) on August 1st, of the same year. This Church was commenced by the Rev. Peter McLaughlin but his pastorate, like that of his successor, the Rev. Anthony Farrelly lasted only one year. The next pastor was the Rev. Andrew Bohan, who ministered to the wants of his people for more than ten years. The Rev. John Crimmins, who was pastor of the church from 1879 to 1883 made some improvements and the Rev. M. F. Murray built a most needed pastoral residence. The present pastor is the Rev. James Taaffe, (brother of the Rev. Thomas Taaffe of St. Patrick's.) Father James was born at Dromard, County Longford, Ireland, and completed his preparatory studies at Clongoes Wood College, where he graduated in. 1872. His ecclesiastical studies were made in France, partly at the College Ste. Marie, in Toulouse, and at the famous St. Sulpice, in Paris. He was ordained in 1878 and, on his arrival in this country in 1879 he was appointed assistant at St Patrick's. Here he labored with the zeal peculiar to his family, until his appointment as pastor of the Church of the Immaculate Conception, in 1887. Father Taaffe's first care was the erection of an Academy which was in due time opened and placed under the care of the Sisters of St. Joseph, who also have charge of the parochial school.   '

In the same year, 1853, St, Thomas' Episcopal Church, Bridge Street, near Willoughby Avenue, was purchased by a new German congregation and was solemnly dedicated to the service of God, under the invocation of St. Bonifacius, on January 29th, 1854. The dedication was performed by Rt. Rev. Bishop Loughlin. His sermon on this occasion was pronounced one "of great power and deep reflection." The early pastors of this church seem to have been the same as those who attended St. Benedict's.

The Church of the Visitation on Verona Street, was founded in 1854 by the Rev. Timothy O'Farrell. It was a plain brick building, and was replaced in 1880 by a very fine structure of blue stone, seventy-five by ninety feet. This splendid church was finished under the pastorate of the Rev. John M. Kiely. It was dedicated in March 1880, by the Rt. Rev. Bishop Loughlin. Solemn Pontifical Mass was then celebrated by the Rt. Rev. M. A. Corrigan, D.D., Bishop of Newark, and the sermon was preached by the Rt. Rev. J. F. Shanahan, D.D., late Bishop of Harrisburg.

The year 1857 was marked by the erection of two more churches, the Church of Our Lady of Mercy, in Debevoise Place, near DeKalb Avenue, and St. Anthony's, Greenpoint. Both these churches have been replaced by larger and more commodious edifices. Rev. John McCarthy was the first pastor of the Church of Our Lady of Mercy, and Rev. John Brady was the founder of old St. Anthony's, on India Street. This structure has since been transformed into a school-house, and a large gothic church, erected on Manhattan Avenue, has taken its place. During the pastorate of the Rev. P. F. O'Hare, the present incumbent, the Church has been greatly improved, a new pastoral residence has been erected adjoining the church, and one of the finest parochial school buildings in the city is now in course of construction.

The corner-stone of St. Peter's Church was laid September 4th, 1859, by the Right Rev. Bishop Loughlin. The task of building the church was entrusted to the Rev. Joseph Fransioli, then an assistant to Dr. Pise, at the Church of St. Charles Borromeo. Father Fransioli was born in the canton of Ticino, Switzerland, November 30th, 1817, and after making his studies in two famous seminaries in Italy, was ordained in 1840. He labored in Ticino and afterwards as Director of the Government Normal School at Milan, where he did much to advance the cause of education. After a career of almost unbroken labor his health failed, and he was permitted by his superiors to come to America. He offered his services to the Bishop of Brooklyn, who, as has already been stated, assigned him to the church of St. Charles Borromeo, in December, 1856. He immediately set to work to master the English language, and such was his success in that direction, that three years later, (1859) he was entrusted with the formation of a new parish. The wisdom of that confidence on the part of his Bishop is manifested to-day in the beautiful church; the flourishing schools, with their 2,000 children; the kindergarten; the parish library; the splendid hospital; the public hall and the endless societies for old and young, for males and females, with which Father Fransioli's energy and foresight have adorned the parish. After a pastorate of nearly a third of a century, during which he gained golden opinions from all who knew him, Father Fransioli passed to his eternal reward in October, 1890, while the Diocese of Brooklyn was celebrating the golden jubilee of its honored Bishop.

Hardly had St. Peter's Church been erected in South Brooklyn when it became necessary to erect another in the vicinity of old St. James'. On the 20th of August, 1860, the Rev. Bartholomew Gleason broke ground for the erection of St. Anne's Church, at the south-west corner of Front and Gold Streets. In the Eastern District English speaking and German Catholics were also increasing. The year 1863 saw the erection of two new churches, that of St. Vincent de Paul, at North Sixth Street near Fifth, under the pastoral care of the Rev. Bernard McGorisk, and the German Church of the Annunciation, under the care of the Rev. John Hauptmann. St. Vincent's Church, (originally an old frame Presbyterian Church) was replaced by a much larger and handsome gothic edifice of Belleville graystone, with Ohio stone trimmings, in 1868, by the Rev. Daniel O'Mullane. It was dedicated on October 17th, 1869. Father Hauptmann enlarged the Church of the Annunciation in 1870. He also built a school and convent for the Sisters of St. Dominic.

In 1866 a church on Carroll Street, near Hicks, was purchased from the Episcopalians by Rev. O. J. Dorris, and placed under the invocation of St. Stephen. In 1873 the Rev. E. J. O'Reilly began the erection of a new church at the corner of Summit and Hicks Streets, on lots that had been purchased some years before, and in October, 1875, the new St. Stephen's Church was dedicated. The old church was converted into a school and placed under the care of the Sisters of Charity.

Two years later, 1865, the German Church of St. Nicholas was erected at the corner of Powers and Olive Streets, by the Rev. C. Peine. It was enlarged in 1877 by the Rev. John P. Hoffmann, who has also erected handsome school buildings, which he has placed under the care of the Sisters of St. Dominic.

The Diocese of Brooklyn has had but two congregations of priests within its limits. The first to come were the Lazarists or Priests of the Congregation of the Mission. In the spring of 1868 the Rev. Edward M. Smith, C. M., was sent by his Superiors to Brooklyn, to open a new home for the special work of his order. He was fortunate enough to secure a whole block of ground bounded by Lewis, Willoughby and Stuyvesant Avenues and by Hart Street. It was purchased by the Right Rev. S. V. Ryan, D. D., C. M., the present Bishop of Buffalo, who was then Visitor (or Provincial) of the Congregation of the Mission in this country. There was a little cottage situated upon this ground and it was soon transformed into a Community house. A room was fitted up as a chapel, and here, on the 12th of July, 1868, the first Mass was celebrated before a congregation of not more than twelve or fifteen persons. On the same day the corner-stone of the temporary wooden church was laid by the Right Rev. Bishop Loughlin. It was a mustard seed which was then planted; but, under the protecting care of St. Vincent de Paul, it was destined to grow into a flourishing parish. In the following year, 1869, the Bishop laid the corner-stone of the new College of St. John the Baptist, and in September, 1870, it was opened under the Presidency of the Rev. John T. Landry, C. M. Father J. Quigley succeeded Father Smith in the pastorate of the church on Christmas, 1868; but Father Smith returned in 1870 and resumed the pastorate, and continued in that capacity until March, 1874, when he went to La Salle, Ill. On February 9th, 1875, Father Landry resigned the Presidency of the College and his unexpired term was filled out by the Rev. J. A. Maloney. In September fol-

lowing the Rev. P. M. O'Regan became President, and
Father Maloney became Pastor of the church. In September, 1877, the Rev. A. J. Meyer became President of the
College and continued in that capacity until February, 1882,
when the Rev. Jeremiah A. Hartnett, C. M. became its
President.

In the meantime the mustard seed had been growing
and Father Hartnett's Presidency fell at a time when zeal,
energy, patient endurance and hard work were demanded.
The congregation had outgrown the old church ; the College
had increased in the number of its pupils because its standard had been raised to meet the wants of the times ; the
neighborhood which in 1868 consisted largely of open fields
and scattered dwellings, was now built up and populated. A
new church was needed, and on June 24th, 1888, the Rt. Rev.
Bishop Loughlin laid the corner-stone of one of the largest
and finest churches in the state. It is two hundred and eight
feet long; nave, including side chapels, eighty-five feet; width
of transept, one hundred and thirty-five feet : depth of chancel fifty feet ; height of ceiling from floor, ninety-five feet.
The material used in the construction of the church is blue
granite; the style of architecture is Roman. The building is
now ready for the roof and there is, as yet, *no debt upon it.*

In October, 1890, Right Rev. Bishop Loughlin celebrated
the Golden Jubilee of his ordination to the priesthood. His
devoted clergy wished to signalize the occasion by a testimonial that would be pleasing to his pastoral heart. No
personal gift would have found favor in his eyes ; this they
knew too well. It was then decided that this testimonial
should assume the form of a monument that would continue
the good Bishop's work long after he had ceased "to fight the
good fight." He had long cherished the idea of building a
Diocesan Seminary, and the clergy decided to cheer his heart
by the realization of this desire. The Bishop selected the
ground adjoining St. John's College as the site for his future
Seminary, and work was commenced at once. The Lazarist
Fathers were to be the trainers of his future clergy, and upon
the broad shoulders of Father Hartnett fell the task of erect-

ing this building. The corner-stone was laid on Sunday, September 29th, 1889, and the work was pushed forward with all speed possible. The style of the new building is Romanesque; it is built of brick, with terra cotta and stone trimmings and is three stories high, with mansard roof. The Lewis Avenue front is sixty feet in length and the depth of the building on Hart Street is one hundred and eighty-five feet. At the end of this wing is a beautiful chapel adorned with stained glass windows and handsome frescoes, representing St. Thomas Aquinas and St. Catherine. The altar is of white marble and of beautiful design. Over the chapel will be the Library. The class rooms, study halls, dormitories and refectory are large, well ventilated, furnished in hard wood, and heated by steam. It is expected that the new Seminary of St. John the Baptist will be opened for the reception of students in the fall of 1891.

In connection with the Sacerdotal Jubilee of the Rt. Rev. Bishop of Brooklyn, it may be interesting to know how many of our Bishops have celebrated Silver and Golden Jubilees. The annexed table has been prepared with a great deal of care and is as nearly accurate as such a table can be.

ARCHBISHOPS AND BISHOPS OF THE UNITED STATES WHOSE
EPISCOPATES HAVE REACHED OR EXCEEDED
TWENTY-FIVE YEARS.

Name.	Born.	Ordained.	Consecrated.	Died.	Years of Priesthood.
Carroll,	1735	1759	1790	1815	56
Neale,	1746	1773	1800	1817	44
Marechal,	1768	1792	1817	1828	26
Whitfield,	1770	1809	1828	1834	25
Eccleston,	1801	1825	1834	1851	26
Kenrick, F. P.	1796	1821	1830	1863	42
Spalding, M. J.	1810	1834	1848	1872	48
Bayley,	1814	1844	1853	1877	33
Gibbons, Card.	1834	1860	1868		31
Cheverus,	1768	1790	1810	1836	46
Fenwick, B. J.	1782	1808	1823	1846	38

Fitzpatrick,	1812	1840	1844	1866	26
Williams,	1822	1845	1866		46
Vande Velde,	1795	1827	1848	1855	28
O'Regan,			1854	1865	
Duggan,	1825	1847	1857		44
Foley, Thomas,	1822	1846	1870 ·	1879	33
Feehan,	1829	1852	1866		39
Fenwick, Ed.	1768	1800	1822	1832	32
Purcell,	1800	1826	1833	1883	57
Elder,	1819	1846	1857		45
Henni,	1805	1829	1844	1881	52
Heiss,	1818	1840	1868	1890	49–6
Dubourg,	1766	1793	1815	1833	40
De Neckere,	1800	1822	1830	1833	11
Blanc,	1792	1816	1835	1860	44
Odin,	1801	1823	1842	1870	47
Perché,	1805	1829	1870	1883	54
Leray,	1825	1852	1877	1887	35
Janssens,	1843	1867	1881		22
Concanen,			1808	1810	
Connolly,	1750	1774*	1814	1825	51
Du Bois,	1764	1789	1826	1842	53
Hughes,	1797	1826	1838	1864	38
McCloskey, Card.	1810	1834	1844	1885	51
Corrigan,	1839	1863	1873		28
Blanchet, F. N.	1795	1819	1845	1883	64
Seghers,	1839	1863	1873	1886	23
Gross,	1837	1863	1873		28
Egan,	1757*	1781	1810	1814	33
Conwell,		1776	1820	1842	66
Neumann,	1811	1836	1852	1860	24
Wood,	1813	1844	1857	1883	39
Ryan, P. J.	1831	1852	1872		39
Rosati,	1789	1815	1824	1827	12
KENRICK, P. R.	1806	1832	1841		59
Cretin,	1800	1824*	1851	1857	33
Grace,	1814	1839	1859		52
Ireland,	1838	1864	1875		27

Diego y Moreno,	1799*	1824	1840	1846	22
Alemany,	1812	1837	1850	1888	51
Riordan, P. W.	1841	1865	1883		26
Lamy,	1813	1838	1850	1888	50
Salpointe,	1825	1859	1869		32
Conroy. J. J.	18—	1842	1865		49
McNeirny,	1828	1854	1872		37
Baltes,	1827	1853	1870	1886	33
Loughlin,		1840	1853		51
Timon,	1797	1825	1847	1867	42
Ryan, S. V.	1825	1849	1868		42
de Goesbriand,	1816	1840	1853		51
England,	1786	1808	1820	1842	34
Reynolds,	1798	1823	1844	1855	32
Lynch, P. N.	1817	1840	1858	1882	42
Northrop,	1842	1865	1882		26
Rappe,	1801	1829	1847	1877	48
Gilmour,	1824	1852	1872	1891	39
Rosecrans,	1827	1852	1862	1878	26
Watterson,	1844	1868	1880		23
Carrell,	1803	1829	1853	1868	39
Toebbe,	1829	1854	1870	1884	30
Maes,	1846	1868	1885		23
McMullen,	1833	1858	1881	1883	25
Cosgrove,	1834	1857	1884		34
Macheboeuf,	1812	1836	1868	1889	53
Matz,			1887		
Resé,	1797	1821	1833	1871	50
Lefevre,	1804	1831	1841	1869	38
Borgess,	1826	1848	1870	1891	43
Foley, John,	1833	1849	1888	1891	42
Loras,	1792	1817	1837	1853	36
Smyth,	1810	1844	1857	1865	21
Hennessy,		1850	1866		41
Young,	1793	1817	1854	1866	49
Mullen,	1818	1844	1868		47
Luers,	1819	1846	1858	1871	25
Dwenger,	1837	1859	1872		32

Dubuis,			1862	
Gallagher,	1846	1868	1882		23
Richter,	1838	1865	1883		26
Melcher,		1830	1868	1873	43
Krautbauer,	1824	1850	1875	1885	35
Katzer,			1886	
Shanahan,	1834	1859	1868	1886	27
McGovern,		1861	1888		30
Tyler,	1806	1828	1844	1849	21
O'Reilly, Bernard,	1803	1831	1850	1856	25
McFarland,	1819	1845	1858	1874	19
Galberry,	1833	1856	1876	1878	22
McMahon,	1835	1860	1879		31
Brondel,	1842	1864	1879		27
Hogan,	1829	1852	1868		39
Flasch,	1837	1869	1881		22
Miége,	1815	1847	1853	1884	37
Fink,	1834	1857	1871		34
Byrne,	1802	1827	1844	1862	35
Fitzgerald,	1833	1857	1867		34
Flaget,	1763	1786	1810	1850	54
David,	1761	1785	1819	1841	56
Chabrat,			1834	1868	
Lavialle,	1820	1844	1865	1867	23
McCloskey, William,	1823	1852	1868		39
Baraga,	1797	1823	1853	1868	45
Mrak,			1869	
Vertin,	1844	1860	1879		25
Portier,	1795	1818	1826	1859	41
Quinlan,	1826	1850*	1859	1883	33
O'Sullivan,			1885	
Amat,	1811	1830	1854	1878	42
Mora,		1856	1873		25
Miles,	1791	1816	1838	1860	44
Whelan, James,	1823	1850	1859	1878	28
Rademacher,	1840	1863	1883		28
Chanche,	1795	1819	1841	1852	33
Martin,	1803	1825	1853	1875	50

Durier,			1885	
Blanchet,	1797	1821	1846	1887	66
Junger,	1838*	1862	1870		29
Wigger,	1841	1865	1881		26
Wadhams,	1817	1850	1872		41
O'Gorman,	1809	1823*	1859	1874	51
O'Connor, James,	1824	1848	1876	1891	43
Spalding, J. L.	1840	1864*	1877		27
O'Connor, M.	1810	1833	1843	1872	39
Domenec,	1806	1839	1860	1878	39
Tuigg,	1822	1850	1876	1889	39
Phelan,	1825	1854	1885		37
Bacon,	1814	1838	1855	1874	36
Healy,	1830	1854	1875		37
Hendricken,	1827	1853	1872	1886	33
Harkins,			1887		
McGill,	1809	1830	1852	1872	42
Keane,	1839	1866	1878		25
Van de Vyver,	1845	1870	1889		21
McQuaid,	1823	1848	1868		43
Manogue,		1861	1881		30
O'Connell,	1815	1842	1861		49
Pellicer,			1874	1880	
Neraz,	1828	1853	1881		38
Gartland,	1805	1832	1850	1854	22
Barry,	1799	1825	1857	1859	34
Verot,	1804	1828	1857	1876	48
Persico,	1823	1846	1854		45
Becker,	1832	1850	1868		32
O'Hara,	1818	1842	1868		49
O'Reilly, P. F.	1833	1857	1870		34
Moore,	1835	1860	1877		31
Ludden,			1887		
O'Farrell,	1832	1855	1887		36
Bruté,	1799	1808	1834	1839	31
Hailandiere,	1798	1825	1839	1882	57
Bazin,	1796	1820*	1847	1848	28
St. Palais,	1811	1836	1849	1877	41

Chatard,	1834	1862	1878		29
Whelan, R. V.	1809	1831	1841	1874	43
Kain, J. J.	1841	1866	1875		25
Hennessy, (Wichita)			1888		
Curtis,			1886		
Bourgade,	1845	1869	1885		22
Manucy,	1823	1850	1874	1885	35
Marty,	1834	1860	1880		31
Lootens,	1825	1851	1868		40
Glorieux,	1841	1867	1885		24
Haid,			1888		
Seidenbush,	1830	1853	1875		38
Zardetti,			1889		
Scanlan,			1887		

* Dates marked with a star are approximations.

MEETING OF THE UNITED STATES CATHOLIC
HISTORICAL SOCIETY.

The United States Catholic Historical Society held a public meeting on the evening of 25th May, 1891, at La Salle Institute, New York.

The meeting was called to order by Judge Morgan J. O'Brien, the retiring president, in the presence of a large and representative audience, estimated to have numbered five hundred.

Having expressed the gratification felt by the Society at the presence of so many interested in its work, he spoke a few words as to the object of the Society and of its rise and progress; of the many difficulties met and the cheering hope that at last they could look forward with some certainty to the advancement of the project for which they were incorporated, and to the general co-operation of the public at large.

The Judge then announced that at last they had succeeded in persuading the man of all others most fitted to preside over the Society and be their trusted pilot, who had until now modestly held back, but who at length, yielding to their united wish, had consented to become their presiding officer; and that he felt pleasure and honor in introducing the new President, Dr. John Gilmary Shea, the Catholic historian.

Dr. Shea expressed his thanks for the kind reception accorded him and for the all too flattering words of the late and highly esteemed president of the society, Judge O'Brien.

He spoke in terms of praise of the progress of the society under Judge O'Brien, whom he succeeded in office, of his able and wise administration.

He then informed the assemblage that Cardinal Gibbons although prevented by suddenly imposed duties from attending, had sent an interesting paper embodying some personal reminiscences of his missionary labors in North Carolina, and that in his absence the paper would be read by Rev. James J. Dougherty, director of the Home of the Immaculate Virgin in this city. The Reverend gentleman was then introduced to his audience. At this point Archbishop Corrigan arrived and was warmly greeted by all present. When he was seated the Cardinal's paper was read.

When this was finished it was moved, seconded and unanimously carried (Dr. Shea putting motion) that vote of thanks be expressed to his Eminence for his highly valuable and entertaining paper, and to Rev. Mr. Dougherty for his masterly delivery of the same.

The Doctor then announced the paper to follow : " The Surratt Case," a True Statement of Facts, by Rev. Jacob A. Walter, of Washington, D. C., and introduced Dr. Sloane, who had kindly consented to read Rev. Mr. Walter's paper. The paper was then read.

Rev. James H. McGean moved that vote of thanks be offered Rev. Mr. Walter for his clear and explicit statement of the facts in the case. The motion having been seconded the Archbishop put the motion which was unanimously carried. Dr. Sloane also received vote of thanks.

At the *urgent* request of Father McGean Archbishop Corrigan made a few remarks.

He expressed his own belief in the innocence of Mrs. Surratt, spoke of the scope of the Society, of the great and good work that it was accomplishing, and of the debt under which all Catholics rested to Dr. Shea for his own personal, historical labors, and of the bright prospects of the Society in the near future, and wished them every success in their valuable labors.

Rev. J. H. McGean then read the report of the nominating committee, and the following officers were duly elected: Most Rev. Michael A. Corrigan, Honorary President; John Gilmary Shea, President; Charles Carroll Lee, M. D., Vice-President; Mare F. Vallette, L.L. D., Corresponding Secretary; Joseph T. Keily, Recording Secretary.

On motion of Dr. Vallette, seconded by F. D. Hoyt, the following resolution was adopted :

WHEREAS, the increase of a library for Catholic History must depend mainly on the collection of Catholic newspapers, periodicals, pamphlets, circulars, documents, material which cannot be bought, but must be collected,

The Librarian is hereby authorized to appoint a solicitor of such material in each diocese, and furnish him with proper credentials.

A vote of thanks to the Christian Brothers of the Christian Schools, for their kind courtesy in granting the use of their hall, by the Society, was then adopted and the Society adjourned.

NOTES.

LETTER OF JUDGE HORSMANDEN TO CHRISTOPHER COLDEN. From on board Admiral Winne, near the mouth of the Highlands, Aug. 7th, 1741.

Dear Sir.

After a long cessation of correspondence, I take the liberty of resuming the pen, partly with design of apologizing and also not without view of provoking you to renew the combat which may be engaged in with honor, without loss of blood.

A. Ever since the fire at the Fort, which was on the 18th of March, I've been engaged in perpetual hurry, insomuch that I've been forced to dedicate part of my resting time to the public service, in prosecuting an enquiry into the rise and occasion of our late disorders in the city of New York ; but I think the labor bestowed has not been in vain, for though the mysteries of iniquity have been unfolding themselves by very small and slow degrees, it has at length been discovered that Popery was at the bottom, and the old proverb has herein also been verified that there is scarce a plot but a priest is at the bottom of it, or as the like pert priest Eury said upon his defence at his trial (though sarcastically) "according to the vogue of the world, where there is a plot, the first and last link are especially fastened to the priest's girdle;" but he must excuse us in his case, if the last link be fastened to his neck, for he is convicted as one of the principal conspirators, and is condemned to be hanged on next Saturday night.

He appears to have been a principal promoter and encourager of this most horrible and detestable piece of villainy, a scheme which must have been brooded in a conclave of devils, and hatched in the Cabinet of Hell, so bloody and destructive a conspiracy was this, that had not the merciful hand of Providence interposed and confounded their devices, in one and the same night the inhabitants would have been butchered in their houses by their own slaves and the city laid in ashes; and this was to be perpetrated under the obligation of an infamous oath, administered to the conspirators (most negroes and some soldiers and other whites, the more's the shame) by John Hughson, now in chains, and this way the priest, by whose craft they were perverted, and in expectation of a (fool's) paradise. baptized into the most holy Roman Catholic faith, and under color of absolution and pardon of sins, past, present and to come; and while they were going to sacrifice to the devils, were made to believe by destroying of heretics, they would do God good service. Tantum religio potuit suadere malorum !

And though we have been so successful in prying into this scene of darkness and horror, as to bring to light near ninety negroes and I think about a dozen whites engaged to be actors in this black tragedy, of the former whereof thirty odd have been executed, and this priest makes the fourth white. And though the town were well pleased with the first fruits of our labors and inflicting the deserved punishment on the offenders, yet when it comes home to their own houses, and is like to affect their own properties in negroes, and conscienceship in others, then they are alarmed and they cry out, the witnesses must needs be perjured, and so we come under a necessity of making a sort of stand for the present, and it is almost incredible to say that great pains has been taken by some among us to bring a discredit upon Mary Burton the original witness, whom Providence, one would think had designed for the happy instrument of all this dis- covery, and whose testimony has been confirmed by several negroes in flames, who obstinately denied their guilt till they came to the stake to be burnt. So soon have her services been forgotten ! and a stop affected to be put to her doing any further !

B. As to the characters of other witnesses who have been acomplices in this wickedness designed against us, what can be expected to be said for them? They are such as the wisdom of the law allows to be legal and good evidences and that from the necessity of the thing. For how can a discovery of such works of darkness be expected but from some of the confederates themselves? And if the witnesses are kept apart, and ex- amined apart as most of them have been in most instances upon most, if not all the trials, their respective testimonies tally and agree, what better evidence can be desired, or expected.

C, And though Mary Burton has from the beginning been an unwill- ing witness through the terror of having her life threatened both by blacks and whites, and though she has declared from the beginning, that should she tell all, she knew people would not believe her; and though she has been prevailed upon' after being threatened to be imprisoned, upon her standing mute and obstinately refusing to name any names, though she confessed she knew more; yet, when she did name them, we could not but be shocked, the persons mentioned being beyond suspicion, and the consequence followed that great clamor has thence been raised against her, and now by some she must be esteemed a person of no credit. I do think her case is attended wifh singular hardships, and at the same time the things she says cannot but stagger one's belief in some measure; but I must observe this is not the first time her examinations have had that effect upon me, but several times from my first taking her in hand; yet 'till now everything that has come from her has in the event been confirmed; but here must be a suspension of credit for a while and time only can clear the matter up.

D.   I must own I am glad I have got an opportunity of little relaxation from this intricate pursuit, though at the same time from the length of my letter you may take occasion to imagine I'm not quite tired of it; but if my design of this imperfect narrative, by way of amusement may be thought to answer that intention, it will at the same time in some measure apologize for former defects and also vindicate my sincerity.

And now it is almost time to release you; but a few more words and I have done.

Peter Winne desires me to inform you that as to the land at Anthony's Nose, he forgot to carry down the Indian deed with him, for want whereof he could not get the certificate which he was to send you; but he'll send the deed down by return of the vessel, in hopes that you will soon be at York, and that the Governor may see it and the business be forwarded.

And as to Sakendagat affair the Governor said, that could not be proceeded in titl he was informed of all the names in the petition, which he was nat able to do by memory,

I am dear Sir etc.

My humble service to Mrs. Colden and all the family.

I hear you are returning sone upon the business of the commission to Connecticut, so I'm afraid, I shall not have the pleasure of seeing you till after your return, being going to Albany upon a commission of good delivery. I hope to be down in less than three weeks.

A new Governor I presume is no news to you.

CATHOLIC CHURCH, SCRANTON, PA., FROM AN OLD DIRECTORY. Among the earlier settlers of Scranton, those professing the Roman Catholic refigion must have been few. No record, however, has been handed down from which facts might be gathered. The only authentic account extant dates 1846, when Rev. P. Prendergast, residing at Carbondale, paid the first visit to these scattered few, and after organizing the little band and securing for their use a small room in a private dwelling on Division Street, continued visiting occasionally and attending to their spiritual wants. Thus matters went along for two years, at the expiration of which the congregation had grown in numbers sufficient to warrant, with the timely aid of the Lackawanna Iron and Coal Co., in the shape of a large plot of ground, free of charge, for church and grave yard use, the speedy erection of a small building 35 feet in length 25 feet in width, and which was immediately commenced and the following year finished by the Rev. J. Laughran, who at this time had assumed the temporal and spiritual charge. The Rev. J. Cullen took charge in 1852, and finding the congregation had outgrown the small building on Division Street, soon commenced a very substantial frame edifice 96 feet in length and 45 feet in width on Franklin Avenue, nnd which was completed the following year, 1854, by Rev. M. Whitty, who, by this time, had been appointed to the charge. The congregation now growing rapidly, the pastor found it necessary to provide more church room, and in 1856 succeeded in getting built a good frame church 75 feet in length and 45 feet in width, in the village of Dunmore (Rev. E. Fitzmaurice soon after taking charge) in order to accommodate that part of the Parish, who, to this time, had been worshipping at Scranton. The members still increasing, it was deemed desirable to provide still further, which was done by the speedy erection in 1858 of a frame church 70 feet long and 30 feet wide, near the village of Providence (now within the city limits) for the use and benefit of that part of the Parish, which, up to the time, had also worshipped at Scranton. By this judicious arrangement the congregation were enabled once more to appreciate the comforts from which an overcrowded church had estranged them. Time rolled on in this way until the year 1864, when Scranton, it would seem, called for a building worthy its fame and population. In the fall of that year the pastor, Father Whitty, commenced on Wyoming auenue, one of the largest and perhaps handsomest church edifices within the State of Pennsylvania. The church is built in the Grecian style of architecture (designs furnished by J. Amsden, architect) and is 158 feet in length and 68 feet in width inside.

INDEX.

www.ingramcontent.com/pod-product-compliance
Lightning Source LLC
Chambersburg PA
CBHW030328120726
47901CB00007B/1714